Praise for
Yesterday's Promise

"Prepare for adventure, romance, and intrigue in nineteenth-century South Africa. Linda Lee Chaikin has done her homework, exploring the world of diamonds and goldmines in the land that would become Victorian Rhodesia. A page-turner of a story told by a veteran novelist."

—LIZ CURTIS HIGGS, best-selling author
of *Thorn in My Heart*

"Linda Lee Chaikin never fails to deliver a dynamite story! In *Yesterday's Promise* she weaves the complications of love and history into a storyline that is a sheer joy to read. I can't wait for book 3 of the East of the Sun series!"

—DIANE NOBLE, award-winning author of *Phoebe*

"I love, love, _____ I'm
looking for _____ me,
believable r _____ t,
I wouldn't ___

Praise for
Tomorrow's Treasure
Book 1 in the East of the Sun Series
by Linda Lee Chaikin

"*Tomorrow's Treasure* invites the reader to look closely at God's fatherly care for his orphans and widows, particularly those whose families were martyred on the mission field. An engaging historical novel!"

—C. HOPE FLINCHBAUGH, author of *Daughter of China*

"Absorbing human drama, intriguing mystery, heart-pounding love interests, a dramatic setting—this novel has it all, including a good message expertly woven into the greater story. I can't wait for book 2!"

—LISA TAWN BERGREN, best-selling author
of *The Captain's Bride*

"Adventure. Intrigue. Romance. Settle back for an enjoyable read. *Tomorrow's Treasure* is as old-world as the setting yet as contemporary as the human heart."

—KATHY HERMAN, best-selling author of The Baxter Series

"Linda Chaikin has created a wonderful page-turner with this engaging historical novel. Her sense of time and place is exquisite, her characters so real they seem ready to step right off the page. This is a story rich with conflict, triumph over adversity, and wondrous testimony to God's grace. Your heart will sing as you read."

—DIANE NOBLE, award-winning author of *Heart of Glass*

YESTERDAY'S
PROMISE

YESTERDAY'S PROMISE

EAST *of the* SUN 2

LINDA LEE CHAIKIN

WATERBROOK
PRESS

YESTERDAY'S PROMISE
PUBLISHED BY WATERBROOK PRESS
2375 Telstar Drive, Suite 160
Colorado Springs, Colorado 80920
A division of Random House, Inc.

All Scripture quotations are taken from the *New King James Version.* Copyright © 1982 by Thomas Nelson, Inc. Used by permission. All rights reserved.

The characters and events in this book are fictional, and any resemblance to actual persons or events is coincidental.

ISBN 1-57856-514-6

Library of Congress Cataloging-in-Publication Data

Chaikin, L. L., 1943–
  Yesterday's promise / Linda Lee Chaikin.— 1st ed.
      p. cm. — (East of the sun series ; 2)
      ISBN 1-57856-514-6
    1. British—South Africa—Fiction. 2. Conflict of generations—Fiction. 3. Gold mines and mining—Fiction. 4. Women—England—Fiction. 5. South Africa—Fiction. 6. England—Fiction. I. Title.
      PS3553.H2427Y47 2004
      813'.54—dc22
                                                                          2003019786

Printed in the United States of America
2004—First Edition

10 9 8 7 6 5 4 3 2 1

To Pegg Hill,
a friend, a lover of the peoples of South Africa,
and a faithful missionary of our Lord.

*For God is not unjust to forget your work
and labor of love which you have shown toward His name,
in that you have ministered to the saints, and do minister.*

HEBREWS 6:10

ACKNOWLEDGMENTS

Peggy and David Hill served as missionaries in South Africa from 1974 until 1990. Peggy was exceedingly helpful by sharing an understanding of her birthplace and the tribes. She sent me rare books and articles as well as conveyed many of her own exciting experiences with wildlife—which I was able to incorporate. Thank you, Peggy.

Peggy's parents, Eldon and Florence Sayre served as pioneer missionaries in Rhodesia from 1945 until September 1977, when they were forced to leave due to the unstable conditions at that time.

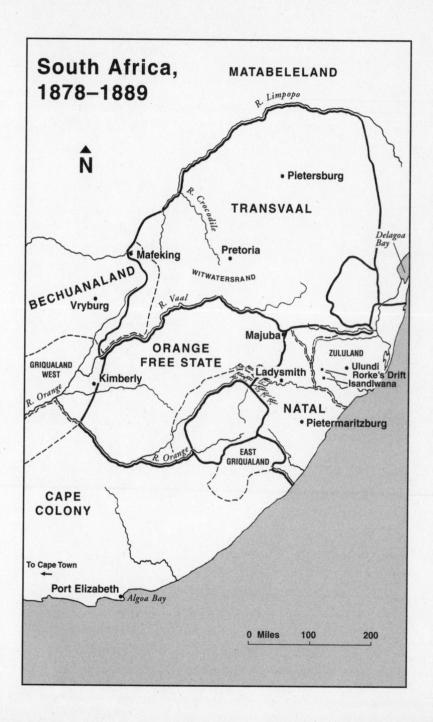

South Africa, 1878–1889

MATABELELAND

N

R. Limpopo

• Pietersburg

R. Crocodile

TRANSVAAL

• Mafeking

Pretoria
•

Delagoa Bay

WITWATERSRAND

BECHUANALAND

Vryburg
•

R. Vaal

Majuba •

ZULULAND

ORANGE
FREE STATE

Ladysmith •

• Ulundi
Rorke's Drift
Isandlwana

GRIQUALAND
WEST

Kimberly
•

NATAL

R. Orange

• Pietermaritzburg

R. Orange

EAST
GRIQUALAND

CAPE
COLONY

To Cape Town
←

Port Elizabeth

Algoa Bay

0   Miles   100   200

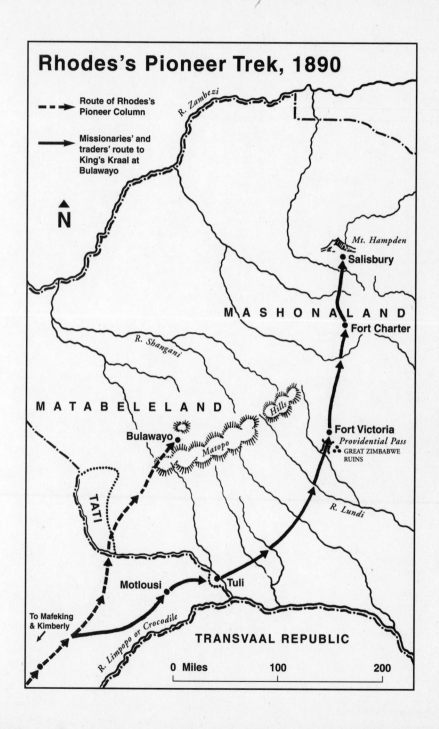

Rhodes's Pioneer Trek, 1890

- - - - ▶ Route of Rhodes's
Pioneer Column

━━━▶ Missionaries' and
traders' route to
King's Kraal at
Bulawayo

**↑
N**

R. Zambezi

Mt. Hampden
Salisbury

MASHONALAND

Fort Charter

R. Shangani

Hills

MATABELELAND

Bulawayo

Matopo

Fort Victoria
Providential Pass
GREAT ZIMBABWE
RUINS

TATI

R. Lundi

Motlousi

Tuli

To Mafeking
& Kimberly

R. Limpopo or Crocodile

TRANSVAAL REPUBLIC

0 Miles   100   200

PART ONE

Treasures of wickedness
profit nothing.

PROVERBS 10:2

CHAPTER ONE

Grimston Way, England
31 October 1898

On the perimeter of the village green, a thick stand of ancient trees with half-clad branches trembled in the rising wind. Dark clouds obscured the cheerful face of the sun, and like a harbinger of events to come, a thunderhead cloaked the afternoon sky.

The first smattering of rain dribbled down branches to a crisp carpet of burnt-orange leaves. Though the countryside seemed draped with a fall gloominess, laughter still danced on the wind from children who joined hands and skipped in a large circle while singing "London Bridge Is Falling Down" and giggling as they dropped to the damp grass.

A tall white cross graced the village green near the twelfth-century rectory of St. Graves Parish. Below the cross some of the village girls were adding last-minute touches to the outdoor fall decorations. Chains of red pomegranates, yellow gourds, and dried cornhusks, plus bundles of tied grasses and bunched leaves gave a warm touch of color to the festive gathering. This was October 31, Allhallows Eve, the yearly celebration recalling brave Christian heroes and heroines of the past who had faithfully labored for Christ. The outdoor activities in Grimston Way would end at eventide with the lighting of candles, a chapel service, and a friendly supper inside the parish hall.

Evy Varley, who had grown up as the niece of the now deceased

Vicar Edmund Havering and his wife, Grace, emerged from the ancient gnarled oak trees, where she had been gathering dried lacy moss hanging from ghostly branches. She was quite accustomed to the church holidays, spring fetes, and summer bake sales, for she'd been reared to become a vicar's wife, but Providence, so it seemed to her, had intervened, and she'd been blessed to study music. She had recently graduated from Parkridge Music Academy in London and, by means of a loan from Rogan Chantry, had opened a small music school here in her home village.

As she paused to take in the view of the village green, however, she now felt strangely alienated, as though she were an outsider looking through a window at a nostalgic scene. Had she been affected by the sudden gloominess? Perhaps it was the odd restive spirit she had sensed for the past few days that seemed hidden in the shadow of her subconscious.

The sensation intensified to the point that Evy turned away from the singing children and looked toward the fast darkening Grimston Woods. She suddenly remembered an incident in her girlhood—the day when a stranger had stood watching her from these very trees. The man had appeared kindly back then, even sad when he spoke to her, but she now experienced less benign emotions as the dark memory clouded her mind. There was nothing she could describe as out of the ordinary, yet she remained conscious of an inexplicable unease.

She turned away and quickened her steps back toward the village green, seeking the children's laughter and their innocent faces as they prepared for the evening's festivities. Perhaps her wary mood was due to the season. September had been unseasonably warm and cheery, but the inevitable cold October weather had finally arrived.

Ahead, Evy heard grave voices coming from behind some old hemlock bushes. She recognized the voices of the twin Hooper sisters, Mary and Beth, who were students in her piano class. The two schoolgirls emerged from the bushes carrying wicker baskets filled with dried lavender and lemon grass, and their pretty blue calico skirts flared in the chilling breeze that sent leaves scattering about their feet.

They both wore spectacles and had corn-colored hair that was braided and looped. The only noticeable difference between them was that Mary wore a red-and-white polka-dot ribbon.

With them was Wally, son of the village carpenter, a tall boy with long arms and big hands, which he had shoved into his too-short, faded breeches. He was listening to the girls with his head bent, his longish brown hair ruffling beneath a floppy hat.

The three huddled together like guilty accomplices, with Mary's solemn voice taking the lead, as usual. She seemed to be trying to convince Wally of something.

"…it's got to do with murder."

Evy's fingers tightened around her basket as a chill breeze reached the back of her neck.

"Murder runs in family blood, you know," Mary stated matter-of-factly. "Science says so."

"Poppycock," Wally scoffed.

"Science is never wrong." Beth nodded in grave agreement, adjusting the spectacles on her snub nose. "And Mary is always right."

"We both are," Mary agreed with a polite nod to her twin.

Evy remained still so the brittle leaves beneath her shoes would not announce her presence and embarrass them.

"Science ain't always godlike, and murder don't run in the blood, 'cept if you're talking about sin. And sin be in the human nature of us all. Even the dowager, old lady Elosia Chantry. A more stuffy aristocrat you never seen than her."

"That's what I mean, Wally. Lady Elosia's heard how Miss Varley was born out of wedlock."

"You be meaning the wrong side of the blanket?"

"That is quite what Mary means." Beth nodded knowingly.

"Lady Elosia wants Master Rogan to marry a lord's daughter, Lady Patricia Bancroft. That's why Lady Patricia's sailing to Capetown in the spring to marry Rogan. And there's plenty the Chantrys wish to hush up about their family history. Henry Chantry was Miss Varley's father.

He brought her back from Capetown and gave her away to Vicar Havering."

"So then, Miss Varley *is* Miss Chantry."

"No, Wally!"

"You just said Master Henry was her father."

"He and her mum weren't *married.*"

"So? He'd still be her father, you silly goose." Wally's voice became wearied.

"Well, that may be, but the vicar and his wife took Evy in out of kindness."

"Everyone knows that. They had Christian hearts."

"But…Henry Chantry died before his time!"

"Uds lud!" Wally said. "Everybody in Grimston Way has heard that old tale. He done kilt himself in his study on the third floor at Rookswood. Room's haunted."

"He was murdered," Mary repeated. "And Miss Varley's mum from Capetown is the murderess. Vengeance was the motive, because he betrayed her."

"How could she have done it if she was dead already?" Wally mocked.

"Her ghost came and did the dark deed."

The twins nodded sagely at each other and then at Wally.

"Even I know that's impossible," Wally scoffed. "Uds! Look, Twins, it's your mum. She's beckoning."

"If she learns we've been playing Scotland Yard again, she'll take away our science books. Hurry, Beth."

They ran across the green toward the rectory. Wally turned and headed for the road, as though he knew the twins' mum did not approve of them being close friends with the carpenter's boy.

An icy gust of wind took Evy's breath away and sent the hem of her dark hooded cloak billowing around her ankles. She looked after them, a little amused by the absurdity of their reasoning, yet disturbed as well about Lady Patricia Bancroft.

From Mike:

To Jon Shafqat—
With many thanks . . .

From Tricia:

To Katie—
Having you join our family has been
as priceless as the *Mona Lisa*

Was it true? Was she voyaging in the spring to Capetown to become Rogan's bride?

The dry leaves rattled through the overhead branches, while a withering blast of wind swept through her lonely heart, leaving desolation in its wake. Rain, like cold, wet fingers, spread across her face and neck. Drawing up her shoulders in a little shiver, she lifted the hood of her cloak over her thick, tawny hair.

Any interest she'd had earlier in the candlelight supper at St. Graves parish hall was now extinguished. She must get away. She must think things through. Little else would solace her spirits except retreating to her beloved piano to play her favorite pieces. She could lose herself in Mozart's Piano Concerto No. 21 in C, and her heart would stir with a desire to worship.

Evy hurried toward the road, keeping close to the hickory trees so as not to be noticed. It was to her advantage that most of the folks had deserted the green in order to congregate in the warm parish hall. Questions beat like the wings of a trapped rook against her restless soul.

Yes, secrets and suspicions abounded around the Chantry family. The theft of the famous Kimberly Black Diamond still remained unsolved after all these years. And then there was Henry's mysterious death at Rookwood. The authorities had ruled it a suicide, but even Rogan believed his uncle had been murdered.

The wind and cold rain drove against Evy as she slowly made her way up the dirt road that ascended to Rookswood Estate. She was soon soaked to the skin, her cloak billowing and whipping with each gust. The wind filled her ears as it rushed through the great trees that loomed overhead like sentinels guarding the only entrance that led to the ancestral home of the Chantrys.

She neared her rented cottage, which stood well back from the road, tucked among the trees, with Rookswood Estate as her nearest neighbor. The bungalow's isolation, however, did not trouble Evy. The cottage was perfect for her music classes, with room in the large parlor for her grand piano. In fact, the term *cottage* was rather misleading, since it contained six ample rooms and an attic.

She looked again toward the tall trees of Grimston Woods, now encroaching on the side of the meandering road and growing darker by the minute. She could imagine Rogan Chantry emerging from those trees riding his fine black horse, just as he had on the day she first met him, back when he'd been a spoiled, arrogant boy, determined to lord his station in life over her. She could see him now as that youth, his glossy dark hair waving past his forehead, his flashing brown eyes and taunting smile that insisted she would be his one day whether she liked it or not.

As Rogan grew up, however, he had matured and mellowed and had been much kinder to her. He had gone so far as to arrange a loan so she could complete her final year at the music academy. He had even given money through Vicar Osgood to start her own music school, enabling her to live independently.

Will I ever see him again? she wondered. *And if not, will it matter to him as much as it does to me?*

A creaking sound broke her reverie, and as Evy approached the cottage, she noticed the front wicket gate was open. The wind must have loosened the latch after she left for the rectory. The gate was swinging so hard that if it had a mind of its own, it should be quite dizzy. Her own feelings were being buffeted in much the same way. Wisdom argued with folly, and she knew wisdom should easily win, but when it came to her will, it was not so easy to yield her desires to the Lord. She must pray about that harder.

Despite the rain, she paused by her gate. From here she could look straight up the dirt road to the forbidding Rookswood Estate. The towering stone gate, weathered by generations of time and decorated with leering faces of medieval gargoyles, was bolted shut against her, serving as a stern reminder that Rogan Chantry was not only gone from Rookswood but also from her life—perhaps forever, if the Hooper twins were right.

The rain continued to descend in torrents, bouncing off those hideous stone creatures of man's twisted imagination. *Hee, hee,* they seemed to mock with bulging eyes as the rainwater came gushing from their open mouths and over their protruding tongues. *My own imagination is perhaps as wild,* she thought. Even as a girl, in the company of Rogan, she had not appreciated those gargoyles; nor did she now. She glared at them, then turned away and entered her yard, securing the gate latch against the tugging wind.

The sturdy cottage, with its white walls and green shutters, withstood the storm as bravely as it had for generations, but she noticed an open shutter on the high window near the peaked roof. The dark pane stared back, looking opaque and silent as the rain slashed against it.

She came up the walk past whipping vines that reached their tentacles toward her and shaking bushes now devoid of autumn's golden flowers.

Rogan... Her feelings, unlike the twins who seemed to agree on everything, argued between desire and anger, but when it came to Rogan Chantry, it seemed neither emotion won. Hadn't it always been so— even when she was a girl? There were times when her frustration over his failure to write made her angry enough to throw things, but she had been brought up too well for such childish displays of unbridled anger. On more frequent occasions it was not anger, but a deep longing she felt, a keen desire for Rogan's company. Denied this, she at times wilted under an intense sadness that often reached the level of pain. One day she loved him and remembered in detail his fiery kiss good-bye, then she loathed him the next when the post delivery continually passed her by.

"No mail today, Miss Evy," old Jeffords would call out when he came by in his pony-trap to deliver the post and saw her on the porch busily pretending to care for a potted flower. She was sure the news spread around Grimston Way how Miss Varley waited for an envelope postmarked from South Africa.

The barbed words of Mary and Beth claiming that Lady Patricia would leave in the spring to marry Rogan left her more distraught than angry. What if it were true?

Evy ran up to the front door and found her key in its usual place in the pot where one of Aunt Grace's favorite geraniums grew, transplanted from the rectory. She steeled her emotions. *I won't think about Rogan.* But she knew she would; she usually did.

For some reason her door key always needed to move about in the lock until it finally clicked open. Battered by the wind and cold rain, she at last unlocked the door and rushed into the dry, comfortable cottage with a sigh and quickly closed the door behind her. Safety at last.

She hastened to remove her drenched cloak and sopping shoes, leaving them to drip on the rain cloth spread beneath the hat tree. She would put water on to boil, then change into some dry clothes. By the time she returned to the kitchen, the water would be just right to add the robust dark tea leaves. A nice hot cup with bread and butter would make her feel alive again, ready to enjoy a crackling fire and her music! *Remember that delightful evening at the Chantry Townhouse in London when Rogan played the violin just for you?*

The memory made her pause for a moment, causing a small twinge of regret, then Evy shook her head and padded off to the kitchen pantry. The kettle was where Mrs. Croft had left it. Enough water remained, so Evy struck a match and lit the burner.

She set her jaw. If only she could come up with the money to pay Rogan's loan back. That would let him know she did not need him, that she was not mooning about, forlorn and wan, waiting for his crumbs of attention!

With the water on to boil, she went straight to her bedroom to dry herself and put on fresh stockings and a warm woolen dress. She brushed and pinned up her wavy, sometimes unruly, tawny-colored hair. Her amber eyes with flecks of green looked back at her from the mirror. In all honesty, she had no cause to deny that God had made her fair to look upon. It wasn't wise, but she went ahead and compared herself to Lady Patricia, certain it wasn't her own lack of charm that had detoured Rogan's feelings.

Thunder muttered overhead. She hastened back to the kitchen and poured the boiling water into the pot. While the tea steeped she went to the parlor, where her precious piano awaited her. Here she would relieve some tension by playing her favorite pieces.

It was not to be, for a rush of wind invaded the parlor, scattering sheets of music across the piano and down to the floor. An open window? Evy turned to see ballooning brocade draperies reaching to ensnare her.

She remembered now. The morning had been deceptively sunny, and she had opened it a few inches to let in some fresh air. *Oh dear,* she thought, *by now the rain will have blown in and wet the rug.*

She hurried to close the window and was startled by a streak of white that flashed across the black sky, followed by a thunderous boom, then rumblings through the darkened woods of Grimston Way. More rain followed, pounding the pane with fists like mystical goblins riding on the fall wind.

She wondered that her fingers shook, that she reacted so emotionally. *What is the matter with me? I've lived through hundreds of storms.*

The wind swept over the cottage, howling, repeating the word she least wanted to remember at this moment. *Murder.*

Evy had been a small child when Henry Chantry's life was taken. The murderer, who'd managed to get away, still had Henry's blood on their hands. Had the murderer located the Kimberly Black Diamond and escaped with it? The very thought rankled her because her mother had been blamed for its theft so many years ago. By now the perpetrator would be far from Grimston Way—there'd be no reason to stay. Even so, her skin prickled at the thought. Nor could she keep the twins' unlikely words that Henry was her father from churning in her mind. *What if he was?* She paused, letting the implication flutter around in her mind before rejecting it. It couldn't be true—that would make Rogan a blood relative.

Regardless of the silly talk about her mother coming to Rookswood to take revenge on Henry, someone may have done just that, but not Katie—she had died along with Dr. Clyde and Junia Varley at Rorke's

Drift mission station on the day of the Zulu attack in 1879. No one could possibly have survived that onslaught.

Overhead, a floorboard creaked, bringing her back to the moment. Her gaze lifted to the attic. *It's just the dampness, is all,* she told herself.

She remembered what Rogan said before sailing for the Cape. In spite of the authorities' conclusion that Henry Chantry had taken his own life, he suspected otherwise, believing that someone in the extended diamond family may have killed him for more than the Black Diamond. Why *more?* What could be *more* than that rare diamond from the Kimberly fields? The map? Ah yes, there was that. The precious map that Henry Chantry had left in his will to Rogan, promising gold on the Zambezi.

From Evy's limited knowledge of the diamond dynasty family, the shareholders and inheritors consisted of Bleys, Brewsters, and Chantrys. Never was there any mention of her mother's family, the van Burens. Evidently, Katie, under Sir Julien's guardianship, had not been left an inheritance, which meant, of course, there'd been nothing left to Evy. Not that she expected otherwise. Dreaming of diamonds had never been one of her weaknesses. However, she did care deeply about Katie's reputation—and her own.

According to Rogan, who hadn't explained how he knew, some members of each family were in England on the night of Henry's untimely death. All seemed capable of the short trip from London to Grimston Way to meet with Henry…and murder him?

The floorboard creaked again.

Evy snapped from her thoughts and turned toward the ceiling. *Rats?* Ugh… Maybe, but this was a heavier creak. *Footsteps?* Now she was really allowing her emotions to run wild! Her musings about Henry were unsettling her nerves.

She rubbed her arms and glanced around her in the dimness. Maybe she *should* have stayed for supper in the parish hall after all. A bit of company on a stormy evening would have restrained her imagination, but she set aside any notion of returning to the rectory in weather like this. By the time she arrived, she would be soaked once again, and there'd be plenty of explaining to do, especially to Mrs. Croft, who treated her as if she were her own granddaughter.

Evy squared her shoulders. There was only one way to handle her edginess. If the Hooper twins and Wally could play Scotland Yard, well, so could she.

She walked to the kitchen, where the tea was ready to pour, but instead of enjoying a cupful as she had intended, she went to the pantry. A small table held the oil lamp. There were no windows, only a small vent for the warm months. She struck a match and lit the wick. A flight of steep steps beside the wall led to the attic. Holding the flickering lamp, she forced her spirit to bravery, lifted her chin, and climbed.

The wavering lamplight revealed yellow daisies on the fading wallpaper, which appeared comfortably familiar in a moment like this.

Rain continued to lash the cottage walls. She could imagine a giant standing outdoors with booted legs apart, whip in hand, trying to bring the house down.

It was really quite silly to allow her nerves to imagine footsteps from just a few creaks in the attic floor! After all, who would wish to look up there? There was absolutely nothing of value—just some personal belongings from Uncle Edmund and Aunt Grace—certainly not the Kimberly Black Diamond!

The wind plowed against the cottage, threatening to penetrate the weathered planks. The steps creaked beneath her feet, yet she was certain no one could hear her approaching over the noise of the storm.

She reached the final step and lifted the lamp. Standing near the door, she paused to rouse her courage again before stepping up to the small landing. The door whipped open, and she gasped.

A figure, apparently draped in a dark sheet, rushed at her with hands extended. A violent force shoved her and caused her to lose her balance. As she started to fall backward, she reached in vain for a rail that wasn't there. The lamp crashed down the steep steps, and her head struck something hard.

A deep growl of thunder shook the cottage. Lightning dazzled the dark sky. Evy Varley lay in a crumpled heap on the pantry floor, the paleness of death upon her cold, still face.

Henry Chantry's murderer lifted the dark shawl and stepped down the stairs to kick away pieces of the shattered lamp and beat out the flames before they could draw attention to the cottage. With the fire now extinguished and everyone else away at the dinner, there was time enough to search.

The murderer returned to the attic, threw open the drawers of an old parson's desk, and tossed its contents aside impatiently. A stack of envelopes were illuminated by the glow of a candle. One envelope in particular had its edges yellowed with time. It was written in Henry Chantry's hand, addressed to:

Vicar Edmund Havering
St. Graves Parish

It had been sent from:

Henry Chantry
Rookswood Estate

Then Henry had not been bluffing that night in the office chamber on the third floor of Rookswood. Henry said he had suspected me of taking the Black Diamond from him in the stables.
But had he told me the truth about Vicar Edmund Havering?

Kill me and you won't get away with it. Do you think I'm a fool? I've left a record with the vicar of what really happened that night. Your name is in that letter.

The murderer's mouth twisted grimly.

Yes, and that is why Vicar Havering had to die. Because he finally grew wise enough to look on me with suspicion. He was asking too many questions at Rookswood. But I got away with it, Henry old boy, just the way I got away with silencing you forever. To this good day they still think the old vicar's death in the buggy on that stormy night was an accident. No one had enough sense to notice the wheel spokes had been altered. After that, all it took was a rifle shot from Grimston Woods as the vicar drove by in a hurry to get home in the rain. The horse bolted just as I had hoped. A clap of thunder and a flash of lightning were an added stroke of luck.

The letter read like a confessional. Yes, Henry had assisted Katie van Buren in taking the Kimberly Black Diamond from its secret hiding place in Sir Julien Bley's library at Cape House. They had intended to travel to the mission station at Rorke's Drift to locate her baby, then leave for England, with Katie going on to America to begin a new life. But when Henry entered the stables, he was struck from behind. After he regained consciousness, both the Kimberly Diamond and Katie were long gone.

I now believe it was Katie van Buren who struck me down in the stables and took the Kimberly Black Diamond. Certain information has come my way convincing me she was waiting in the stables that night in 1879. So convinced, I have spent months now, searching, and I believe that I am close to proving this. I am asking you to say nothing of this to anyone until I return from a trip to South Africa, which I intend to make next month.

Upon my return I fully expect to exonerate my own tarnished honor, as I continue to live under a cloud of dark suspicion.

The murderer's hand trembled with rage. *Henry deceived me into thinking he named me as the thief instead of Katie! And the message I sent him—he lied to me, saying he had kept it for Scotland Yard, when all the time I had fooled them all! There was no reason to have fought him… And when the pistol went off—*

"All for nothing… Henry had not even suspected *me!*"

In a surge of rage, the murderer crumpled the letter and reached for the candle, then on second thought decided against burning it. The murderer moved from the attic to the steps and looked down into the gathering dimness to Evy Varley's crumpled body.

All for nothing. You, too, could have been spared. If only you had stayed at the church supper as you were supposed to, none of this would have happened. Foolish girl. You always were too adventurous for your own good.

But now I'm certain I know who is hiding the Kimberly Black Diamond. I will yet possess it. It is only fair. It was meant for glory, and it belongs to me, to us! If I must kill again to have it, then I shall. Too much is at stake.

The figure went down the steps, pausing again to look down at the body lying on the floor, still looking so fair and innocent.

Then quickly, as thunder rumbled in Grimston Woods, the murderer fled into the raging storm.

PART TWO

Then you will lay your gold in the dust…

JOB 22:24

CHAPTER TWO

South Africa
July 1897

Who murdered Uncle Henry?

Rogan Chantry felt calmly convinced the question would find its answer among the extended diamond dynasty members scattered throughout South Africa and England—three families related by marriage, but with little else in common except diamonds...and the greed that surrounded the sparkling gems. Chantrys, Bleys, and Brewsters, all ruled by one man, Sir Julien Bley—sometimes ruthless, always dictatorial.

Rogan sat brooding over the two objects sitting on the mahogany desk in his cabin aboard the HMS *King George* bound for Capetown, South Africa.

The ship, now three weeks into its voyage from London, had come up against an uncommon storm for the season of seagoing travel. Shadows lengthened across the dark, mountainous swells as the ship rolled and pitched, its aged timbers creaking and moaning in harmony with the howling wind.

The lantern above his desk seemed to sway its own cadence in some macabre waltz. His focus shifted from his uncle's unexplained death to the two objects—now starting to slide across his desk. As they neared the precipice, he fetched them back.

Two objects, both important, both reaching a generation into the past: a portion of Henry's diary, and the map Henry had drawn to what he said was a gold deposit in the Zambezi River region. The map, once smiled upon as Henry's Folly, was now seen differently—as a golden light shining on a path to another famous rand, like the first great gold discovery at the Witwatersrand in 1886. The British had shortened the name to The Rand, and so the big gold owners were now called randlords.

Rogan drew the map toward him. As his fingers touched the heavy paper with pencil lettering, now beginning to fade on the yellowing sheet, his mind stepped back into that night at Rookswood when he'd located the treasure map he'd been searching for since boyhood...

It happened toward the end of a summer at Rookswood Estate. Rogan had been attending geology studies at the university in London and was at the top of his class. Upon returning to Grimston Way, he found the vicar's niece, Evy Varley, grown up...and very much to his liking.

He encountered her one afternoon at the summer fete while he and Lady Patricia Bancroft were out riding past St. Graves Parish. Evy and Derwent Brown, son of the vicar, were putting up a booth on the village green, with Evy doing most of the hammering. The sight had amused him, and ignoring Patricia's peevish protests, he had ridden up. The fete, which he'd had practically no interest in, was a benefit sale to help the vicar with his orchard. Rogan decided right then to attend the village event in order to admire Evy. Her green-flecked amber eyes and tawny hair were enough to catch any young man's fancy.

He had to admit, though, that it was not just her appearance that captured his interest. He knew many lovely girls in London, some of them daughters of lords and earls, but their beauty alone was not enough. The other girls he could always catch, but they soon bored him with their self-centered ways and shallowness, Patricia Bancroft included. Evy Varley had intelligence and wit, and she had not fallen adoringly at his feet the way the others had done. They were only interested in the title that soon would be his, upon his father's passing: Sir Rogan Chantry of Rookswood Estate.

What had started out as a game to add Evy to all the others had proven disturbing. From the time he had first met her, she made it quite clear that she was not impressed with his aristocratic station in life. In fact, there were times when she made him feel humble, and he found that he liked that about her. And Evy was confident in her Christian beliefs. He rarely, if ever, saw her compromise on any issue. And unlike his sister, Arcilla, with her beautiful clothes and flirtatious ways, Evy could stand her own in any group, regardless of whether or not her dress was the prettiest. She always showed a confident self-possession about her, whether she was in the company of common villagers or those with titles who often visited Rookswood. Somehow Rogan knew that it had something to do with her strong faith, perhaps because she believed Christ possessed her.

The fete was held the next day, and after attending, Rogan had ridden his horse back to Rookswood with Evy on his mind. Patricia had left early in the morning to return to Heathfriar, her ancestral home. When he came through the front door, he found Heyden van Buren standing in the Great Hall. Rogan had never seen the young man before, and he had the audacity to show up uninvited by anyone in the family.

"This is Heyden van Buren from the Transvaal," his father, Sir Lyle Chantry, had said. "Heyden, this is my youngest son, Rogan. Heyden is in London on business. He's a secretary to one of the men in the Boer government of Paul Kruger."

"Seeing I'm in England traveling with our Boer president, your father's kind hospitality has proven quite acceptable."

Rogan disliked Heyden from the beginning, though he could not say why. He claimed to be an Afrikaner—a descendant of the Dutch settlers in South Africa. He said his family had come to South Africa from Holland during the 1600s, when the Spanish Inquisition raged in the Netherlands against the Protestants. He boasted a good deal about the stalwart Dutch and their Boer Republic, and it did not take long for Rogan to understand that Heyden gazed at his world with the zealous perspective of Boer politics.

Rogan, a steely eyed English lad, found Heyden's boasting irritating, for he himself supported a far-flung British Empire from London to Calcutta, from Egypt to Capetown and beyond.

Heyden's fair appearance was burnt brown by the African sun. His smile was amiable, his accent not unlike Uncle Julien's, but his frozen pale blue eyes convinced Rogan he could not be trusted. Later, when Rogan asked his father why he allowed Heyden to stay at Rookswood, his father raised his brows.

"Out of social courtesy. He'll soon be leaving."

"I'll be content when he does. His ruddy Boer bragging wears on my patience. He's no blood of ours, is he?"

"No, but he's affiliated with Sir Julien through his late former ward, a young woman. I must say, though, with all his feverish discussion of possible war between us and the Boers, it shouldn't bode well for him in Julien's estimation."

"Nor mine. For an uninvited guest to allow himself to become so predisposed about Boer rights shows him a bit moldy of manners."

"Julien sent a wire saying not to receive him, that he was trouble, but that was after I had asked him to stay. One night won't matter that much."

"A night that tries my patriotism," Rogan said dryly.

"Do not forget your social duty, son. I am the squire of this fine village, and someday you will inherit not only my title but my role here. And Heyden has come all the way from London."

"I wonder why?"

His father shrugged, then turned back to his books and the research paper he was writing on the history of Grimston Way and its lengthy line of squires.

"Did Heyden learn of us through Julien?"

"Yes, though Julien shares your apparent impatience with him."

Rogan avoided the Afrikaner after dinner, wishing to suspend debates over British policy. He went up to his room early in order to think about a way to convince the rectory girl to go riding with him while he was home. He had noticed she usually went for long walks from the bungalow to a little-used path into the private woods of Rookswood. There was a hill that he could see from his bedroom window. He would often see Evy go there toward sunset and, evidently, daydream. He decided to keep an eye out for the next time she left, then saddle his horse and follow.

He picked up a geology book and sprawled upon his divan to read. It must have been around 10:30 P.M. when he heard stealthy footsteps down the corridor. Rogan listened. He suspected it was the Boer. He waited, snapped his book shut, and got to his feet. A minute later he stepped from his room in time to see Heyden taking the stairs to the third floor.

Third floor? Now why would he be going up there? That was a section of the house he should not be visiting. Henry's room was located up there.

Rogan followed. If it became necessary to forget his "social" manners, he'd toss him out on his ear.

Rogan walked past the nursery, where, as boys, he and Parnell had suffered the regiments of boring governesses and stuffy male tutors, and where Mrs. Grace Havering, the deceased vicar's wife, had come with her niece, Evy, to teach his sister, Arcilla.

He soon reached the steep steps leading up to Henry's old study and silently climbed toward a narrow corridor.

The door was open a crack, and a thin ribbon of light fell onto the corridor above the steps. Rogan's eyes narrowed. His uncle's study had been his secret room since childhood, and now this tiresome Boer was snooping around like a common thief. There could be but one reason. He must know about the Black Diamond—but not about Henry's map, Rogan hoped.

This room was usually locked. It was considered an unpleasant place in the house, a room to be avoided by nearly everyone in Rooks-wood, except Rogan. Sir Lyle had never come to grips with his younger brother Henry's untimely death. It had been more than a heartbreak, and all these years it had remained a scandal on the Chantry name that his brother had taken his own life.

Sir Lyle had a key to the room, as did Rogan. He'd had the key since he was a boy. But as far as he knew, no one outside the household had a key, so how did Heyden unlock the door?

Rogan set his jaw and pushed the door open. Heyden was standing in the middle of the room. He didn't move or seem to hear him until Rogan stepped in and closed the door with a deliberate click.

Heyden turned with a smile.

"Oh, hullo. Hope you don't mind?"

Rogan did, and he was about to throw the man out, when Heyden spoke up again.

"I've heard all the old tales of 'Henry's ghost,' and I suppose there's still enough boy in me to be intrigued." Heyden chuckled. "Maybe I should have waited till the old grandfather struck twelve?"

"It's wise you didn't. I might have shot a prowler. How did you get in?"

"Lizzie, cute little maid. We got to talking about ghosts and what-not. You know how it goes. One thing leads to another, and soon I asked to see the room. She promised to leave it unlocked. Bless her heart, she did. Hope it's all right, Cousin? I should hate to get the girl a scolding."

So now he was a *cousin*, was he? A smooth talker, this Boer. Lizzie, the silly chatterbox, would easily fall for his feigned attentions, warming to the dashing stranger from South Africa who wished to see the famous Rookswood "ghost."

"She told you where the room was?"

Heyden looked at him, still grinning in his own musings. "Yes. I wouldn't have known otherwise, now, would I?"

"No. Unless you've been here before."

Heyden turned full circle, looking about the room as though it were a museum. "Not much chance of that, is there? This being my first trip to England. I'm not much older than you and Parnell. Strange, isn't it, how ghost stories get bandied about until a generation or so later the tale is chiseled in stone?" He looked at Rogan. "Makes for good family history and amusing gossip in the village, I suppose."

"So does the tale of the Kimberly Black Diamond. You've heard that one, too, no doubt."

Instead of showing embarrassment that Rogan's bluntness had caught him off guard, Heyden drew his golden brows together.

"The diamond. Ah yes, ah yes. There's hardly a soul who's worked for Sir Julien at Cape House these past years who hasn't heard of it. It was monumental news when it happened. I was just a child, but I remember how Henry Chantry stole the Black Diamond and ran off to London with it." He looked at Rogan with apology.

Rogan folded his arms across his chest and leaned against the door, offering a faint smile. He saw mild surprise in Heyden's eyes, as though Heyden had expected outrage over the accusation about his uncle Henry.

"My uncle was a rascal. I've not much doubt Julien is right. Henry was involved with a beautiful woman at Cape House, and the two of them ran off with it. Diamonds are all in the family, you know," he said, deliberately glib.

Heyden's smile vanished. "Yes. There was a beautiful woman. But they say it was Henry who brought the Kimberly Black to England. Strange that it's never shown up on the world markets, though, don't you think? I wonder where it could be. Did your uncle ever discuss it?"

Rogan measured him carefully. As if he would answer such a question! Heyden wouldn't get any information from him.

Rogan tried to surprise him.

"You think Henry was murdered in this room for the Black Diamond?"

Heyden's mouth slipped open. He stared at Rogan. "Murdered—

you cannot be serious! I surely would not dare say such a thing. Lizzie says he killed himself."

"And we can count on everything Lizzie tells us."

"Well, Sir Julien says the same. It's no secret in Capetown that Henry Chantry took his own life."

"No, I don't suppose it is."

Heyden gave him a sudden searching look. Rogan stared back evenly.

"The Kimberly Diamond was never returned to South Africa."

"No, and through the years, I'd say just about everyone in the family has made their pilgrimage here to Rookswood to Henry's room hoping to find it tucked away in a cobwebbed corner. This appears to be your pilgrimage, van Buren. Am I assuming too much? But you'll also leave empty-handed because Henry left no clue as to where he hid it. It's likely not at Rookswood at all."

"Me?... Looking for it? You misunderstand, Rogan. It was a lark I came here at all. Shouldn't have, I suppose."

"Maybe not. But you're not the only one who still believes it's hidden somewhere here. Julien thinks so too. He's been coming here searching every year since Henry died. Not that he'll admit it."

"I don't know what Julien thinks. I doubt the Black Diamond was his discovery to begin with. But I don't think your uncle was murdered for it. That's a serious charge to make, and very macabre."

"By all accounts."

Heyden measured him. "Who are you suggesting would do such a thing?"

Rogan shrugged. "Your guess may be as good as mine."

"I don't know why. I'm not in the inner circles of the diamond family. I spent my whole life growing up in the Transvaal. But I'll give you my best guess. I doubt he was murdered for the diamond, even if he did steal it from Cape House. He took his own life, perhaps out of guilt. Because of his wife, Lady Caroline Brewster. She was your mother's sister, I believe? She died of African fever on one of his treks into Mashonaland.

And wasn't she with child? It must have been hard on him. Especially in his later years. Not an easy burden for a man to carry. It's likely it got to the poor devil in the end. That, plus the theft of the Kimberly Diamond. The Africans say it belongs to them, and they believe in curses, you know. The Zulu and the Ndebele tribes are cousins."

Rogan considered Heyden's words, then laughed. "Curses and witch doctors? Henry scoffed at such things. Are you now suggesting he wasn't murdered through malice, but rather a nameless curse walked into his bedroom and shot him?"

"Mock if you will. I am an Afrikaner. Born and raised in South Africa, as my parents and grandparents were. We know the ways of the tribes there. They set great store by such beliefs." Then, suddenly, Heyden spread his hands. "But as you say, if he hid it somewhere here at Rookswood, it's not likely to ever be found."

"In a mansion this size, it could be anywhere. We could tear it apart stone by stone and still not find it. It looks as if the diamond is forever lost."

"Yes…" Heyden looked about soberly, shoving his hands into his trouser pockets. "Yes, anywhere, including the estate grounds."

"A man could spend his entire life just searching." Rogan gave him a sharp look as, unexpectedly, something dawned on him. He stared at Heyden, but Heyden didn't appear to notice.

"I suppose you've checked in here already?" Heyden asked, looking about.

Rogan forced a forbearing smile; his silence was answer enough.

Heyden grinned and shrugged. "Yes, as you say, this room would be the first place people would look. But they could all be wrong, you know. The crypt might be the place. That would go along with his knowledge of curses." He chuckled. "Your uncle has hidden it well. And so, the mystery survives—and the ghost tale? Your descendants will have quite a story to pass on, Cousin Rogan. It should give them hours of amusement fifty to a hundred years from now. Who knows? Maybe one of *them* will find the Kimberly Diamond!"

"I'll keep that in mind." Rogan held the door open, pointedly.

"Yes, well, good night."

"You can find your bedroom all right?" Rogan inquired innocently.

Heyden laughed. "Yes, second floor, fifth door. You and your father have been kind hosts." He bowed lightly, turned, and left the room, going down the steps.

Rogan was not smiling as he listened to Heyden's steps fade away. His heart was thudding—not about the Black Diamond, but about Henry's map. Words that awakened him ran through his mind again and again: *He could have hidden it anywhere on Rookswood, including the estate grounds... A man could spend his entire life just searching... In a mansion this size it could be anywhere. We could tear it apart stone by stone and not find it.*

Of course! Henry was no fool. Why didn't I think of this sooner?

Henry had willed Rogan the map because he *wanted* him to find it and use it. It would have defeated his purpose to hide it so well that he would have no clue where to look.

"And he didn't," Rogan murmured decisively.

He stood still, considering again every meeting he'd had with Henry here in this room. He had often come here, and Henry had filled his ears with adventurous tales of Africa.

"There's gold north of the Crocodile River, Rogan. Plenty of it. Enough to make a man a gold rand. Here, take a look at this." He placed a rock in his hand. "Keep it. I may never go again. But you will. This is a sample. And I've drawn a map from memory that will help you find it. I wish I could have drawn a more detailed map, but we were under attack. We had to get out of there fast. My guide, Bertrand Mornay, was killed. You've heard me talk about him before? Yes, a solid man. A *Frenchie*. There was no better hunter-guide than he. The little Hottentot, Sam, was the one who told me about the gold, but he was killed too. I've done my best in drawing the location, but details fade in the heat of battle. By the time I made it out alive to Kimberly, the memory of its location was already a bit muddled. The shock and terror of fighting do that to a man. The bloody deaths of close friends. But the map has enough information for you to stake a claim if you use that head of yours. You take after me, Rogan. You'll do it. I'll wager my reputation on you, boy. Just wait till you grow up."

Henry had taken him by the arm and led him into the other room. "Remember, boy, if something happens to me, I've left the map to you. I'll mention that in my will. And the picture I painted... Take a good look at it. Remember it, Rogan. It's yours, understand? That will be mentioned in my will too. You do understand, don't you, boy?"

Yes, finally...now I understand.

Rogan shut the door and slid the bolt securely closed. His mind grabbed hold of the realization and wouldn't let go. He laughed at himself for having been dense for so long.

Rogan went straight across the room toward the small bedroom Henry had used when working late at night and entered.

This was where he'd hidden Evy the time Uncle Julien surprised them by coming here.

Rogan looked straight at the painting on the wall, the one Henry had willed to him along with the map. Henry said he had painted it upon returning to Rookswood after the Zulu massacre at Rorke's Drift. Rogan stared, as if seeing it for the first time. He remembered Henry pointing at it, telling him the details again and again. The battle of Isandlwana, Rorke's Drift, of the strong Zulu warriors called *impis*. He remembered how Henry would talk about his map at the same time, repeating that if something happened to him before he could return to South Africa, the map was Rogan's.

The map...and the painting.

With one swoop, Rogan lifted the painting from the wall and turned it over. He pulled the tacks from the frame, removed an outer backing, and...saw something folded, concealed between the painting and the false backing. The map...and something else. His heart began to race with excitement. An envelope with some pages, torn from what must have been a diary of sorts. Rogan recognized Henry's writing. He had expected a letter addressed to him from Henry, but there was none. Just the map and the diary sheets his uncle had put away securely early on, even while Rogan was yet a boy. Now he was even more convinced that Henry had not expected to die as suddenly as he had. Henry was normally very methodical about everything. If he had planned to take his life, he would have written a letter first and placed it here with the map. Rogan could hardly wait to get alone in his room to study the diary pages and the map!

He put the painting back together and replaced it on the wall. No one would ever guess these clues had been hidden there all these years.

He smiled. This was his secret now. He would tell no one. He would quietly finish his remaining years at the university, do his intern work at the family diamond business in London for a year, and then set sail for Capetown with Henry's map. He would arrange his own private expedition. Somehow he would convince Derwent to come with him. He could trust Derwent, who grew up in the rectory with Evy, as he could trust few others.

Now, what was the name of the son of Bertrand Mornay, Henry's guide? Henry had mentioned his guide's son several times. Giles, that was it. According to his uncle, Giles Mornay would follow in the steps of Bertrand to become a hunter and guide as skilled as his famous father. One day he would locate Giles Mornay in Kimberly. He was the right man to take up where his father had left off. Together, with Derwent, they would discover the gold deposit on Henry's map…

The ship pitched again in the storm raging outside, and the lantern swayed. Rogan turned his attention back to the yellowed pages from Henry's diary. Though the writing was indistinct in the lamplight, he read again Henry's warnings…

Chapter Three

22 October 1879
Pietermaritzburg

The Zulu War is about over. After the massacre the impis committed at Rorke's Drift at the Varley Mission Station, I've small pity left for the Zulu. Great warriors they are, but showing scant mercy. I blame Julien for what happened to Katie. I told him so to his face when he showed himself at Lady Brewster's. He believes the baby is dead too. I think he's actually relieved. Even Lady Brewster was offended with Julien's manner and kept the infant's whereabouts a secret. I confess she does not know all the truth. She will help arrange our travel home with a nursemaid to England.

Julien believes that I have the Black Diamond, but it must be under the rubble and stench at Rorke's Drift. Where else, if it was Katie who took it from me in the stables? Yet due to the secret love I hold for her, I will keep silent and take the blame for now. But I won't let this matter rest. I shall continue looking into it. Could it have been Katie who struck me from behind? Reason says yes, but I am not fully satisfied.

5 November
Aboard the Victoria, *headed for London*

In the end, even Lady Brewster, Caroline's aunt, turned against me. Julien has convinced her I was to blame for Caroline's death on the last trek. I've written Honoria, brother Lyle's wife and Caroline's sister. Dear Honoria is a good person. She wrote me back a most compassionate letter, saying she does not hold me responsible. Caroline wanted to go on the trek with me. She was an adventurous young woman.

When I went to produce this letter from Honoria to show Lady Brewster the thoughts of her other niece, the letter was missing. Did Julien find it and destroy it? He was there in the estate at Pietermaritzburg. Lady Brewster now believes I have the B.D. She is backing Julien in refusing me a shilling of my rightful inheritance. Curse the day old Ebenezer Bley made every family member's inheritance contingent on the agreement of Julien and Lady Brewster. It will become even worse when Lady Brewster passes on and Julien becomes the sole arbitrator.

10 November

Storms. Will we even make it home alive to beloved England?

The infant cries constantly. Thank Providence she's with the nursemaid and not with me!

January 1880
Home in England, Rookswood

I've delivered the baby to the London Missionary Society before arriving at Rookswood. I have requested they make arrangements with Junia Varley's sister, Grace Havering, to take her. All seems to be going well in that regard, but it is wise the baby's whereabouts remain a secret from those in Capetown. I've told this to Vicar Edmund Havering. I have given some white diamonds secretly to the good vicar to raise the baby well.

3 August

Old Ebenezer Bley still had his wits about him when on his deathbed he gave his son, Julien, controlling interest over the family inheritance. The security of the diamond investments motivates all of Julien's ruthless decisions. Family members are of little consequence to Julien Bley. Be cautious of him. When Julien perceives the diamond company is at risk, he can be as deadly as a provoked cobra. Julien sees himself a guardian angel over all, but angel of greed fits his patriarchal charade far better.

I remember the way his one good eye looked at me on a particular morning I entered his office at Cape House last year. How he told me I would receive no assistance for the gold expedition to the Zambezi. On that instance the Black Diamond was sitting on his desk. It glittered under the light of his lamp! As big as a hen's egg!

We got into a discussion about a loan for my next expedition, and that led to bitter disagreement. "It was Sir George Chantry, my father and Lyle's, who found the Black Diamond back in 1868," I told Julien. "Lyle and I both want what belongs to us," but Julien scoffed. "Everyone suddenly claims to have found the Black Diamond. I have witnesses who swear by the law that I found it, and the Kimberly mine as well."

He does have authority behind him, he and some others in De Beers Consolidated, including Cecil Rhodes. Rhodes, by all accounts, controls Kimberly. When I told Julien I discovered gold and needed some of my own money to stake an expedition to the Zambezi region, he mocked me. Henry's Folly, he called my gold claim. One day he will be striving to gain control of Henry's Folly. When I insisted on a loan, he actually drew a pistol on me and ordered me out of Cape House and out of his life.

31 October 1884

I'm remembering an incident about Julien that lately has been troubling me. I walked into his library office at Cape House in 1875, and I caught him unprepared. He sat at his desk with that black patch over one eye, his face fixated upon a set of sixteen bones, called hakata, sitting there in front of him. I recognized them at once. I've had experience with the dark superstitions of the nganga, or witch doctor, on my various treks deep into Matabeleland and Mashonaland. I don't know where Julien got the hakata bones. But a nganga uses the hakata for different things, including "sniffing out" an evil spell, an omen, a necromancer, or a caster of spells.

I saw Julien, that stalwart Englishman who attends the Anglican Church, paying heed to those bones. They're made of wood, from the mutarara tree, the tree that keeps evil spirits away. It's often planted over graves for that purpose. All this may seem mere mumbo jumbo, but witchcraft abounds. To this day I do not know what Julien was doing with the hakata. Katie once told me that Julien was studying about the Umlimo, a god of the Ndebele, who they believe lives in the Matopos Mountain Range by the Bulawayo region. There is a spirit guide who lives in the caves who reportedly speaks dark sayings for this god. I still ask myself why Julien would be studying about the Umlimo, and about bone casting for divination.

Of this I am certain. When it comes to diamonds and gold, I'd trust him no more than a banded cobra.

Rogan looked up from the yellowing sheets. The ship's groaning timbers gave voice to mental images of Sir Julien Bley engaged in divination. The idea seemed ludicrous from what Rogan knew of him. Odd…was it so? Sir Julien Bley involved with African witchcraft? Old practical Julien would have been the last person he'd ever suspect of dabbling in superstition. Was there power in such nonsense? Rogan tried to think back to his growing-up years in the church under Vicar Edmund Havering. He couldn't recall the vicar ever discussing anything diabolical.

I'll have a look into this myself. Derwent might know a few things. Does the Bible speak about it? Just what was Julien trying to do when Henry walked in on him?

Rogan drew his brows together. Along with his blood uncle's warnings, his own suspicions grew stronger. Henry had his faults, but he had never been ruthless in the hardened way Julien was.

Julien's presence at Rookswood made Rogan wary, even as a boy.

After Henry's will was read and his bequest of the map known to the family, Julien would come from Capetown and seek him out alone to "have a small chat." By the time Rogan turned twelve, he didn't trust Julien. He would sense being "watched" from the shadows of the mansion, or in the garden. Julien would come to Rookswood each year to visit "the dear family," something he had never made much of before the reading of Uncle Henry's will. More than clever for his age, Rogan began to turn the tables on Sir Julien. He would follow him at night to the third floor and watch him enter Henry's old rooms to search time and again.

Was Henry killed for the Black Diamond, or the map? Was it Uncle Julien who murdered Henry? With his powerful influence, Julien could have easily arranged things at Grimston Way to cover over anything that might point to him.

Rogan reached for the other item on his desk, perhaps the more important, the map. The ship pitched again, and Rogan held a column to steady himself. He squinted for perhaps the hundredth time at the emblem of a bird—or birds. He'd long pondered the meaning of the symbols Henry had drawn on the map. Could it represent a falcon, a hawk, or some fowl peculiar to that area? Perhaps he was making too much of it. In all the meticulous research he'd done in London since locating the map, he had yet to find anything significant about a bird in the region north of the Limpopo River. Henry had also drawn a lion and a baobab tree.

Perhaps the trek itself would shed light on any obscure meanings contained in the wildlife symbols. Was it possible that Henry had nothing more in mind than adding a touch of artistic flair to the painting? If so, its application here would merely have detracted from his usual clarity.

Rogan's thoughts roamed to his grandfather, Sir George, who died at sea on a return voyage from the Cape in 1869. Rogan knew him only by his grandiose portrait displayed above the stairwell in the Great Hall at Rookswood with the rest of the Chantry squires.

Soon after discovering the map, Rogan had asked about his grandfather. One day he found his father busy writing a history of Rookswood. He looked up from his books with typical impatience, brows twisted as though hooked together over the bridge of his aristocratic nose.

"My father found the Kimberly Diamond? Balderdash! What is this, Rogan, more of Henry's Folly? I wish that will of his had never mentioned leaving you a map."

Rogan held his questions and, after that meeting, never again went to his father on the subject. Had he tried to justify himself, showing the map or diary pages, the news would soon have reached Julien in Cape House. Rogan had long been rankled by the way he saw his father submit to his stepbrother. All through the years he had grown up at Rookswood, he had longed to see his father confront Julien head-on. But whenever opportunity arose, his father, Lyle, always backed down, insisting, "Conflict is foolish," and would withdraw to another room to lose himself in his private interests.

Rogan replaced the map and diary pages into a leather envelope he wore on his person to guarantee safety, then glanced at his pocket watch. It was close to midnight. Tomorrow the ship would be entering the Cape harbor. That is, if the storm did not delay them. Sir Lyle or Aunt Elosia would have wired Cape House that he was aboard the HMS *King George*. Would Julien be waiting? More than likely he would be riled that Rogan had not completed a full year in the family diamond business in London. Rogan knew his uncle would assume he had found the work too tame and, longing for action, had grown restless.

To occupy time alone in the cabin, he picked up a pencil and turned his attention to his personal journal. He had begun writing down what he knew of Henry's death when he'd departed London. Then, as ideas accumulated, he grew interested in trying to make more sense of his mysterious death.

Rogan scowled. He looked at the last entry he'd made the night before, dated the first week of July. He mused over his own words as he reread them.

Henry Chantry was not the manner of man to snuff out his own life. He was not prone to any emotional disheartenment that might provoke such an act. He would be the first to scoff at such a notion if he could have attended his own inquest. He was too bold to leave his burdens behind for others to carry.

As far as I know, my uncle was not a religious man, but he did respect the church. I do not believe he would look upon the doorway of death as an escape, if he were unsure what lay ahead for such a man as he. Taking his life would be too easy for my uncle. He had fought wildly and bitterly to stay alive when under attack by Shona tribesmen on his last expedition near the Zambezi. He had lost his guide, Bertrand Mornay, and a bushman called Sam in a wild scramble to survive. No, Uncle Henry would not have committed suicide.

Then what happened that night?

Members of every branch of the family were all reported to be in London at a family wedding the night of his death. But I have ridden the late train from London to Grimston Way enough times to know that any one of them might have done the same, taking the short trip to Rookswood and then returning without being missed.

Henry had been working at the estate in his upstairs rooms. The murderer must have known this and gone up to the third floor. But who?... Julien, Anthony Brewster, Lady Camilla? Yes, even my own father Lyle or my maiden aunt, Lady Elosia? Any one of them might have come to meet with Henry about the Black Diamond or the map on that fatal night.

If I hadn't been so young, I might have been awake to hear footsteps inching their way up the stairs, across the second floor hall, and the steps up to the third floor… I might have heard the pistol go off. If only…

Rogan tapped his chin and sighed. He snapped the journal closed and placed it inside his leather satchel. Outside, the wind increased. Restless and eager to disembark, he stood up just as the ship pitched violently, and losing his balance, he struck his head on the protruding cabin bulkhead. Leaning on one knee while propped against the wall, he narrowed his eyes and gritted his teeth. *One thing I am glad of. I won't ever need to be a sea captain!*

He crawled to his bunk and tied himself in for the rough night.

He thought of Evy Varley…those amber eyes with green flecks, and wavy, tawny hair… Where was she now? What was she doing? He imagined her playing her piano. Was she also remembering him?

CHAPTER FOUR

Capetown

Even though Rogan was out at sea, the distant sight of Table Mountain, appearing to rise above the watery horizon, with white clouds draping its flat top, roused his imagination. Later that afternoon he was standing on the ship's deck with his back to the stiff landward breeze as they neared Table Bay and Capetown, when an old sailor he'd spoken to on the voyage came up beside him and gestured to the mountain range.

"Stirred many a sailor's hopes, that mountain. Been a cheery beacon for ships comin' out of some of the worst storms a man ever did see.

"Table Mountain, she's called. Them's her two companions, Devil's Peak and Lion's Head. That there mountain range 'tween 'tis the backbone for the Cape peninsula. Only thing is, I'da called her Angel's Peak. That there devil gets too much publicity."

Rogan held to the ship's rail and squinted across the water to Table Bay. "Sir Francis Drake described it as 'the fairest cape we saw in the whole circumference of the earth.'"

"Did he, now? Well, aye, so she is. Mighty fair. The Almighty knew what He were doin' aright," the old sailor agreed. "He made Table Top flat so as it gathers all that moisture. Then that purt cloud just comes rollin' over the edge nice 'n' neat as a lady's crocheted dining cloth."

"What makes the cloud drape across the mountain slope and stop halfway down where it does?"

The old crewman scratched his locks. "Well, sir, I wouldn't be knowin', but today 'tis truly earning its name, 'Tablecloth.' "

Rogan studied the tablecloth cloud through his binoculars. The way the cloud rolled over its northern edge and stopped—draped just so far down the slope—reminded him of a waterfall wrapped in mist. "It looks to me as though the wind is colliding head-on with the mountains on the peninsula, getting forced up the steep slopes. That would drop the temperature and start condensation, apparently just where the thick cloud edge appears."

"Aye, suppose you be aright. Wind screams throughout the year 'round the Cape o' Good Hope. Seldom's the day when there be none. Been in many a bad storm and ocean swell comin' round that tip of southern Africa. Storm t'other night was small turnips compared to the ones I seen. Been sailin' since I were a cabin boy, only a young'un of nine years." He studied Rogan. "You be goin' to the diamond mines at Kimberly, I suppose?"

"For a short visit. I've family there."

"Most folks go to Kimberly and stay."

"See that mountain? I've plans for an expedition that will bring me far beyond, to the Zambezi region, to gold, perhaps emeralds, too." Rogan looked at the old man and grinned. "You can come with me if you like. Ready to give up the sea?"

The old sailor chuckled. "Yer pullin' me leg, lad. Ne'r catch me beyond the land of the Dutchies. Sooner face dragons o' the deep than giant savages with spears. Heard tell they pulls out yer heart and eats it alive. If you can get yer gold and emeralds and make it back to merry old England alive, you be deservin' ever' last one of 'em."

It was dawn the next morning when the HMS *King George* slid through the rippling water of the Cape into Table Bay and docked at the wharf. Impatient to be about the coming adventure, Rogan hefted his bag over his shoulder, grabbed his hat, and bolted from the cramped cabin, heading topside to the deck.

His booted feet took the steps with the same confident ring that drove him forward toward his desired destiny.

On the deck, he set his bag down and stood feet apart, one strong hand bracing himself against the rail. Even at dockside, the wind blew in from the sea, but now the salt air mingled with the enticing fragrance of a strange new land. His shirt, partially opened over his bronzed chest, tossed as freely as the new liberty pulsing through his veins. The adventurous wind, like a woman's seductive fingers in his dark wavy hair, was welcoming him, drawing him, toward an uncertain future.

Table Mountain dominated the view, with the mountain range forming a half circle around Capetown, Devil's Peak and Lion's Head on either side. Rogan could see Capetown spread around Lion's Head with some red-roofed, white mansions and smaller bungalows, which clustered near the bay.

The sky was clear as he walked down the ramp to the dock, which teemed with workers awaiting the ship's cargo. A fiery hue touched with gold colored Devil's Peak. Rising thirty-five hundred feet, Table Mountain was unveiled, showing off its glory, its huge mass close enough for him to see the clefts and ravines. Its long flat top stretched behind Capetown, with the blue sky above like a canopy.

Rogan strode along the crowded dock with his heavy bag over his shoulder, taking in everything he could see. Barrels and crates were stacked everywhere as they were hauled from ship to shore on the sweating backs of both Europeans and Africans. The Bantu workers wore short knee pants, their backs bare. One-horse taxis and private coaches jostled for space to greet the disembarking passengers.

Rogan stopped on the wharf to survey the vehicles waiting for passengers. To his surprise, he saw Arcilla seated in an open carriage attended by two Bantu. She was smiling and waving for his attention. One of the serving boys ran over and relieved him of his baggage.

Should he be surprised to see his sister? His father or Aunt Elosia must have wired Cape House about the ship he was on. Then Julien must know he was here. Rogan set his jaw. He wasn't ready to meet Julien yet. He wanted to go alone to Kimberly to locate Derwent, who had written him from there. Parnell was at Kimberly too, working at the Company office.

But he didn't see Julien or Arcilla's husband, Peter. She was alone, and a pretty picture she was in a lacy pink hat and white blouse with puffed sleeves. He walked toward her carriage, with the Bantu following, carrying his baggage.

Arcilla Chantry Bartley recognized the forceful young man standing at the ship's rail even before the unloading ramp had been secured in place. She smiled with sisterly pride over his handsome, rugged appearance. The confident line of his tanned jaw revealed a hardness of purpose she knew well from their growing-up years at Rookswood. His dark hair curled slightly, and a thin mustache had been added since she'd seen him last, perhaps grown on his voyage to give the appearance of maturity when dealing with gold rands and diamond moguls who would be dogging his steps once they knew of his plans for an expedition to find gold. It also added a certain rakish charm that fit him well. She laughed, thinking of Evy Varley. As if Evy hadn't fallen for her brother years ago. Evy hadn't fooled her a bit, despite all her dignified ways and pretense and all that silly talk about marrying the vicar's boy, Derwent Brown!

Arcilla sighed. But how she missed Evy! If only she were here with her now. At least the vicar's niece was a loyal friend, someone she could trust. Darinda Bley was a thorn in her side and she spent most of her time in Kimberly helping her grandfather, Julien Bley, with the diamond business. The other married women, whose husbands worked for the Company, were even more insufferable. Two-faced and catty, all! She hadn't a friend to confide in anywhere in Capetown.

Is it my fault men prefer to dance with me? If I'd known last week that old lady Willowby would be there spying on my every move, I would have stayed home and not even bothered going to the silly old Company ball, anyway.

Arcilla swished her fan with renewed vigor. Now there was gossip buzzing in all the social circles, saying she was "carrying on" behind Peter's back. She chewed her lip. If Peter ever found out…

There was also Captain Retford. At Peter's request the captain had been removed from regimental duty and sent to work as his personal assistant in an administrative capacity. Arcilla moved uncomfortably on the carriage seat. Was it her fault he was terribly handsome and that Peter often used him as her personal guard when she had business of her own to attend to about Capetown? But today she had refused his escort, knowing that idle tongues were already wagging and that Sir Julien was furious with her conduct. But she was growing tired of the expectations placed on her by her uncle. Oh, to be free and home again at Rooks-wood with her indulgent Auntie Elosia, and her preoccupied father, Sir Lyle. At least they allowed her to live her life as she pleased.

But naturally, the gossip was all a pack of lies. Well…almost all. It was just that they didn't understand her, these hard-nosed ladies in black. And they most certainly didn't understand her constant need to be flattered. And Peter was always gone—and when he was home with her, his attention was on matters that bored her to tears.

"You weren't this stuffy in London," she had accused him.

"The honeymoon, my dear, is over. It is time to settle down and be about our work. What you need, Arcilla," he said tenderly, "is a baby…"

"I don't want a baby! I want to dance and go places and have lovely people around me, the way it was in London. I want to go home!"

Peter had looked at her bewildered, worried, and then had clumsily tried to make her "happy" for the evening by talking about how brilliant Cecil Rhodes was for wishing to bring all South Africa under the scepter of Her Majesty. Arcilla had thrown a book at him, then raced up the stairs to their room and locked the door. The next day he had left with Parnell for Kimberly after receiving a message from Rhodes.

Those women…the old cats! They were jealous, that's all, because they were all getting old and wrinkled, and men like Captain Retford didn't look at them with interest any longer. They had little else to do but make her life miserable here in Capetown.

She swallowed an unladylike chortle. Imagine! That old dowager Jane Willowby daring, yes, *daring*, to come to Sir Julien on the matter. Arcilla felt her face turn warm over the humiliating memory of Colonel Willowby's wife coming to Cape House to talk with Sir Julien about the "untoward behavior" of his London niece.

"I do believe, Sir Julien, that the girl, married though she be, is young and willful. She needs an older, more sensible woman to keep an eye on her. I only mention this for her own good."

And then the final veiled threat. "I should hate to trouble Lady Elosia Chantry back in England. Elosia has been such a *good* friend of mine through the years that I wouldn't want to bring her worry unless it became quite necessary…"

Arcilla snapped her bright red fan open and closed. She didn't want to bother Elosia, indeed. *Why, I'll wager she can hardly wait to write her, filling Auntie's mind with all kinds of silly lies.*

And now! Worst of all, Uncle Julien had called her into his office yesterday morning and lectured her on her "untoward behavior." She had bridled, a grave mistake when it came to Julien. He instantly became angry. Once he mistakenly called her "Katie." Who was Katie?

"I'm bringing you to Kimberly," he had said, standing and lighting a cheroot. "You can join Darinda there at the house. I'm already making plans with Peter to send him to Rhodes's new colony. He'll be assistant commissioner to Dr. Leander Jameson, Rhodes's partner. And as Peter's wife, you are going with him."

He looked at her with that one eye of his, so cool and impervious to argument. "I've no time to play mother hen, Arcilla. Politics and power are at stake here. Peter cannot afford to have his young wife carrying on with other men behind his back."

"Lies! The old biddy lied—"

"Whether she exaggerated or not matters little to me. The problems for Peter remain the same. I have important plans for him, and it's crucial you do nothing to offend the wives of important men who can make it possible. Believe me, they wield more influence over their husband's decisions than anyone cares to admit. If they think Peter's wife is a tart, he will suffer for it by losing positions that are key to South Africa's future."

"Have you told any of this to Peter?"

"No—not yet. And I won't need to if you make up your mind to cooperate. Thankfully for you, he's in Kimberly, and gossip is slow to reach him."

"I won't go to Kimberly. And I certainly won't go to the new colony and waste my life fighting insects and enduring heat and savages. I'm going home to London."

She had turned to flounce from the room when his words stopped her.

"You will not go home to London. You will do as I say, Arcilla."

She wheeled in surprise, and the look on his hard face froze her to silence. For the first time since she had married Peter and come to Capetown, she was afraid.

"You are a grown woman. You are married to Peter, and with Peter you shall go. You will be leaving with me for Kimberly in a few days. See that your bags are packed. Plans are being discussed for an expedition north. I won't have him burdened by your tantrums. Just remember, he needs you."

Needs me? Peter hardly knows I'm around. She shared nothing of his life. When he discussed things with her, he treated her as if she were a child, incapable of understanding anything of import regarding his plans for South Africa. Oh, she understood all too well! Only two weeks ago there'd been the deaths of some white farmers near Matabeleland. What would it be like deep into the north near the Zambezi River?

Sitting in the carriage on the wharf, she shuddered at the thought. Oh, if only Evy were here, she could tell Evy anything. Though Evy was too religious, she did not condemn her friend. Evy knew the worst about her yet still remained a friend—like her brother Rogan.

Rogan… Her hopes stirred to life. Rogan had always protected her, and he would help her now. She felt the same release that she'd felt after the wire arrived from Aunt Elosia.

Auntie had wired Julien that Rogan would be arriving in Capetown on the H.M.S *King George,* due in Capetown around the fifteenth of July. Julien hadn't been home when the Bantu delivered the wire, and she had confiscated the happy news and hushed it up all to herself, quite pleased that she had a secret Uncle Julien knew nothing about.

Each morning she'd sent the Bantu down to the harbor to see if the ship had arrived. The ship was three days behind schedule, but yesterday the boy returned with a grin. The *King George* was anchored in Table Bay, and word about the dock area was that the passengers would disembark the next morning very early. Arcilla had slipped from Cape House unseen, and it seemed as though Providence was now like the wind at her back.

She must convince Rogan to accept the offer Julien would make him to become part of the BSA—Cecil Rhodes's British South African Company. But she knew Rogan and Julien had been at odds for years, and she desperately feared Rogan would refuse.

What can I do to convince Rogan to join Peter in the Company? There must be a way! She needed Rogan on that expedition north. She couldn't bear the thought of having to suffer such a long and difficult expedition without the comfort of having Rogan along. Desperately, she wrung her Holland lace handkerchief, trying to think of a way to convince him to accompany them.

She saw him nearing her carriage and opened her arms to welcome her favorite brother. "Rogan! This is absolutely too grand to have you here." She broke into a tinkling laugh as he climbed in beside her, grinning.

She hugged him, and he planted a kiss on her cheek.

"What's this, little sister, drenching yourself in diamonds already?" His dark brow lifted with amusement as her bracelet flashed and her earrings sparkled.

"They must weigh a ton. Is it safe?"

"Peter gave me these diamonds"—she flashed them deliberately—"for my birthday last month."

"Where's old Peter?"

"Kimberly." She laughed. "But it's safe here. Don't worry." She thought of Captain Retford and blinked the memory away. No good to bring him up now. "My two Bantu boys are both loyal. They'd fight to protect me. But that's not needed in Capetown. It's that horrid trek north that frightens me, fraught with dangers and beasts and wild savages. Spiders, they say, as big as your fist. And snakes, black mambas and cobras…ugh."

He laughed at her. "My sister, always the little coward except when it comes to the real dangers. So how is my prestigious brother-in-law doing in the BSA?"

She shrugged. "Nothing ails him ever. His work for Uncle Julien and Mr. Rhodes proceeds nonstop. And you, you naughty boy. You didn't even send me a letter."

"Aboard that stuffy ship?" he grimaced. "It was all I could do to keep sanely occupied. How did you know I was arriving today, or need I ask? Elosia, I suppose."

"Yes, Auntie wired Julien a week ago telling him you'd arrive on the *King George*. He wasn't there to receive the message, so I rallied to the cause. I'm glad Julien was away when the wire came, but he's back now." She glanced at him. "I didn't think you'd wish to meet him here when you first set foot in Capetown."

"Brilliant, my little sister, as always. But he's at Cape House now?"

She nodded, and he looked concerned. "Don't worry. No one saw me leave. I needed time alone to discuss things with you, just the two of us." She saw his quick glance, searching.

"Everything going well with you and Peter?"

"It's dreadful."

"As I suspected. How do you find his work?"

"Totally boring. Oh, Rogan, I'm so glad you've arrived. I couldn't be in a more horrendous situation than I'm in right now."

"Come, it can't be as bad as all that. Any man who weighs his wife down with diamonds is bent on keeping her happy."

"Oh, you are joking."

"All right, what is it you've done? Stole the Governor General's heart so every decent woman in town is after your scalp?"

"How did you know—" She stopped as the corner of his mouth tipped downward. "But not the Governor General, silly. I've never met him. Well, I did meet him once at a ball, but he's very old with arthritis in his knees, so he couldn't dance. No, it's that frightfully impossible dowager, Lady Jane Willowby."

"One of those…"

"Yes! And she knows Auntie too."

"Worse luck."

"And she's gone to Uncle Julien and accused me of absolutely outrageous things."

"None of which are true, I hope?"

"Of course they are not true. She's a gossipy old biddy, that's all. Jealous and mean-spirited."

"Well, I can't say what the woman is like, but knowing you, she may have a point or two."

"Rogan."

He smiled. "Cheer up. Whatever you've done should eventually blow over."

When she said nothing he looked at her, this time more gravely, as he must have realized there was more to the storm than her girlish pranks.

"Or will it?" he asked quietly.

She looked down at her lap and fussed with her fan. "Julien doesn't think so. He's threatened to tell Peter about things if I don't fully cooperate with his wishes."

Rogan's gaze turned into a hard glitter. "Best tell me all of it."

"It's nothing, really. Just a passel of old black-gowned dowagers who went to Julien and demanded he talk to me about my behavior." She looked at him and added quietly, "Oh, Rogan, I played the fool." Her voice trailed to a whine as she saw his jaw tighten.

"Go on," he said.

"I went to the Government House Ball two weeks ago and went into the garden with Elizabeth's fiancé, and…well, I didn't mean to flirt, but I caught my skirt on those absolutely horrendous rosebush thorns an inch long, and I couldn't pull it loose. So Thomas tried to help me, and then his shirt sleeve got stuck. We were both caught and standing quite close, and I don't know how it happened, but somehow I was in his arms when Sally Horn came out and saw us. Oh, it was horrid! But I didn't mean anything serious by it. Then she told Elizabeth, and Elizabeth slapped Thomas and—well, you do see how it went?"

"Yes."

How could he say so much with one word? Arcilla plucked a crimson feather from her fan and dropped it on her lap. It ruffled in the wind. Rogan reached over and took the fan from her clutching fingers. She bit her lip to keep back tears.

"And now I'm the topic at all the tea parties in town. The engagement is broken between Elizabeth and Thomas, and Lady Willowby has called on Julien. She'll write to Aunt Elosia if he doesn't do something."

Rogan was quiet, then said, "Peter doesn't know?"

She sniffed, shaking her head. "Not yet. He's still at Kimberly."

"Arcilla, you were very unwise. You've Peter to think of besides yourself now. This isn't London, and Peter isn't the calm, unruffled Charles Bancroft."

"I wish he were Charles," she murmured, taking a handkerchief and dabbing at her cheeks.

"Enough of that. Regardless of how you feel, you are married now. A few more *accidental* forays into the garden with willing young gentlemen, and you won't have a reputation to worry about. You'll be like Anne."

She looked at him. "Anne?"

He waved a hand airily. "What did Julien do about all this?"

"That's the worst part. He's taking me to Kimberly soon, where Peter is, and he insists both of us are going north to the new colony. Rogan, it's horrid. I don't want to go, but I've no choice with Julien insisting, and I…I'm afraid of him." She looked at her brother with wide eyes. She took some comfort in seeing a flash of anger in his dark gaze. Though he disapproved of her follies, she sensed the anger was not toward her, but toward Julien.

Though she knew Rogan would not insult her, she took courage that he hadn't threatened to disown her. It was so good to see him after all these months that Arcilla rushed headlong now to pour out all her woes about what Sir Julien had said concerning Peter's promising career and his need for a prudent wife.

"Julien should have thought about that before he insisted you marry Peter," came Rogan's blunt retort. "I warned him repeatedly that the marriage was all wrong."

She looked at him, suddenly offended at his frankness. She drew back against the seat. "You told Julien about *me?*"

"Of course. Oh, Arcilla, don't look so betrayed. You're undisciplined and foolish at times, and your lack of discretion is known to both of us. So let's not pretend. But now you're a married woman, and there's no changing any of it."

"Oh, I know all that," she said hoarsely. Rogan could talk to her like this, and she didn't find it as threatening or offensive as when Julien looked at her with his cold eye, or when the haughty face of Lady Willowby watched her at the ball with lifted silvery brow filled with judgment.

"Then if you know these things, you must begin to grow up. You must think of your husband, too, not merely waltzing the night away under the Capetown stars taken with some handsome soldier."

"Thomas isn't a soldier."

"Beside the point. And"—he gave her a dry glance—"Julien would hire pirates to capture the ship you were on before he'd allow you to escape to London. He wanted you to marry Peter for a reason: diamonds. And Peter's family is extremely powerful in politics. Julien has definite plans for you and Peter, plans that will suit his own greedy purposes. Now, that's no surprise, is it? You knew as much from the beginning. We both knew."

Yes, she knew, only too well. Life in Capetown was far different from what she had expected. But things hadn't seemed as dreadful back in England. She hadn't wanted to come to South Africa, but Peter convinced her it wouldn't be as odious as she had feared. But it was worse!

She frowned at Rogan, but under his wry gaze, she broke into a smile and then laughed, an uncomfortable laugh. "Oh, Rogan, how well you know me. You and Evy, both. And how I've missed you. And Evy, too. I wish she were here now to lecture me. How is Evy, by the way?"

He did not answer at once, and she gave him an amused, searching glance. "You have your own problems, I see."

"There are no problems," came the smooth voice. "Evy was fine when I left Grimston Way, though Grace Havering died."

"Did she? How unpleasant for Evy. She's all alone now."

"She has Mrs. Croft," came his firm voice, as though he didn't want to think otherwise.

Arcilla thought it was because he did not want to worry.

"Mrs. Croft, that dear old bastion of strength, is as much of an 'Auntie' as Evy could wish for. Evy also went back to music school. In fact, she'll open her own school soon."

Arcilla winced at the boring thought. Piano... She had always loathed piano because it meant long hours of tedious practice.

"Far better Evy were here with me. Do you suppose—"

"No. She has her own life to live, and you have yours now. I'll tell you what I think, Arcilla. I think Julien is right to a certain extent."

"Julien, right?" She could not hide the surprise in her voice. This she hadn't expected from her brother, who normally went along with her wishes.

"Yes, I don't really approve of the long, perhaps dangerous trek to the Zambezi, but since Peter is going and will help represent Rhodes's company at the colony, you would do well to be with your husband."

"But Peter is so dreadful," she said, trying to make light of his suggestion. She didn't want to admit Rogan was right. "I shall never forgive him for doing just as Julien wants. Parnell, too. He and Peter both are at Kimberly doing whatever Sir Julien bids them." She looked at him with a little caution. "If Julien knew you were here, he would be upset. You were supposed to finish out your year at the business in London."

"I find diamond cutting interesting, but for me—an unnecessary skill, and the shipping aspect, much too routine."

"What does the proper rectory girl think of your restless temperament?"

Rogan changed the subject as smoothly as turning a page. "I endured the shipping for almost a year after my graduation from the university. You know I've long had plans of sailing here to the Cape to pursue my own dreams. It's never been far from my thinking."

"Julien will be surprised." She read the hard set of his jaw.

"For the present, it's just as well he doesn't know. I plan to go straight to Kimberly to look up Derwent. So then..." He studied her face before continuing. "Can you help Peter understand? I'm sure he'll try if you give him a chance."

"It's not all Peter," she admitted, throwing up her hands. "He's kind enough to me...but he's away so much of the time at Kimberly."

"Well, then, go to Kimberly and remind him he has a wife. That will get his attention."

She smiled, amused by Rogan's boldness. "I have gone to Kimberly several times. The family has a beautiful house there. In fact, Cousin Darinda is there now. She spends more time in Kimberly than she does here in Capetown. She's dreadful, so unamusing. She thinks like a man."

Arcilla saw a smile on his face.

"How interesting. I should think that would make Parnell happy."

"On the contrary, Parnell is furious. She keeps him dangling."

"I'm sure Julien will put an end to the dangling when he decides Parnell deserves the prize of his granddaughter."

"Prize? Hah. She wants to travel the diamond and gold fields with her grandfather—imagine that! So absurd, but Julien seems pleased to let her accompany him wherever he goes. It is quite annoying how he dotes on her every wish. She can do what no one else can, twist him around her little finger."

"Can she? How interesting." He stroked his mustache.

"Don't get any ideas, my dear brother. Parnell is quite enraptured with her and will demand a duel of anyone else who tries to win her affection," she said cheerfully. "She can even shoot. She likes to hunt with Uncle Julien."

Rogan merely lifted a brow at this news. She hurried on. "But it's not Darinda, or Peter. It's Julien sending us to the colony that is so positively ghastly. Darinda wants to come too. Oh, Rogan! You simply *must* be with us and Peter on the venture. If you'd only cooperate with Julien on that gold prospecting dream of yours, it would solve everything."

She saw the hard glitter in his eyes beneath the slashing dark brows.

"I refuse to join forces with Sir Julien. What I plan to do, I'll do on my own without any help from him." Then his tone relaxed. "But I am sorry about the trek north. It will be hard on you, no doubt, but that's where Peter comes in. Really, Arcilla, you ought to be able to talk this through with him."

Her frustration broke. "Talk to him? I might as well talk to *Jasper* for all the good it does. At least Jasper listens to me."

"Jasper?"

She saw his eyes darken, and she smiled sweetly and picked up her little poodle that had been sleeping at her feet. "How's my precious, sweetie Jasper? Oh, you're such a darling." She kissed the dog's little ears, and it licked her cheek.

Rogan's mouth twisted. "Really, Arcilla."

"I'm serious, Rogan. If you don't join Rhodes's company, you won't amount to anything in South Africa. And besides all that, I need you on that trek north. I'd feel so much better if you were there. And Peter needs you too. When he learns you're here, he'll be so pleased."

Rogan looked immovable. He folded his arms in a stance she remembered all too well.

"Isn't Parnell going with Peter?"

The suggestion that Parnell's presence would make matters better for her and Peter was dismissed with a toss of her head.

"Yes, he's coming, I suppose, but that doesn't much matter. He's no help to me at all. Although, he's not keen on going either. He and I do share that in common. We both abhor uncomfortable lifestyles. Heat, dust, insects—oh, the insects! Horrid, beastly things! They scare me out of my wits. And Parnell, well, he's merely going because of Darinda. He'd go to the moon to be with her if she had a notion it was possible to go there." She looked over at Rogan, adding in a quiet tone, "Besides, Parnell's worried about Captain Retford and Darinda."

"Captain Retford? Who is he?"

His alert gaze made her wish she hadn't been so quick to mention him.

"He works for Peter. A personal assistant of sorts. He's a soldier. He's with Peter now."

Under her brother's long and searching look, she felt her face turning warm and slanted her eyes away. She fussed with Jasper, straightening his jeweled collar.

"You see, Parnell thinks Darinda is attracted to Captain Retford."

"Is she? That's rotten luck for poor old Parnell. He's had his cap set on Darinda for years."

"Darinda is hard to know… I must admit the captain *is* quite handsome. A bit like you, actually."

"Arcilla."

His stern but soft voice brought her hurried denial. "Don't be silly, Rogan. After that simply ghastly situation with Elizabeth's fiancé, do you think I'm witless enough to get myself entangled in such a mess again?" *Anyway, Peter would be there.*

"Please see that you don't forget discretion, sister dear. For Peter, as well as yourself."

"You sound as prudish as old Derwent. He's at Kimberly too, but you know that." She laughed suddenly. "Alice makes his life miserable." She mimicked the girl's nagging voice: "Where's all that gold, Derwent? Where? Where is it? You promised me. You promised Mummy and Daddy we'd be rich when we go home to Grimston Way. You promised Rogan Chantry knew where the gold was, and all you do is work for that nasty hunter, Mornay."

Rogan's head turned sharply. "Derwent works for *who?* Mornay? You don't mean Giles Mornay?"

His robust interest surprised her. "Why, yes… I think that's his name. Alice mentioned him several times. She writes me, complaining all the time."

"Well, well. Again, I've underestimated the jolly Derwent."

Arcilla wondered at his thoughtfulness and distracted smile. "Why does Giles Mornay interest you?" And then as he stared back evenly, she sucked in her breath. "Oh. Now I understand. He's a hunter and guide. So that's why Derwent is with him. Alice couldn't understand it. She wrote me begging to get Derwent a job here in Capetown. Tell me seriously, Rogan. Are you and Derwent going on a trek of your own? I mean, how can you? Wouldn't it be so much easier to join Rhodes's company and go with his pioneers? You know so little about this dreadful Africa."

"Dreadful? You goose. It's wild and passionate! It sends my heart thudding and my energies swimming upstream."

She laughed. "Same adventurous brother. Well, you can have it."

"Of course, I don't know the land yet. That's where a good guide comes in. Giles Mornay knows the land and the tribes better than most. I've studied everything I can get my hands on for years—you know that. I've a degree in geology. But nothing will make up for solid field experience. Though I'm determined to learn quickly."

"As if we all didn't know that. For years and years, it was that silly old map of Uncle Henry's. I'll wager he lied about a gold deposit, anyway. And you've not the foggiest notion where to look on the Zambezi—or whatever that area north of us is called."

He laughed at her, and she tackled the subject again, still hoping. "Rogan, please, you will cooperate with Uncle Julien, won't you? You will come with us and work for Peter at the colony?"

"No."

She frowned at him. "You'll be sorry if you don't."

"More sorry if I do."

"Julien isn't a man to fight against, Rogan. He always has his way, and he always wins."

"Not this time. I know all about dear Uncle Julien, so save your breath. Look, Arcilla, I'll share something with you I haven't told anyone else—" He hesitated, barely able to restrain the excitement in his voice. "I found Henry's map."

"You found…" She drew in her breath and stared at him, knowing her eyes must be wide, for he grinned down at her.

"I told you I would one day, did I not? Well, I have it. And I want to form my own expedition under Giles Mornay. He's the son of Bertrand Mornay, the guide who first led Uncle Henry to the Zambezi region years ago."

"Then Julien doesn't know about the map? He'll be absolutely dazed."

"I don't want him to know until I'm safely across the Limpopo River headed toward the Zambezi."

"Well, if anyone would know about guides besides Giles Mornay and Derwent, it would be Darinda. I told you, didn't I, that she admires hunters and guides, soldiers, those sorts of brave men. It's one of the reasons she's doubtful about marrying Parnell. She told me she fears he won't have the courage to stand up to Julien."

"An odd statement seeing as how she likes to be with her grandfather. Didn't you say she wraps him around her little finger?"

"Coming from her, that sort of statement is reasonable. I told you. Darinda is odd. Anyway, she may know Giles Mornay."

"Thanks for the tip. But if she's as close to her grandfather as you hint, I wouldn't trust her with my plans. I'll talk business with Mornay before it can get back to Julien. He'll be onto me faster than a crocodile after a drowning swimmer if he knows I've got Henry's map."

"Where did you find it?"

Rogan laughed. "Remember the painting Henry did of the battle of Isandlwana?"

Arcilla wrinkled her nose. "That simply horrid thing, yes. Don't tell me—"

"Yes. Amusing, isn't it? All those years it was under my very nose. I should have known. Henry hinted enough about that painting."

"Did he? Well, what does it look like? The map, I mean. Show it to me, Rogan."

"Not now. It just looks like an old map."

"Julien will find out, you know." She looked at him warily. "You can't hide anything that valuable for long. If you'd join the Company now, the way he wants, you could use the map to make your own terms."

"Crafty, aren't you, little sister? Maybe I could, but I don't trust him."

She remembered Rogan as a boy trying to outfox Julien at Rookswood. He had deliberately kept some old maps in an ottoman just to fool Julien if he caught Rogan in Uncle Henry's room. Arcilla shivered. She hated those awful rooms on the third floor.

"Look, I'll talk to Peter about you," Rogan said, but there was a hesitancy in his voice as if he, too, wondered what good it would do. "I'm sure he'll do something about your concerns, Arcilla. You say he's at Kimberly with Parnell?"

"Yes. Julien sent him there to talk with Mr. Rhodes's man, Dr. Jameson. Something about Bulawayo and that African chief who lives there with his warriors. Anyway, I'll be going to Kimberly soon myself with Julien. Talk to Peter if you will, but he won't make a move unless Julien gives him permission." She snatched her red feather fan from the carriage seat where Rogan had placed it and swished it nervously.

"When you agreed to marry Peter, you promised to stand with him wherever he went," Rogan said gently. "You knew of Julien's plans to send him to the new colony. We discussed all that in London on more than one occasion. Remember?"

"Of course I remember, and I remember how I loathed the idea the first time I heard it. What choice did I really have?"

"Practically none," he agreed and looked angry but restrained. "I talked to Father about it. I wish he had listened. You could have fought harder for Charles. I was surprised when you didn't."

She looked at him startled. "Fought harder for Charles Bancroft? I did, for days. Don't you remember? It was Charles who didn't fight for me!"

"Yes, perhaps because his father was rather against the marriage."

"Well! I…I didn't know that." She fumed, feeling hurt and disappointed. She had always thought Lord Bancroft approved of her.

"I thought you would surely go to Aunt Elosia and appeal to her," Rogan said. "She would have backed you up. I'm not saying Julien would have given up his plans to have you and Peter marry, but the four of us together might have at least delayed things."

The *four* of us. That meant Rogan would have fought for her too. The idea both depressed and encouraged her. If Rogan had been willing to stand for her back then, why not now? Rogan was strong, whereas she was afraid. And dear Peter couldn't see further ahead than his duty and honor to the British Empire.

"Well," he said quietly, putting an arm around her shoulders and giving her a squeeze, "that's all behind us. We must move on. Come, Arcilla, it's not as bad as all that, is it? I mean, you *do* like Peter, don't you?"

She looked at him and saw that he was quite grave, and suddenly she laughed. "I had better, don't you think?" She waved her wedding ring, and the large diamond and gold shimmered.

Rogan covered her hand with his and said soberly, "Remember that next time when some soppy-eyed dandy asks you to step out into the garden."

She dropped her gaze. "It won't happen again… I promise. But you've got to make Peter understand if Julien tells him about the garden incident."

Rogan's eyes narrowed thoughtfully. "Julien will say nothing. He could lose Peter if he did."

She looked at him hopefully. "Do you think so?"

"I'm fairly sure."

"Well, I'm not as certain."

"I don't think Julien will tell him. He was trying to bully you. It's his way to threaten to get what he wants. But this time I agree with Julien, not in bullying, of course, but I, too, want you with Peter, sister dear."

"I hope you're right…about not telling Peter. That trek north through savage country, wild animals, and horrid weather is going to be awful… Oh, I detest the very thought. Yet, I think you're right." She looked at him again. "If you were with Peter helping him at the new colony, I would feel so much better about everything. Including Peter. He needs you, Rogan. So do I."

She could see her words brought him concern, and she knew she was unfair in taking advantage of his brotherly loyalty, but what else could she do?

"Please, Rogan!"

"I'll consider," he said flatly, "but I won't promise you, Arcilla."

She was far from satisfied, yet knew she could go no further with him for the time being. Still, there had to be a way if she thought about it long enough.

"Enough of unpleasant things for now," she said with forced cheer. "If you won't go see Julien now, and insist on going to Kimberly, then I'll bring you to the train depot. On the way you must tell me all the news. Tell me about Evy, Grimston Way, and what girl Charles is seeing now…"

CHAPTER FIVE

Rogan had managed to deliver his baggage to the railway and purchase a ticket for a sleeping compartment. It was several hundred miles northeast to Kimberly. The train rattled over the track northward through a wide, flat plain dotted with thorn scrub and grasses. Rogan stood at the back of the train enjoying the wind, the fragrance of the open veld, and the expansive view. Before darkness fully settled, he saw some steenbok antelope and a pair of solitary gray duiker that were early morning and evening feeders. He watched the pair through his glass, noting the variable color from grizzled gray to a yellowish fawn, with a dark stripe down the nose. The male had long, slender upright horns. As the intruding train neared them, he watched their zigzag run and plunging leaps as they darted across the golden veld to take cover in thicker brush.

With the darkness came a stillness, except for the lonely rhythm of the train's engine passing through the wild, open land. He looked up at the dark, star-tossed sky until he found the constellation of the Southern Cross. An awesome longing came over him at the realization of the greatness of God, a longing he could not satisfy. He tried to think of what Evy might say if she were here now.

The first rosy glow of sunrise in the eastern sky tinted the distant, brooding hills to salmon, while a delicate mist garlanded the rocky crests. A short time later that morning, the train pulled into Kimberly's switching line yards where much activity was under way.

Rogan jumped down onto the platform as the locomotive slowed to a stop. Heaving his bag over his shoulder, he turned to the conductor.

"Where's a good room with a bath and something decent to eat?"

The man gestured his head up De Beers Road. "Blue Diamond." He looked Rogan over. "Mighty expensive for a new digger, though. What's your name, young man?"

He refrained. He might learn more if he acted like a busted prospector newly arrived from England.

"Heard of Julien Bley?" He kept his voice casual.

Rogan saw the man's mouth tighten.

"That Sir Julien Bley's an important man in Kimberly. That, and the Chantrys, too. There's a Chantry who's come recently from England. Works over at the fancy De Beers building." He nodded his gray head once again down the street. "Important people. Knee deep in diamond shares of De Beers Consolidated. Tati gold fields, too."

Rogan nudged, for he could see something just below the surface that was goading the old man.

"What kind of a man is Julien Bley? A fair man, is he? I heard he's in thick with Rhodes."

A look of anger flickered in the watery gray eyes as the conductor pushed his cap back and glanced down De Beers Road as if he could see the men in question. He turned and studied Rogan.

"It wouldn't be smart for me to say, now, would it, sir? They got enough power to run me out of Kimberly."

"Why would they bother, rich and important diamond rands like that?"

The old man looked sheepish. "No reason." But then he seemed to change his mind, and his cheeks became florid.

"Diamonds aren't enough for men like that. Too greedy wanting to own everything, they are. Not that Rhodes lives high, mind you. Dresses casual, no more style than I have. Doesn't spend lavishly on himself either. No, it's what the diamonds and gold and land can do that Mr. Rhodes wants. He wants an empire for England."

Rogan was nettled. "If England doesn't step lively, Germany, France, or Portugal will colonize it. England's shown in the past that we bring civilization wherever we go."

The man eyed him more cautiously, then Rogan smiled quickly. "Not that it matters to me. But you seem to dislike Rhodes."

"Not Rhodes so much, but—"

Again, he looked at Rogan and seemed about to back off. Rogan offered him a cheroot, and the man bit off the end and bent to light it from Rogan's match. Rogan peered into his eyes. "You mean Sir Julien Bley, then?"

"If you wanna know, I hate him."

Rogan dropped the match and stepped on it. "A real bloke, is he?"

"Neither diamonds nor gold is enough. He's got to have the coal, too. Though he didn't discover it. Him and those lawyers at De Beers—Wolf Pack, I heard some call 'em. Don't know how many there are, but maybe a dozen, maybe less. They form some sort of board that interprets the mining laws and such. There are those who say the laws all favor Rhodes's company. I wouldn't trust any o' them."

Rogan felt his own jaw tensing. "How did you hear about the coal?"

The old man drew himself up. "Johnny discovered it, that's why. Johnny Sheehan, my nephew. They're stealing him blind. Julien Bley is taking it right out from under him. The Wolf Pack says he didn't abide by the mining laws, so he's lost his claim by a hair. Rubbish! They got some skinny crack in the law they can slither through and steal the coal claim, is all. Johnny's trying to fight them, but what can he do against such powerful men? But he'll try. He's meeting with them this afternoon at De Beers."

Rogan studied the old, weathered man bent with age, and then he saw a young man coming toward them, walking with a limp.

"That's my nephew here now, Johnny Sheehan. Irish lad, he is, through and through. He's a fighter, that one. But sometimes fighting ends up getting you hurt. That's how he's got that bum leg. He came here when he was sixteen with a dream. Worked long days and nights in the diamond mines. He got injured, and there weren't any doctors around in these here parts to patch him up, so the bone's still not set straight. Too late now. But he don't cry none about it."

The young man walked up. He was tall and skinny with alert blue eyes and fair brown hair.

"Morning, Uncle. How was the run from the Cape?"

"Fine, fine, nice stop at Mafeking. Johnny, this is—" Suddenly the old train man looked at Rogan, realizing he didn't even know his name.

"Rogan," he said simply.

"Johnny Sheehan, Ireland. England, are you? Aye, it tells." He grinned. "Looking for work? You can always find it at the Big Hole."

"Big Hole?"

"Sure, that's what everyone calls the diamond mine. It's as deep as a large crater now. Diamonds are coming out of there every day."

"I was telling Mr. Rogan about your coal find," the old man said, and Johnny's face went stolid.

"Let's not talk about that now, Uncle Gerald."

"You keeping that meeting with those lawyers from De Beers?"

"You bet I am." He pulled out a scrap of paper from his pocket and squinted at it. "Tomorrow at eleven in the morning."

"You need them spectacles. You be careful, now, Johnny boy, when you're talking to them. You be dealing with spittin' cobras. A whole mess of 'em."

The willowy Irishman waved off his uncle. "You know me. I'm always careful."

He looked at Rogan, and friendliness returned to his face. "There's a good eatery not far from here. Kittleman's, it's called. Fair prices. They give you a good breakfast. No cheating on the eggs and mealies."

Rogan had already learned that mealies were some sort of a grain cereal popular with the Boers.

"Thanks. I think I'll try it. You going that way?"

Johnny Sheehan looked at him a moment. "Don't mind if I do." He turned to his uncle. "See you later."

Kittleman's eatery was warm and clean with plain tables and dishes. It was owned and run by an Australian couple who had come to Kimberly in the 1880 gold rush on the Witwatersrand. They hadn't struck it rich, but they'd made enough to settle down and feed miners and prospectors instead of resorting to a pick and shovel.

Rogan ordered his breakfast of eggs, bacon, and coffee. He avoided the mealies, which reminded him of bland mush, a breakfast he had turned down when a boy at Rookswood. As he ate with John Sheehan, the Irishman loosened up, and the talk soon turned to the coal deposit he'd found farther north. It was just as the old train man Gerald had said. John had pegged a claim, and now the Rhodes's company was disputing it.

"It's Sir Julien Bley," Johnny was saying over his bowl of mealies. "He wants that claim all for himself."

Rogan felt empathy for the young Irishman as he thought of his own interests in the Zambezi and the clutching hands of his uncle.

"I'd better tell you who I am," he said over his coffee. "My name is Rogan Chantry. Sir Julien is an uncle."

Sheehan's face seemed to lose its blood. Rogan saw his fingers tighten on the spoon in his hand.

"So that's it. He's hired a spy. You're laying a trap with my own mouth."

"No." Rogan set his cup down. "I'm not working for my uncle. I'm here on my own. I'm headed north of the Limpopo on an expedition. I want no part of my uncle. I like my independence."

The young man relaxed a little but looked wary now. Rogan didn't blame him.

"Maybe you can put a word in for me with Parnell Chantry over at the mining office of De Beers. I suppose you two are related?"

"My brother. I can't promise anything, but I'll talk to Parnell." Rogan knew Parnell could do little on his own. He answered to the Company, to Julien in particular. Unless Julien agreed, Parnell wasn't likely to change matters.

"I don't want anything that isn't mine fair and square, Rogan Chantry. That entire claim I filed legally. And I intend to keep it."

"Don't blame you. Fight for it if you will. I'll mention you to Parnell."

"You're a fair man, Rogan. I believe you."

They talked on for a while until Rogan finished his coffee, then he paid for the food and left Sheehan pondering over his coffee.

A short time later Rogan entered the room at the hotel, preoccupied and restless. He felt a strange kind of anger that didn't come often. Coal wasn't as glamorous as gold and diamonds, but it could be worth millions. The establishment of the Rhodes colony in the north and the growth of this entire area, including Kimberly, would depend on a constant supply of energy. Naturally, De Beers and Julien wanted that coal deposit that young John Sheehan had filed on.

Rogan was still frowning as he heard the Bantu workers stoking wood into the hotel boiler beneath his window, affording him all the steaming water he wanted for his bath. He shaved with a straight razor while serving boys unpacked his trunk and a valet made sure the trousers and shirt were neatly pressed, his boots polished to a shine.

A little while later, dressed smartly, his dark hair still damp and smelling of the hotel brilliantine, he left his room, the leather envelope containing the map worn safely in the leather strap beneath his shirt, and strode up De Beers Road.

At 10:15 he entered the De Beers Consolidated Mining Company to locate Parnell. He smiled to himself. His brother, two years his senior, would be taken aback to see him here now. Rogan wondered if Peter was here too. He might be down at the mine, or off somewhere on business.

The man who met him was dressed circumspectly in a uniform fit for Queen Victoria's private guard, white gloves and all. It was on Rogan's tongue to ask if Her Majesty was holding court today, but he held his flippancy and asked studiously, "I'd like to speak with Mr. Parnell L. Chantry. And if he's not in his office, then I'll speak with Mr. Peter J. Bartley."

"Mr. Parnell L. Chantry is, indeed, in his office. May I tell him who is here to see him?"

Rogan could hardly keep from smiling as he said, "Mr. Rogan H. Chantry from Grimston Way, England, is here to call upon his brother."

At once the dutiful man mellowed with a swift and flowing apology.

"We've never had the privilege of seeing you here before, Mr. Chantry, sir. I should have known, sir. You do look a bit like your brother."

Rogan smiled at the man's words. Actually, Parnell and he looked less alike than most blood brothers, not that it mattered.

It was a showy building, and in some unholy way it suggested to Rogan a religious edifice dedicated to secular achievement. Fancy balconies made of intricate white ironwork graced three floors. The walls were made of red brick. The corners of the walls were stylishly made of hewn-out stone blocks, adding to the grandeur. The windows were of stained glass, and all the door fittings were shiny brass.

The equally fancy guard, if that's what he was, brought Rogan up a sweeping staircase to the third floor.

"Here you are, Mr. Chantry. This is your brother's office. Shall I show you in, sir?"

"No, I'll surprise him. He thinks I'm still in London."

"Oh, I see, sir…yes, indeed. A pleasant surprise."

MR. PARNELL L. CHANTRY, ASSOCIATE, the brass plate read. Rogan opened the door and entered. Parnell was not sitting at his huge desk, but standing before a large map pinned to the wall. His back was toward Rogan when he shut the door.

What would his meeting with Parnell reveal of Julien's plans?

Parnell turned, and seeing Rogan, he first showed complete surprise, then recovered.

"Rogan!"

Parnell was a slim, agile young man, an inch shorter than Rogan, with curling chestnut hair and a dark mole on his chin that women seemed to find attractive. He was vain and at times imperious. He wore an impeccable shirt of Irish linen, and the blue cravat was of the finest Italian silk, all typical of Parnell.

Rogan smiled and walked toward him. "Hello, big brother. Looks like you're doing well for yourself." He glanced about at the fine furnishings and large windows. "A splendid office you have here. You must be earning your keep with Uncle Julien."

Parnell laughed shortly and came to meet him. They briefly grabbed each other by the shoulders and shook hands.

"It's been three years," Parnell said thoughtfully, measuring him. "You're looking well. But what are you doing here this soon away from the London shipping office? I'll wager Julien doesn't know."

"No, I didn't ask his permission," Rogan said, feeling irritation. As always, it was Julien. Rogan walked over to the double windows and door that opened onto the balcony. He looked out over the family mine, the BCB, standing for Bley, Chantry, and Brewster.

"So that's it," Rogan said, hands on hips, as he looked below. "Not much to look at, is it?"

Parnell smiled. "It's what's hidden in the ground, dear fellow—what gets honed from the kimberlite. They call the diggings the 'Big Hole.' They've been excavating diamonds out of there since the 1860s, and there's no end in sight. The quarry's almost a mile across."

Rogan was intrigued that even looking down from three stories up, he could not see into its depth. The Hole looked as if a meteor had struck and ripped through the ground. He saw what were known as donkey engines being used to keep water out of the Hole. Diggers—black, white, and in-between skin colors—were all grubbing around in that giant hole scratching and sweating with backs bent beneath the broiling sun for the enigmatic stones, not for their own gain, but for the Company. He knew that guards painstakingly searched each digger before they left at the close of each day, making certain that diamonds were not being smuggled from the mine. Even so, there were always a few who somehow managed to spirit one or two out. These ended up being sold to a smuggling ring and then into the world on the black market.

Parnell pointed through the window. "Each day we burrow deeper and deeper into the Big Hole, following the blue kimberlite conglomerate downward. Already that Hole's produced ten million carats of diamonds." His hazel-green eyes burned. His mouth widened into a grin. "And Mr. Rhodes's company owns it all." Parnell's voice came off proud and satisfied. "That means 'our family' owns plenty, and Uncle Julien is the manager."

"Unfortunately."

Parnell chuckled, then glanced over his shoulder as if he were worried that someone might have overheard and caught him laughing. His laughter ended abruptly, although no one was there. He caught Rogan looking at him soberly, and his gaze slanted away and out the window again, as though he knew Rogan's thoughts.

"Julien is not a man to lock horns with. Anyone foolish enough to try ends up the loser. I don't need to warn you. We both know what he's like from our days at Rookswood. That's why I'm worried you're here now." Parnell looked at him. "He won't like it, you know. I wish you hadn't come now."

"Arcilla feels quite the opposite."

Parnell looked suddenly alert. "You saw her already at Cape House? But Julien is there."

"I didn't go to Cape House. I came straight here to Kimberly. She met me at the harbor." He could see Parnell's curiosity and surprise as he tried to understand how Arcilla, and not Julien, knew of his arrival.

"Elosia sent a wire, but Arcilla intercepted it in Julien's absence."

Parnell jammed his hands into his expensive trouser pockets and shook his head. "She shouldn't have done that. It's not wise to keep things back from Julien. He has spies everywhere. He'll find out, and she'll be in more trouble than she is now."

Rogan did not like what he saw in his brother. Parnell had always wanted to please Julien because he had dreams of getting greater wealth and prestige through marriage to Sir Julien's granddaughter. That had been no secret. But Rogan noticed Parnell seemed more driven now, not by ambition alone but by worry. He'd grown more tense since Rogan last saw him in London.

"Everyone's afraid of Julien. It's disgusting. Arcilla, now you. What could be worth living in the shadow of his displeasure or favor?"

"Julien knows what he's doing. He has great plans, Rogan. He and Mr. Cecil Rhodes, both."

Rogan already knew that Julien was more than a well-placed partner in De Beers Consolidated. Julien was allied with Rhodes in his determination to forge South Africa into a British colony.

"Naturally, Uncle Julien is temperamental, maybe even ruthless at times, but the cause is so great, the burden on his mind so heavy that he needs our understanding."

Rogan gave a short laugh. "If that isn't rubbish, I don't know what is. He's driven by a selfless cause, is that it? Like Rhodes—it's all for Her Majesty and the good of the world. What about that young Irishman, Sheehan? Is Julien also trying to steal his claim on that coal deposit north of here for an honorable, selfless cause?"

At the mention of John Sheehan, Parnell looked away. He walked over to his polished desk and arranged a stack of already neat paper.

"Who told you about Sheehan?"

"I met him by chance when I got off the train this morning. We had breakfast together, and he told me his unhappy story. What do you know about this?"

"I can't talk about business dealings, and you know that. But I do know Sheehan's a feisty troublemaker. The mining laws rule here, Rogan. Fair and square."

"Fair and square? You're sure about that? Then he should have no trouble, right? Everything out in the open?"

Parnell's mouth thinned. "Don't get involved. This doesn't concern you."

Rogan read the warning in his brother's voice, almost a plea.

"I didn't come all the way from England to Kimberly to play advocate for John Sheehan. I can't help it if Julien's mask is slipping a bit and what I'm seeing is rather ugly. Not that his ruthless ambitions ever fooled me much. I always knew he was a hard man, one I wouldn't trust. But a hard man is one thing…a common thief is another."

"If he heard you talking like that—"

"Oh, I know. He'd be tempted to use that sjambok he favors so well." A sjambok was a Boer whip made from rhinoceros hide, used by Boer farmers to drive oxen and, more recently, for flogging trouble-makers and slaves. "He'd best not give in to his rage with me. Wise up, Parnell. You'll get nothing decent submitting to his greed, just dirty hands. You want Sheehan to lose that claim?"

"I told you," he said miserably, "I don't make final decisions here. I obey them."

"And you like that?"

"Of course not."

Rogan placed his hand on the desk and leaned toward him, smiling almost boyishly. "Then do something, big brother. You've got the means and methods. Look it up, check the wires, find out what happened to that claim he filed. Is it held up somewhere? Who's behind it? Julien? Rhodes himself?"

Parnell drew back in his leather chair, his Irish linen shirt so white it had a bluish cast. The gold ring and diamond pin at his cravat glittered.

"And get demoted if they find out?" Parnell choked. "If I got in his way, what would he do about Darinda? He'd rule against me for sure. I'd never get near her again."

Rogan straightened, disturbed at the sight of his brother cowering under Julien's constant control. "Has she no say about seeing you again? And what would Darinda think about you if she knew that you helped Julien in that kind of dirty deal?"

Parnell picked at his manicured fingernails.

"What Darinda thinks she keeps to herself."

Rogan folded his arms. "Sounds a pretty mess, if you ask me."

"Well, I'm not asking you. Stay out of it, Rogan. I know what I'm doing."

Rogan wondered but kept silent.

Parnell came from behind the desk and circled the lavishly decorated room. "It's you who'd best be on guard," Parnell said as he looked at Rogan seriously. "Henry's dreams about gold beyond the Limpopo may not be as foolish as everyone once thought. That puts you in a precarious spot."

Alert, Rogan looked at him, studying his tense face.

"Go on."

Parnell shrugged, looked as if he wished he had kept silent, then gestured to the large map on the wall.

"We had that drawn up by Giles Mornay."

Rogan stood still. "Mornay?"

"Ah…I see you understand. Yes, Giles is the son of Bertrand Mornay, who worked with Uncle Henry on that Zambezi expedition you've been so fond of all these years."

In three strides Rogan was standing before the map, his jaw set, studying the drawing meticulously to see how much it matched Henry's. His anger boiled.

Parnell shoved his hands in his trouser pockets and looked sullen.

"Julien's been very interested in Henry's touted gold deposit for a few years now. You know that as well. It's one of the reasons why he bought in so quickly with Mr. Rhodes's idea of an English colony north of the Limpopo. Remember? It's also one of the main reasons he wanted Arcilla and Peter to marry, so he could send them north. It was on your sixteenth birthday, I think. I told you even back then what I thought was the cause behind Julien's interest in a new colony."

Rogan was hardly listening. His mind was racing with the sickening thought of his uncle's discovering what he had dreamed of since he was a boy. He'd been a fool. He should have known Julien would try to locate Giles Mornay.

Derwent! Why hadn't the boy contacted him, warning him that Mornay and Julien were working together?

"You'll have to join the BSA along with the rest of us," Parnell said.

Rogan turned sharply, his smile sardonic, and challenging. "Maybe not."

Parnell's eyes came alive. "What do you mean? You're not much better off than that Irish kid with his fool claim to the coal. I've told you Mornay was paid to make that map of the Zambezi. I could risk Julien's displeasure in even telling you that."

Rogan knew he would need to be careful about sharing too much with Parnell. Unlike Arcilla, Parnell was Julien's man because of Darinda. A marriage to Darinda meant that together they would inherit a greater share in De Beers Consolidated after Julien's death. Julien would leave Darinda a large fortune. With this glittering promise dangling above Parnell's head just out of reach, his loyalties were likely to side with the one man who could fulfill his dream.

Parnell was watching him. Had he given anything away in his expression?

"So that's the crux of it, is it?" Parnell said. "That's why you're here now instead of next year. You've found out something… Haven't you? About Henry's map?"

Rogan started for the door. He had to find Derwent and talk to Mornay as soon as possible.

Parnell was at his heels following Rogan to the door. He took hold of Rogan's arm. "You found it, didn't you?" Some emotion brightened his eyes.

Rogan didn't like the look of it, but he could not be sure of what it meant. He looked at Parnell evenly, disappointed in the change he saw, or was it change? Had it not always been there, but now was growing stronger in this ripe environment of greed?

"Breathe a word to Julien, and you'll regret it, big brother."

Parnell stared back, then his hand dropped from Rogan's arm. He let out a slow breath. There was no excitement now, just a sober look. "Rogan, promise me you won't lock horns with him over this."

Rogan was taken aback by the unexpected look of worry. "I can't promise that, and you know it."

"I know you, and I know Julien—better than at any time in my life. That's what worries me. He will have his way, and no one will stop him. For one thing, he's close to Rhodes. If there's any English loyalist more determined than even Julien to control mining rights in the north, it's Rhodes. They both see a new colony as a means to provide the wealth that will help them build a powerful empire for England. Rhodes envisions an Africa 'all red,' as he puts it. A Commonwealth belonging to the throne. He's a driven man…a clever man…and an intelligent man. You can question his motives, you can doubt his right to proceed, but you won't be able to stop him. Nothing will stop him—or Julien. They will squeeze the life out of you as coolly and methodically as a python and will think little about it—a mere sacrifice for a greater purpose. There is no law that can stop them. In many ways, Mr. Rhodes and the Company are the law."

Rogan thought of John Sheehan. His hand was still on the door-knob, gripping it hard.

"Julien will get Henry's map over my dead body."

Parnell went white around the mouth. "Don't even joke like that."

His brother's response did more to shake Rogan than anything he'd heard. A moment of silence passed between them, like a ripple of wind passing through an open window. Rogan deliberately smiled to ease the tension.

His mind went back aboard ship to the pages from Henry's diary: "When it comes to diamonds and gold, I'd trust him no more than a banded cobra."

They looked at each other soberly, then Rogan threw the door open and walked out.

He was sure now that his brother would not tell Julien that he'd found the map. Ambitious, Parnell was; Darinda, he wanted. But it was now clear that Parnell feared Julien in a far more serious way than Arcilla feared him. Arcilla was apprehensive over Julien's interference in her frivolous social life. But Parnell feared him because he was convinced Julien could commit murder if anyone got in his way.

CHAPTER SIX

Grimston Way, England
Rookswood

A week later, Sir Lyle Chantry and his maiden sister, Lady Elosia, conducted a meeting in the Rookswood parlor with Dr. and Mrs. Tisdale, and Vicar Osgood and his wife, Martha. Mrs. Croft was there as well, sitting in a corner wringing her hands. She knew her eyes were red-rimmed from crying as she twisted her damp handkerchief, now and then blotting her pointed nose.

When Evy had not shown up for Allhallows Eve Supper at the parish hall, she had grown worried and sent Wally to the cottage.

"In the rain, Mrs. Croft?"

"In the rain, Wally. Now, scat with you. She should've been here by now."

"Aye, then you be saving me some of that pumpkin pie, else it'll soon be gone."

"Run along. I'll save you a piece."

He had come running back dripping wet, eyes wide, yelling that Miss Evy was dead. It had taken some minutes to quiet everyone down to discover that Wally wasn't sure that Evy was dead, but to him she sure looked it. He said he found her lying in an awful state at the bottom of the attic steps, and he didn't think she was breathing.

Dr. Tisdale and Sir Lyle had rushed to the cottage with a few of the leading citizens of Grimston Way. Mrs. Croft had followed, arriving some twenty minutes later, huffing and puffing her way along the edge of the muddy road through wind and rain, all the time her heart in her throat and a prayer for the mercies of God upon her trembling lips. By the time she entered the bungalow, she was in such a state of exhaustion and emotional distress that Dr. Tisdale had Mrs. Tisdale treat her with a mild sleeping powder while he gave his full attention to Evy. Mrs. Croft lay down on the divan and remembered nothing until her niece Lizzie shook her awake an hour later.

She awakened to a cup of strong tea and Lizzie hovering about her like a nervous swallow. Lizzie had come down from Rookswood with the latest news and to bring Mrs. Croft up to Rookswood. Dear Evy was not dead, although she was gravely injured.

"The poor darlin' lost her footing, she did. It were dreadful, Aunt Edna, just dreadful. I was there when they carried her up the stairs and put her in her old room near the nursery."

Lizzie told her how the squire and Lady Elosia had insisted Evy be brought immediately to Rookswood. They had put her in the very bedroom she had used as a girl when Mrs. Grace Havering lived with her at Rookswood as Miss Arcilla's governess.

Lady Elosia wanted Mrs. Croft to pack some of Evy's things and come and stay with her in the alcove beside Evy's chamber. Although Mrs. Croft wouldn't come out and say so, she had long considered Evy like a granddaughter. She had loved her dearly from the time Evy was in braids and would sneak into the big rectory kitchen for freshly baked scones.

Now sitting off by herself in the Rookswood parlor, Mrs. Croft looked up from her wet handkerchief as Dr. Tisdale, a tall gaunt man with a two-inch-wide silver bar mustache, was gravely answering Lady Elosia's question. Mrs. Croft had been so upset, she hadn't heard what the question was.

"As to that, Lady Elosia, I cannot say. That will be for experts to decide. Whether Evy ever walks again is too early to determine. We'll know more as we observe her recovery, which, quite frankly, might be rather slow, given the seriousness of her injury."

Mrs. Croft choked back a sob. *Never walk? Oh, the cruelties of life.* Dr. Tisdale went on to state that Evy's back was not broken, but although he could not prove it, he believed there was damage to her spine.

"She will benefit from treatment I cannot give here in Grimston Way. She will need to go to a hospital in London."

"This is, indeed, a great tragedy," Vicar Osgood said. "But we must trust God's good providence in all this. Not to say we take this lightly. No, not at all." He was short and plump with a shiny scalp. "We should at least try to contact any of Evy's direct relatives."

"Yes, a shame," Martha Osgood said. "Such a lovely girl like that, alone in the world and without mother, sister, or even an aunt of blood to step forward to care for her. We simply *must* do something, Lady Elosia. I always did think it a trifle unhealthy for her to be living alone in that cottage."

"Not to say Grimston Way isn't a perfectly safe and secure village," Sir Lyle said flatly, as though his squireship were being faulted. "It's not as though she lived in the East End of London where thieves abound thicker than rats."

"Oh yes, surely," Mrs. Tisdale nodded vigorously. "Quite safe. It would be scandalous if it wasn't, wouldn't it? I mean, my dear Alice grew up here. Such a *splendid* child she was. And now she's off in that savage land of Africa— I do hope Derwent discovers gold—"

The squire stood, shoving his hands in his trouser pockets and frowning, looking nothing like his handsome son Rogan Chantry, Mrs. Croft thought. *That scoundrel, Rogan. Ought to be here now at a time like this.*

Sir Lyle looked somewhat embarrassed by Mrs. Tisdale's little speech. Of course, it had nothing whatever to do with poor Evy. Mrs. Croft turned an irate glance on the doctor's wife, but the poor woman seemed not to notice that the squire had cut off her rambling. So like

Mrs. Tisdale. Always bragging silly like about that Alice Tisdale, now "Mrs. Derwent Brown." Mrs. Croft shook her head. Dreadful mistake, that was. Alice had stolen that decent boy right from under Evy's nose. Shameful, it was. All so he could go looking for gold in Africa. Such piffle.

"Her accident had nothing whatsoever to do with being alone in the cottage," Sir Lyle stated.

"Of course not." Mrs. Tisdale seemed to shrink like a fading rose beneath his gaze.

"We should make certain a rail is put on those attic steps," he told Lady Elosia.

"They *are* steep," Lady Elosia said with a frown and a shudder. "Poor child. The thunder and lightning must have startled her."

Vicar Osgood nodded in agreement. "Nonetheless, Martha has a point. Evy ought to be with family."

Martha Osgood nodded. She was a slight woman with graying hair and patient ways. She sat still, her wrinkled hands folded quietly on her lap. She seemed to watch the squire with compassion, Mrs. Croft thought.

"Not that we haven't tried to be her family," Vicar Osgood said. "We even invited her to live at the rectory and take her old room, but she wouldn't hear of it."

"Too many memories, no doubt," Martha said.

"And an independent spirit," the squire added. "Trouble is, Vicar, Evy has no blood relatives in England."

"It's such a grief Grace Havering died so young," Mrs. Tisdale said. "A fine woman. Treated Evy like her daughter."

Lady Elosia stood, all six feet of her, with a dignified lift of her head, her gray-gold hair smoothly wrapped into a chignon. She seemed to have had enough of the confab and took matters into her own hands, as usual. She touched the diamond brooch on the bodice of her pinstripe satin blouse with leg-of-mutton sleeves.

"We will need to contact Julien about Evy's unfortunate accident,

Lyle. There's no way around this. She ought to be placed in a London hospital. She will need money for her expenses."

Every head present in the little confab appeared to turn her way, including Mrs. Croft's. *Sir Julien Bley in Capetown? Now why would Lady Elosia be saying that? Miss Evy is no relation to that evil-looking Julien with his one eye and black patch.*

"Don't you think so, Lyle?" Lady Elosia urged when the squire was silent a moment too long.

He turned toward his older sister, and it seemed to Mrs. Croft that he sighed.

"Yes. But there won't be a need to wire him. Anthony's in London."

"Oh? Well, tush," Lady Elosia said, brows lifted. "Of all things. And I didn't know."

Lady Elosia knew just about everything there was to know, thought Mrs. Croft.

"And he hasn't called at Rookswood?"

The squire cleared his throat. Immediately, Mrs. Tisdale's hungry eyes were alert and interested.

That got her hair prickling. Soon Mrs. Tisdale would be gossiping, asking questions about why Anthony Brewster didn't call at Rookswood, and suggesting reasons she knew nary a thing about.

"He's at the diamond-cutting business," Sir Lyle told his sister.

"Ah, well," Elosia said reflectively. "That rather explains things. Then Anthony can wire Julien."

Mrs. Croft noticed that Mrs. Tisdale's eyes narrowed thoughtfully.

In the meantime, Lady Elosia decided that Evy would remain at Rookswood and that Mrs. Croft and Lizzie would tend to her needs. That was just the way Mrs. Croft wanted it.

"I'm certain Julien will have something to say about this tragedy, as well as its aftermath," Sir Lyle stated.

"Quite sure," Lady Elosia said.

CHAPTER SEVEN

Kimberly, South Africa

Rogan strode up De Beers Road scowling to himself over the disturbing turn of events.

"Mr. Rogan!"

He stopped and turned. A familiar young man, slim and wiry, with russet hair beneath a floppy hat came hurrying across De Beers Road and caught up with him, grinning widely. He stood shaking Rogan's extended hand.

"Am I glad to see you, Mr. Rogan. This is a grand surprise. Thought you wouldn't arrive for more'n a year. Was just on my way up to the Blue Diamond to wait for you."

Derwent and his wife, Alice, had arrived in Capetown a short time after Arcilla and Peter married and sailed to the Cape. But even after a year beneath the African sun, his fair skin had refused to tan, except for the freckles on his gaunt nose, which had deepened into a toasty color. He was the same old Derwent Brown, and Rogan found himself relaxing and smiling at his boyhood village friend, hitting him good-naturedly on the shoulder.

"Good to see you've survived all the lions and snakes, Derwent. How is Alice taking it all?"

Derwent's nervous fingers removed his floppy hat and then put it back on again as he continued to smile.

"She's doing dandy, but missing Grimston Way, to be sure." He changed the subject a little too quickly. "I daresay I was mighty surprised to get your message this morning. So was Alice. This is good news, sir! We're both hoping you'll come to supper tonight."

"I'd be glad to come." Rogan strode along toward the hotel, and Derwent's long legs kept up.

"I just left Parnell at De Beers Consolidated Mining Company. Do you know what's on the wall?"

Derwent looked suddenly dismal. "Aye, sir, I saw it…a map, drawn by Giles Mornay."

"Aye, indeed," Rogan countered curtly. "The very man I've been telling myself I'd hire for the expedition north. And now what do I discover on my arrival?"

Derwent rubbed his nose. "That I've been working for him—an' he's drawn an expedition map, and not for us—but for the BSA."

"Exactly." Rogan narrowed his eyes as he peered at Derwent. "How did you allow that to happen, I'd like to know?"

"The map wasn't anything I ever expected, Mr. Rogan. I'd never have guessed he was doing it at all, leastwise for Sir Julien. Mr. Mornay sure did keep it from me. Not that I told him about you," he hastened, "or mentioned our—your plans for the Zambezi expedition. I was waiting for your direction. I figured when you were ready, you'd let me know, and then I'd talk to him about doing the trek with us, try to line him up early so he wouldn't hire out on one safari or another. Those Europeans sure do think highly of shooting big game for their fancy."

Rogan stopped on the busy street and pushed his hat back. Had he heard right?

"What do you mean, waiting for my direction?"

"Aye. Didn't think you'd want me to talk money with Giles, since it wasn't wise to talk about the trek north until you sent me word for the go-ahead. Besides, you hadn't authorized me to talk money, an' there's no telling how much he wants. Could be costly, I daresay."

"Hold on." Rogan was baffled. "Are you telling me you already wired me in London about locating Mornay?"

Derwent, too, looked baffled. He crinkled his eyelids against the bright morning sun. "Sure I did, Mr. Rogan. 'Twas the first thing I did. Thought you'd want to know how I managed to hire on with him. Seemed like the wise thing to do, getting to know Mr. Mornay like that."

Rogan pulled his hat lower. "So it was. Clever of you." His suspicions rose, not of Derwent, but of Parnell. Something was wrong, terribly wrong.

"I wasn't trying to be clever, sir. Just thought it was a good thing to do."

Rogan stood still, hands on his hips, thinking, then scowling to himself.

"So why did I not get that wire?" he mused aloud.

"Now, that's an odd one, sir. I sent it straight to the train junction in Grimston Way." Derwent shook his head. "Something went wrong, then."

"Something did," Rogan said. "And I doubt if it went wrong at Grimston Way." His anger flared like a match. Julien again, who else? Or even Parnell, that weasel brother of his pretending to worry about him when all the time—Parnell had mentioned Company spies.

"From where did you send it? Kimberly, I suppose?"

"Aye, from the train depot." Derwent hunched his shoulders in a glum stance. "What do you think it means?"

"Spies."

"Spies?"

Just how pervasive was the Company's spy ring? "Do you remember what you wired me?" It would be worse if he'd mentioned Henry by name.

"Don't recall everything I said. Just that I'd made contact with Giles Mornay, son of Mr. Henry's hunter-guide to the Zambezi, the man you mentioned to me. And should I try to hire him for the trek?"

Rogan tipped his mouth into a quirkish smile. "Anything else?"

"No, that was it."

And that was enough. Enough to let either Parnell or Julien himself know of Rogan's plans to hire Giles Mornay.

"I didn't know Giles was doing the map until Mr. Parnell and another man from the Company came to pick it up and bring it to Sir Julien Bley. Guess he didn't think it was important for me to know."

"I studied that map, and it's uncomfortably close to what Henry drew and left me in his will. If I don't move fast, Julien and the Company will be ahead of us, and all my planning will be for naught."

Derwent looked startled. "Aye, Mr. Rogan, you're not saying, are you, that you found that old map of Henry Chantry's?"

Rogan grinned and threw an arm around his friend's slim shoulders. "That's exactly what I'm saying, Derwent, but don't breathe a word to anyone. That includes Alice when you're with her at night."

Derwent flushed. "No, I wouldn't say a thing to anyone. Does this mean you'll be wanting to arrange that expedition soon, then?"

"You bet I do. But I want the best guide available. That means Giles Mornay."

"Looks like I made a blunder sending that wire the way I did. I should have been more careful and sent a letter, Mr. Rogan."

"Forget it. There was no way you could know of BSA spies crawling around like rats. Cheer up, friend Derwent, we're not beaten yet. Henry's map includes information even Mornay doesn't know." He thought of those strange symbols Henry had sketched. If Giles Mornay did have knowledge of the symbols, he hadn't included them on the map hanging in Parnell's office.

"If Giles Mornay knew where to look, he'd have gone there himself by now," Rogan said. "That means we are still a lap ahead in the race, Derwent. But we have to start as soon as possible."

"Spies," Derwent was saying, shaking his head in disbelief. "Seems folks will do most anything for diamonds or gold. What was it Vicar Havering used to tell us on Sunday mornings?"

"I don't remember," Rogan said. "Come on, take me to Mornay's shack. We've got to get things moving." *Before Derwent starts preaching!*

Derwent smiled suddenly and snapped his fingers. "Aye, I've got it. 'The love of money is a root of all kinds of evil.' Something like that. I'll need to look it up—in First Timothy I think it is."

Rogan, too, remembered. The strange thing was, the more he tried to push aside spiritual teachings he'd grown up with, the stronger the memories became.

"Where does Mornay live?" he asked abruptly.

"A few miles outside Kimberly. We'll need us horses, for sure. He just came back from a safari. Some Germans hired him. They were up hunting around the Limpopo River."

"All right. Where can we buy some good horses? Not the broken-down animals I've seen since arriving."

"Sheehan has good horses. A Dublin man, he was. Just like you when it comes to knowing a good horse, Mr. Rogan."

"John Sheehan, with the bad leg?"

"Aye, that's him, all right. You know him?" Derwent sounded surprised.

"I met his uncle on the train from Mafeking." He didn't mention the problem with John Sheehan's claim, but Derwent already looked upset about it.

"John's filed on a high-grade coal deposit in the north. He's waiting to find out if the mining board approved his register yet. He's a good fellow, Mr. Rogan. A man to trust. It worries me, all this trouble he's been having."

"Yes, well, I've enough troubles with the Company myself."

"Seems like the BSA wants that claim too. Doesn't seem just."

Rogan didn't like the implications on that coal deposit claim, either. He had liked what he saw of the young Irishman. In fact, the way the mining board was keeping Sheehan going round in circles made Rogan just plain angry.

"Let's go see those horses of his."

They strode on. "We'll need to take a taxi, Mr. Rogan. Sheehan's farm is a ways from here. I'm glad we're going there, though. Maybe you can help John. Seeing as how Mr. Parnell is your brother and all, and Sir Julien your uncle."

Rogan remembered telling John at breakfast that he would speak a word for him to Parnell. That discussion had screeched to a dead end.

"I already mentioned Sheehan's problem to Parnell. I don't know what good it will do."

Sheehan wasn't at his farm when they arrived in the old mule-drawn taxi trap, but his uncle was there, and the old man recognized Derwent. As Gerald Sheehan walked closer, carrying a rifle, he seemed to recognize Rogan as well. If anything, there was relief on his lined face. Rogan supposed he carried the rifle for protection against the wilds, but from what he'd gathered in the short time he'd arrived, there might be human dangers as risky as poisonous snakes.

"Horses?" he said when Rogan asked to buy them. "Aye, me lads, we have us good horses aright. Fair uns too. But Johnny's not here now to make the sell. I was expecting him back this mornin', but he hasn't shown up yet. Suppose he's looking into the claim he pegged."

"He didn't come home last night, Mr. Sheehan?" Derwent asked. "Now, that's a mite strange, sir. It isn't like John."

"Yer right, laddie. It isn't the least like my nephew, but he was determined to see Mr. Cecil Rhodes himself about that coal claim before tomorrow's meeting with the lawyers. Johnny won't be doing less than going to the big man himself about it."

"Then he ought to go see Sir Julien Bley," Rogan said dryly. "I doubt if Rhodes is the one holding up the legality of that claim file. Can I have a look at your grandson's horses?"

"You can, but I'd rather Johnny were here himself to deal with you."

"We need horses right now, Mr. Sheehan," Derwent urged. "Mr. Chantry, here, is wanting to pay Giles Mornay a visit out at his bungalow."

The old man scratched his beard and seemed to hesitate.

"I'll pay you more than a fair price," Rogan said. "Or if you can't sell without your nephew's approval, let them to me for a few days. I'll pay twice the usual rate."

"Sounds good, me lads. But Johnny wouldn't take double. He believes in being fair to a fellow. I'll let them out to you for a deposit now. Then you come back in the next few days and settle on a price with Johnny."

"More than fair." Rogan shook hands with him, pleased to see the man's honesty.

Gerald Sheehan led as Rogan and Derwent walked to the stables in back.

Rogan liked the condition of the horses, and John Sheehan knew a good breed. These appeared to have strength and staying power. Rogan settled on a large black one. It reminded him of his prized horse, King's Knight, back home in Grimston Way.

He helped Derwent choose a mount more suited to his riding style, a calm roan gelding.

Rogan handed over several gold pieces for the use of the horses and saddles, thanked him, and then they rode from Sheehan's farm at a fast gait.

"Next, I want a good gun or two, plenty of ammunition, and the right clothes."

"There's a Boer family near Mr. Mornay's bungalow. They sell all manner of guns and leather goods. Best leather is Boer leather. Best hats, too. No nonsense to 'em, and plenty rough." Derwent grinned. "To your liking, I'll wager."

They paid the Boer farmer a visit, and Rogan bought the goods he wanted, a Winchester rifle and two .45s in an oiled gunbelt. By the time they rode into the fenced dirt yard encircling Mornay's thatch-roofed bungalow, it was nearing midafternoon.

What Derwent called mopane trees grew as a border for Giles's big yard. Rogan found the dark red, heavy timber attractive, thinking it would make excellent and beautiful building timber. The unusual butterfly-shaped leaves were stiff, with clear cells that were apparent when held to the sunlight.

"Leaves are good fodder," Derwent added, pointing out some bucks munching them on the ground. Their arrival spooked the animals, and they ran off.

If I weren't interested in gold, Rogan thought casually, *I'd be interested in horticulture.* The flowers and trees he'd seen on his travel in and around the Cape were unusually beautiful at times, and distinctly different from the plants back in England.

He was still turning over the stiff mopane leaf in his hand when several Bantu came forward and gestured to lead the horses to shade and water. Rogan looked toward the porch. Giles Mornay must have heard them approach, as he had come out and stood waiting.

He was somewhat older than Rogan had expected. Yet that might be to their advantage, for he should have a fair memory of his father's expeditions.

Giles Mornay was of French blood. Like the Hollanders, his ancestors had come to Cape Colony in the 1600s to escape the persecution of Protestants by monarchies loyal to the Roman Church.

Mornay wore a small, pointed silvery beard. His hard face was long and bony, and charred as brown as wildebeest hide. His almond-shaped, deep-set black eyes looked back with an awareness and appreciation, but with little warmth. He seemed sure of himself. Rogan had seen that look before—wisdom mixed with apprehension. He knew it would take some effort to convince him to trust them.

Mornay greeted them politely and offered them coffee and beer on a rickety wooden table on his porch. He seemed oblivious to the constant teeny flies that would have distracted Rogan to frustration had he permitted. Mornay opened a box covered with old rhino hide that held cheroots, small, square, untapered smokes with both ends open.

Derwent chose coffee, but Rogan wanted to see what African beer tasted like. Mornay lit a cheroot.

Rogan felt Mornay's eyes, chilly as black stagnant pools, studying him, making their own silent appraisal. "I have heard of you, monsieur. My father knew well your uncle, a bold man."

Rogan kept his steady smile. "You speak of Julien or Henry?"

The humor was not lost on Mornay, and his mouth turned above his beard. "I speak of Henry Chantry."

Rogan leaned back in the chair, putting his booted feet on the wooden footrest.

"Your father brought my uncle to the Zambezi region in the north."

"He did. A very long, hard, and dangerous trek."

"If I may get right to the point, I'm here from England in the memory of my uncle. A blood uncle I was fond of, and respected, despite the flaws in his reputation—some of which are unproven, by the way."

"The theft of the Kimberly Black Diamond, yes?"

"Then you know."

"As do most who have been born and raised here, monsieur. It is a famous tale one grows up with." His black eyes took on a flicker of malicious amusement. "Like the great deposit of gold reported to have been discovered north of here by your uncle and my esteemed father, Bertrand."

Did Giles believe the report? Rogan was cautious. Could he be trusted? He had to proceed carefully, but time was of the essence. If he was to proceed north before Julien, Rogan had to know where Mornay stood.

"I take it you have doubts about the gold find?"

Mornay spread a hand expressively. "My father died on the journey, as did the Hottentot, Sam, who is reported to have led them to the deposit. Only your uncle made it out alive, so how can one say for sure?"

"Because my uncle spoke to me about it many times before his death," Rogan stated, placing his boots on the porch floor and resting his elbows on the table between them. He met Mornay's gaze steadily, narrowing his eyes. "And I'm going to find it."

Mornay was quiet a moment, brows lifted with a debonair expression. "Ah?" was all he said, but it gave away enough that Rogan grinned.

"And what's more, you don't fool me at all," Rogan said, standing. "And I think it is only recently that you have had serious thoughts on the matter. I suggest that what affected you was the sizable amount of money that my brother Parnell Chantry was willing to pay you to sketch your recollection of the trek north by your father and my uncle in 1877. He came to you at the request of Sir Julien Bley for De Beers Consolidated."

"Ah, monsieur, the sizable amount, as you English say, should it not have been as great as the renown due my father for his brilliant guidance?"

Rogan looked at him a moment, then sat down on the edge of the porch. "I suggest that the amount you were paid was due more to the possible size of the gold deposit than to any of your father's due renown." He smiled. "I want to trek north of the Limpopo, Mornay, as soon as possible, traveling on the same route your father led Henry."

Mornay, an unhurried man, considered his words before answering. "You are at odds with the Company, then?"

"Let's be forthright, Mornay. The BSA and I have competing goals. You and I both know there is gold on the Zambezi. And the BSA knows it as well. But I intend to stake the claim first on the deposit discovered by my uncle years ago. It's no secret I'm green when it comes to the ways and wiles of this great land. I'll need an experienced guide to bring me into Mashonaland. A guide who isn't afraid of Sir Julien Bley and Rhodes's company."

Mornay chewed the end of his cheroot while studying Rogan. Then he looked at Derwent, who sat quietly but alertly.

"So this is the monsieur you claim is more worthy than his brother and uncle."

"Aye, Mr. Mornay, this is my friend."

"Odd, you would have a friend like this one." Mornay jabbed his cheroot in Rogan's direction.

Rogan, surprised by what could be construed an affront, merely watched Mornay, who then offered a suave smile—perhaps the most that could be gotten out of the man.

"Derwent, your friend is a bold and brash young man. But I like him."

Derwent cleared his throat and looked from one to the other. "I'm glad you see it so, Mr. Mornay, because Mr. Rogan's been a true friend to me since we were boys in England. His father is Sir Lyle, the squire of Rookswood. It was Rogan here who taught me to ride and shoot. Long he's been planning this expedition, and he'll do it too. Just you wait and see."

Then Derwent surprised Rogan by standing and saying calmly but pointedly, "He'll do it with or without you, sir. And I'm going with him. And he'll do better with the gold than either Sir Julien or Mr. Rhodes. So that's how I see it."

Rogan felt a prick to his conscience. Derwent's guileless ways and loyalty occasionally contrasted with his own tendency toward ruthlessness. He glanced at Mornay to see how he'd taken the little speech.

Mornay looked neither impressed nor offended.

"What do you know about my uncle's expedition back in the seventies?" Rogan asked mildly.

"I was seventeen, and I knew the Hottentot, Sam, who first told Monsieur Henry of the glitter of gold near the Zambezi. I sat and listened by the hour to their plans, their route, their excitement to find a great treasure of gold. I wanted to go with them. Had I gone"—he gestured dramatically—"I, too, should be dead. I doubt I would have survived the Shona attack. Only one man made it out. Your Monsieur Henry. Why?... Luck was with him, monsieur."

Rogan looked at him skeptically.

Mornay lifted a silver brow. He shrugged. "The only thing that saved me, monsieur, was an unflattering sickness that laid me low. I wept after the expedition party moved out." He waved his glass of warm beer. "Luck, she was with me, too."

"More likely, the good Lord was showing you kindness, Giles," Derwent said cheerfully.

Mornay looked across the porch at him, unsmiling. "Perhaps, yes. And sent you along later to preach at me these many long months."

Derwent laughed, and Mornay looked at Rogan. "I can bring you to the Zambezi. How much will you pay for my services, monsieur?"

"Name your price," Rogan stated boldly, confident, hiding his immense satisfaction that what he had come looking for was almost his.

"Fifty thousand pounds. Up front. It is, as you say, a very dangerous trek." Mornay drew on his cheroot calmly, watching him, a sparkle dancing in his black eyes.

Rogan emptied his glass of warm beer, looking down at him over the rim. *Is he out of his mind? Fifty thousand pounds! Up front? The arrogant goat!*

Rogan tried to look calm. He knew he could not get money from Julien without forming the partnership Julien wanted. And the last thing he would do was play into his uncle's greedy hand. Not that Rogan was without funds. As an inheritor, he had plenty of shares in the diamond mines at Kimberly, but access before his thirtieth birthday was another matter. Again, Julien held the purse strings, and he held them tightly. Parnell faced the same predicament regarding his inheritance. Rogan would one day have Rookswood, his father's estate at Grimston Way. But that awaited the time of Sir Lyle's passing, and Rogan wished not to dwell on it.

Except for his yearly allotment—of which he had already spent a good portion on a loan for Evy's schooling and her music school—he hadn't anything even close to fifty thousand pounds. Yes, he could understand Henry better now, and how he must have felt returning to England after being foiled by his stepbrother from finishing his expedition.

Rogan was angry that this imperious old bushman would want to lay down such an impediment.

Well, he'd call his bluff straightaway. Rogan set the glass down firmly on the table, looked Giles squarely in the eyes, and said, "No guide is worth that much. Not even your father, Bertrand Mornay."

Mornay's eyes widened slightly, and he removed the cheroot from his mouth.

Rogan sensed Derwent moving uneasily in his chair, as though he guessed Rogan's temper was igniting like a dry grass fire.

Derwent stood quickly, catching up his floppy hat and jamming it on his head.

"Say, you'll surely need to sleep on this, Mr. Rogan. Like you said when we were boys, most decisions can wait till morning." He looked at Mornay, nodding his head as he did so. "Don't you think so too, Mr. Mornay?"

Mornay stood, not looking at Derwent but at Rogan. Mornay looked like a brown wolf with amused black eyes.

"Then we can meet again in three days, Monsieur Rogan."

Rogan looked at him, feeling his jaw set like a rock.

"Best we be getting back," Derwent said again. "Alice will have that supper ready for us."

Mornay shouted to the Bantu in their dialect, and they came bringing the horses.

Rogan leaned a hand against the porch post, looking hard at Mornay, trying to read him, then said, "Make it a thousand pounds, and we have an agreement. I'll leave you to think it over. Au revoir." He turned, went down the porch steps, and strode to the black. He mounted and wheeled the horse to ride out the gate, raising a small cloud of silty dust. Derwent was quickly in the saddle.

Rogan cantered out of the yard, and when Derwent caught up a minute later, Rogan drew up under some trees by the path. He gazed back toward Mornay's bungalow.

"I don't understand it," Derwent said. "He wasn't this way before. He didn't charge a tenth of that much when he took Baron Frederick von Kessler on safari. Why, it was almost as if he was making it hard for you on purpose."

"He was." Rogan's voice was cold. "He's been bought, Derwent."

"Bought?" Derwent looked at him, brows pinched in puzzlement.

"I'll wager he's been bought by Julien. Parnell will tell me the truth this time. I'll force it from him if I have to."

"Mr. Rogan, it's been a mighty long day, and it's been a disappointment, to be sure. You're angry, and they're all plotting against you, it seems. And this is no time to talk to your brother. I wish you'd come to the house first and sleep on all this. Mr. Parnell will be at the mine in the morning. He comes early. There's little we can do now, and all our problems will still be there staring us in the face come daylight. And I heard Peter Bartley will be there tomorrow too. What do you say? Will you come over for supper?"

Rogan knew he had to concede. Another meeting with Parnell in his present heated state would be detrimental to any plans he had for an expedition north to the Zambezi. He needed time to think about all that was happening and try to decide what Julien had in mind. He was hungry and in need of a good night's rest. He looked toward Derwent and smiled suddenly.

"You're right. I'm starving."

Derwent laughed, and turning their mounts, they rode off side by side down the track back toward town.

The first flush of sunset in the western sky was painting the polished rock of distant, brooding hills a rosy gold. Rogan saw a large flock of birds on their way to roost for the night, their colors faded to dark profiles sweeping across the veld. For a few quiet minutes the sunset slowly rinsed the grasses from a pale eggshell green to a colorless shadow, and the new light of a white moon inched above the hills. Somewhere a hyena laughed in the darkness.

CHAPTER EIGHT

Rogan rose early the next morning, saddled his horse, and rode out to the diamond mine. European, African, even American diggers were already there, clambering about the Big Hole under the watchful eyes of guards and overseers.

Rogan stood on the edge of the giant hole, hands on hips, watching all the activity and thinking of all that had led up to this point. From childhood, the history of the first diamond discoveries was drilled into his thinking until he'd become bored with the familiar saga. Perhaps it was the reason Henry's mysterious expeditions to find gold rather than more diamonds had caught his fancy as a young boy.

Diamonds were first discovered in diggings close to the Vaal River in the Boer Republic of the Transvaal, then again, twenty miles away at Colesber, on a rocky flat-top hill the Dutch called a kopje. The kopje, which was "pudding-shaped," later developed into what was now known as Kimberly. The kopje was now the "Big Hole." Rogan had heard it said that it became the largest man-made hole in the world. After the diamond discoveries, the revenue of Cape Colony rose five years in a row as thousands of diggers from around the world came to Kimberly to muck the blue mud in search of wealth.

This was the very region where Sir Julien and his partner Carl van Buren were said to have found the Kimberly Black Diamond, where Carl died in a mining accident, and where Julien lost an eye. Here, too, according to Henry's diary, was where Sir George Chantry had found the diamond—was it true? Just *who* had found the Black Diamond?

The debate between the Boers and the English over who owned the area where the diamonds were found had raged for some years until England managed to gain control. Finally, in 1872, Cape Colony was granted self-rule. What had Heyden said that night in Henry's rooms? "By all rights the diamonds of De Beers Consolidated belong to the Boer Republics."

Heyden... Where was he? The Transvaal, still working in Paul Kruger's government, no doubt, hating Britain and hoping for war. Rogan hadn't thought too much about war recently, nor did he wish to waste time doing so. He heard a coach coming on the road. He turned, catching the wind in his face.

The fancy gilt-edged coach was pulled by four fine horses. The driver looked English, and beside him rode another man, muscled and blond. A guard?

Rogan narrowed his eyes suspiciously. The door of the coach opened. Parnell stepped out, followed by a young woman who must have been Darinda Bley. Next Sir Julien stepped out and stood, dark and forbidding, his strong features scorched a leathery brown by his hard life in South Africa. Except for the deepening white in his sideburns, he seemed not to have aged since Rogan last saw him. His black eyepatch added to his enigma, and Rogan could imagine the one good eye burning like blue fire. He was staring straight in Rogan's direction.

Arcilla had said he wouldn't arrive until next week. What happened? Julien had to have left Capetown soon after he did! Had Arcilla told Julien, after all?

Rogan armed himself for confrontation.

Surprisingly, it was Darinda who left Parnell and her grandfather and walked toward him, shoulders thrown back. She was young, perhaps Evy Varley's age. Unlike Evy, Darinda was a brunette. She was tall and slender, and as she came near, he could see pearl-gray eyes that measured him boldly. Her neat skirt and white linen blouse with pleated bodice looked precise and businesslike. No frivolous Arcilla, this woman. Darinda looked capable of anything. Rogan wondered if she took after her grandfather.

Darinda stopped in front of him, carrying her height well. She looked at him through narrowing eyes with black lashes, a coquettish smile on her full lips.

"So this is Parnell's younger brother."

Rogan smiled. "So *this* is Julien's granddaughter. I hear you're giving my poor brother a strenuous time."

Instead of becoming angry, she laughed. "You're not like Parnell, are you? He's afraid to contest me."

"Is that what you want, to be contested?"

Her dark brow lifted, and she scanned him again. "Welcome to South Africa, *Cousin* Rogan."

"Welcome? I wonder…" He gestured his head toward Sir Julien. "Does he have his sjambok with him? Or is that two-hundred-pound guard the whip carrier?"

"Oh, you mean Jorgen?" She glanced toward the big man who climbed down from beside the driver. "He does get carried away at times…and Grandfather always has a sjambok near at hand," she stated with indifference.

"Better tell him I'm no longer a boy."

"Anyone can tell that." Her eyes met his evenly.

Trouble. He looked away toward Parnell. His brother was glowering as he walked up, and Julien walked into De Beers Consolidated. There would be no confrontation yet.

"I see you two have met," Parnell clipped.

"Unfortunately, just now," Darinda quipped with innocence to her voice.

Rogan knew the retort was anything but innocent, and he did not look at his brother. It was apparent that she had some of Julien's cool determination running in her veins.

"I've heard so much about you, Rogan. Not from Parnell, but from Grandfather."

"Then I imagine you carry a derringer in your handbag," Rogan said smoothly.

Again, she laughed. "Oh, I always carry a gun," she quipped. "Any smart woman around here will. I keep telling Arcilla that, but she blanches each time she sees it."

"Arcilla is from London," Parnell said, his voice crisp, and it wasn't clear whether he was telling her she needed some of the polish of proper British ladies, or defending his sister.

"She'll learn," Darinda said, then turned her attention back to Rogan. "Are you joining Grandfather on the expedition?"

"No. I came with my own plans." Yet he wondered if his plans were already being thwarted by his uncle. He thought of Mornay and the money he needed for securing him as his guide.

"Grandfather needs you," she said. "You simply must come on the pioneer trek north."

"I doubt if Julien needs anyone except you, Miss Darinda," Rogan said quietly.

She seemed to like that. "I wish Grandfather recognized that. For some reason he thinks he must have a male heir to run the family diamond business here in Kimberly. So he adopted Cousin Anthony. But Anthony is a Brewster through and through."

Rogan wondered what she deemed lacking in the Brewsters. It was Parnell who shed some light.

"Anthony Brewster doesn't like confrontation. Business partners walk all over him. He'd much prefer to go off on some safari, not to actually hunt, but merely to take photographs of big game."

"It's Camilla, of course," Darinda said. "Her mental illness has robbed him of courage."

"Bah, Lady Camilla is as sane as you or I," Parnell countered. "She stays in her bedroom at Cape House because she doesn't like your grandfather."

"Most people don't like Grandfather," she agreed soberly and looked at Rogan again.

"Where's Peter?" Rogan asked Parnell.

Parnell showed unease. "At the house. Julien surprised us all, didn't he, Darinda?"

"Grandfather always surprises people. And I think he enjoys it. In fact, he wasn't due here until next week, but something has changed his mind." She looked at Rogan again. "I suspect it was your arrival. He showed up last night with Arcilla."

Then Arcilla must have told him of his arrival. Again, she had disappointed him. But had she mentioned Henry's map?

Darinda laughed. "Arcilla is still in bed. How on earth does Peter think she can survive the trek north?"

"Better ask your grandfather," Rogan said smoothly. "It is Julien who insists she go. As well she should. A wife's place is beside her husband."

"I always thought so," she said cheerfully and smiled at Parnell, but there was more taunt in her eyes than sincerity. "Parnell thinks the opposite, don't you? He thinks a woman should remain safely in Capetown. I'm glad you don't feel that way, Rogan. Parnell, you have so much to learn from your younger brother."

On guard, Rogan warned himself dryly. *This woman means trouble. Worse yet, she is very attractive. For Parnell's sake, I better stay far away.*

"I'll get Grandfather," she said suddenly and turned toward the De Beers building where Julien had gone. Either he was in no hurry to confront Rogan, or there was something important he wanted to check in the mining office. Whatever the reason, Rogan felt sure it would not be to his benefit.

Parnell turned on him angrily when she was out of earshot.

"Stay away from her, Rogan," he warned grimly, his face flushed with frustration.

"Look, you ruddy clod, I've no interest in Darinda Bley. Take it easy. All I want is to be about my own expedition, free of Julien and the BSA. Tell me the truth about Mornay."

"What?" Parnell now looked distracted, caught off guard. He calmed, straightening his cravat over a watered silk vest. "I don't know what you mean," he said, slanting his eyes away.

"Come off it, Parnell. Someone paid him to draw that map. I've a good reason to think he was also warned to not hire on as my guide. He asked for a king's ransom to head up my expedition. It was deliberate."

Parnell shook his head, then glanced back over his shoulder toward De Beers. "I was told to hire him to do the map. That's no secret. I already told you yesterday."

"By Julien, no less."

Parnell failed to reply, confirming his statement.

"Derwent and I rode out to Mornay's bungalow. He'd been warned I was coming. He demanded an unreasonable wage for his services. Derwent tells me Mornay just came back from a safari with a German baron. He didn't charge the baron a tenth of what he demanded of me."

Parnell shrugged impatiently. "I don't know about that. How could I have warned him? I didn't know you were here until you walked into my office yesterday."

Rogan looked toward De Beers Consolidated Mining Company. "All right, Julien then. But how did he know?"

Parnell smoothed his hair, which glistened like a polished chestnut beneath the bright sunlight.

"You should know the answer to that question." His voice was quiet. "Arcilla's returned with him. You heard Darinda."

Rogan didn't want to believe Arcilla would betray him like this.

"She promised to say nothing until I got my expedition together."

"Look, Rogan, we know our sister. We know she means well, but she's...she's Arcilla. Doesn't that answer it?"

It did. But Rogan didn't want to think of it. Arcilla truly wanted him on the BSA expedition north. She'd made that clear at Capetown. Had Julien caught her returning to the house and forced it out of her? *Yes, that had to have been it.* Arcilla would have been no match in a confrontation with Julien. He could be quite intimidating. She might admit the truth and then make an excuse for her failure in doing so. The worrisome thing was the map. Had she told Julien that he might be led to the gold by Henry's map, which Rogan had found?

"Julien's coming now," Parnell said. "Excuse me. I don't want to be here for this. I'm going to my office to find Darinda." He turned and walked briskly across De Beers Street to the three-story edifice.

Rogan waited for his uncle by marriage as he walked toward him. For a moment Julien stood there measuring him. What Julien thought could not be discerned from his stoic face. Yet Rogan could sense a controlled anger as his uncle stared at him with his one eye.

"You've thrown aside the family's wishes and indulged your restless nature, I see. I should have known a year in London with Anthony was too much to expect from your adventurous sort. Henry, that's who you're like. If I didn't know better, I'd swear Honoria—"

"Don't say it, Julien," Rogan cut him off in a deadly quiet voice. "One word about my mother, and I'll live up to your insults and flatten you."

Julien's mouth slipped open. He glared at him. Then the dark eye glinted like the mysterious diamond itself. His lower lip pulled into a smile.

"Yes, you would, all right. You'd enjoy it too, wouldn't you?"

"Not particularly."

Julien gave a snort of laughter. "I won't give you that satisfaction, my boy. Come. We need to talk business."

He turned his back and strode toward the edge of the Big Hole, where countless workers continued their busy activity. The wind caused his jacket to flap like crows' wings. No matter the weather, Julien always wore English black and fastidious white Irish linen shirts.

Rogan watched him a moment, then followed him to the rim of the mine. He didn't wait and took the initiative.

"Was it you who warned Mornay not to work for me?"

Julien took a gold case from his pocket and removed a slim Turkish cigarette. He lit it, cupping his hands against the wind.

"Mornay is now working for me," he said matter-of-factly. "I pay him a ridiculously high wage for doing very little. The only advantage this offers me is that he will not lead your expedition. Why? Simple. I need you on Rhodes's expedition north."

Rogan tried to bluff. "Mornay's not the only experienced guide in these parts." But he was the best one for following Henry's map, and they both knew it.

"Few are capable of leading you deep into Mashonaland, because few have ever been there. I know of only one other guide who's better than Mornay, Frank Thompson. He is a Rhodes man. So, Rogan, you might just as well forget this nonsense of yours and come along with us. You're anxious for adventure, so you'll do well as Peter's assistant. There will be hard times ahead with the Matabele chief, Lobengula. The tricky old devil is backtracking on his agreement with the BSA. He squats at Bulawayo, his warriors making raids against the Shona in the north. It's time to be rid of him once and for all. They want a bloody fight, and we ought to give it to them."

Rogan could think of little about Julien that he liked. His greed, his arrogance, all served to strengthen Rogan's stance against any coopera-tion. The idea of ending up like his brother, a tool in Julien's hands to do his bidding while Julien held the key to something he needed badly, was worse than losing his inheritance.

With Julien there was no middle path; it was always all or nothing.

"Forget Mornay," Rogan countered. "Somehow I'll find a way. You'll have to accept things as they are this time, Uncle Julien. For years I've planned to finish Henry's expedition, and nothing will stop me now—not even you."

"Commendable. Nostalgic, I suppose. Carrying on your beloved uncle's big dream—"

"A dream you mocked back then too. Henry's Folly, wasn't it? It looks as if it wasn't Henry who was so foolish."

Julien inclined his head. "A point to your credit. Yes, I was wrong, and I've admitted it a hundred times. If I could do it over, I'd not only have given him the money for the expedition, but I'd have arranged to go with him."

"We cannot go back. And Henry is dead." *Should I have said murdered, or do I wait?*

"No, we can never go back and retrace our lives. But the gold remains. And the shareholders in Rhodes's company will find it absolutely necessary to stop you. Unless, that is, you form a partnership with several in the Company, including myself. Cooperate with me, Rogan, and there's no need for Rhodes to know."

Rogan studied him, surprised at his offer. This was a step he'd never thought Julien capable of. Forming a partnership behind the back of the BSA. It said even more about Julien Bley's all-consuming greed.

"Henry's gold deposit will remain in the family, adding to our power and wealth in the next generation. Strike out on your own, a greenhorn who knows nothing of this land, its peoples, or the determination of Cecil Rhodes, and you'll break your back against a solid wall."

"Even Rhodes knew little about Africa when he first came here to dally on the rim of the Big Hole, talking of his big dreams to anyone who would listen. And you? How much did you know when you and Carl van Buren began to grovel for diamonds in the pit as young men?"

At the mention of Carl van Buren, Julien turned full face to look at him. It was a searching look that left Rogan wary.

"You misunderstand," Julien said. "I recognize your potential. You could be a great asset to me, like Darinda, or you could turn out to be nearly useless as Anthony has proven himself to be. The biggest mistake I made years ago was adopting Anthony and making him a son. He hasn't a fire warming his blood. And now we're discussing you, and what can be yours, and what can benefit the entire family dynasty for generations to come."

Flattery and threats. It was typical of Sir Julien's rhetoric.

"Peter tells me you found Henry's old map. We'll keep it a secret from Rhodes. We'll keep this in the family, and we'll both have what we want. You will have your adventure, and your gold, and whatever charming young woman suits your fancy. And I shall have the other half. With it we shall sponsor new and even deeper colonies into the Zambezi, even beyond into the Portuguese port at Beit. Rhodes isn't the only pathfinder capable of building empires."

This Rogan had not been expecting. *Peter!* Peter had told Julien he'd found Henry's map. Rogan could hardly believe his ears.

Julien's eye wore an amused gleam now as his flaming rhetoric about building great empires cooled. He had the arrogant look of confidence of an expert chess player who had just called checkmate on his opponent.

"Don't be too outraged with Arcilla. Naturally, she had no intention of the news ever reaching me, but Peter, dedicated Company man that he is, came straight to me."

Rogan was too disgusted with himself for having confided in Arcilla to be angry with her. He should have known better.

"Yes. I've had it for several years, in fact, just biding my time. Your knowing complicates matters, the way it has with Mornay. But I won't let this change my decision."

Julien's patient smile was a facade. Rogan could see the temper beginning to boil behind his one eye.

"I congratulate you, Rogan. I never thought to look behind that worthless painting. I suppose that's why he placed it there, mentioning it in the will, knowing we wouldn't bother with it. He was smart to mention leaving you the map in his will too. Separating the map and the painting. It naturally led me in two very different directions. Very astute of him. And of you to find it. I'll make you a generous offer."

"No offers, Uncle Julien."

"You'll have to come around and face the inevitable sometime. There's no way you can escape it. I'll give you time to think it over. You're family. But in the end, my boy, we'll sit down and talk it over— or I will utterly destroy you. It's that simple."

Rogan looked at him for a long moment. As desensitized as he was, Julien's calm, steady but coldly pointed gaze left him feeling sick. Julien was absolutely ruthless and would go to any lengths to get what he wanted. He meant every word he said. Rogan knew Julien would seek to destroy him if he did not cooperate.

Rogan set his jaw. He thought of what Parnell had warned him about yesterday in his office. Parnell was right, after all. His brother knew Sir Julien. No doubt, he submitted out of fear.

But not Rogan. There was just enough stubbornness and iron in him to demand that he resist this ruthless ultimatum. If necessary, he would resist to the bitter end.

"I'll destroy Henry's map first."

"Don't be a fool, Rogan."

"I won't become another lackey like Parnell."

"You blasted young buck! I could make you one of the most powerful men in all of South Africa. Do you realize what I'm offering you? You needn't work with Rhodes. You could share a full partnership with *me*. I'll even give you Darinda. A marriage to her would give you more shares in the diamonds."

Rogan's contempt grew. This was not the kind of man he wished to be. Lording it over others, making them grovel by tempting them with their heart's desire until they buckled under and gave in, compromising their integrity. Julien was turning Parnell into a cowering slave who obeyed his every command. And years ago he had humiliated Uncle Henry as well. Everything that Julien Bley had become made Rogan recoil. He would not fall to one knee before Sir Julien Bley and—

Rogan heard a ruckus breaking out behind them. They turned, and Julien shaded his eyes.

Rogan saw Parnell hurrying from the De Beers building, with Darinda close behind. But ahead of them, coming straight toward Sir Julien, was the young Irishman John Sheehan, followed by what looked like three or four men in business suits—lawyers?

John, in spite of his limp, won the race and hailed Sir Julien with a loud voice. A crowd began to gather, and as Rogan watched Julien, he could see distaste written on his face at the sight of Sheehan, but also something more—uncertainty.

Julien turned abruptly away and called to his driver and guard. Rogan looked on amazed at the scene that broke. The guard came forward, armed with a belted pistol and carrying a sjambok.

"Jorgen," Julien called. "Remove this troubling Irishman from hounding me about that blasted coal."

"No, wait, Mr. Bley," John Sheehan called. "I want no trouble, sir. But I want justice. I pegged that claim on a bed of coal on the fifteenth of last month, and by law that file is in my name. Now your lawyers—"

"They are not my lawyers, Sheehan. They are Company lawyers."

"Oh, I know all about those lawyers. The Wolf Pack, Mr. Rhodes calls 'em, and *wolves* they do seem—"

"I beg your pardon!" one of the lawyers said with aggrieved dignity. He turned to Julien. "We have tried to show Mr. Sheehan that he is not in conformity with the mining laws instituted by Mr. Rhodes, but he refuses to listen, Sir Julien."

"The law remains, regardless." Julien turned to John Sheehan. "The date for filing on that claim was twenty-fours too late. There is nothing to be done about that. I advise you to prospect elsewhere."

"Twenty-four hours too late! Too late for what? It's still my claim."

"Nevertheless, that's what the legal authorities are saying, Sheehan. The best thing you can do is get over it and get back to farming. Now, young man, you are blocking my path, and I wish to get in my coach. Step aside, or I shall have Jorgen forcibly remove you."

Sheehan turned a pasty white beneath his brown skin.

"You won't get by with this. Thieves, that's what you are. You and the whole lot of your smooth-talking business-suited vultures. I discovered that bed of coal. I filed on time, and I'll not be taking no for an answer. You're stealing me blind, that's what you're doing."

Julien gave him a cold look and without a word reached an arm out to brush him out of his path. But Sheehan grabbed his arm in a heat of emotion.

"You lying cheat!"

Rogan had made a move to come between them, to pull John aside. But the guard's whip was faster. The whistle of the sjambok cut through the morning heat and caught John Sheehan around the shoulders and jerked him abruptly back.

Sheehan lay stunned in the silty dust, blood seeping through his shirt.

At that moment Parnell tried to keep Darinda from coming forward to look at the man in the dust. She broke free and rushed to Julien, as though she thought it was he and not John down on the ground. When she saw the Irishman lying in a crumpled heap, his bad leg twisted grotesquely, she stepped back, her arms going rigid at her side. She stared at him, then looked at Julien with a blank face. Then she turned to the guard, and her face went rigid.

"You beast!" she cried. "What have you done?"

"Stay out of this, Darinda," Julien stated. "Get into the coach. Parnell, help her in."

But she stepped toward the guard and tried to wrench the whip away. The Afrikaner staunchly held on as she attempted to take it. Parnell rushed in between them and pulled her away, escorting her against her will to the coach, and all the while, Darinda let him know her fury at the brutality she had just witnessed. A moment later the coach door slammed shut, keeping Parnell and Darinda out of sight of the gaping onlookers.

Rogan grabbed the guard's arm and ripped the sjambok free, hurling it beyond reach into the dust. Jorgen seemed about to jump him, but Julien shouted a command. The Dutchman's chilling blue eyes spat hatred at Rogan, who wished Jorgen would disobey Julien so he could thrash him.

Jorgen dutifully backed off and was leading Julien away toward the coach when Sheehan managed to crawl onto all fours and call out after Julien.

"You can't get by with this, sir!"

Rogan's blood turned cold when Julien turned and looked down at the defeated and bleeding Irishman and "smiled."

"I have already gotten by with it. You need to buy yourself a pair of spectacles. When you signed that paper in the office this morning, you signed away all rights to the claim. It now belongs to the Company."

Rogan watched Julien walk to his shiny black coach, back straight. Rogan was still staring when the coach drove away, kicking up fine dust.

"All right, you pack of jackals," the main foreman called to the diamond diggers, "mind your business and get back to work. The day is just beginning."

The crowd drifted away, and few were left when Rogan turned to John. Rogan's heart sank like a rock. Never had he seen a more pitiable expression as the one on John Sheehan's smudged face.

"He beat me," Sheehan whispered from a dry throat. "I signed that paper, aright. Signed it right in front of the Wolf Pack, just as sure as I'm sitting here."

Rogan clenched his jaw and went to lift him to his feet. Sheehan's weak knee nearly buckled again, and Rogan held him steady.

Rogan brought him over to a rock and lowered him upon it.

Someone brought a bucket of water and sloshed it across Sheehan's back and shoulders where the whip had cut the flesh. The sun had dried the blood, and the shirt stuck as Sheehan tried to tend to his wound.

Rogan stood thinking, his fevered mind struggling with a deep anger he found difficult to shake.

Julien Bley was powerful and rich, yet unsatisfied, seeking to quench an insatiable thirst. John Sheehan was a humble Irish immigrant who had stumbled upon a coal deposit that would have etched his name in stone and made him a wealthy and respected figure in history. Now he sat beaten, bloody, and at rock bottom, his hopes dashed. Cheated from his claim by clever lawyers working for the invincible De Beers Consolidated Mining Company. Two men. Two very different roads. Rogan knew with a certainty that he would not follow the crushing footsteps of Uncle Julien. He did not want to be consumed by the same greed and lust for power, inevitably using the same ruthless tactics to get what he wanted.

Nor did he wish to be like Sheehan, beaten and licking his wounds.

Strangely, at that moment, he thought of Evy. She deserved a man of honor, a man who, if he gained wealth and power, could be respected by men like Sheehan for honesty and fairness in all his dealings. Right there Rogan resolved to forever turn away from the wiles of men like Julien. What Julien had extolled as virtues, Rogan clearly saw as despicable vices that had distorted and twisted his uncle into the tyrant he had become. Unlike his uncle, Rogan would make his search into the Zambezi to find Henry's claim, "fair and square," as Sheehan liked to say it. There would be no injustice. And the last thing he would do was to treat his fellowman the way Julien and his henchmen did.

"What happened, Johnny lad? What happened to you?"

Rogan looked to see John's uncle hurrying up toward them.

"Oh no, Johnny. What'd he do to ye? What happened?"

"It's all right, Uncle. Just get me back to the farm… I'll be all right. We will be starting over, is all. We'll make it…"

Rogan watched the two hobble away, arms wrapped around each other so neither would fall. A young man with a broken dream and an old man with no dream at all. Gerald Sheehan had his Johnny boy, and for the old man that seemed to be enough. Poor and broken they were, but he decided they had more of the real treasures of life than Sir Julien as his gilt-edged coach disappeared down De Beers Road. Inside, they wore sparkling diamonds, but their hearts were as bruised as Sheehan's shoulders and back. A concoction mixed up by Gerald Sheehan and applied to his nephew's lash cut would heal the laceration in time. But what would heal the empty heart of Julien? What would destroy the idolatrous shrine to diamonds that his uncle had built over the years? Rogan shook his head at the thought that Parnell was trapped too and blinded by Darinda. Was it really Darinda he wanted, or was it what Julien said she could bring him in the way of diamond shares in the future?

And Darinda?

"Mr. Rogan!"

He turned as Derwent Brown hurried toward him unaware of all that had just occurred, a grin on his face.

Rogan relaxed, recalling the quiet, pleasant supper he'd shared with Derwent and Alice last night in their modest bungalow in Kimberly. Even Alice had changed some since her days in Grimston Way, though gold dust still shone the brightest in her visions of the future. Rogan had liked the way Derwent had prayed, thanking God for their supper before they ate the roast chicken. He remembered the verse Derwent had slipped unobtrusively into his prayer at the dinner table. "What profit is it to a man if he gains the whole world, and loses his own soul?"

A profound question with a profound answer—nothing. Rogan reached down as Derwent chattered and scooped up a fistful of warm dry silt. As he let it fall through his tanned fingers, and the wind carried it away, he heard the distinct sound of picks and shovels chipping away in the Big Hole.

"Mr. Rogan, you're not listening," Derwent said.

"What did you say?"

"Mr. Mornay's changed his mind."

Rogan looked at him, becoming aware at last.

"What do you mean he's changed his mind?"

"About working for you. He's quit working for Sir Julien and says he'll lower his wage. Says if you're interested, he's waiting outside the Kimberly Club to talk to you. He'll begin arranging the expedition to the Zambezi just as soon as you and he come to an agreement."

Rogan looked at him, surprised at the sudden turn of events. He smiled at Derwent and slapped him on the back, and they took off down De Beers Road toward the hotel.

The expedition was on! And he had survived the first battle with Sir Julien.

CHAPTER NINE

London
Mercy Hospital

When Evy opened her eyes, she was a girl again in Grimston Wood, and a man was watching her from the trees. The thunder growled a warning, and raindrops were beginning to wet her face.

No—she blinked her eyes. She was not gathering fall leaves for decorations for Allhallows Eve. She was lying in a bed somewhere. She tried to focus her eyes, but the surroundings were hazy. She did sense they were strange surroundings, that she could smell the odor of medicine…rubbing alcohol… Why, she was in a hospital! This couldn't be Grimston Way. London?

She turned her head to look again at the figure standing beside the bed. The one thing that seemed the same, but not quite, was the face of the man looking down at her. Light blue eyes…pleasant features, platinum hair, skin browned by the sun… He was older, of course, with gray at his temples, yet retaining a handsomeness, and strong shoulders.

She blinked, trying to rid her mind of fuzziness.

Her throat was dry, and she tried to swallow. "I've seen you before… a long time ago…"

The corners of his mouth turned upward, but his eyes held no smile. "A very long time ago. In Grimston Wood, wasn't it?"

"I think so… You remember too. Who are you?"

110

"Anthony Brewster."

His voice bore that pleasing lilt she had heard from others in from South Africa, like Sir Julien Bley. Cousin Heyden's guttural accent was even stronger, with a Dutch flavor. Anthony Brewster and Julien Bley had more English aristocracy to their vowels.

"I'm Sir Julien's nephew from Capetown. You've met Camilla, my wife."

Anthony Brewster... Camilla... Lady Camilla, yes. Yes, now she remembered.

"Camilla," she murmured aloud.

"You remember her? She came from Capetown to stay at Rookswood when you were a girl. She gave the impression she'd come alone, but I voyaged with her as far as London, then I went on to New York on some business."

There was something bewildering in what he said, but her back hurt too much to try to think through it.

"I'm visiting in London on my way back to the Cape. Sir Julien asked me to contact the family at Rookswood. I did so at once, and Lady Elosia told me about your tragic accident. Julien, too, sends his regards and good wishes for your swift recovery. It was a pity you fell from the attic steps like that."

"It wasn't an—" She stopped. *I didn't fall!* she wanted to shout. It wasn't an accident. Her heart was pounding now.

No, say nothing...keep silent...

The bland blue eyes looked back. "Yes?"

Evy shut her eyes tightly to block out everything around her. *Father, help,* she prayed. *I can't think straight, I'm afraid, and I don't know what to do.*

Her head ached, and when she tried to move her legs, they seemed stiffly bound. Nothing seemed to work, and her arms felt very heavy. Panic threatened, and she made a feeble cry.

The man leaned over her. "Don't worry, my dear. Everything is going to be all right. No need to talk about it now. I should not have brought it up. You must rest and grow stronger. You will be well taken care of. I've already spoken to your physician, Dr. Snow. He says you will walk again one day."

She fluttered her eyes open. Walk again? But of course! Why would she need to be told that?

"After six months to a year, with a little help from crutches, Dr. Snow believes you'll be getting around just fine."

Crutches! After a year…no. No! "W-What are you saying?"

"We want you to rest assured you'll be more than adequately cared for, Evy. Sir Julien and I both. We don't want you worrying about finances, just about getting well again. Vicar Osgood has said you are a high-spirited young lady who can face the disappointments of life. Your strong faith in God will sustain you."

She shut her eyes tightly to hold back the tears. It was too much to think about now, too horrid to accept. Naturally she would walk again. She would run. Crutches? No… The very thought made her senses recoil.

"We think it best that you convalesce here in London instead of Grimston Way. Lady Elosia has suggested you stay at the Chantry Townhouse. We all concur."

The Chantry Townhouse. Evy winced, remembering. That was where she'd dined with Rogan after her piano concert, where he had played his violin for her. A night she would never forget.

"Mrs. Croft will come and stay with you. We understand you get on well with the woman. There will be a live-in nurse for as long as you need her. Hopefully, that won't be for an extended period. Dr. Snow will take care of all the necessary arrangements. Also, I'll be here in London longer than I'd expected. Sir Julien has asked me to oversee matters in the family diamond business. So I will be around to see you. Later, when you're feeling stronger, the family lawyer will contact me about setting up a fund for your needs."

All Evy could do was look back at him blankly.

"A fund? I don't understand any of this, Mr. Brewster. Why should you or Sir Julien Bley—"

"The fund is an inheritance. Sir Julien has asked me to arrange it for you."

Inheritance. At present it seemed the least important thing on her mind. Someone had tried to— *No, not yet, don't think of it.*

"I'm confused, Mr. Brewster. What's wrong with me? I must have some broken bones. And…why should you bother to come and say all this to me? Not that your concern isn't appreciated, or Sir Julien's, and an inheritance is too much to think about now. I realize Sir Julien was my mother's guardian, but he hardly knows me…" *Because he wished it so,* she thought. "But why should he, or you, bother about me now?"

His eyes gazed down at her gravely. "I have always cared what happened to you, my dear…from afar, but circumstances were seldom conducive for expressing it."

"And Sir Julien? But why?"

"You are Katie van Buren's daughter." He cleared his throat. "Katie was part of Julien's family. He was her guardian. I think you know that now. And Katie's father, your grandfather Carl van Buren, was his good friend until he died tragically in the diamond mines at Kimberly. Both Sir Julien and I have an interest in you."

She wanted to protest but didn't have the strength. Katie part of Julien's family? Not so. Interest in her? Why now? They were never interested in her while she was growing up in Grimston Way. Why suddenly now?

"Dr. Snow believes you've injured your spine. Whether permanently or not, he's not certain. Only time will tell."

Time will tell. Where had she heard those words before…spoken to her with a far different meaning?

For a moment she was swept away to Rookswood garden on that June morning after Aunt Grace's funeral. Rogan was leaving for South Africa, and he had intimated that time alone would reveal to their hearts whether true love bound them together forever, or whether the passing of time would reveal that what they had felt was also passing.

Passing, like the seasons. She remembered the sweetness of summer near the pond where the gracious swan floated on the ripple of blue, when she'd been in Rogan's arms. Now she felt the chill wind and rain of fall.

"Life's plans are not always tied up in neat little packages," Rogan had said that morning in Rookswood garden. "We find ourselves at unexpected crossroads... Time itself is often the best indicator of which decision to make, for it can tell so many things that are now hazy, don't you think so, Evy?"

"Yes...only time will tell," she had said.

Oh, Rogan. Evy blinked the scalding tears from her eyes, and the face of Anthony Brewster was blurred. She felt his hand awkwardly pat hers.

"I am truly sorry, my dear."

His voice, oddly husky with emotion, confused her even more. This man was a total stranger. Why should he feel any emotion at all except casual sympathy?

She was able to move her right arm, and she brushed the tears from her face. She tried to focus on his face.

"I'm the one who's sorry. Aunt Grace would be disappointed in me. I'm being too emotional at a time like this."

"Who wouldn't be? That was a nasty fall."

Yes, quite nasty. She refused to see that figure rushing at her. "Did you know my mother, then?"

A long pause followed, and she wondered why he looked at her with pain streaked across his face. It was because she looked so horrible...bruised and broken. That fall—that terrifying fall down the steep steps, that ghoulish figure in black that had come rushing at her—how could she explain it to anyone? How could she get them to even believe such a wild, ghostly tale? And how could she even know whom to trust with it?

Someone had been hiding in the attic—someone real. Someone either in London or Grimston Way had rushed at her and deliberately pushed her down the steps—but who, and why? She trembled at the memory. She trusted no one enough to explain what had happened. Except Mrs. Croft. And Evy hadn't been able to see her here in London.

Anthony Brewster stepped away from the hospital bed when the door quickly opened and a nurse in white pinafore and cap entered, the red cross clearly visible. Evy was relieved to see her. Even though Anthony Brewster seemed curiously empathetic, his presence in London near the time of her accident in the cottage pricked her suspicions. Maybe what she saw in his face was not sympathy at all, but guilt.

But how could she think such a thing? It was preposterous. Why would anyone wish to harm her? It was all a coincidence. It had to be. A common thief must have hidden in the attic, that's all…passing through Grimston Way, perhaps thinking to take shelter from the storm. And she'd come upon him, startling him into reacting in a dangerous way. Yes, that must be what happened. Anything else was too horrible to contemplate. She'd been foolhardy to go up those steps to investigate the sound she had heard. She'd been trying to prove her independence, to tell herself she was capable, though living alone. And now she had brought more trial upon herself. She wasn't independent. She needed friends. She needed God most of all.

Crutches—after weeks and months…

"I'm afraid she must rest now, Lord Brewster."

"Yes, certainly." Anthony looked down at Evy. "You heard the nurse, Evy. You must rest. We will talk again in a few days, and you'll be feeling a little better by then. We'll save your questions for later. Good day, my dear."

When he'd gone and the nurse drew the window shades, Evy tried to sleep. Questions hammered at the door of her mind. Questions that had no satisfying answers. She drifted off into an uncertain sleep, whispering a portion of Psalm 37 she had learned while growing up in the rectory: "The steps of a good man are ordered by the LORD, and He delights in his way. Though he fall, he shall not be utterly cast down; for the LORD upholds him with His hand."

CHAPTER TEN

Limpopo River

Dry summer winds swept across the open veld, rippling golden tussock and the assegai grasses camouflaging a pride of lions. A thin cub panted beneath the scorching South African sun. Above, a few puffs of white cloud glided across an expanse of blue. In the indigo shade, among some bleached boulders, the male lion, alerted to man's presence by the sound of hooves, stood, making a throaty noise that carried on the wind.

A few minutes later, when the riders passed by, the pride had slipped away through the grasses unnoticed.

At a brisk canter, those same horsemen, equipped with rifles and belted pistols and followed by three Bantu guards, rode toward the kopje, hunting not lions but gold.

The forceful young man in the lead, wearing a Boer leather vest laced over a canvas shirt and a wide-brimmed leather hat, brought his black gelding to the rocky rim facing the veld with an easy grace. His eyes were as electric as a thunderstorm as he surveyed the grassland that spread between the Limpopo in the south, and the River Shashi in the north. His handsome face and muscled neck were brown from weeks in the harsh African elements, and his dark hair had grown a bit longer, dusting his collar.

Two men drew up beside Rogan, stirrup to stirrup, their horses snorting uneasily as they sniffed the wind, giving a shake of their manes.

"Trouble, do you think, Mr. Rogan?"

Rogan followed Derwent's gaze in the direction of their small base camp not far from the Limpopo, or "Crocodile" River. He reached for a small telescope and trained it on the distant wagons formed into a Boer-style laager.

Mornay grumbled. "Visitors."

Rogan drew his dark brows together, and his mouth turned under his narrow mustache. *Intruders* was more like it. The Capetown gold-bugs and randlords were still sniffing his trail like half-starved hyenas trying to lay a trap.

"Let's find out," he said, then turned his horse to ride down the hillock as Derwent fell in behind. Mornay turned in his creaking leather saddle and gave a swift order to the Bantu, who followed, alert.

They came down onto the veld and rode through the short grasses, keeping a safe distance from the riverbank. Even so, pink and white flamingos nervously swooped away in a pastel haze of wings, causing a great whooshing sound that scattered other birds into their wake. A crocodile basked on the slippery bank under the hot sun. Its six-foot-long body of greenish-gray armor appeared still and lifeless, its deadly mouth wide open as tiny, courageous birds picked particles of food from between its large teeth.

Rogan entered the base camp, which his crew of Bantu workers had set up under Mornay's orders two weeks earlier. The sun was beginning its retreat behind distant hills, painting the boulders with golden-rose tints. Rogan surveyed new Capetown carts, surreys, and covered wagons, some of which had settled in and formed an overnight camp with their own. He did not like what this implied and exchanged concerned looks with Mornay.

The silver-browed Boer of French descent did not try to hide his tension. Rogan knew the split between Mornay and Sir Julien over the unexpected decision to work for him instead of Julien had left rancor between them. He also knew that Julien would do everything within his power to stop his expedition.

Mornay, loyal to the Boer Republics, was not in sympathy with the Company's goals to turn the region "all red," as Cecil Rhodes envisioned. Mornay had admitted to Rogan when he agreed to lead the expedition that he had only made the map because of the high price Parnell had paid him. He had worked for Julien for the same reason. Now he was working for Rogan for less money but with a greater ease of conscience, or so he said.

Rogan drew rein and studied the well-fed horses, oxen, and mules before dismounting. The other animals were being attended by more than thirty chocolate-brown Bantu servants, lithe and straight-shouldered.

Rogan swung down, his boots hitting the powdery dust that was everywhere, and dropped the reins on a thorn bush. One of his own Bantu led the gelding away to be rubbed down and fed.

The luxuriant camping scene of the newcomers convinced Rogan he was right. The unwanted company were diamond rands from Kimberly.

Purple twilight filtered through the lemon-flowered acacia trees, offering speckled shadows. The breeze kicked up, warm and thick with the pungent smells of a wild land, setting Rogan as much on edge as any hunted animal.

Footsteps crunched over the warm ground behind him. Rogan turned, suspecting he would see that swarthy, one-eyed tyrant uncle of his, and instead confronted the pearl-gray-eyed Darinda. He muttered his frustration under his breath. A girl, a pretty one at that, was the last thing he wanted to trouble with now, and this one was not past wandering the camp as freely as she pleased.

At least she was dressed for the rough in what looked like a specially designed hunter's outfit of tan, in the style of a riding habit. He noted she wore a belt and a smaller pistol, probably a .38.

Aware that she had spoken, Rogan roused himself and smiled—casually, he hoped.

"What are you doing here, Darinda?"

She walked toward him. "I told you at Kimberly I intended to join the expedition north."

He managed a disarming smile. "If your grandfather and Parnell agree to let you face lions and hippos on the Company trek north, far be it from me to raise dust over it, but not on this expedition, Cousin."

He tried to ignore that she stood too close, hands on hips, her dark head tilted, looking up at him to see what he would do. He had a mind to let her know. He chuckled and gave her chin a little flip with his finger that broke the spell she was trying to weave.

"No women allowed. Not even the granddaughter of a diamond rand."

Her eyes turned cool, and she stepped back.

"We will see. This may not be your private little expedition much longer."

That should have warned him, but perhaps he had grown too confident in the past two months since the confrontation with Julien at the diamond mine. He had avoided the family since then, working with Mornay to arrange his own trek. Then two weeks ago they had made camp here by the Limpopo River. Things were still unsettled. The best trekking season wasn't for a few more months.

"How did Julien know where I was?"

She shrugged. "Really, Rogan, you need to ask? Grandfather has spies everywhere. We knew when you left Kimberly and moved out to Mornay's place. A Bantu reported to Parnell the day you arrived here on the river. Grandfather's been a regular porcupine ever since you succeeded in hiring Mornay away from him." She glanced over toward the old Frenchman and Derwent, who were both keeping their distance near the campfire.

Mornay, as hard as a piece of biltong, that sun-dried strip of salted meat, regarded her with no expression on his leathery face. He stooped and, as an apparent dismissal, removed the tin mug he kept on a hook on his belt and filled it with inky coffee from the pot perched on the hot coals. The old bachelor turned his back, showing that he considered the opposite sex about as welcome as a mosquito.

But Derwent smiled shyly at her, removed his hat, and offered a small bow that reflected upon his years in Grimston Way, when he would bid good evening to the squire.

"Hello, Derwent. Alice will be joining you soon?"

"No, Miss, she'll be staying on in Kimberly with church folks."

"Oh, surely she'll change her mind when she hears I'll be going along on the expedition."

Derwent remained silent and glanced sideways at Rogan.

Rogan stood with his arms folded, jaw set. She didn't seem to notice his coolness, or else she didn't care.

"So you've won over the dour old Mornay. Lucky for you, though. He can speak Lobengula's language. But as you must know, the risk is great. The old Ndebele warrior is in no generous mood." She looked directly at Rogan's revolver. "They say you are a dead shot."

Rogan knew about the risk, but he kept from smiling his irony, since she wasn't likely to understand the risk facing him in the guise of the Capetown randlords, of whom Sir Julien was one. The "white peril" was perhaps as threatening to his safety as the Ndebele warriors, who, like their cousins the Zulu, used the sharp assegai, a slender iron-tipped spear made of the wood of the assegai. An army of mighty impis abode near Bulawayo, where their king, Lobengula, had his great kraal.

In order to reach the Zambezi, Rogan would need to pass through Lobengula's Matabeleland, which presented serious dangers if indeed the old chieftain was riled. But Mornay had hinted of a route that might avoid Lobengula's land and thus his warriors. In past years Lobengula had warred with another tribe, the Shona to the north, and had invaded and conquered the Shona, making them slaves and incorporating some into his army. In his own words, Lobengula had made them his "dirt-eating dogs," and now he considered Mashonaland an extension of Matabeleland.

Darinda had said *we* when she first mentioned finding his camp, and Rogan looked toward the lighted safari coach. Not even Darinda would be allowed to travel alone.

"Where is Julien?"

"With the others. All anxious to meet you. There's been a great lot of talk about Sir Lyle's 'other son from England.' Grandfather has told them obstacles don't easily deter you once your mind is made up." She looked intrigued by this.

"Parnell must be here too. I doubt he'd let you out of his sight."

Darinda looked bored. "Parnell bullies me."

Rogan smiled his skepticism. "I imagine it's the other way around."

"I've told Julien I'll marry whomever I wish," she stated firmly. Her eyes found his.

Why tell him?

"You underestimate me?"

His tight smile continued. "Never."

Someone stepped from the tent, silhouetted in the flickering lantern light. Rogan would recognize his brother anywhere.

"Darinda? This is no place to be wandering about alone. Sir Julien is asking for you. Hullo, Rogan."

"You see?" she whispered with a smile. "A bully. I wonder what he's so cautious of?" And placing a hand on Rogan's arm again, she slowly withdrew it and walked ahead to the tent.

Rogan watched her until she pulled open the flap and stepped inside.

Parnell walked toward him. He was unsmiling, but apparently this time he seemed undisturbed that Darinda had come out to greet him. Yet Rogan did not miss the gravity of his brother's look.

"I warned you back at Kimberly, Rogan. I told you Julien wouldn't sit by idly and allow you to lead a rebellion against his interests. You see? I was right, wasn't I? You have a lot to learn, Rogan." He seemed satisfied that he thought so. "Your expedition won't proceed without him. Not even if you've managed to snare Mornay. A clever move, by the way. Even Julien's money couldn't hold the cold fish for long."

"Maybe Mornay has reasons for avoiding Julien's gilded pond."

"Oh, sure, the old Boer has his patriotism, love for the independence of South Africa, and a ruddy dislike for the British Union Jack! But his French pride won't deter Julien. He's a master at strategy."

"He's had years to sharpen his craft," Rogan said dryly. "I wouldn't be boasting, if I were you." He gestured toward the elaborate camping rig. "What do you have there? Looks like a traveling safari."

Parnell chuckled at Rogan's wry description of the outfit of tents, wagons, and surreys.

"You're not far from the truth. There's even wine from Paris." His hand on Rogan's shoulder held him back a moment longer. Parnell lowered his voice.

"Darinda told you Julien's here?"

"I recognized his golden gelding as soon as I rode in. Look, Parnell..." He felt a weighty spirit settle over him. "We discussed the expedition back at Kimberly. I've already explained my plans to you. You were to make my intentions clear to Julien. And since then, nothing has changed."

"Ha! Since when did I need to explain your intentions? You made them quite clear yourself at De Beers two months ago. I thought Julien would take that sjambok from his guard and try to use it on you. He was livid that night at Kimberly House. He fired Jorgen, did you know?"

That, Rogan had not heard. "But he hasn't decided to play fair with Sheehan and his uncle."

"He won't. Best forget that. Sheehan's into farming now."

"This meeting won't change my mind," Rogan insisted, remembering the ugly scene at the Big Hole.

Parnell slowly shook his head in doubt. "I wonder. This isn't even Julien's idea, though he bought into it quickly enough. Coming here was Mr. Rhodes's idea. He's here, and so is Dr. Jameson."

Cecil Rhodes, here? That surprised Rogan. Rhodes owned the Royal Charter from the queen, which authorized his British South Africa

Company to sponsor a colony in the north. The man controlled millions in diamonds and gold.

"You'll need to cooperate with him," Parnell said. "It'll pay off in the end, though. You're likely to end up one of the moguls yourself."

"That's your dream, Parnell, not mine. You've given in to Julien too easily. He's had your cooperation since before we went to university in London."

Rogan softened the mild rebuke with an understanding smile, though his brother's decision troubled him.

"You want Darinda too much."

Parnell's sharpened gaze swung to Rogan. "Why discuss her?"

"Julien knows what you want. He weighs everything in the balance of getting a good return. He'll turn you into his indentured servant until he agrees to release her in a marriage that suits his purpose. Like poor Jacob dealing with his Uncle Laban, Uncle Julien will make you serve double time before you get her."

Parnell loosened his shirt collar. "You're being a bit dramatic, aren't you?"

"But truthful."

"Yes…you're right. But Julien will make sure you give in too. Don't think you'll get away with this trek a free man. There's no way around him without cooperation. Look, Rogan, don't rile them tonight. For your sake. Please play along and be the gentleman. Will you?"

Rogan drew his mouth into a smile that showed his cynicism. "Be compliant, a piece of clay in the hands of the great nation builder, Cecil Rhodes." He shook his head. "One thing's wrong with that. Rhodes isn't the Divine Potter."

Parnell jerked his shoulder. "You've been listening too much to old Derwent. He should have stayed back in Grimston Way and become the vicar. Look, I've already told you back at the Cape you don't have to like the leaders in the BSA. Few of us do. But you do need to look at things as they are, not as you'd like them to be. Rhodes is a powerful man and owns *millions*."

"Understood, only too well. Money speaks." As Rogan said it, he was still remembering Sheehan, remembering also that he still needed more money to sponsor his expedition. True, he had made arrangements with Mornay, but money was still needed up front for supplies, extra oxen, horses, mules, fodder, and the hiring of a few more guards with guns. Guards were a necessity. This experience with money was becoming too familiar, bearing a marked resemblance to Henry Chantry's early days.

"Well, we were always told money was power, weren't we?" Rogan said, his voice sharp. "Power to rule. We knew it even as children at Grimston Way when Father's position as squire meant we owned the village and just about everyone in it."

Parnell tilted his head. "What's come over you? Blackwater fever?"

"Maybe I just don't approve of the dirty deal done to Sheehan. I don't agree with a lot of things I've seen since arriving."

"You sound like a peasant with rebellion brewing in your mind. I'd swear you've changed since you arrived in Africa," Parnell said, his chestnut brows tufted together.

Maybe he had. The land…the people. The sight of John Sheehan lying bloodied in the dust, his claim on the coal deposit stolen legally.

"Speaking of money and all it brings, I wouldn't join the peasant's march too soon," Parnell goaded lightly. "The ditty about carving up the king's head on a platter for all to share—it might turn out to be your own. It's you who will inherit Father's title and estate. And an even bigger title when you and Patricia wed. You'll be marching to the tune of Lord Rogan Chantry."

Parnell laughed suddenly, good-naturedly. They both did.

"Maybe you should go ahead and toss Henry's map to the fires of Africa and return to England," Parnell said, "making the rounds of the royal parties with little to worry about but sumptuous meals and wine."

"It has its allurements…" Rogan said with a sigh. "And its boredom."

Parnell laughed. He shrugged his shoulders. "C'mon, His Majesty Rhodes is holding court, and you're an honored guest."

CHAPTER ELEVEN

Night began to settle, casting velvet shades of darkness upon the veld, but the expanse of cloudless sky still retained some indigo where the first star gleamed with brilliance. Soon a plump white moon rose from behind the hills and scattered a shimmering of gold and diamonds across the sky.

Gold…that mysterious map. Unnoticed by the two Chantry brothers, Darinda narrowed her lashes as she stood near the covered mule coach watching them. They talked alone for a few minutes, now and then exchanging smiles, or laughing, now and then serious and challenging, especially the younger one. That one was trouble! He would be difficult to overcome.

Parnell frustrated her! He was weak. By now he should have discovered where his brother kept the map and delivered it to her. If he were as strong as Rogan, he would have succeeded by now. Too bad she and Rogan were not on the same side. Unlike Parnell, she might be able to fall for him, but doing that wasn't in her plans. Nor was she going to marry Parnell. If he were clever, he would have guessed by now that she cared nothing for him. Parnell was all Grandfather's idea.

Yes, Rogan would be difficult. Her mild flirtation with him had merely been a test to discover whether he was susceptible like Parnell. Rogan was on guard. She could feel the armor in place each time she came near him, yet she sensed something else about him too. He was a man, and he found her attractive. That gave her hope. If she could break through his defenses, she might accomplish her aims without Parnell. She had decided tonight she could not use the same tactics she had with Parnell. Parnell had fallen into her hands like ripe figs. He would do anything for her. But Rogan would not be won by mere flirtation. Maybe there was another way… She would need to discover his strengths and weaknesses. Meanwhile, all she needed to do with Parnell was to work on him awhile longer. Eventually, he would succumb and somehow get the map from Rogan. It must happen on this expedition.

If only Captain Retford were here. She might be able to use him, too. A captain in the military might be vulnerable to the sparkle of a diamond inheritance and a woman who found him irresistible. She would keep him in mind. That foolish nitwit Arcilla! Flirting with Captain Retford. She didn't deserve Peter Bartley. Now, there was a sensible man she could have married and at least been comfortable with. A good, solid, practical head on his shoulders. Poor Peter, married to a silly schoolgirl who couldn't think a whit beyond what pretty frock to put on and what diamond to wear! Grandfather had been cruel to poor Peter by insisting he marry the Chantry flirt. Oh, well. She could live without the men on the expedition. Like Grandfather, she preferred power and fear and respect rather than love. At least she told herself so…

She came alert. Parnell and Rogan were walking toward the tent where the meeting with old man Rhodes would take place. She wanted to be there to study all the men and their weaknesses. That map and new rand somewhere in Zambezia was going to belong to Darinda Bley. When she accomplished that feat, Grandfather would see his mistake in choosing a male heir instead of her. And Uncle Anthony Brewster! Grandfather needed to change his will and place her in charge of the diamond dynasty. She was far more clever than Anthony. She would prove it too, by astounding her grandfather when she presented him the map.

Darinda backed away silently into the warm dark night until she had circled Cecil Rhodes's big meeting tent. She slipped in through the back opening and found her place beside Grandfather Julien just as Parnell and Rogan entered through the front tent flap.

She was smiling and pleased when she saw both Chantry brothers look over at her. What's more, *both* men noticed her. *Really* noticed her. That was a strong beginning. Her eyes met Rogan's and boldly suggested that she, too, noticed him. It rankled her when a flicker of amusement showed in his dark robust eyes. As though he saw through her facade and found her plans amusing and challenging. For a moment, while he scanned her, her heart skipped a beat. A frightening thought came that made her consider her own weaknesses. That look of his almost said he welcomed the challenge and would beat her at her own game!

Oh no you won't, Rogan Chantry.

Darinda looked across the tent and was surprised to see Captain Retford, Peter's assistant in military affairs, at the meeting. *Oh, what a delightful surprise! But where are Peter and Arcilla?*

Grandfather had placed Captain Retford in Peter's service, but neither the captain nor Peter realized that it was *she* who had recommended him. Darinda had noticed the captain on a trip to Capetown to see Arcilla and thereafter used her position with her grandfather to gain access to Retford's personal records. His reputation as a soldier was impeccable, his schooling was traditional at the Honourable East India Company's Military College in Addiscombe, and he had served with distinction and received a brevet for courage in the fighting in Sudan.

Captain Ryan Retford was extremely handsome and very precise. He might be as difficult to crack as Rogan Chantry, but he, too, was a possibility. She knew he had a mother and sister in London who were barely making ends meet partly on his wages. His generosity showed admirable responsibility. Darinda knew her power and money could mold him into exactly what she wanted.

Darinda caught Captain Retford's gaze. He looked away. She felt her lips curve into a satisfied smile. Yes, he, too, had noticed her from afar.

Rogan, who had entered Cecil Rhodes's meeting tent with Parnell, took a moment to measure the man. Mr. Rhodes was the real power behind the BSA and De Beers Consolidated Mining Company, and the political force behind carving a British Empire in Africa. But he looked anything but a great king with the steely ambition to enforce his dream. He was a ponderous man, his skin showing the results of cyanosis from a long-standing heart ailment. His somewhat copper-colored hair was streaked at the temples with gray, and his sleepy, turtlelike eyes gazed steadily from the closing folds of skin around his eyes. Although worth millions, he was not a fastidious dresser like Uncle Julien. Mr. Rhodes's Norfolk jacket was rumpled, hanging askew on his soft, sagging shoulders. He sat slumped forward in a camp chair, his elbows resting on a long trestle table, with his entourage around him.

Cecil Rhodes had first come from England to South Africa years ago to nurse his frail health and be with his brother, who was working in the diamond mines. It was reported that Cecil Rhodes would sit by the rim of the diamond pit at Kimberly by the hour with his legs crossed, watching and talking. He loved to talk more than listen, and he would tell his "big dreams" to anyone willing to listen. Instead of succumbing to his ailments, he outlived his brother and joined with partners to consolidate De Beers into a near diamond monopoly. Now it was gold that had claimed his attention. Gold, and an empire with his name.

Rogan felt Mr. Cecil Rhodes's deceptively sleepy blue eyes appraise him, and he seemed to waste no time drawing conclusions. His thick hand gestured to a chair at the table, his voice brusque.

"So! Rogan Chantry! Julien tells me interesting things about you. I think I'll not be disappointed. Sit down," he repeated. "Darinda, would you serve my best wine?"

"Delighted, Mr. Rhodes… I believe it's in the back? Perhaps Captain Retford would bring the lantern for me?"

"We trail well equipped," Cecil told Rogan, gesturing that the captain should help Darinda.

Parnell started to get up from his camp chair, but Sir Julien lifted a silent hand to stop him. Parnell sat down, and Rogan recognized the tightness around his mouth. Rogan's anger rose at seeing his brother treated with contempt. How could he get him to see he was being used and break with Sir Julien Bley?

"Sit down, Rogan," Rhodes all but commanded.

Rogan looked at the man, feeling his fur ruffled in the wrong direction, yet he remembered his manners and pulled out a chair. He felt he was approaching a monarch and his attendants.

Julien sat at the end of the table. Their gaze held steadily, but surprisingly the violence Julien had displayed when at the Kimberly diamond mine was no longer noticeable. Maybe that should worry him even more.

Darinda returned with Mr. Rhodes's expensive bottle of wine and, with practiced flair, went around the table, serving Mr. Rhodes first, then the others. Her fingers were bedazzled with diamonds as she deliberately rested her hand on her grandfather's shoulder, parading the close relationship between them in a way that would assure any onlooking male of her heiress status.

Mr. Rhodes pushed a silver box holding cheroots toward Rogan, who selected one.

Julien leaned over and struck a match to light it. Above the sharp flame, Rogan looked into his one eye, which reflected the searing white flame.

"Send for Mornay," Cecil Rhodes told Parnell. "He'll need to be included in our discussion. We'll need him for the trek north."

Rogan turned his head and looked at him. "He's not for hire, sir."

Rhodes gazed at him unblinking. "What are you telling me?"

"I'm saying, sir, Giles Mornay has quit my uncle's service and is now working for me as a guide."

There was another man present, sitting comfortably in his camp chair, holding a glass of wine, legs crossed at the knees. He spoke for the first time, as though only roused from his evening leisure when there seemed a need to rally defenses in support of Cecil Rhodes.

"Not for hire?" came the quick demand from Dr. Leander Starr Jameson, the personal physician and right-hand ally of Rhodes. "Mr. Rhodes hires whomever he needs," Dr. Jameson stated. He appeared younger than Rhodes and was a pleasantly featured man with a dark mustache.

Jameson's autocratic manner rankled Rogan. "Mornay has agreed to lead my expedition to Mashonaland, but why it should concern anyone other than myself is curious."

Jameson lifted his head, as though Rogan were an impudent young chap, but Cecil Rhodes waved his hand as if to stop the matter from being chased by Jameson.

"On the contrary, Chantry. Your bold but unacceptable expedition interests me and the Company very much, and also worries us."

"How so?" Rogan knew why but was delaying. He could see he was squarely up against some very strong and high-handed men who could not see themselves as ruthless or unfair. They pompously viewed themselves as the self-appointed custodians of an empire they wished to procure for the good of all, especially themselves.

"Sir Julien has explained about Henry Chantry's map—of what could be a large gold find in Mashonaland, or the Zambezi region, as it is sometimes referred to. We think it's well worth the Company's sponsorship. The gold must be in responsible care."

Responsible care. For one brief moment a dark thought came: How he could tighten his hands around Cecil Rhodes's throat.

"The British South Africa Company," Rhodes said reasonably. He lifted his crystal glass and drank.

"Naturally, you will reap a bounty. Members of the Company are prepared to offer you handsome shares in the BSA, which can certainly be appreciated by a young man with your ambition and talent. Personally, I could use someone like yourself in a key position once we settle matters between us and the Charter Company. You can discuss that with Sir Julien or Dr. Jameson. Your future can be as bright as your ambition and loyalty shine. I understand you'll need funding for the expedition. There's really no reason for that. You can simply merge with our expedition, which will leave as soon as matters with Lobengula are settled."

Rogan looked back into his level gaze. He knew he shouldn't be surprised by this autocratic move, but he was, even though he'd expected them to oppose him in some way. That Cecil Rhodes would do it in so reasonable a manner angered him more than if the man had pounded the table with his big fists and threatened him. The reasonable threats crawling just beneath the surface of his cool manner seemed more dangerous than even Julien's rage with the sjambok.

Rogan looked over at Sir Julien. Wisely, Julien was not looking at him, but studying his wine glass with deep interest. Darinda was standing behind him, her hand on his shoulder, and she watched him as pertly as a cat. Her eyes were bright, as though excited by the tension that filled the tent.

"Mornay won't cooperate. Even Grandfather couldn't buy him back from Rogan," Darinda spoke into the silence.

Parnell stood in the background without moving. Rogan knew that his brother wanted—no expected—his simple capitulation, to which they all felt entitled.

Dr. Jameson broke the silence. "Forget Mornay, Cecil. I always did say he never measured up to his father. Giles is an arrogant devil. A friend of the Boers. That accounts for his stolid, unimaginative ways. Frederick Selous is the guide we want. A far better man."

Captain Retford turned toward Mr. Rhodes. "If I could speak, sir. I was talking to Mr. Peter Bartley just a few days ago. There may be good reasons for delaying the expedition. Any foray into Matabeleland could risk a bloody attack from Lobengula. Our spies there report he is upset over what he believes was our betrayal."

Rhodes looked undisturbed as he exchanged glances with Dr. Jameson.

"That's why we must have Lobengula's permission before we leave," Mr. Rhodes said. "And we will. We already have it, don't we, Jim?"

Dr. Jameson nodded. "We have his concessions on paper. He signed it with his elephant seal."

"I'm sending an official entourage to meet with him at Bulawayo," Rhodes stated. "Dr. Jameson here, for one. You too, Captain Retford." He turned his steely blue gaze on Rogan. "We'd like to have you with us, Rogan."

Rogan had been silent, not trusting himself to speak. He fought down his growing anger at these men who had calmly moved against him and claimed what was his.

"You see, there is only *one* expedition going from Lobengula's kraal into Mashonaland, an expedition with a Royal Charter, the British South Africa Company. We will begin a colony near Mount Hampden in the north and plant the British flag. Your expedition must merge with ours under the charter."

"And if I refuse to join?"

"I hope you are wiser than that. I believe you are." Mr. Rhodes's voice was reasonable and placatory, but those eyes revealed an iron core to the man. "Sir Julien tells me you have what it takes to excel."

Rogan did not look at his uncle. He sat face to face with Rhodes, hands folded firmly on the table.

"Did my uncle also tell you I refused this same offer back in Capetown?"

"There can be no refusal," Rhodes said coldly.

Rogan stood. "Henry Chantry planned this expedition years ago, long before you received your Royal Charter. When he came asking for financial backing from Sir Julien, he was turned down. I'm going to carry on his work, and that means sponsoring my own expedition."

Darinda walked over to Parnell and looked at him, taking hold of his arm.

Parnell's face had turned a sickly color beneath his tanned skin.

"Listen to common sense, Rogan. We're not at war with you. Can't you see the Company is inviting you in? Think of the power and prestige this can bring you!"

Darinda dropped Parnell's arm and walked up to Rogan. "They are right, Cousin. Mr. Rhodes is offering you substantial compensation. Land, gold claims, anything you want." Her eyes held his.

For the first time Rogan noticed the glow in her eyes, and he wasn't conceited enough to think he himself was the cause. Darinda, too, wanted the map as much as her grandfather and, now, Rhodes.

Rhodes leaned back in his chair. "I want you with the entourage we're sending to Lobengula's kraal, Rogan. We're going to sign a treaty with the Ndebele king for mineral rights. He has already agreed on an expedition through Matabeleland, but we need that agreement to be legal. As soon as we have it, we're heading toward Mashonaland. I'm willing to make you an official in the British South Africa Company for your willingness to join hands with us."

"I can't accept your offer, Mr. Rhodes. I enjoy my freedom too much."

Rogan nodded in their direction and stood. He turned to leave, when Rhodes said without emotion, "Very well, then." He looked across the table at Julien, who until now had been mostly silent. He said to Julien coolly, "Then there's no way around this. I had hoped for willing cooperation. You were right. I see he's going to be difficult." He placed his heavy hands on the table and pushed himself up. "You'd better have a private talk with him, Julien. Explain clearly how things are."

Cecil Rhodes gestured to Dr. Jameson and then left the tent in a bearlike gait, the doctor following.

Rogan did not wait to talk to Julien as Mr. Rhodes had stated. He too turned and left the tent. He'd not gone far toward his camp when Parnell caught up with him.

"Wait."

Rogan stopped and turned, knowing his anger showed.

Parnell looked pale and tense beneath the moonlight. For one moment Rogan felt pity for his brother.

"I'm sorry it turned out this way, but I tried to tell you back in Kimberly that you couldn't win. Might as well face the mighty Victoria Falls as think you can stop Mr. Rhodes. That goes for Uncle Julien, too. They are all one and the same."

Rogan glared at him. "It's you I'm worried about. You've become a pawn to them. Father should see you."

"Father!" hissed Parnell in unexpected openness. "What did he ever care? We were all property for Julien to divvy up and use the way he thought best for the family dynasty."

Rogan caught his breath, surprised by Parnell. But his brother quickly withdrew again behind his old facade. He hurled his frustration at Rogan as though he were the one really to blame.

"Why couldn't you have just cooperated? It would have been for the best."

When Rogan found his voice, it was rough with emotion. "Cooperate. It's always that with you, isn't it, Parnell? Even when a sjambok is used on a near helpless man like Sheehan and the coal deposit he pegged is stolen by ruthless men. They'll get by with it, Julien and the Company, but that doesn't bother you enough to force you to break away from them, does it? Nothing will force you to choose between right and your own desires."

"Right? And what is right?" Parnell fumed.

"If you don't know," Rogan said sharply, "it won't help for me to spell it out." He turned and walked to the campfire. Derwent and Mornay waited there, as though they knew nothing of the meeting in Rhodes's tent.

Darinda had followed Parnell when he'd left and called out to his brother to wait. She'd not been able to pick up the brief but heated exchange, but she could tell by Parnell's unhappy face when he walked back toward her that what was said had not gone as he'd hoped.

Darinda drew Parnell aside near the mule coach. In the moonlight and warm wind, she listened to the canvas flapping and heard a far-off animal cry that stabbed the night.

"Could you make him see some sense?" she whispered.

"I've told you he doesn't think the way we do."

"Then get the map, Parnell. You should know where he keeps it. You'd have more excuse than the rest of us to be around his bedroll, or that black gelding of his. Or have one of the Bantu search his things when he's occupied elsewhere. I could have done it myself while everyone was at Rhodes's meeting."

"What you ask is crazy."

"You've as much right to the map as he does. Henry was your blood uncle as well. The map belongs to all of us, to the family. Why settle for less? You saw the way Rogan stood up to them. There's a chance he won't cooperate. Then what?"

"He'll cooperate." Parnell's voice was bitter. "When your grandfather's through talking to him, Rogan will have no choice but to join the Company."

"I don't believe it. I saw what kind of man Rogan was tonight. But even if he does agree, so what? Why allow old Rhodes to get his hands on the map? If *we* found it and brought it to Grandfather first, he'd finally recognize how he doesn't need a male heir to run the family diamond mine after his death. I have more right to be in control than Anthony Brewster. I'm a full-blooded Bley!" Darinda smiled to soften her words, for she could see Parnell's emotions beginning to recoil. She laid a gentle hand on his forearm and smiled up at him.

"You want to know how you can please me, Parnell? How you can make me happy...so that you and I can marry at last?"

She heard his breath catch and saw the kindled warmth in his hazel-green eyes. His hand hesitated and then found hers. She nearly winced at the strength of his fingers. But a wince would spoil her gentleness.

"If you get the map," she whispered, "and we bring it to Grandfather, then I'll tell him I want to marry you at the end of the expedition."

"Darinda…"

She allowed his arms to enfold her, allowed his lips to press against hers, then she pulled quickly away and hurried toward her wagon.

Chapter Twelve

Rogan straightened from the campfire and lifted his tin coffee mug to his lips as he surveyed the encampment, now quiet under the vast African sky. Not all were asleep, however. Derwent and Mornay had been sharing this evening watch with him, joining in a thoughtful discussion of the day's events. And on the far side of the laager, the sides of Rhodes's big tent still glowed with lantern light.

Just as Rogan started to return to his seat, he saw Sir Julien push the big tent's entrance flap aside and step out into the night. Then Rogan turned quickly at a rustle behind him to see Captain Retford walk into the firelight from another direction and speak to Mornay.

"Mr. Rhodes wants to talk to you."

Mornay glanced at Rogan, then rose and accompanied the young captain across the laager.

Derwent's worried gaze shot to Rogan. "Looks as though our plans may come tumbling down like the walls of Jericho, Mr. Rogan. Pardon my saying so, because he is family, but I don't put much past Sir Julien Bley. Not after what was done to John Sheehan. I'm glad John wasn't married yet, with a baby or two to feed."

Rogan remained silent. He stared at the dark dregs in the bottom of his tin cup.

"Strange," Derwent mused, "how far some folks will go to get what they think they have a right to, isn't it?"

Pricked, Rogan snapped, "Nothing strange about it."

"Seems to me there is. Now, Sheehan was a little different. He could accept the loss after a while. I saw him a month ago, and he and Mr. Gerald were doing a whit better then they were at first. If a man like John could go on being happy after losing all that coal, and not let bitterness and hate eat him up, he's discovered some of the best of all God's treasures."

"He had no choice but to accept the outcome," Rogan argued. "He came up against a brick wall, and only a fool keeps throwing himself against it."

"Aye, that's true enough, but a man could accept the reality of that brick wall and still be bitter as hemlock. But peace in the heart and contentment come when a man can leave vengeance to the great Judge of all, knowing even gold rands and diamond moguls will give an account to God. Well, a man who's been cheated can sleep better knowing he doesn't have to be the one to bring in justice. What do you think, Mr. Rogan?"

Rogan gave him a narrow look. "I think you've already made it clear."

Derwent smiled, then took his small, black Bible from his pocket and opened it. "I was reading this awhile ago when you all were in the tent with Mr. Rhodes and Sir Julien. 'Woe to him who builds a town with bloodshed, who establishes a city by iniquity!' "

Rogan looked at him. "All right, Vicar, you can go to bed now."

Derwent grinned and put his worn Bible away.

Rogan smiled faintly.

Derwent stood from the fire and glanced in the direction of Rhodes's tent. "Oh, here comes Sir Julien."

"Better leave me so I can handle him. Peaceful like."

"Sure, I was just going to turn in. G'night, Mr. Rogan."

When Derwent had left, Julien walked up to the fire. He accepted a tin mug from the washerboy, stooped, and poured his own coffee.

"Looks like poison."

In the tense silence that followed, Julien added quietly, "You were unwise to contest Rhodes the way you did earlier. Angering him will only add to your problems. The BSA is law in this section of Africa, and remember, it was Cecil Rhodes who started the Company."

Rogan shrugged off the accusation. "When is it ever safe to question a tyrant's wisdom?"

"Come, come, Rogan. You're exaggerating. Cecil Rhodes is one of South Africa's leading British colonials."

"I don't question his commitment to building a British empire. I question the tactics. I'm not forgetting John Sheehan. In some ways the BSA is little better than the buccaneers in the Caribbean. The Company's in this for itself, to gain control of wealth."

"I wouldn't be too quick to brand the Company as a brotherhood of lawless profiteers if I were you, young Rogan."

Rogan loathed being called "young Rogan." The silly term "my boy" was equally abhorrent to him.

"What do you call your expedition into Mashonaland?" Julien challenged. "And Henry's in the 1870s? Wasn't it for personal ambition and gold?"

Rogan drew his brows together and was silent. The wood crackled and cast a flurry of red sparks into the air.

Julien's mouth twisted. He drank his coffee. "You, too, can be called a buccaneer."

Rogan threw the remains of the bitter coffee into the fire, causing the flames to hiss. "Henry didn't intend to subjugate a land for Her Majesty. Nor do I. And if I recall, Queen Victoria sent word that she does not approve of the BSA taking African land and subjugating it. The trouble with Rhodes, as I see him, is that he's a law unto himself." He tossed his empty mug to the washerboy and turned to stride away. "Good night, Uncle."

"Rogan!"

Rogan paused and turned. He knew he had riled the cobra.

Julien stood, formidably. The firelight cast wild, dancing shadows across his tall, angular frame.

"Direct opposition to our authority cannot be tolerated. This is outright rebellion."

Rogan laughed unpleasantly. "Rebellion against Mr. Rhodes or against you?"

Julien strode toward him. The black patch gave his face a sinister look. Had he still been the "young Rogan" of Rookswood, he was certain that Julien would have struck him. Especially after the events in Kimberly.

They stood confronting each other in the encircling darkness.

"You're forgetting the one important fact, Rogan. The fact of which Rhodes sent me here to remind you. Just as straightforwardly as we can. The queen's Colonial Office in London has already granted Cecil Rhodes that Royal Charter to begin a colony in Mashonaland. You know that. That charter, along with the profits from De Beers Consolidated, officially empowers us to buy and distribute land parcels for farms to its pioneers. It also grants the rights to any mineral discoveries thereabouts. Even if you proceed without us and discover Henry's gold deposit, you will be forced to work through the Company or find yourself in breach of the law."

The dueling words came like short cutting jabs from an expert swordsman, ripping his plans apart. But there was more to Julien's attack this time than just threats. If his claims were true that the Company did hold jurisdiction over all mining rights in what would become Rhodesia, then this could destroy him. It would mean the Charter Company held all power and authority.

Julien did not gloat as Rogan would have expected. His face was sober.

"I see you finally understand Mr. Rhodes. You should have listened to me at Kimberly when I suggested we make the map a family enterprise."

"Wouldn't the Company still have rights?"

Julien was quiet a long moment. "I may have been able to convince him to back off. Now he knows of the map, of Henry, so there's no way out for us. We're both limited to Mr. Rhodes."

Rogan was baffled. "You didn't tell him of the map?"

"No." He drank his coffee.

Rogan studied his face and saw a look of uncertainty. "Arcilla again?"

"No, no, I think it was Mornay."

"Mornay! You've got to be wrong. Mornay dislikes Rhodes. He'd never say anything."

"No? You've still much to learn, my boy, about human nature. Don't think because he quit working for me to become your guide that he did so out of some sudden flare of character. He did so as a bargaining chip with Rhodes."

"I don't believe it," Rogan said angrily. "The very idea of the colony and British rule turn him into a dour old Boer."

"A dour old Boer who will be mollified with British gold so he can settle down comfortably in the new colony."

Rogan considered this and kept silent. It was possible.

"You're a practical young man," Julien continued, more placating now that Rogan was studiously silent. "You heard Rhodes's offer tonight. A fair and generous offer, by the way. But I have something more to add."

Rogan gave him a measuring glance.

"Peter will arrive here tomorrow. He will lead the Company's delegation to Lobengula's kraal at Bulawayo. Peter has specifically requested that you join him on that delegation. Arcilla has begged that you go along. I also want you working with him. Peter has a fine head on his shoulders, but he has his weaknesses. Your particular strengths will make him the better leader once we set up a government for the new colony. We're calling it Fort Salisbury to begin with, after Lord Salisbury in London."

Rogan was irked by his looming defeats and was not in a cooperative mood. "If the Company already owns the land and mineral rights, why the need for a delegation to Bulawayo?"

Julien showed nothing. "Peter will discuss it with you tomorrow. He'll want to depart for Bulawayo in the next few days. The parley with Lobengula is urgent before we go any farther into Mashonaland."

Rogan placed hands on his hips and returned the level stare. He was curious about the urgency, but also wary of what Julien could be planning.

"I haven't even said I would go."

"I think you will. You've responsibilities to your family name, my boy. It concerns Arcilla."

Rogan's fingers clenched at the veiled threat.

Julien produced a cheroot, and a match flared. "Peter is to work with Dr. Jameson and others in overseeing the new colony. That gold on the map must be somewhere in the vicinity. With Henry's map we'll find it sooner. If you cooperate, Rhodes will give you fifty percent. That is more generous than his usual way."

Rogan couldn't resist the hypocrisy of it all. "More generous than the treatment afforded Sheehan?"

"That land where he found coal is Company land."

The tip of Julien's cheroot glowed red.

"Peter will be helping to lead the pioneers this June. Herein lies the problem, my boy. We had planned to have the colony settled with security forces and farm productivity in place before the women joined their husbands. Unfortunately, there will be an exception when Peter begins the trek. You see my dilemma? Both Arcilla and Darinda will be coming on the expedition. Perhaps even Derwent's little wife. You have an obligation."

Rogan's jaw clamped. He wouldn't bring up Arcilla's foolish indiscretion at the Government Ball in Capetown, nor the fact he agreed she should be with her husband.

Rogan had been protecting Arcilla from her impulsive whims all his life, and he understood her sometimes unwise spirit. This time her behavior had him cornered.

"This land will destroy Arcilla. She doesn't have the frame of mind to handle the raw and wild surroundings. She and Peter ought to be sent home to London. You could arrange for Peter to have a government job there, perhaps in the Colonial Office."

The smell of tobacco drifted downwind toward Rogan.

"Perhaps. But not at this time. Whether I do anything about this in the future will depend on your cooperation with the Company."

Julien would always have more traps to snare him. Julien understood the leverage to be gained by using Rogan's concern for Arcilla. Julien had learned such tactics from old Ebenezer Bley. Perhaps Ebenezer had recognized the cold, hard face of power and ambition in his young nephew.

Julien calmly smoked his cheroot.

Anger smoldered in Rogan's chest. He'd been thwarted, and by the one man he had long suspected of murdering his uncle Henry.

He might not win now where Arcilla was concerned, but there must be a door out of bondage to the Company somewhere. Rogan told himself he wouldn't quit searching until he found it.

It was foolish, however, to continue the duel now. He must wait for a more opportune moment, a time when he could win against Sir Julien. He must locate a sharper sword to defeat his nemesis.

Rogan affected his most disarming smile and bowed.

"It looks as if there is little choice other than joining hands on the trek to the Zambezi."

"And Henry's map?"

"Regardless of the Company's exclusive mining rights, the map remains my private property."

Julien looked thoughtful. As Rogan smiled without feeling, Julien answered with the same affected ease. "I'm sure our difficulties will be smoothed over in time. Map included. We can use you, Rogan. I learned even when you were a boy just how formidable an opponent you could be."

Julien laughed, and Rogan joined in, though coolly.

"I won't disappoint you."

Sir Julien glanced at him, brow lifted in question, but Rogan continued to smile.

When Julien had walked away toward the safari wagons, Rogan gazed after him. He saw little room to maneuver. Yet every fiber of his will abhorred submission to an arrogant man like Julien. He had outsmarted Julien on more than one occasion at Rookswood as a boy and had taken great satisfaction in doing so. Now he found himself cornered, with apparently no way out. Could he cooperate with their plans without compromising his independence?

He must think. He must plan. He did not want to follow in the footsteps of formidable men like Rhodes or Julien, not when simple men like John Sheehan could be trampled on without so much as a backward glance or a twinge of regret for the pain and disappointment.

He would fight on. He would not give the Company the satisfaction of the map. They would need to work hard to find the gold without any help from him and Henry.

And his own dreams of the great gold deposit? Once again, the dream must wait until he believed it was safe enough to pursue it. He would go on the expedition as they wished, he would try to protect Arcilla and aid Peter, but his plan to find the gold would be put away with the map until another time.

He always carried the map on him, trusting few, now that ambitious men knew he had it. And ambitious women?

He thought of Evy. How different she was from the cool and calculating Darinda Bley and his unwise sister. Evy's character seemed to shine even brighter out here among the lions hungrily stalking prey.

Thinking of Evy's virtuous character reminded him of his own shortcomings. She deserved a man who would be faithful on a distant shore, a man of integrity with the strength to resist. With God's help perhaps he could measure up, but he was also wise enough to know that opposition lay ahead like a cobra poised to strike.

Chapter Thirteen

With the coming of dawn the veld turned golden once more, and the Limpopo came alive with birds of many colors. In the distance a herd of chocolate brown sable antelope were grazing, their tails flicking nervously. The herd's mammoth buck walked forward, sniffing the breeze while lifting its head, crowned with curved, ridged horns—always alert to approaching danger. Its wide shoulders were shiny black, the underbelly white as snow. Then, tossing its shiny mane, it turned and thundered across the veld, the herd swiftly following its lord.

Rogan recognized the man on horseback riding boldly into camp leading a Company delegation, his brother-in-law Peter Bartley, son of Sir Reginald Bartley, appointed commissioner in Lunjore, India. Julien, for reasons of his own political choosing, had used his connections in the Colonial Office in London more than two years ago to have Peter assigned to South Africa.

Peter, at thirty-two years old, though young for his appointment, was schooled in the ways of Her Majesty's Colonial Office, and his position as a diplomat somewhere in the vast and still growing British Commonwealth of Queen Victoria was certain.

Peter was dusty after the long trek from Kimberly, which lay more than a hundred miles south of Rogan's camp. But garbed in a uniform of fitted jacket, vest, and hat, he looked well suited to the distinguished position that had been conferred on him. Riding beside him on a mare was Arcilla, looking like a disgruntled queen. Rogan grinned to himself.

Peter dismounted, leaving his horse's care to one of the Ngwato workers, and came around to help his young wife off her own mount. Arcilla looked about with dismay clearly etched on her tired face. Her ebony hair was tangled from the wind, and her two-piece suit of inappropriate ivory and emerald satin now looked wilted and a trifle downcast along with its owner after the long journey.

Seeing Rogan, Peter saluted in a friendly gesture and said something to Arcilla, as though trying to boost her spirits. Arcilla looked quickly toward her brother, and a sincere smile of relief turned her pouting face into something special to see.

"Rogan," she cried and came hurrying toward him. "Oh, thank God you're here. It's been positively beastly! Hours and simply hours of horrid riding. Why, it's a wonder I can walk. And Peter was absolutely dreadful. He wouldn't even stop and let me rest. I shall die before this expedition is over! I know I shall."

Rogan patted her shoulder as she fell into his arms with a sob. His gaze went to Peter and saw both guilt and impatience.

"They are all miserable to me," she wailed, "both Uncle Julien and Peter. Oh, how I wish I were back home in Grimston Way."

"Hush," he said in a low voice. "You'll soon have everyone else wishing the same, including your husband."

"Good!" She lifted her face from his shoulder and sniffed loudly, glancing over her shoulder toward Peter, who walked toward them with strained dignity.

"It wasn't quite all that dreadful, my dear. You are exaggerating. We went quite slowly for your benefit. We could have made better time alone."

She pushed away from Rogan, nearly losing her balance and whirled, glaring at her husband. "Then I shan't trouble you any further. Go on *alone*. Serve your precious Company *alone*. I—"

"Darling, I didn't mean—" began Peter.

Rogan smoothed his mustache with a finger. This was going to be a very engaging expedition. Never mind Arcilla. Could he himself endure all this?

Darinda Bley came out of her wagon when the entourage arrived, and now she stood looking across at them. At length she came strolling over.

"Oh, come, Cousin Arcilla. It's not as bad as all that. Come with me. I'll see you to a wagon. You can rest and wash some of the dust off you. Then I'll bring you some coffee and breakfast. You'll soon feel much better. One of your problems is those clothes. You can't very well run about out here on the veld looking as if you're going dressed for a London tea."

"I happen to utterly *loathe* London teas, and I won't cavort around in Boer leather with a pistol slung over my hip."

Darinda dropped her hand from Arcilla's arm, and her face grew serious. "You may wish you had when you come face to face with a spitting cobra."

She turned and walked away, and Arcilla hesitated, then followed her toward the wagons.

Peter looked on helplessly.

Rogan stood watching the three of them, hands on hips.

When the women had disappeared into one of the wagons, Peter turned and met Rogan's gaze. After a moment they both smiled.

They shook hands, exchanging greetings, but Rogan could see by Peter's expression that he was uneasy over more than his wife. Rogan guessed that his brother-in-law might wonder how matters had gone with Sir Julien over his private expedition. Peter seemed to put off the issue for as long as possible.

"I told Julien that Arcilla should remain at one of the British outposts until after my meeting at Bulawayo. Darinda would be wiser to join her there too."

"Julien isn't going to agree with that. He's permitted his granddaughter to join us. At least they'll be company for each other."

Peter frowned. "I wish the two women could make friends. It doesn't help with Darinda goading her about her sensitivities to the elements and insects."

"If all we'll need to worry about is insects, we'll have smooth traveling. What is this I hear about Lobengula's impis urging him to attack the white devils?"

"I'm afraid what you've heard is true. Our spies report much restlessness among the warriors.

Rhodes had pulled out before dawn, and Rogan wondered about Julien's plans. "Is Julien going to Bulawayo?"

"No. He'll remain here at camp until he learns how the meeting at Bulawayo turns out. Then he'll report to Rhodes when he returns to Kimberly."

Peter frowned, but it wasn't clear to Rogan if the cause was Julien's presence or something else.

"Let's go for a stroll, Rogan. We need to talk."

After obtaining sidearms, they walked from the camp toward the blue Limpopo River. The distant hills that braced the base camp wore a misty veil this morning. The far-off land of the Zambezi continued to pull him, beckoning. Who knew what awaited? Diamonds, gold, emeralds, danger, perhaps even death?

"Obviously, there won't be a town north of the river until we build it," Rogan said. "You're quite sure, Peter, this is what you want to do with your life—and marriage? It's going to be rough. You don't need me to tell you that. You know this land and people better than I. You could still tell Julien you've changed your mind and return to London. My father would welcome you both back with open arms. You've been to Rookswood. You've seen how it is. It offers a good life, a comfortable one, and there's no financial lack."

Peter rubbed his aristocratic chin, a thoughtful gleam in his eyes. "A pleasant reverie, but one has his duty, as you well know. I cannot turn back now."

He stood, hands behind him, looking grim. It was a familiar trait of his, an almost pious, sacrificial loyalty to the BSA.

Rogan thought he could have boxed his ears, but he kept back the wry curl of his lip.

"I am worried about Arcilla, though," Peter admitted.

From the look in his eyes, Rogan could see he was sincere.

"I tried several times to enlighten Julien on the dangers, and he wouldn't see it." Peter straightened his shoulders and gazed off toward the river.

Rogan didn't explain the reason for Julien's failure to be enlightened.

"It will be a year before it proves safe enough for any women to join us at the colony," Rogan suggested again, still hoping Peter would reconsider and return to London.

Peter shook his head. "Even then, it's going to be difficult. I'm surprised she came, considering how difficult it is on her." Peter's voice took on a strained edge. "She'd much rather stay at the Cape. The social life and all, you understand." Peter shot him a glance, then looked away again. He drew his shoulders back and stared toward the hills.

Rogan recognized Peter's grim determination. Could he know about his wife's indiscretion in the garden?

Peter snatched his pipe from his jacket and clamped it between his teeth, arms behind his back.

"Arcilla would just as soon voyage back to England, but I refuse to give her an excuse. I'd have thought she would be proud of my dedication to England, but she takes her patriotism quite shabbily, I'm afraid."

Rogan looked at him, surprised by the sudden frustration in his voice.

Rogan arched a brow. "Oh, come. She's very young, Peter."

"So is Darinda, but she is a fervent supporter of the push northward."

Rogan's first instinct was to draw sword in defense of his sister and make a comment about Darinda, but he refrained. It was more important to let Peter know he could confide in him.

Rogan held no flowery illusions about Arcilla. He knew that she was self-centered in some ways and much too vain over her appearance. But she had sacrificed her heart's choice of Charles Bancroft to accept the family's wish for her to marry Peter. He had already mentioned this to her in Capetown. He had his own struggles with bucking the will of the family. What he did know was that Arcilla had relented with dignity and grace in marrying Peter. She'd also been reluctantly willing to go on the planned trek to the new colony before she married Peter, so there was no making excuses for her now that the time had come. She must grow up. In fact, they all had some growing to do.

He wished Peter had taken a stand against Julien when he insisted Arcilla join the trek.

Of course, Peter wouldn't know that Julien had meant to use Arcilla to force a decision from Rogan.

"So, the marriage is going badly, is it? Ruddy luck, but you're more mature than she is and ought to know how to work matters out."

Peter opened the door to his frustrations even wider.

"I don't see that it can get much worse. She won't explain her feelings to me. Insists I wouldn't understand if she did. A cold fish, she calls me. More interested in what the Company wants than in learning to understand her."

Rogan knew he was no expert at understanding women. He had certainly learned a few things going head to head with Evy on many occasions. But he had notions of his own on marriage.

"Of course, that goes both ways. She needs to try to understand your obligations."

"She flounces off in a huff every time I try to talk about the importance of my responsibilities here. It's either tantrums or giddiness. Never logic. Quite annoying. Yes, *most* annoying."

Rogan didn't dare smile. "I warned you she was young and spoiled before you married her. Maybe you should have taken the advice of her brother to heart."

Peter laughed suddenly. "So you did." He filled his pipe with tobacco and struck a match to it. "Don't misunderstand. This in no way diminishes my devotion to her. She worries me, though." He frowned as he looked off toward the river.

Rogan, too, was concerned. He had seen Captain Retford about camp, and the young man could catch the fancy of many young women. Rogan had already noticed that Darinda had looked the captain's way, and he hadn't forgotten that Arcilla mentioned him in Capetown. He glanced thoughtfully at Peter. Did he suspect? Was that what worried him?

Anyone thinking straight should have known Arcilla's temperament was wrong for the role of wife to a bureaucrat like Peter. Yet now, they had both willingly vowed to each other before God.

"I tell you, Rogan, there is plenty to be concerned about with Lobengula. This visit to Bulawayo will not be an easy one. Nothing is simple in South Africa. You'll come to appreciate how polarizing different ambitions and conscience can be when there are two sides to every issue."

"Mornay claims the dispute between Rhodes's delegation under Charles Rudd and Lobengula is the result of Rudd's tricking 'the old savage,' as some call him, into signing the concession paper."

Peter waved his pipe. "Nonsense. Mornay is an excellent guide, but he's extremely biased against the British. Rhodes's delegation met with Lobengula at Bulawayo to convince him to sign, allowing the Company to dig for gold, and he agreed. We've Lobengula's mark on the official document to prove it. It's an elephant head ring made for him in Europe. Well, my good fellow, on the ride back to Kimberly, Rudd was so anxious to get there he nearly died of thirst and lost the paper.

"Rhodes set sail for London at once to show the paper to the British government. That's when he received the Royal Charter."

"Then, what's Lobengula's complaint?"

Peter shrugged, but the gesture lacked enthusiasm, which prompted Rogan to dig further for the facts. Finally, Peter admitted the problem.

"A rival gold company headquartered in London, which had men operating in Bechuanaland, apparently had the same idea as Rhodes about moving north from the Limpopo into Mashonaland. As soon as Rhodes's delegation scrambled out of Bulawayo, the rival delegation under Lieutenant Maund arrived at the kraal.

"It didn't take the clever lieutenant long to find out his delegation had been bested to the task by Rhodes, so he came up with a scheme of his own." He hesitated, puffing his pipe.

"Which was?"

"The rival informed Lobengula that Rhodes's delegation had lied and cheated him. The rival told Lobengula that all his own group wanted was to dig for gold but that Rhodes also wanted their land—the truth is, we did, and still do. Lobengula sent two of his elderly *indunas* to London with Lieutenant Maund to decry what happened before the British government. Meanwhile, Rhodes was not idle."

"I could never see Mr. Rhodes idle," Rogan retorted.

"He began buying out his opponents, or rewarding them as shareholders in the new company if they joined forces."

"Sounds familiar," Rogan said and thought of the meeting in the tent the night before.

"Soon, even the rival company in London, for which Lieutenant Maund worked, made a settlement. They all agreed to use the mechanism of a British public company empowered by a Royal Charter to govern and develop the territory of Mashonaland in the name of the queen, using gold discoveries to pay for the colony."

"That was then. What about now?" Rogan remained doubtful of Rhodes's tactics. He had seen them at work more recently and had felt the stinging cut of the sword.

"Now," Peter said, "as you say, we have had a serious problem on our hands. Some of Lobengula's indunas at Bulawayo are giving the BSA the evil eye."

Peter bit his pipe stem. "He's listening to his indunas who are calling for war. Like their cousins the Zulus, they want to 'wash their spears in blood.' So far he's quieted them down and told them to go home, but he's refusing to honor the concession he signed."

Peter hesitated, as though he couldn't fathom such unwise behavior. "He agreed we could build a road from his Matabeleland into the north, but he's reneged. Now the indunas are grumbling. Their impis are shaking their spears and stamping their feet. So you see our work is going to be difficult when we ride to Bulawayo."

The African sun was growing hotter and burning against Rogan's shoulders and back. "I thought it was something of this nature." Rogan shook his head. "I'm liking what I hear about the concession less and less. This is about as sticky a situation as can be. If Lobengula thinks his rights were violated, and misunderstandings abound on both sides about what those rights are, little good will come from it. Why not renegotiate?"

"Are you mad? He would refuse. We must make him see he's already committed himself."

"That leaves a troubling situation, Peter. Justice is too easily open to disagreement and eventually leads to bloodshed."

Peter's lips thinned, as he obviously didn't like what he'd heard.

"You don't really believe Mr. Rhodes would have brought the concession paper to London if he thought his delegation had deceived Lobengula?"

Rogan arched a brow. "I've seen them at work in Kimberly," came Rogan's cold reply. "You must have heard what happened to John Sheehan and the coal deposit he pegged at Wankie. Do you call that justice?"

Peter's face turned a rosy brown. "Really, Rogan, you are a cynic. You simply do not like Rhodes and his partners."

Peter puffed rapidly on his pipe as they strode on toward a small rocky hill with a flat top.

Unexpectedly, Rogan remembered the words from Scripture that Derwent had quoted last night at the campfire. "Woe to him who builds a town with bloodshed, who establishes a city by iniquity!"

"Old chap, you're not listening to a word I've been saying," Peter complained when they'd reached the top of the hill.

They stood looking down upon the winding river and the distant crouching mountains of the north toward Zambezi.

"Sorry... You were saying?"

Peter's brows pointed together. "Naturally, I wasn't at Bulawayo when Rhodes's delegation first met with Lobengula. That was a few years ago. So I cannot attest to every bit of propaganda that comes out about how the BSA hoodwinked him. But it's all a misunderstanding about land rights. He insists none were given. But Great Scott, man! We've got to have land rights to settle the pioneers. What good is a colony without property rights?"

Obviously, the chieftain of the Ndebele tribe had not been expecting a colony when he'd agreed to let the Company dig for gold.

"This isn't my fight, Peter. I came to seek gold on the Zambezi, not to conquer a land."

"Conquer! Rubbish. Better our flag than France's or Germany's. Or would you rather see the Portuguese or Belgians colonizing all of Africa? And don't think they won't come. If England doesn't do it, someone else will. It's only a matter of time. And what of those cantankerous Boers? That ruddy Dutchman Kruger has had plans to push from the Transvaal Republic into Mashonaland for months. War with the Boers is inevitable. And I doubt any people other than the English would be any wiser in handling the tribes. Good grief, man! Do we want the Africans to remain naked savages, steeped in diabolical witchcraft for more generations to come? We need to bring education, put an end to witchcraft."

"The Bible and the plough"—that was missionary Robert Moffat's philosophy. It had worked for Robert Moffat at his mission compound, Kuruman. But the BSA was not patterned after Robert Moffat. Maybe Peter actually cared about bringing civilization to the African tribes and ending demon worship, but that was not the motivation of Julien or the BSA. It was gold, diamonds, and political power.

"I agree with part of your argument, Peter, but not all. And while we may share a similar interest in gold, there is a difference. I intend to leave eventually, but you and Julien and the others want to stay and expand the British Empire. That in itself is neither bad nor good, but I can't support tricking an old savage who can't read the fine print. We may conquer them, Peter, but it won't work in the generations to come unless we win their hearts as friends."

"Yes, yes, I realize all that. Friends come to help, to teach, to lift up—to treat with dignity, to grieve for their condition as fellow men."

Rogan quoted the words Derwent had read last night. "If we don't come as friends, then one day the new Rhodesia will come tumbling down."

"You sound like one of the confounded windy missionaries…or worse, like those dour-faced women in black at the London society for the protection of the so-called aboriginal peoples! And I've no reason to believe the Company deliberately lied to the Ndebele chief. If the confusion boils down to anything, it's due to the differences in language and culture. Dr. Jameson was one of the men who met with Lobengula in a second parley not long ago. The good doctor insists everything was done decently and in order. A missionary was present who read the conditions of the agreement aloud to Lobengula, making sure he understood. I believe Dr. Jameson. It's intransigence on Lobengula's part. And we cannot allow that to happen."

It wasn't Rogan's intention to change Peter's mind, or change the BSA. He was content to be out of the fray. All he wanted was his independence. As for Dr. Jameson, Rogan had little liking for him, and it was easy to believe he had used deception in his dealings with Lobengula.

"The real truth of what happened between Rhodes's delegation and Lobengula may never be fully known."

"Yes, yes, probably not, but what can we do about it? We can't change the world, and life goes on. It's far better that it proceed under the Union Jack."

Rogan laughed and started back down the kopje in the direction of camp.

Peter followed. "So we must have another meeting at Bulawayo to convince Lobengula. Dr. Jameson is coming with us. He's learned Lobengula is suffering again with gout. Maybe a bit of kindness from the doctor will show the poor devil our good intentions. If not, we will go anyway with an armed guard."

Rogan squinted toward the clear sky, watching a vulture gliding high over the river on wide, dark wings.

As Peter went on coaxing him, Rogan listened, but so far all the talk of political power and the subjugation of Africa left him unmoved.

Peter must have understood this, for he sobered. He stopped near the camp and faced him.

"There's another reason for wanting you along. I'm not speaking for the Company now, but for myself...for Arcilla. I'm second in command under Dr. Jameson at the new colony. I need someone I can have confidence in—who will tell me before it's too late if I'm headed in the wrong direction."

"Ah yes, the way I did earlier?"

Peter shrugged at his brother-in-law's wry voice. "We may not always see eye to eye, Rogan, but I'll still want your valuable insight. And I have confidence that you're not after my job. I don't always trust Julien when it comes to his wishes for himself and Arcilla. At any rate, having my brother-in-law at hand is important to me. Arcilla feels the same way."

She was wise to be afraid. Peter, too, was afraid behind his blustering determination. Perhaps they all were, himself included. That Peter admitted his need with surprising humility did more to persuade Rogan to stand with him than anything else he'd argued in the last hour.

Rogan liked Peter and wanted him and Arcilla to succeed in their marriage and Peter's pursuits in Africa. And yet...he had his own life to chart. His own heart to understand, and to make right, his own conscience to listen to when the voices, true and false, fell upon his ears like the beating of war drums.

And there was also Derwent Brown to think about. Honest-hearted

Derwent, the most loyal of friends. Derwent had his own dreams too. Derwent would want to go on the expedition even under the flag of the British South Africa Company. How could he disappoint him after all these years? From their teen years he had filled Derwent's mind with his own big dreams. Perhaps dreams not so different from Rhodes's dream of a far-flung new colony bearing his name delivered with pride to Queen Victoria.

Rogan stood looking off toward the base camp. The white canvas on the wagons billowed. He felt the wind ruffle his hair and cool his skin.

Besides redeeming Henry's lost expedition, what did he, Rogan, really want in life? Restlessness stirred his heart like the distant call of the wild beneath the bright African sun.

He heard Peter asking, "What do you say, Rogan? For you it's locating the gold deposit from Henry Chantry's map. For me it's claiming this land for the British Empire. Together we can do both. When we plant the Union Jack for Her Majesty below Mount Hampden, I want you standing with us shoulder to shoulder."

Rogan found that he could give no clear and certain answer, not yet.

"I'll go with you as far as Bulawayo," he said slowly. "After that...I don't know. I'll give you and Julien my answer then."

Peter smiled. "Fair enough."

CHAPTER FOURTEEN

The next morning at dawn Arcilla managed to rise and face Peter before he rode out to Bulawayo. The night had been a miserable one. Stinging insects had pestered her until Peter finally struggled from his blankets inside the wagon and dug something from his satchel.

"Try this, my dear. Rub it on your skin, and it will keep the insects away."

She opened the bottle and gagged. "Oh, Peter, it's positively ghastly. Smells like something from the barnyard."

"Arcilla," he stated with dignity, "your language surprises me."

"Oh, Peter, you're silly. It smells horrid. What is it?" she asked suspiciously.

"Now it is you who is being silly. It's oil from herbs and plants used by the ngangas."

She gasped, tossing the jar aside with a thud. "A witch doctor? Now you're trying to cast a spell on me."

Peter scrambled to retrieve the jar before the ointment began flowing onto the floor.

"Now it is you, my dear, who is being foolish. Put this on your face and arms, or I shall do it for you."

She snatched the jar from him and, holding her breath, smeared on the greasy ointment, holding back her tears. "And I brought French p-perfume… You hate me… I know you do, I know you do, Peter."

"Oh, Arcilla, darling, my dear, I care for you very much…"

She jerked away from his arms and, still whimpering, pulled the bedding over her head. As it became too hot and stuffy, she threw the cover aside and listened to his snoring. After what seemed countless miserable hours, she finally fell asleep. She awoke to his gently shaking her shoulder and handing her a tin cup full of something dark, hot, and bitterly strong and offensive.

"Coffee," he said. "We're leaving for Bulawayo, Arcilla. I won't be back for a week or so. You'll stay here with Darinda and your uncle Julien. We've left an armed guard, and you'll be safe enough."

She made a face as she took a gulp of the disgusting coffee.

"Are you going to get dressed and come out to see us off?"

She recognized the hopefulness in his voice. She supposed it would look good for Peter Bartley's wife to be on hand as he rode out with Dr. Jameson and the others to represent the Company. In London she had tried to present herself as the dutiful wife, but she was still emotionally wrecked from the long trip from Kimberly, and she'd had little sleep. Life had taken on a dark, hopeless cast, and she was in no mood to be dutiful about anything.

"No," she said and hoped Uncle Julien would not take it upon himself to lecture her after Peter rode out. "I have a dreadful headache." She scratched at the insect bites on her arm and noticed how unattractive they made her once lovely white skin.

Peter squared his shoulders, and his face became hard. "As you wish. Then I will see you on my return."

"Good-bye," she said with a lift of her chin, looking straight ahead.

He hesitated, then turned on his heel and walked away into the dawn.

Guilt now added to her misery. She should have kissed him goodbye. In frustration with herself as well as her surroundings, she opened the back canvas of their wagon and tossed out the nasty coffee. As she did, she had a full view of the entourage prepared to ride out to Lobengula's kraal. There were a half-dozen men on horseback, a handful of armed Bantu, and packhorses.

She also saw Darinda Bley. The young woman was up and dressed impeccably in a stylish riding outfit, her dark hair smoothed back and perfectly coiled.

Arcilla grudgingly admired her cousin. Whatever was driving her certainly made her a bold and stark contrast to herself. Darinda was carrying her bedroll, a rifle, and a gunbelt draped flatteringly around her hips, Arcilla noticed and felt disdain twist her mouth. Whose attention was she trying to get besides poor Parnell's? Every male eye seemed to survey Darinda as she came walking up.

"I'll be perfectly safe," Darinda's voice carried. "Someday I'll want to write my book about the expedition north. I want to see Lobengula for myself."

Rogan all but shook his head in amusement, but Parnell looked sullen as he sat reluctantly on horseback. So he had decided to join the negotiators. That was curious. He'd told her last night he had no wish to go to Bulawayo. Something had changed his mind.

"You must stay here, Darinda," Sir Julien said, and after some protestation, Darinda gave up and walked over to Parnell, seated on his horse.

Parnell leaned down to hear her words. Arcilla was surprised when her brother lifted Darinda's hand to his lips and kissed it. Were things progressing between him and Darinda at long last?

Arcilla's gaze strayed to Captain Retford, who rode beside Peter. He, too, had something of an amused smile as he watched Darinda and Parnell saying good-bye.

Arcilla thought Captain Ryan Retford a handsome young man, and she believed that Darinda thought the same. He had flinty blue eyes and sandy hair. His confidence and strength of purpose reminded her of Rogan, though they looked nothing alike.

Her eyes swerved to Peter, and her guilt returned. Then Darinda walked up to Peter and said something, and they both laughed. Arcilla stared hard. *Why, that little tart! How dare she flirt with my husband!*

She swallowed hard. *I'll make Peter a good wife yet,* she decided. She grabbed her clothes and scrambled into them, then brushed her hair. There was no time to put it up in any dignified fashion, but this would do. She pulled on her boots and climbed down from her wagon and ran toward the horses—

Arcilla stopped. "Drat!" She watched the small procession disappearing through the laager gate.

Darinda wore a cool expression as she sauntered closer. Her eyes twinkled as she said, "You're too late now."

She strolled past Arcilla toward her own wagon. Arcilla turned and glared.

Bulawayo lay in the middle of a grassy plain dotted with mimosa trees. Lobengula's kraal was a large oval circle of mud and thatch huts plastered with cow dung. Twelve miles to the south, the Matopos Mountain Range, focus of superstition to the Ndebele and Zulu alike, thrust its reddish-brown rock formations above the horizon, overlooking a vast and majestic but otherwise empty expanse.

Dr. Leander Jameson and Frank Thompson had conducted the earlier meetings with Lobengula, which resulted in the concession paper, giving Rhodes what he needed to present in London to receive the Royal Charter. Now the two men once again headed the team of negotiators to reconvince Lobengula of their right to pass through his land.

Rogan accompanied Peter and his aide, Captain Retford, and Parnell had joined them at the last hour. Derwent had come along to help with the cooking, and Mornay rode beside him, silent as usual. Three more of Cecil Rhodes's men came along in the party, as well as a small number of Bantu.

Near Bulawayo they made camp by a baobab tree, a strange specimen with swollen trunk and branches that reminded Rogan of a tree planted upside down with gnarled roots reaching hopelessly toward the sky. Like himself, Mornay was interested in the fauna and flora of Africa, and that had bonded them into a kind of friendship.

"The trunks are often hollowed out and used for a variety of purposes," Mornay said as they rode along. "The young leaves can be eaten as a vegetable, and the seeds can be roasted and eaten."

They made camp and prepared to move out to approach Lobengula's kraal. They were already under watchful eyes from behind trees and rocks, and Parnell appeared to shudder.

"A cat walked over my grave." He hunched his shoulders as though prickled by goose bumps.

It was necessary to move with caution, to show no action that could be construed as belligerent or proud behavior.

"No brandishing of weapons can be tolerated," Peter told them gravely. "The indunas are already riled. Any misunderstanding of our intentions, and we will find ourselves hopelessly surrounded by impis with sharpened assegai pointed at us."

"I hope we're not blundering into something we'll be sorry for later," Parnell complained.

"Why'd you decide to come? You surprised me," Rogan said amiably.

Parnell avoided his brother's gaze and busied himself with the cinch on his saddle. "If I hadn't, Darinda would think me a coward," came his quiet reply. He looked toward Captain Retford, who didn't seem to notice them as he wrote something into his log. "I don't trust him," Parnell said in a low voice.

Rogan glanced at Retford. "Seems all together to me. I rather like him. Looks like a man who'd stay beside you in a fight."

"Looks can be deceiving, my good brother."

Rogan smiled. He turned his reins and rode ahead to Captain Retford. Rogan thought it was more jealousy that troubled his brother than any issue with Retford. Rogan had heard of the brevet he'd earned in Sudan in the heat of battle.

"What do you know about the Ndebele?"

Retford squinted against the hot sun. "Lobengula has one of the most feared armies of any African kingdom. Some fifteen thousand Ndebele warriors are organized in impis like their Zulu cousins, who also carry the dreaded assegai.

"The tribe lives mainly by raising cattle—and raiding cattle from other, weaker tribes. Especially the Shona in the north. They broke away from the Zulu."

Captain Retford looked at him with hard blue eyes and said, "Though my business is to follow orders and leave politics to others, I've also questioned the BSA's motives. But it's fair to say that Lobengula controls Mashonaland because he, too, invaded and subjugated the Shona tribe."

They slowly approached the chieftain's kraal, dismounting and waiting until they were approached by the indunas.

Dr. Jameson and Frank Thompson led the procession toward the oval circle of mud huts.

The tall, chocolate brown warriors watched them with immobile faces, but it was clear to Rogan that the associates of the BSA were not liked here.

A fixed guard of indunas came forward and stared at them one by one, as if trying to smell out their evil intent.

Thompson and Dr. Jameson were the key spokesmen. Thompson, an explorer, spoke Sethuana, which was understood by the Ndebele and Lobengula.

Mornay murmured, "Monsieur Thompson has a loathing for the Ndebele. When he was a boy he saw his father killed by some of their warriors. They forced a ramrod down his throat."

Parnell made a choking sound and stepped farther back. Rogan walked slowly ahead beside Peter and Captain Retford, with Jameson and Thompson in the lead. They entered a second circle.

"This is the royal enclosure," Peter said.

With avid interest Rogan looked about. Lobengula had set up his palace here, made out of a trader's covered wagon. His throne, constructed of wooden crates, had once stored tins of condensed milk.

After a considerable wait, Lobengula finally appeared. By some who had dealt with him in the past, he was considered "a shifty customer." He looked to be about Rogan's height, six feet, but weighed around two hundred and eighty pounds. He was naked except for a small loincloth and a Zulu ringed headband. He wore what seemed to be a monkey-skin cape. A gold chain hung across his broad chest with an array of diamonds, and leather bands that sported fringes were tied around each of his calves.

Peter had already warned about the severe customs extracted from any visitor to the king, so Rogan expected the meeting to be tense. But when he saw Thompson, Jameson, and the others go down on all fours in the dust, a wave of revulsion swept over him.

Being the only one standing, he immediately felt like the three Hebrew children refusing to bow before Nebuchadnezzar's golden image.

The viciously sharp iron tips on the assegai threatened as the sullen eyes of all the indunas singled him out. Rogan felt Derwent yanking at his trouser cuffs urging him down.

Rogan stooped reluctantly, hot dust beneath his sweating hands. Insects buzzed near his face and ears, and he wanted to wave them away. He felt annoying, stinging bites.

"Crawl forward," Peter whispered, "and don't swat the flies.

Thompson and Dr. Jameson were creeping ahead toward the wooden crate throne. Now Rogan, Peter, and Retford moved forward on all fours, slowly following. Mornay, Parnell, and Derwent crawled behind them.

They waited in the hot dust until Lobengula stepped onto his throne above them. Not permitted to stand, they squatted before him in the broiling sun while insects continued to pester them. After several minutes, Dr. Jameson began talking in a quiet voice, and Thompson translated into the Sethuana language. The long parley with the primitive king had begun, with cajoling, dickering, and endless flattering.

"The mighty king should know," Dr. Jameson was saying slowly so Thompson could translate, "how Mr. Rhodes has the blessing of the great White Queen across the sea. King Lobengula must honor the paper he signed with his great elephant seal. This agreement will protect the king and his tribe from the Boers and other gold seekers who can't be trusted."

Rogan could see the suspicion in Lobengula's eyes as his gaze pinned Jameson to the spot where he sat cross-legged.

"The tongue of the white doctor sent by the queen speaks many languages. All do not say the same thing." His lips spread into a mocking smile. "What language should I believe?"

Rogan was not surprised; the man was shrewd. He must have known how the Swazi ruler, to whom he was related, had lost most of his land by concessions to the Europeans. And he for certain knew about the humiliating defeat of the Zulus in 1879.

"It's all a bundle of wicked lies, what our enemies are telling you. All we want to do is dig for gold, just ten men as it was told to you. We want no land. We have no designs on Mashonaland."

Rogan looked at Peter. Peter kept his eyes ahead of him.

Rogan noticed one of the indunas staring at him. He was tall and lean with tight muscles. He wore a short leopard-skin cape and the head ring of the Zulus. Why had he singled Rogan out from the others, or was he imagining it? Rogan looked back, and the induna slowly looked away.

"You lie," Lobengula told Jameson and Thompson. He flashed a malicious smile. Then he pointed to Frank Thompson, pronouncing his name "Tomoson."

"Tomoson has rubbed fat on your mouths. All you white men are liars. Tomoson, you have lied least. I said to your White Queen across the waters, 'A king gives a stranger an ox, not his whole herd of cattle. Otherwise, what would other strangers have to eat?' There will be no road to Mashonaland. You white men are troubling me much about gold. If the queen thinks that I have given away the whole country, it is because you lie."

Rogan glanced casually at the indunas and impis. The atmosphere was hot and tense, thick with danger that seemed to be growing by the minute. He caught Peter's eye.

Peter nodded faintly. The kraal was alive with menace. The induna who had been looking at Rogan earlier appeared to notice it as well.

Another induna stepped forward, spear in hand and an angry look on his hard-boned, sweating face. He lifted the spear, and a stir arose among the impis like a sigh, then it turned into a long, low moan. Then—

"White men lie. We will push the white man into the sea!"

Again the sucking in of breath as one man, the exhaling as a low, frightening growl.

Dr. Jameson raised a hand. "We do not want Ndebeleland. Only a road to Mashonaland to find and haul the gold. The mighty king has given his word to let us build the road from Bulawayo north. The elephant seal does not lie."

"Jee!" hissed the lead induna, the deep, drawn-out war chant of the fighting impis. Some of the others took up the cry and began to move from side to side under the force of the chant, their faces suffused with a fighting madness.

Lobengula stood and spoke sharply to the induna, and those following him grew quiet, then silent.

The induna Rogan had noticed watching him stepped forward and faced Lobengula. He raised his spear. "Bayete!" came the familiar royal salute, and the other indunas all turned as one man. "Bayete!" they shouted, and suddenly the angry murmur fell to a strained silence.

Rogan saw Lobengula looking evilly at the induna who had started the protest.

It was Lobengula who ended the meeting. He would rest. Dr. Jameson explained that his sickness was troubling him again.

"The white men must go now," Lobengula said as he stood. "I will send for you again later."

With Thompson in the lead, they crawled away from the wagon into the second circle, where they were permitted to stand. They were then escorted out of the circle of mud huts and through a line of young impis armed with assegais.

Rogan felt the menacing gaze of the warriors as he walked slowly through their ranks, refusing to show fear. They did not part to give them room to walk until the last moment. Rogan smelled the dust, the sweating bodies, the harsh breathing, the barely controlled hatred.

"I've a feeling they'd turn on us in an instant if they could," Peter said in an undertone.

"Let's get out of here," Parnell muttered, wiping the sweat from his forehead with the back of his arm. "This is the last time for me. Never again."

"Relax, gentlemen. I've been through this several times before," Dr. Jameson stated. "This is their way. The old savage won't turn on us. He knows he will come to the same end as Cetshwayo."

Rogan found himself wondering again about Dr. Leander Jameson. He looked more confident than the situation warranted. Then he remembered he was a doctor and that he had treated Lobengula in the past for his sickness.

"What's wrong with the king?"

"Gout. Very painful," Dr. Jameson said over his shoulder. "I brought morphine along with me. I thought he might need it. It will come in handy indeed." He looked at Frank Thompson, but Thompson looked nervous.

"Whew," Derwent murmured. "I thought we'd had it for sure this time, Mr. Rogan. Did you notice that one induna looking at you?"

"So you noticed too."

"I wonder why. Sure was a tight spot, I'd say, even if Dr. Jameson doesn't seem worried. Just think, Mr. Rogan, how that great Scottish missionary Robert Moffat came to these parts with no protection but the Lord's. He sure was a brave man."

"We could use some of that protection right about now, Derwent," Rogan said.

"Well, sir, I've been praying for that ever since we walked into Lobengula's kraal."

They mounted their horses and rode slowly away so as not to give the impression they were intimidated.

The fresh wind, though warm, felt good as it blew again through Rogan's damp shirt.

"Guess Robert Moffat knew the Lord had specially called him to bear witness to His grace," Derwent continued thoughtfully. He shook his head, took off his floppy hat, and put it back on. "They sure do need to hear the gospel of Christ. Made me sad to see such great men all bound up in superstition and witchcraft. They were made in the image of God… And now…" He shook his head again. "How Satan must enjoy seeing Lobengula and all of them, bound with chains of darkness. Wish I could speak that Sethuana language. I'd tell them myself."

"You just keep that rifle of yours loaded, Derwent."

"Aye, I'll do that all right, Mr. Rogan, but somehow I just wish…," and he sighed.

Rogan was watching. It didn't surprise him to see the sincere grief in Derwent's face. He, too, had been moved by the spiritual darkness binding the Ndebele.

"You know, Derwent," he said quietly, "I like you."

Derwent looked at him, surprised.

Rogan glanced ahead at Dr. Jameson riding along with head high. The smile left Rogan's face. "You bring me a clear distinction between men's motives, Derwent. Jameson called Lobengula an old savage, which he is, don't get me wrong. But where he showed contempt, you show compassion and sadness for those, who, as you say, were made to know God."

Derwent turned an unflattering pink beneath his freckles and fumbled with his bridle.

Rogan edged his horse away and rode up beside Peter.

"Thanks, Mr. Rogan," Derwent murmured after Rogan had ridden ahead of him.

CHAPTER FIFTEEN

London
Chantry Townhouse

Six months after the dark, mysterious incident on the attic steps, Evy wrestled with her disappointment. Dr. Snow had told her she would walk with a limp for the rest of her life. Walking about her room was not that difficult now. She had been improving, regaining some of her strength, but she was far from strong, and further still from coming to peaceful acceptance of the sudden and unwelcome hindrance in her life. It seemed unfair, needless, and cruel. Had she not loved God? She'd not been willfully disobeying Him.

Evy was living in London now at the Chantry Townhouse. It was as she remembered from that magical night so long ago when Rogan had played his violin for her. It was situated amid other two-story houses in the socially elite Strand, known for royalty and titled families.

The last place I belong, she thought morosely. The elegance emphasized her defect and made her feel more acutely the gulf between her and Rogan. Inheritance or not, she felt inadequate. Perhaps the thing that grieved her most was living in the place where memories of her crowning musical achievement seemed most acute…and mocking. *Why, heavenly Father?*

She limped her way, clumsily at first, using crutches, into the same room where she'd supped with not only Rogan, but Arcilla and Peter

Bartley, now Arcilla's husband. The lovely room was still and empty. On that night after her recital, she had worn a beautiful gown, her hair styled in high fashion. Candles had gleamed, and the atmosphere had been warm and romantic.

She fumbled her way into the same chair where she'd sat near Rogan. Deliberately, she relived each moment, feeling the sting of her present loss, tasting the bitter contrast. She remembered every detail of the conversation, the way Rogan had looked at her. As she sat quietly, she could hear in memory the violin playing, see the romantic challenge in his gaze.

How hopeful that night had seemed! How broken now, the delicate dream that lay smashed. Except for Simms and his daughter, servants of Lady Elosia who kept the Townhouse running smoothly, and Mrs. Croft, the dwelling was deserted. Only distant memories were here, memories that would never live again.

Never again would she waltz in a beautiful gown on the polished floor the way she had done one Christmas with Rogan at Rookswood. Crutches were a part of her life now, and crutches were not romantic. If Rogan were to see her now—

No, no, never. Her pride insisted that she must not suffer such humiliation.

For weeks she wrestled with her uncertain future. This couldn't be happening to her. How could she live with the reproach of deformity? Rogan was perfectly handsome, rugged, confident. But even if he should suddenly return to London, she would not meet with him. It was too late for that. He would show pity, and the very thought caused her to lift her chin. She wanted no pity, especially from him.

She was strong enough to get outdoors now. With early spring upon them, she would sometimes venture out with Mrs. Croft to one of the nearby parks or public gardens to sit on one of the benches and enjoy the fresh air. But she found the crutches awkward, especially when she needed to carry something or get in or out of the coach, and using them in public made her self-conscious. She imagined the stares of young women looking in pity, relieved *they* had been spared such uncomeliness, and the embarrassed glances of men meeting her eye, then looking quickly away.

"Horsefeathers! You imagine it," Mrs. Croft said. "I haven't seen a man yet, be he young or old, looking at you any differently than they ever did. Why, anyone could sprain an ankle or break a leg and look the same way as yourself."

Perhaps Mrs. Croft was right, but Evy's feelings were too raw to see things that airily. Besides, a sprained ankle usually healed, and since she was painfully aware of the seriousness of her injury, perhaps others could sense it in her eyes.

"You'll get stronger, Evy," Mrs. Croft encouraged. "The doctor says you may need only a cane later on. The stronger you get, the more you'll see it's so."

"Maybe, Mrs. Croft. But I'll always feel odd around people. I'm different now."

"No you aren't, child. If anything, you're even more unique. Always thought so anyway. As for that no-account Rogan Chantry, I wouldn't be wasting my tears on the likes of him."

"Who says I'm shedding any tears over him?"

Mrs. Croft paid no mind to her defensive tone.

"His running off the way he did to live among natives, promising you he'd write and never taking the time. He's no better than that rebel Derwent, going off to hunt for gold, when his father, the good Vicar Brown, wanted him to enter the church and marry you. Alice Tisdale…poppycock. I'll wager he's groaning about the whole thing by now."

Mrs. Croft had never trusted Rogan, even when he was a boy, and she was still miffed that Derwent had married Dr. Tisdale's daughter. Evy loved Derwent as a Christian friend, nothing more, so she could smile over Mrs. Croft's loyalty to her in thinking he'd jilted her, but Evy felt no consolation over Rogan.

"I don't want to talk about Rogan, Mrs. Croft."

"And it's no wonder."

Night was the worst time for fears and disappointments to loom large as mountains. It was then, alone in her room, unable to sleep, or waking at odd hours in the long night and being unable to return to sleep, when she knew that if she wasn't vigilant, her imagination would run astray. Feelings of isolation threatened to engulf her. Her new sense of weakness would sometimes drift toward panic, so that she would need to sit up and light the bedstand lamp.

During such times she discovered she could bring her spiritual struggles into subjection by filling her mind with the Scriptures she'd memorized since childhood.

Vicar and Mrs. Osgood came to call on her a few weeks after she'd left the hospital for Chantry Townhouse.

"We brought the things you wanted from the cottage, dear," Mrs. Osgood said when the doorman hauled in a trunk.

"The piano, and your aunt and uncle's trunks in the attic, we left until you're sure of your plans," the vicar said kindly. "Sir Lyle and I thought it best to just lock up the cottage for now."

Evy shuddered at the idea of returning to the cottage alone. The mere thought of it brought back fears of that terrible night of the thunderstorm...and the stranger.

Mrs. Osgood looked about the room, clasping her thin, veined hands together in unselfish delight. "I'm so pleased you're here at Chantry Townhouse, Evy dear. Lord Brewster is such a fine man to have arranged it all."

Anthony had remained in London, where he was dealing with problems in the family diamond business. Evy was expecting him for luncheon tomorrow, when he would explain her financial situation. His motives remained unclear, and that worried her. Lord Brewster had assumed a protective attitude that seemed odd, considering she hardly knew him. His explanation was simple enough, though—he was carrying out the wishes of the family patriarch, Sir Julien Bley.

Lord Brewster treated her kindly, and though she was cautious, she rather enjoyed the long chats with him about her music. He was nothing like Uncle Edmund Havering, with whom she'd enjoyed a warm relationship while growing up in the rectory. Anthony Brewster was sophisticated, yet he was awkwardly kind to her.

So far, she had not dared tell him about the ugly incident at the cottage, afraid he would think her too imaginative. Everyone continued to assume she had fallen, but no one had bothered to ask why it happened or observed that such a fall might be unusual for her. "It was a wicked storm, all right, all that thunder and lightning," was all Mrs. Croft had said when Evy had once broken her silence on the subject and suggested that her fall was a bit strange.

Later in the afternoon, outside in the Chantry garden, Evy poured tea for the vicar and Mrs. Osgood. The song sparrows trilled in the garden trees, and the London sky was blue for a change, without a trace of gray mist anywhere.

Mrs. Osgood chatted about the village news. "Lady Patricia Bancroft left Rookswood and returned to Heathfriar, her father's estate." Evy remembered how much time Rogan and his brother, Parnell, had spent there during their school years in London, horseback riding and attending all the elite socials.

"You mean she didn't sail for Capetown?"

"No, she hasn't left yet. Very disappointed too, poor dear. She was quite morose when she left Rookswood with Lord Brewster."

"Lord Brewster?"

"Oh yes, he brought her home here to London, or hereabouts. I'm not sure where Lord Bancroft's estate is located... Anyway, Sir Julien Bley postponed her going out to Capetown for as much as another year."

Another year—that would be enough to infuriate Patricia. Evy almost felt sorry for her. Even with all her prestige and family money, she was having a difficult time capturing Rogan Chantry.

"It's the new colony," Vicar Osgood commented over his tea, "the one Cecil Rhodes has a Royal Charter to create in the Zambezi. It seems a woman won't be safe out there for some time. So Lord Bancroft finally agreed with Sir Julien that it was best for her to wait."

Evy wondered about her childhood friend. She knew Arcilla well, and Arcilla would have loathed the hardship of trekking into Africa to start a colony. Her marriage to Peter Bartley had been arranged against her will by her family, with Sir Julien pressuring Lyle to choose Peter. The marriage needed much prayer, and Evy worried about their future together. Sometimes it helped that the dignified Peter was ten years Arcilla's senior, but in other ways it proved harmful. Peter was not the sort of man who enjoyed being married to an immature girl. Would the wilds of Africa eventually tear them apart?

"And what of you, Evy? How are you adjusting to changes?"

The vicar's logical question, asked calmly, without clerical pressure, helped her to relax and express her genuine feelings. She was not doing well. The struggles were continual, almost unbearable some days.

"Sometimes I feel angry," she confessed. "Angry that God took both Uncle Edmund and Aunt Grace, leaving me alone just when the real trials in my life started. Grace Havering was a relatively young woman… Why did she need to become ill with her lungs and die so early? And now *this*." She glared at the crutches leaning against the tree. She wanted to add, *And now I've lost Rogan, too.*

Vicar Osgood didn't answer, and for a moment she felt the heat of shame steal into her cheeks, thinking she had shown herself a faithless creature, and that her honesty had offended him and Martha. But Martha looked calm, sipping her tea as the vicar munched thoughtfully on his crumpet, in no apparent hurry to counter her thoughts.

Evy hastened, "I know God is good and all-wise, and He doesn't make mistakes…only…well, I just don't like what He allowed to happen to me."

Vicar Osgood finished his crumpet and wiped his fingers on the snowy napkin, then drank his cup of tea. He cleared his throat and, as though he hadn't heard a word she'd said, pointed toward a small garden tree that had blown down, its roots clearly displayed.

"What happened to it?" he asked indifferently.

"What? Oh, that." Evy felt nettled. She had bared her heart while he seemed only to have gone off in another direction, more interested in botany.

"The wind blew it down in the last winter storm," Evy stated. "I understand it wasn't doing well, anyway. The gardener hadn't planted it correctly. You can see the roots never went deeply into the soil, so its growth was stilted."

The vicar nodded in hearty agreement. "Exactly so. A root problem. That's why it blew down. We noticed many trees that survived the winter storms coming up on the train. Didn't we, Martha?"

"Oh yes, dear, many, standing tall and strong. Now the storms have passed, and spring brings out new leaves. It's marvelous."

"An object lesson, Evy. Those with deep roots survived the winter gales, but the shallow-rooted trees blew down. The survivors remain tall and grow still stronger."

"Yes, indeed," Martha said, nodding emphatically.

"So it is with us when the winds of adversity buffet our lives," the vicar said, pouring more tea into his cup. "How we respond to trouble often decides the direction our lives will take. If we surrender to bitterness, it can harm us far more than the trial. But if adversity causes us to run to our heavenly Father, we can profit spiritually from a far deeper relationship with Him." He reached over and laid a hand atop his wife's. They looked at each other lovingly, as though Evy were not there. Despite their silver hair and the lines of time in their faces, it was clear that they cared as much for each other now in the sunset of life as they had when the glow of youth shone in their faces.

"Adversity knocks on all our doors at different times in our lives."

Martha nodded. "Like when Billy died. I watched him fall into a lake and drown before I could reach him... He was our one and only baby, just three years old."

"That was thirty years ago," her husband said and glanced from the small dead tree to the blue sky. A calm, confident smile touched his mouth. "Thirty years since our baby first saw Jesus."

Martha nodded. "The winds of disappointment and loss can blow very strongly. For a time after Billy's drowning, I could find no words to describe my pain and disillusionment. My heart was like a grave. But God has power over the grave. Adversity is a challenge, but with it, God gives us opportunity."

Vicar Osgood looked across the table at Evy. His eyes were sober, but she saw some of God's compassion in the depths.

"Don't listen, Evy, to false expectations promising that His children are to be exempt from suffering. Search the Scriptures and see what God did in the lives of the saints in the Bible. Some of His greatest servants advanced spiritually not through good health and prosperity, but through adversity. Why should we be any different?"

Mrs. Osgood nodded her gray head. "At first I looked for someone else to blame for my loss. Then I went into denial. But my faith has now grown deeper and stronger all these years."

"The same as that tree, Evy," the vicar said quietly, "and those dead, dry, shriveled roots. Some of us, sadly, when trouble knocks us down, are not deeply rooted in Scripture, so it's easy for doubt, depression, and hopelessness to defeat us."

Quite casually he reached over and took Evy's hand into his. Martha laid her wrinkled hand on his, so that the three of them were holding hands.

"Surrender your will to Him, Evy dear. He can build strong roots in your life. Yield all your dreams and tomorrows, pray for understanding, and then rest in His trustworthiness to see you through your valley."

Yes, she must accept loss and disappointment or grow lukewarm and shrivel, bearing no eternal fruit.

Martha reached down into a large straw handbag and handed her husband his Bible.

He patted his frock coat, looking for something. Martha handed him his spectacles. He placed them on his nose and opened the Book.

"Habakkuk chapter three, verses seventeen through nineteen: 'Though the fig tree may not blossom, nor fruit be on the vines; though the labor of the olive may fail, and the fields yield no food; though the flock may be cut off from the fold, and there be no herd in the stalls—yet I will rejoice in the LORD, I will joy in the God of my salvation. The LORD God is my strength; He will make my feet like deer's feet, and He will make me walk on my high hills.' "

He closed the Bible and bowed his head and prayed for Evy.

Afterward, Evy was silent. She had heard every word. Like seed falling upon the soil of her hurting heart, God's Word would take root. A little sunshine, a little rain, and the seed would germinate and grow.

Chapter Sixteen

Bulawayo, South Africa

Soon after leaving Lobengula, the Company entourage rode into their small camp about a mile away. The Bantu were waiting nervously under a mimosa tree, watching them ride in, no doubt curious about how the meeting with the feared king of the Ndebele had gone.

Thompson had the shakes the whole time they rode back. Rogan didn't blame him, considering how they'd brutally killed his father. When they reached camp, Thompson dismounted and removed a flask of liquor from the satchel near his bedroll. His hand trembled as he drank. Rogan, even with his .45 pistol belted in place, had felt like a skinned rabbit on a spit, walking into Lobengula's kraal.

Dr. Jameson had taken refuge from the sun under a makeshift awning that had been set up earlier. He was conferring with Peter, who at the moment stood looking down at him with a tense face while the doctor sorted through his satchel.

Rogan leaned against the mimosa tree, watching Jameson thought-fully. The doctor was acting discreetly, talking in a low voice. Whatever he was planning, Rogan didn't want to be a part of it.

Peter filled his pipe as he walked over to where Rogan leaned against the tree, drinking from his canteen.

"Jameson and Thompson are sure they can reason with the king.

We need more time, is all. Lobengula will send for us again, probably tomorrow." He looked toward the bright sun in the azure sky, wiping his forehead with a white handkerchief.

Rogan noticed it was monogrammed. It was like Peter to have such a handkerchief hundreds of miles from civilization.

"What's Jameson got planned?"

Peter looked at him, enjoying his pipe. "What do you mean?"

"I noticed you just now when he was fussing in his bag. You didn't look exactly pleased."

Peter's brows pulled together, and his eyes sparked. "You think we're planning to poison him? Absurd, none of us would even make it out of here alive. They'd find us a week later hanging from a tree with our bellies slit wide open."

"Don't pretend with me, Peter. I'm not talking poison, and I think you know it. We both know Jameson's up to something. How often does he come here to relieve Lobengula's gout pain?"

Peter looked at him hard for a moment. The silence grew between them, then Peter turned abruptly and strode away.

It was toward sunset. Rogan stood off by himself when he heard a soft shuffle of dried grass. Alert, he moved back for cover by the mimosa tree. His hand drifted toward his gunbelt.

From out of the long shadows, a dark form emerged wearing a leopard-skin tunic over muscled shoulders. The induna stood with several impis in an arc behind him, fully armed.

It was the same induna that Rogan had noticed watching him at the kraal. How to communicate?

Surprisingly, the induna spoke some English. "I see you. I am Jube."

"And I see you, Jube. I am Chantry."

"You are a lone spirit. You are not close with the other lying white men. You watch and listen. I will call you Hawk."

Rogan nodded. "You are right. I am alone."

"I remember another Chantry. His name was Henry."

Stunned, Rogan couldn't speak for a moment.

"How did you meet my uncle?"

"Many years ago now. I was young. I saw him in Capetown."

Rogan wanted to ask more questions, but Jube would not discuss more.

"Our king calls for the white doctor tonight, the one named Jameson. He is to come now. The king groans."

"I will tell Dr. Jameson."

"That one is like hyena. He laughs, his laughs fill the air with poison. No one else laugh before Lobengula. No one else stand in the presence of Lobengula."

Now, what would give him so much confidence in the Ndebele king's presence?

"Lobengula is like serpent upon his blanket," said Jube.

"I will call for the white doctor."

The induna turned and walked back into the deepening twilight, disappearing as silently as he had come.

Other footsteps sounded. "Thought I heard you talking to someone, Mr. Rogan. The others are all accounted for, so thought I'd check."

It was Derwent Brown, carrying a mug of coffee in one hand and his Winchester in the other. Rogan noticed he looked uneasy. Derwent handed Rogan the mug.

"Thanks, Derwent."

"That was one of the Ndebele chiefs, wasn't it? The one we saw looking at you earlier."

"Yes. His name is Jube. He had a message for Doc Jameson. The tribal king is sick and agitated upon his bed. He wants his treatment."

Derwent looked surprised at the cynical tone in Rogan's voice, but he seemed to dismiss it. "At least the good doctor can do an act of Christian charity for the chieftain. Maybe it will make them look more kindly upon us."

Rogan looked at him sharply. "If anything, it will cast disrepute upon the white man and his God."

Derwent's rusty brows shot straight up. "Now, why would you be saying that?"

"Between you and me, I think Jameson is resorting to the last and lowest trick in his bag. The Company wants that road built from Bulawayo to the Zambezi. Lobengula refused again this afternoon. You heard. The mood in the king's kraal is growing more dangerous. His impis would like nothing more than to wet their assegais with our blood. I think Jameson plans to use morphine to get Lobengula to agree on building that road."

"You mean get him addicted? Surely *we* wouldn't be doing that?"

It was clear by his use of "we" that Derwent was aligning himself with the English and Boers.

"I wonder how long Jameson has been treating Lobengula for gout," Rogan mused.

"Mornay's likely to know. Why do you think Dr. Jameson's planning that?"

"I've no proof," Rogan said wearily, "just a hunch. Get Mornay, will you?"

When Derwent returned with the Frenchman, Rogan put the question straight to him.

Mornay tweaked at his silver whiskers, his ebony eyes attentive. "I've heard the doctor has been treating him off and on all summer. But what should that mean?" He gestured expressively with open palms. "I can't say. One thing I know—this expedition will go forward one way or another. The BSA has too much at stake to let it fall apart now, *mon ami.*"

Rogan could feel Mornay's inquisitive gaze. He knew what was likely to be on his mind. What did Rogan intend to do about his own plans, and Henry's map? Did he even have a choice? Not if the BSA was claiming control of the Zambezi area in the name of the queen.

Not wishing to discuss the matter now, Rogan went off to find Dr. Jameson and give him Jube's message.

Parnell was there when Rogan told the doctor Lobengula wanted him to come to the kraal to treat him. Parnell looked stressed and said, "Are you going with them to the kraal?"

"Peter expects it, why?"

"Just wondering." Parnell looked away. "Be careful."

An hour later Peter left with Thompson and Dr. Jameson for the king's kraal, but Rogan had changed his plans. If Jameson was going to stoop so low as to use morphine as a tool to get what Rhodes wanted, then he would not be there. He went off by himself to use his telescope on the Matopos Mountains.

He returned at dark, unnoticed. He started toward his horse and bedroll, when he noticed his saddlebags were gone. *Now what?* Then hearing a rustle in the thicket behind the mimosa trees, he stopped, slipping his .45 from his gunbelt. It could be anything from a python to a lion.

A man's heavy breathing convinced him otherwise. He moved with caution toward the sound, pistol in hand. He paused by the clump of bushes, listening. Again, he heard a groan. He moved slowly, pushing the bushes aside.

Then he stopped suddenly. On the ground a man lay in a crumpled heap—Derwent.

Rogan quickly reached him and turned him over to check for wounds in his face and chest, but there was no evidence of blood. He picked him up and carried him back toward the campfire. All was quiet.

"Mornay? Parnell!"

Rogan lay Derwent on his blanket by the fire and was looking at the large lump on the back of his head when Parnell hurried up, rifle in hand. He looked pale.

"What happened to him? Is he all right?"

"Get some water boiling, will you? I'll need to bathe this and get something on his gash. Infection starts quickly out here."

Parnell rushed off for water, and Mornay came up slowly, looking the scene over with a wary eye.

"He was hit from behind?"

"Clobbered, from the looks of the gash."

Derwent stirred, groaning. "Oooh—"

"Take it easy," Rogan told him.

"I'll see if the doctor has anything we can use," Parnell said. "He may have left something."

"Don't need anythin'," Derwent stammered. "I'm all right—just dizzy…"

"Can you tell us what happened?"

Derwent winced as Rogan poured some of Thompson's whiskey on the gash to kill germs.

"Heard something around the horses…thought I saw somebody stealing Mr. Rogan's black. Whoever it was stole his saddlebags, then made for the mimosa trees, so I started after him, then *wham*, I was clobbered from behind. Ouch! Mr. Rogan, don't press on it."

"Did you get a look at who it was?" Parnell asked.

"No— Well…"

"One of the workers. It had to be," Parnell said.

"Don't worry about it now, Derwent. Better get some sleep."

When Rogan had Derwent situated for the night in his bedroll and came back to the campfire, Parnell was still there, watching the flames dance in the night.

"You can't trust those Bantu," he said as Rogan approached. "They'll steal anything if they can get away with it."

Mornay raised his brows with offense. "Not my Bantu. They have been with me since they were children."

"Then one of the others," Parnell said, "from the kraal."

Mornay pursed his lips and studied Parnell. "Maybe, monsieur, maybe. But myself? I don't think so."

"What are you suggesting, then? That one of us was sneaking around Rogan's saddlebags?"

"Never mind," Rogan said. "Where is Retford? Did he go with Jameson and Peter?"

"No," came Captain Retford's voice from behind them. He walked up. "I've been on sentry duty, why?"

"Someone hit Derwent from behind."

Parnell looked at Retford. "I didn't see you go out to the perimeter."

Retford turned toward him. "That doesn't change the fact."

Mornay came back from the mimosa trees carrying Rogan's saddle-bags. "I found them in the brush. Looks like someone was looking for something. Better check them."

Rogan looked through his things. "Nothing missing."

"Odd," Retford said quietly.

"Derwent must have scared the thief off," Parnell said.

"Or what the thief searched for was not there?" Mornay suggested.

Rogan knew exactly what was on Mornay's mind. The same thing that was on his as soon as Derwent had mentioned saddlebags—the map.

Later, in his bedroll beneath the stars, Rogan considered the un-pleasant facts and came to his own conclusion. Either Mornay, Parnell, or Retford had been looking for Henry's map. Retford knew nothing about the map, as far as he knew. So that left his brother and Mornay.

Rogan frowned at the stars. He didn't want to think it so, but he was sure it was his brother. The question was, who had put him up to it? He could confront him and *demand* the truth, but he wasn't willing to do so. Derwent might learn that Parnell had been the one who struck him. There was still enough family loyalty stirring in Rogan to want to protect Parnell.

If he did talk to Parnell about it, it would be alone, and later, after the trouble blew over. He didn't think Parnell would try the search again. He had looked nervous and pale tonight, which could mean someone had arm-twisted him into doing it—and it bothered him.

Had he been sent on this journey for the sole purpose of stealing the map?

The whole attempt looked clumsy and somewhat foolish. It had to have been a plan by someone other than Julien. Julien would know he wouldn't keep the map sitting out in his saddlebag. But would Darinda?

Rogan was sitting on a rock near the campfire the next morning, eating breakfast, when he heard the rapid thud of approaching hooves. He stood, holding his tin plate in one hand, leaving his right near his holster, even though the Ndebele owned no horses.

Peter rode swiftly into camp.

"Watch the dust," Rogan shouted, disgusted, but Peter was down from the saddle in a moment and striding up to him.

His tanned face showed lines of weariness, as if he'd been up all night, but he wore a grin.

"Jameson's done it, chap. He's gotten the wily old savage to relent. We can build the road from Bulawayo."

Rogan sat down on the rock and went on eating the thick slices of smoked bacon, ignoring a side dish of mealies.

"Well, Great Scott, man! Are you just going to sit there? I said Lobengula has agreed at last. We've gotten around the impasse."

"I heard you the first time." His casual tone appeared to frustrate Peter even more. Peter stared down at him with puckered brows.

Derwent, whose head was bandaged, came up, glancing uneasily from Rogan to Peter, then he reached over and filled another tin mug with coffee.

"What happened to you?" Peter scowled worriedly at Derwent's bandage.

"Somebody hit me. They were trying to make off with Mr. Rogan's saddlebags."

Peter looked around for Captain Retford.

"He got away, sir," Retford said. "I checked for tracks this morning, but there were none."

Mornay grumbled and picked an insect out of his coffee. He held it up for inspection. "Locust. Bad omen, messieurs, very bad." He turned his piercing ebony gaze toward the horizon at the first morning sun.

The sky was crimson and gold as the sun began its glorious rise.

"Better have this, Mr. Bartley," said Derwent and handed Peter the tin mug.

Peter drank the coffee, glaring at Rogan, who sat there ignoring him.

Having lost his appetite, Rogan tossed the scraps into the fire and set down the tin plate.

Peter gripped the mug. "Very well, then. I gather you don't agree with the means used to obtain the concession."

His stilted tone caused Rogan to smile crookedly. He snatched his leather hat, first whacking off the dust before settling it on his head. He turned and looked at him.

"Now, why wouldn't I agree? What are a few white lies told to the old savage when so much is at stake? It's a small price to pay, considering we'd have to fight for the land, or see it pass to the ruddy Boers."

The quiet sarcasm in Rogan's voice brought a glitter to Peter's eyes. His nerves seemed to snap after a long night at the kraal, and he threw the coffee aside. "Tastes like mud." Turning on his heels, he marched in the direction of the water hole.

Mornay called out, "Monsieur Peter, let it be known to you that there is a fine fat hippo wallowing there. I do not think it will appreciate your company, yes?"

Rogan went to feed his horse and rub it down with the liniment he'd bought in the Transvaal. Insects of all kinds were a constant torment for animals out here in the bush.

Distant sounds of wildlife hummed in the wind. Insects droned. A rustle whispered through the grasses behind the mimosa trees. Again?

Rogan turned, his hand on his holstered pistol. This time he'd get the scoundrel.

The dark form in the leopard-skin mantle reappeared, two impis behind him.

"I see you, Hawk."

Rogan relaxed his hand.

"I see you, Jube."

The induna stood grave and tense. "I will tell you what happened when the lying doctor left Bulawayo at sunrise."

"I'm listening."

"The young impis are mad for fighting. Our king tells them they will have the white men soon. The shaking like a wind first sounded when Mshete came back from seeing your great White Queen across the waters. Mshete drank African beer from sun rising until sun darken. He told all the indunas how she spoke with him. She said King Lobengula should let no white man to dig for gold, only Lobengula and his servants."

Apparently, Mshete was one of the two elderly indunas who had been sent by Lobengula to London with Lieutenant Maund when he tried to stop the British government from giving Rhodes the Royal Charter to grant mining rights and to start a colony.

"Mshete awakens a great shaking among all the indunas after the lying white doctor leaves Lobengula at sun rising. Lobengula has to quiet the angry spirits. So he has called for Lotshe, who first believed the lies of the man named Frank "Tomoson." Lotshe said the king should believe him and sign the lying words that were brought to the White Queen."

Rogan met the dark, even stare of Jube. "What about Lotshe?"

"Lobengula has sent for him. He will smell him out for witchcraft."

Rogan felt sure that whatever the king would "smell out" would only confirm what Lobengula intended to establish—the guilt of the induna Lotshe. He must want to make Lotshe the scapegoat for his troubles with Rhodes's delegation by blaming it all on the induna's witchcraft against the king.

"Lotshe and all his clan, three hundred Ndebele, will be beaten and hacked to pieces this day. Their blood will soon be warm on the ground. The impis will not be silent."

Rogan kept his emotions concealed.

"The killing will not end yet," Jube said meaningfully. "The hawk should fly at once."

Jube gestured, and one of the ebony impis stepped forward, a large hawk on his leather-wrapped hand. When the induna straightened his arm, the bird spread strong, eager wings, hoping to fly. Jube took a knife and cut the leather strap that bound it.

The bird took off, its wings beating as it ascended in freedom, a moment later only a silhouette as it flew toward the sun.

"Hawk should fly too."

Jube turned and left through the mimosa trees.

Why had he chosen to come and warn him?

Rogan strode back to the camp. Dr. Jameson and Thompson had both collapsed into their bedrolls upon returning from the night spent at the king's kraal. Peter, too, was in a deep sleep. It had been decided earlier that they would break camp early and leave tomorrow.

Rogan gave orders to the Bantu workers to start breaking camp now. He went to Mornay, then to Captain Retford to tell him to post a guard, and lastly to Derwent.

"Rhodes's men won't like this none, Mr. Rogan. They're dog-tired, and Mr. Thompson looked nervous and went to sleep using his flask again. It's going to be trouble awakening him."

"Then pour water on him if all else fails. He'll find that better than facing an army of bloodthirsty impis ready to hack him to pieces."

Rogan explained to Mornay what Jube had said.

Mornay groaned. "Lotshe? A grief. He is Lobengula's principal induna. He is one of the more noble of the indunas."

Derwent gulped. "We're sitting on a powder keg, all right. Why, it's a hundred miles or more back to the Limpopo. If the Ndebele are anything like their cousins the Zulu, they can cover more miles trotting than a man in a wagon."

Mornay's swarthy features showed his knowledge of the imminent danger surrounding them. He glanced quietly about the trees. "Needless to say, *mes amis,* this will not be a place we want to be once the sun sets behind the hills. We have, maybe, two hours."

"I'll awaken Peter," Rogan said. "Bring coffee to Thompson, will you, Derwent? Give him a gallon of it if necessary."

"The news will scare him out of his wits," Derwent said. "After what happened to his father. Got goose shivers running up my back just thinking about it. The Bantu said something wicked was on the wind when they heard how I was hit last night. Then I found that giant spider in the cooking things this morning. Never saw such a big one. Had legs as long as pencils. The Bantu swore it was a bad omen. Spirits from angry dead indunas are prowling tonight. They don't like us."

Rogan grinned and shoved his shoulder. "Don't tell me you're back at Rookswood locked inside the vault with Henry Chantry's ghost?"

Derwent looked at him, clearly surprised, as though suddenly remembering Rogan's boyhood pranks. Then he, too, grinned and looked sheepish. "I'd rather be back at Rookswood spooked by that ghost of yours than facing thousands of impis with assegais."

"I'll get Peter." Rogan walked away, leaving Derwent to rouse Thompson.

The mission to Bulawayo had ended as Rhodes's delegation had hoped, with a concession to build the road, but at what cost? How would this trek into Mashonaland end? With wealth and satisfaction? A new country for the British Empire called Rhodesia? Or would blood and tragedy border the crooked road leading to the elusive gold?

CHAPTER SEVENTEEN

Over a week had passed since the BSA delegation left Bulawayo. Darinda was reading in her private coach and taking tea when the sound of a rapid exchange between the Bantu and Grandfather Julien alerted her.

"They not far away, Baasa! They all come safe."

She tossed her book aside, and her heart began thumping with nervous excitement. Soon she would know if Parnell had been able to get the map.

She quickly dressed in her tan riding habit with shiny copper buttons and smoothed her hair back, this time leaving it loose and tying it with a copper-colored ribbon. She hurried to leave her coach and saw the riders entering the camp.

She waited beneath a shade tree, scanning each rider with indifference until her gaze fell on Parnell. His expression would tell—

Uncertain footsteps approached from behind her, and she glanced around to see Arcilla, looking toward the horsemen as they dismounted and walked their mounts into camp to keep the dust down. Several small Bantu boys ran to lead the horses to water, fodder, and grooming.

"Are they all safe?" Arcilla questioned.

"Of course." Darinda felt impatient. Arcilla had been walking about the camp with the delicacy of a tenderfoot this past week, jumping at every new sound from animal or insect.

Grandfather had come out of the large meeting tent and waited in the shade of an awning.

Dr. Jameson and Frank Thompson walked toward him. Jameson was laughing, an obvious evidence to her of his success with Lobengula. Peter walked to meet Arcilla. Darinda didn't care to see whether they embraced or not. Knowing Peter, he would embrace his wife to make the appropriate impression. Arcilla's tinkling voice rang out, convincing her that Peter had proven himself the adoring husband.

Darinda walked away so she wouldn't need to listen to Arcilla's chatter, concentrating instead on Parnell. He saw her and stopped where he was. His face, she noted, wore a mask of weariness but nothing more. The first flush of disappointment assailed her. He had failed to get the map. She could see it in his stance, the way he did not come immediately toward her.

She felt frustration, then anger. Must he always fail her?

She walked toward him across the yard, so intense on watching him that she ignored her steps—steps too close to some shady rocks and boulders.

A faint movement among the rocks brought a prickle of fear, and she halted. Shock went through her spine when she saw what had caught the corner of her eye. There, not more than six feet from her, a snake coiled and raised itself to an upright striking position while weaving slightly. It was perhaps four feet long, slender, a light gray-brown with black scale edgings. Across its broadly spread neck, she saw a series of irregular dark bands—the deadly spitting cobra.

Darinda froze, while all about her the exchange of talk and laughter mocked the danger she was in. No one noticed her dilemma. At this moment it seemed no one even knew she existed. And she was not armed...but even if had she her pistol, she knew she couldn't draw it. One threatening move, and the cobra would strike, spitting its venom accurately to a distance of eight feet, venom that was ejected straight out of the front of the fangs toward the face of the intruder. Even a drop was extremely painful and injurious if it struck the eyes. She'd once had her favorite guard dog go blind from such an attack.

Parnell. Yes, Parnell had been watching her, and he was armed!

"Parnell," she whispered. Her throat went dry, and the fear sent a trickle of perspiration down her temple. "Do something…" She doubted he could possibly hear her whisper, but he should realize that since she'd stopped dead in her tracks, something was very wrong.

But the moments ticked by, trapping her in fear. She could try to back away an inch at a time, try to fling her hands over her face, but doing all that while the cobra was so close—

She shifted her eyes from the cobra toward Parnell. Why didn't he lift his rifle? Why didn't he save her? He stood staring at the cobra, white faced with a dazed, glassy look in his eyes.

Then she heard a gunshot, and the cobra's head splattered, but not before she felt venom squirt against her face, the warm fluid running down her skin.

Darinda heard Arcilla cry out as she ran across the dusty yard in her direction. Darinda looked and saw that it was Captain Retford who had fired the bullet. In an instant he was at her side, taking her elbow and pulling her quickly toward the barrels of drinking water under the tree.

"Close your eyes and wash it all off," he ordered. "You'll be all right. Just as long as you've no open scratches. That's right, don't get any in your eyes. All right, now?"

Her hands shaking and dripping with the warm water, the front of her riding habit wet, she leaned against the barrels, breathing hard, and looked up at him. Darinda was surprised to see amusement in the flinty blue eyes that gazed back, not alarm, not even sympathy. His white teeth gleamed against his tanned skin as he smiled, the dust of travel and sweat streaking his handsomely rugged face. The wind stirred the hair across his forehead, hair the color of ripened wheat.

He was amused!

"Next time, Miss Bley, watch where you walk—and keep away from the rocks and tall grass." His smile deepened as he pointed his chin back over his shoulder. "I won't always be around to protect you when your future husband freezes."

She could have spat her own venom into his eyes, but she was speechless from shock.

He was still smiling as he lifted his dusty hat an inch from his head and set it back down again. "Good day, Miss."

Trembling from both fear and rage, she leaned against the tree and watched him walk away toward the horses.

She was still beside the water when the others came rushing up.

"Darinda, you're all right, my dear?" Julien asked, his voice tremulous with emotion. He put an arm around her shoulders and drew her toward him.

She nodded. "I'm not hurt, Grandfather. It was my fault. I really knew better than to walk near the rocks like that."

"A cobra…" Arcilla shuddered. "You were brave, Darinda. I should have screamed and screamed."

"And been struck with venom more than once," Darinda managed. "It's silly to scream. What good does it do?"

Arcilla lifted her dimpled chin defensively and stepped closer to Peter. "I wouldn't be able to keep myself from screaming. After all, I've never looked into the eyes of a cobra before. It…it was horrid!" she shivered.

"Those filthy rocks." Julien's anxious voice rose with anger, and he turned sharply toward the Bantu. Several of the younger children and boys huddled together some feet away, looking on and whispering among themselves.

"Omens?" shouted Julien fiercely, turning on them. "You mention omens and spells?"

One of them, the bigger boy of perhaps thirteen, nodded vigorously. "The baasa's daughter was cursed. Someone put a curse on her, and so the spitting cobra waited for her in the rocks."

The look on Julien's face alarmed Darinda. Did she actually see *fear* of witchcraft?

"Who is to blame for this?" Julien demanded. "Didn't any of you attempt to clear this area of rocks and tall grasses?"

"But Baasa, we—"

"But nothing, you useless brats! I should have you all flogged for laziness. My granddaughter could have died because of you," he spat in anger.

"Those are my Bantu, Monsieur Julien," came Mornay's languid voice. He had just walked up with Derwent Brown.

Darinda noticed that Derwent wore a bandage on his head. His face looked pale, as though he'd been sick, and he seemed thinner. What had happened to him? She had always liked the rusty-headed young man because he showed her honest respect, not the feigned kind she was accustomed to from other men.

"They are my children, monsieur," Mornay said in a voice that bespoke trouble. "No one flogs my little ones as long as I am alive."

Darinda felt the chilling silence squeeze them in.

"I'll handle this, Julien," Peter said grimly. "Maybe you'd better get Darinda inside. She's not looking well. That was quite a shock. Arcilla, my dear, will you help your cousin to the large tent?"

"I don't need her help, thank you," Darinda said. She turned to Julien, who stood there stone-faced, glaring at Mornay. "Grandfather?" She laid her hand on his arm, feeling the tension in his muscles. "I want to go inside and change. It's frightfully hot out here. Help me to my wagon, will you? It's silly I know, but that scare has made my knees weak."

Julien shifted his attention to her, and together they turned toward the tents and coaches.

As they walked away, Darinda looked over her shoulder and saw Parnell standing by the rocks staring down at the dead cobra, as though mesmerized. A moment later his face turned pale white again, and he dashed behind the rocks to be sick.

She was feeling sick herself, but now it was over more than the ugly episode with the spitting cobra.

Arcilla followed Peter into their day tent, which was large enough to make a tolerable living space. There were horsehair mattresses, a long trestle table, and comfortable camp chairs, but she loathed it all just the same. How she longed for the comforts of Rookswood, where her every need was abundantly cared for.

"This morning I found a spider walking across the rug," she said, "the biggest one I've ever seen in my life. It was all black and fuzzy with double-jointed legs. I screamed, and one of the Bantu boys came and removed it. Oh, Peter, you're not listening again."

"I am, my sweet, but after a week of sweat and dust, the bath holds more charm for me than your saga of a harmless little spider."

"Harmless!"

"I've just faced Lobengula and thousands of impis anxious to spill our blood with their assegais. You won't mind, will you, if I don't swoon over your adventure with the spider?"

His indifference irritated her. He was making light of her concerns. For a moment she felt a pang of guilt. She should have been concerned about the trip to Bulawayo and asked him about it first, but Darinda's being nearly bitten, then "spat" upon by that cobra, had revived her own frightening experience with the giant spider.

"You were concerned enough about Darinda and that snake. You didn't brush her fears aside, as though they were trivial."

"They weren't. But a spider isn't going to kill you, Arcilla—" He stopped and faced her, looking tired and frustrated. "I'm making a dreadful mess of things. Look, I wasn't more concerned for Darinda than you, my dear— Oh, let's forget it, shall we? Where's that tub of hot water and the soap?" He removed his dusty, smelly jacket and shirt, pulled off his boots and stiff socks, peeled off his trousers, and tossed it all into a corner for the boy to carry off to the boiling pot to be washed.

"The water isn't hot," she said tiredly. "It's cold. And you may find some slimy things swimming about if you're not careful."

"Anything will do right now—" He stepped into the tub and sprawled out with a sigh, sinking low to his chin.

She paced before the tub ready to hand him soap, cloth, and towels, but her thoughts were elsewhere. Uncle Julien had said nothing to her about her "indiscretion" back in Capetown. Had he forgotten it? He wouldn't tell Darinda, would he? Oh, the horror if her cousin heard of it! Darinda was nasty enough to tell Peter. Why did Darinda dislike her so much? Jealousy, no doubt. She had liked Peter before Julien decided he should marry her.

"Have you talked with Julien about Capetown since he arrived?"

Peter was scrubbing himself with gusto. "Your uncle remains adamant that you come with me to Fort Salisbury. You knew what it would be like when we discussed it in London. It isn't as if I've sprung a trap on you."

She had been fearing he'd mention the incident in the garden. She felt relieved he hadn't a clue what she was thinking. In fact, she was so relieved that she smiled down at him and splashed him with a bucket of tepid water, laughing as he spurted and choked.

"The very dignified Peter Bartley," she teased, "choking on his bath water."

He laughed. "Careful, or you'll find yourself in the tub with me."

She backed a safe distance away, still laughing at him. "What happened when you met Lobengula? Tell me, Peter, were they all naked? How tall was he? Some say he is a giant."

"You have an odious curiosity, one I won't gratify. The meeting went as expected. It had its unpleasant, worrisome moments with all his warring impis standing around us. One or two of the indunas wanted to contest him over letting the white man dig for gold. Dr. Jameson convinced Lobengula otherwise. What worries me is whether he'll keep his bargain. Hand me that other towel."

"What if he changes his mind? About building that road, I mean. Would he attack us, do you think?" The security of life at Rookswood seemed a world away.

She knew when he was doubtful or worried by the way his mouth would shut tightly. "Then there's a possibility he will," she said. "Oh, Peter, if only we could go back to—"

"I'm not one to try to shield you from the truth. Yes, he could easily thwart us once we bring in the Ngwato workers to dig the road. It's a miracle everything has gone as smoothly as it has, considering the hostilities we're up against."

Her uppermost thought was that they must have enough guards to protect them against any attack.

"Will you be keeping Captain Retford on?"

"He is an excellent man, and Rogan agrees. Yes, he is going north with us."

"That should suit Darinda. Poor Parnell...I'm furious with the way she's running my poor deluded brother around like a pet monkey on a leash."

"Not a flattering comparison. I wouldn't say that to Parnell."

"I wouldn't. But she has her eye on Ryan, and she doesn't fool me in the slightest bit."

"Ryan?"

"Captain Retford," she corrected quickly.

"Don't let him hear you call him by his first name, my dear. It wouldn't be appropriate, especially since he's under my charge."

"Of course I wouldn't," she rushed.

"Hand me some fresh clothes, will you? I have a meeting with Julien and Dr. Jameson before dinner."

"Will you be late again?" she asked as he dressed.

"I'll be back as soon as I can. It shouldn't take long."

He reached for her, and she came into his arms. "That's better," she taunted. "You smelled as bad as that nasty old mosquito ointment."

He held her close and kissed her. "I'm glad you're here, darling. This is where I want you, with me."

"That's the first time you've ever said that."

"Nonsense," he laughed, "I say it all the time."

"You just think you do. Peter," she said seriously, "after Fort Salisbury, will there ever be a time when we go back to London?"

"There will always be time to return to England. There will be lots of visits to see your family and mine."

"I was thinking... If we had a baby, I should loathe having it this far from civilization and capable doctors... I mean, it would be very frightening for me."

"There's Dr. Jameson. And Dr. Jakob van Buren. His mission station, I believe, is somewhere in that area."

"It's not the same as giving birth to our children in England...at Rookswood, for instance, with Aunt Elosia by my side, and my father."

He petted her cheek. "You won't be the first woman to bear children on the African veld, and you won't be the last. And you have me, dearest. You can count on me being there by your side."

She looked deeply into his eyes, pleasant eyes.

"Will you, Peter? Be there for me?"

He smiled and planted a kiss on her forehead. "Always, Arcilla."

She wondered. And when he had left for the meeting, she stood there in the silence smelling the fragrance of soap. She looked around at the sloppy mess and absently began picking up the wet towels and soiled clothes. Then she dropped them and went to throw open the tent flap. She clapped her hands at the Bantu boy and pointed to the bath area.

Just then she caught sight of a long centipede and recoiled. They bit, she knew that, because one of the poor children had been bitten earlier and had bawled about it for an hour. She directed the boy's attention to it so he could flip the creature away before she walked outside for some fresh air.

It would be a lovely evening with a cooling breeze, but it would never compensate for the evenings at Rookswood. Even the noisome rooks cawing in the trees in Grimston Woods would have been a welcome sound now. She sighed. *I wonder what Darinda is doing after that revolting scare?* Arcilla looked around apprehensively and hugged herself.

Darinda had refused tea and asked for strong black coffee. Imagine that Captain Retford speaking to her as he had. She ought to report him to Julien…but they needed every man they could get, especially with marksmanship like that! He had torn the head off the cobra with apparent ease.

She arose restlessly from the comfortable camp chair and went to the mirror to smooth her hair into place. The meeting over the negotiations at Bulawayo was about to begin, and she wanted to hear what had happened with Lobengula. This was a chance to speak to Parnell, and to show Captain Retford that she hadn't taken to her bed over the cobra incident. That was how Cousin Arcilla would have reacted, not Darinda Bley, future heiress to gold and diamonds, if she had her way.

She went to dress, reaching for a brown riding habit—then changed her mind. Instead, she chose a cool blue Victorian lace blouse and a long skirt. She added a crocodile skin belt with a gold buckle. When she appraised herself in the mirror, she felt quite satisfied. One need not primp by the hour the way Arcilla did to look one's best. She touched her hair again, bringing a strand down to form a side curl at her cheek, then she turned and left for the large meeting tent. Did Ryan Retford have a girl in Kimberly or Capetown? She could find out easily enough through her connections in Kimberly…

The meeting was already under way in the dining marquee when Darinda arrived. The canvas sides had been rolled up to admit the late afternoon breeze, and half a dozen men sat at a long trestle table in deep discussion of Bulawayo and Lobengula, the troublesome Ndebele chieftain.

Darinda slipped in quietly and took a chair near one open side, then glanced at those present. Parnell was there, looking subdued. His gaze had followed her when she entered, and he looked away when their eyes met. *He feels badly that he didn't shoot the cobra.* Captain Retford was present, in his military garb. His flinty look took her in, as though he noticed she wore a blouse and skirt for a change. She turned her head away toward her grandfather and then saw Rogan Chantry. Darkly handsome with a narrow mustache, he looked at her evenly, then directly at Parnell. Did he suspect anything about their designs on the map?

"Doc Jim," as he was called among friends and allies of Mr. Rhodes, was telling her grandfather about his dealings with Lobengula.

He was drinking coffee and explaining to Julien that he was leaving with Frank Thompson to report the success to Cecil Rhodes, who had returned to De Beers in Kimberly.

Darinda noted that her grandfather did not seem surprised that Lobengula had given permission, grudging as it was, for the BSA miners to dig a new road east of Bulawayo to the Zambezi.

But Doc Jim was quick to point out his skepticism. "Let's not think too highly of the old warrior, Julien. I know that man. I've treated him for gout off and on for months. He's as bloated as a python. The best I could get out of him was an admission that he'd never refused the pioneers permission to enter the country. He remains suspicious."

"Mornay seems to think the concession Lobengula held us to many months ago included giving him a thousand Martini rifles," Rogan said.

"You're quite right," Dr. Jameson admitted, pulling out his pipe and crossing his legs at the knees. "We had them sent to Bulawayo in wagons months ago. So far Lobengula has refused to accept the rifles. He knows if he does, it means he's agreed to the contract."

"For the cousins of the Zulus to turn down a thousand rifles tells me Lobengula must be genuinely confused about what he gave up in that concession," Rogan said. Instead of sitting at the table, he was standing, coffee cup in hand.

Darinda noticed the others met his gaze, looking suddenly obtuse, as if he hadn't spoken. The Company men turned to one another over the table and went on talking.

Peter was frowning. He swatted angrily at a large fly and missed. "He was also promised the generous payment of a hundred pounds per month," he parried, obviously trying to put Rhodes in a good light.

"Arming a thousand impis with Martini rifles is like helping dig one's own grave," Rogan stated. "I can only wonder at the wisdom of making such deals in the first place."

"Are you questioning Mr. Rhodes?" came Dr. Jameson's quick, spiked tone.

"In this matter? Yes, I am, sir."

"I never agreed with giving him those rifles either," Julien said. "Rogan has a point. What if he turns around and uses them against us once we cross into Mashonland with our backs to Bulawayo?"

"We'll be ready for him if he tries anything," Dr. Jameson said. "We intend to have a large contingent of armed guards on the trek. Speed is a priority. We can't afford to wait much longer, gentlemen. If we don't cross the Limpopo this season, we could be beaten to the punch by the Boers or the Portuguese. We're nearing the trekking season. Cecil has already proposed that the pioneers be prepared to leave in June."

With that, the meeting ended. Jameson and Thompson, and their traveling workers, departed for Kimberly to report to Mr. Rhodes. The others, with Julien, would wait until morning to leave.

Darinda stayed behind for Parnell, and when he approached, she searched his face. One look convinced her she had been right.

"We can't talk here," she said in a low tone. "Meet me by the mimosa tree at sunset."

Parnell nodded, unsmiling, and went out.

The sunset was a glorious scarlet, and the evening was vibrantly noisy with the chatter of birds and the drone of insects. At the river a hippopotamus was enjoying its mud bath.

Darinda was waiting under the yellow-blossomed mimosa when

Parnell arrived. She wasted no time on meaningless words. "So you failed to find the map?"

"I should have known he wasn't fool enough to keep it in his saddle-bags. The whole idea was foolish. I could have gotten myself shot as a *skollie,* a Cape hooligan. I ended up trapped because Derwent came snooping right at the wrong moment. I hid quickly in the bushes, but his zealous devotion to Rogan wouldn't let well enough alone. He had to come tracking me down. I had no choice except to club him from the back."

She noticed his hands were shaking as he fumbled to light his Turkish cigarette. "I hate violence… I've been feeling ill ever since," The match flared red in the dark.

So that was why Derwent had a bandage around his head. She felt a twinge of conscience. "It wasn't my intention to see anyone injured."

"I know that. But we came close to taking on more than we could handle. I'll have no more of this harebrained idea, Darinda. That ruddy map's been a problem in my family since Uncle Henry left it to Rogan. Well, it's my brother's map now. And I won't be contesting him for it again." He turned on his heel and strode toward camp.

Taken aback by his rash behavior, she ran after him. "Parnell!"

He stopped and looked at her, frowning and looking pale in the rising moonlight.

She looked at him for a long moment, then managed a small smile. "I'm sorry. I didn't realize all this would hurt you so much."

He said nothing and looked down at the toes of his boots. As usual, even out here, they were polished to a shine.

"We'll forget this," he said quietly after a moment. "We won't bring it up again…ever."

She nodded. "I suppose Rogan carries the map on him. That's why no one could ever get it away."

He looked cross. "Yes, and it would be foolish to try. Come, I'll walk you back to your coach."

She shook her head. "You look tired. This long journey to Bulawayo and the unfortunate trouble with Derwent and the cobra have been stressful. You'd better get some sleep."

At the mention of the cobra, he looked pained again. "Good night," he said in a low voice and walked away.

She looked after him. The moon was climbing, and on the river she heard the splash of a crocodile. She lifted her shoulders as if something evil blew against her back. She looked behind her into the deepening darkness but saw nothing. The silly words of the Bantu children came back to her. "The baasa's daughter was cursed. Someone has put a curse on her, and so the spitting cobra waited for her in the rocks."

She remembered the look on Julien's face as if he feared their dark omens. Nonsense, all of it. Devilish.

She turned and ran, and nearly collided with Captain Retford. He must have been out enjoying the evening too, for she could see he was not on duty now. His military jacket was off, and he wore a loose-fitting cotton shirt belted at the waist with his gunbelt.

He caught her arm and looked past her toward the mimosa tree. "Anything wrong, Miss Bley?" His flinty blue gaze came back to hers.

"No, I…I was just out walking." She hated it when she hesitated as if she didn't know what she was about.

"That was Parnell Chantry just now, wasn't it?"

She wasn't going to tell him a thing. She pulled her arm away, and then she remembered…the map. He was the same build and height as Rogan Chantry. If anyone could confront Rogan, it would be this man.

She smiled. "You have it all wrong, Captain. Parnell is *not* going to be my husband. I have something to say about the man I'm going to marry one day."

He looked a little surprised by her openness, and she reminded herself not to move so quickly. It would make him suspicious. She hadn't been friendly toward him before. "I wanted to thank you for shooting the cobra this morning."

"I wouldn't be too hard on Parnell. There are some people who can't face up to violence of any kind. It's just the way they're put together."

"You think that's the way Parnell is?"

"Let's just say that if he ever did provoke bloodshed, he would be pushed into it. He wouldn't seek it on his own."

Under his even gaze she felt the heat burning her throat and face. He couldn't know she'd asked Rogan's brother to get the map. He *couldn't*.

"May I warn you?" He looked at her with tilted head. "Rogan Chantry is no fool. I hope, Miss, that neither am I. We both have a good idea who hit Derwent Brown on the back of the head near Bulawayo. And we both tend to think it was on account of a certain map left to Rogan by an uncle."

Darinda stepped away from him, trying to calm her breathing. *He did know. How? How had he guessed?*

"I haven't a notion of what you're talking about," she said stiffly.

"I've never called a woman a liar before, and I won't start now, but if you are wise, Miss Bley, you would put away this idiotic notion of stealing Rogan's map and put your attention where it belongs. On becoming a young lady of virtue and discretion."

She sucked in her breath and stared at him. "You dare?"

"Yes, Miss Bley. I dare. And I doubt you'll go in a huff to your grandfather, because I believe he would be quite upset if he found out you nearly betrayed yourself as a foolish young woman. He takes great pride in you, as you know."

She did know, which was the reason she had tried to gain the map and impress him even more, hoping he would then make her his heir.

Darinda was glad for the darkness, for she knew her face must be crimson with shame.

"Needless to say, you drove Parnell to a rash and dangerous act. Shall we decide to be wiser people and forget this madness?"

She could think of nothing to say equal to his calm rebuke. She loathed him for exposing her foolishness, yet felt herself strangely drawn at the same time.

"I think, sir," she said coldly, "that you are the most ungallant man I have ever met."

"And you, Miss, if born on the wrong side of town, would surely have turned out a petty thief."

She sucked in her breath. Her palm begged to slap the smirk off his handsome face. Instead she lifted her head, whipped about, and strode back to her mule coach, thoroughly humiliated and wishing she'd never heard of Rogan Chantry's map.

CHAPTER EIGHTEEN

Rogan was walking back to his campsite after the meeting with Julien and the Company representatives when word was brought to him that Julien had asked to see him alone in his tent.

Now what? Rogan wondered with a scowl. He turned around and walked back to the meeting tent.

Julien was waiting. Rogan rejoined his uncle in an airy side room. It was spacious and cool, and netting kept out the irritating insects.

"You wished to see me?"

Julien gestured toward drink and food on a table beside a camp chair.

"Sit down, Rogan, my boy. We've a lot to discuss."

Rogan had removed his hat and sank into the comfortable chair. He sensed that he was approaching a brick wall. He narrowed his lashes, watching Julien, who stood before him looking extremely pleased with himself.

"You heard Doc Jim. Time is of the essence." As if to strengthen his declaration, he paced. "Mornay has been too slow to respond to our request to guide us to the Zambezi. You won him to your side, but I will let bygones be bygones. It no longer matters to me. Rhodes has found the best guide possible, Frederick Selous."

Rogan lifted his glass to his lips and wisely remained silent. *Frederick Selous.*

Julien's mouth spread into a smile. "I see you know of him."

"Who doesn't? Famous big-game hunter—wrote the book, *A Hunter's Wanderings in Africa*. Well done. What did you offer him? A thousand acres in the new colony?"

Julien chuckled, showing that the barb did not penetrate his thick hide. "I see he told you of my offer—approved by the Company, of course. Yes, we're paying Selous well, too. Plus a generous number of gold shares. We also have the blessing of the British government. Lieutenant Colonel Pennyfather of the Sixth Dragoon Guards will lead the pioneers. If things go as now planned, the Pioneer Column will leave in June."

"If Lobengula will allow the road from Bulawayo."

Julien's smile faltered at Rogan's statement. "I'm certain he'll remain a threat. But you heard Doc Jim. We'll have men to protect the pioneers in case he tries anything foolish." He glanced at the .45 strapped to Rogan's hip. "I've heard you can handle yourself well enough."

Rogan helped himself to one of the sandwiches. After eating biltong, the smoked ham tasted more like a Sunday brunch at Rookswood.

"Tell me about Jube."

Julien's words surprised Rogan. Either Peter or Dr. Jameson must've told him. "What more is there to tell? He warned me. That was enough. We scrambled out of there."

"Peter says Jube trusted you. Why would the induna do that?"

Rogan could read the suspicion thick in Julien's voice. It disturbed him. He shrugged and went on eating. "I've no idea. But I wouldn't go so far as to say he trusted me, or anyone else."

"You'd never met him before you went with the delegation to Bulawayo?"

"No. His reason for saving my skin is as much a curiosity to me as to you. I'm grateful he did. He said he had met Henry, though."

Julien stood without moving, clearly shaken. "Did he? What did he look like?"

Rogan described him. Julien shook his head. "It would have been a long time ago... We all change. He must have had a reason..." Julien walked to the table and poured himself a brandy. "The Ndebele are savages. Human life means nothing to them. They slaughter other natives and rejoice at their killing." He took a swallow. "I saw some of another tribe resort to cannibalism once. A sign of victory. The Ndebele are enemies of the Shona, whose land Lobengula plundered and robbed."

"So I discovered."

"Then Lobengula calls Mashonaland his territory. He has no more right to the Zambezi than the white men he loathes."

Julien tossed back the snifter of brandy. When Rogan remained silent, Julien turned his head and fixed his good eye upon him.

"Therefore, the induna must have had a good reason for coming to you. What contact did he have with Henry?"

Rogan was cautious now. "He didn't say."

"Word has filtered back to me. The entire clan of Lobengula's chief induna, Lotshe, was destroyed. Your life would mean nothing to them."

"Maybe Jube had a reason to warn us. He was a friend of Lotshe. Warning us may have been his way of getting back at the other indunas who turned on their brothers. He would have had the satisfaction of denying them our blood."

Julien considered. "It may be that simple. Then again, he may expect something from you later on. You say he had silver in his hair. He may have known the Hottentot Sam, Henry's man. He may have known about the gold. At any rate, be cautious."

Rogan considered his uncle's words. Was it possible Jube's contact with Henry had been on that trek north?

"I'm still waiting for your decision where the Company's concerned, Rogan. This is a historic venture, one you should be proud of joining. But time is running out for you. Either you join our efforts to establish the colony, or your rebellious nature will mean your end. This time it's your final chance to cooperate."

Rogan slowly stood from the chair. He smiled unpleasantly. "What do you plan this time? Another accident? You know I do have Henry's map in my possession." He could have mentioned the attack on

Derwent and the search of his saddlebags, but he believed Darinda and Parnell had done it on their own. "You'll need something other than suicide, though. I'm not known for backing off when I'm right. But then, neither was Henry."

Julien's mouth tightened like a bar of steel. His cheek twitched. He set his snifter down carefully.

"Are you daring to accuse me of killing Henry?"

"Henry was murdered. Even when a boy I could figure out that much. Someone entered Rookswood for the Black Diamond, or was it the map?"

Julien stared at him. As though stunned, he shook his head. "So that's what you think… That's why you won't cooperate with me?"

"The authorities couldn't prove it, nor can I, now. But it's clear that every person interested in the Kimberly was in London the week of his death, including you. I also saw you at Rookswood searching his rooms on more than one occasion when I was a young boy. I knew what you were looking for, and I made it my ambition to find it before you did."

Confronted with the challenge in Rogan's voice and his calm stare, Julien wore a surprised look on his rugged face, his eye as brittle as glass.

"And you were successful," Julien said after a moment. "My hat's off to you. Even at twelve you were clever." He suddenly chuckled, reaching for a camp chair. "Yes, I'll go right ahead and admit to it. I went to Rookswood several times searching for Henry's map."

"And the Kimberly Black Diamond? Or did you already have it?"

"I?" A brow shot up.

"Someone clobbered Henry from behind in the stables. Why not you? You were there that night. You arrived at the stables in time to find him as he was stirring awake. You could have arrived sooner."

"Absurd, Rogan. If I'd had the Kimberly in my possession these many years, I'd have put it on the market. This colony is costing a great deal of money. We're all invested in it." He slapped his hands on his knees and stood. "Very well. I shall be transparent with you. I didn't waste time searching, because I knew Henry did not possess it. Oh yes, in the beginning I thought he'd stolen it, but I learned later I was quite in error. Someone did steal the Black Diamond from Henry in the stables all right, but it wasn't me, and it wasn't Katie."

Rogan's temper simmered. "You knew all those years Katie van Buren didn't steal it from Henry, yet you kept it a secret from Evy?"

Julien lifted his head. "We won't talk about Katie van Buren or her daughter."

"Sorry, Julien, but we *will* talk about them. I told you in Capetown I meant to have the truth. You owe an explanation. And I want it— now!"

"I owe you no explanation. None! Do you understand me? I came here to warn you about your intransigence, and will you now cross-examine me?"

"For Evy *van Buren's* sake."

His emphasis of Evy's true bloodline silenced Julien. For a moment it appeared he would strike him, but when Rogan refused to be intimidated, Julien's stern dignity unexpectedly diminished. He lowered himself back into the chair.

"Sit down, Rogan," he said shortly. "There's no reason to carry on like this. We can discuss this like two reasonable gentlemen. We'll never get anywhere if we don't come to grips. I can see that."

He reached for a box to lift a lid, but Rogan warily laid his hand over the box first.

Julien looked startled.

Rogan opened the lid fully expecting to see a revolver. Inside was a stash of Turkish cigarettes.

Julien chuckled. He reached over, took one, and leaned back in the camp chair, crossing his long legs, watching Rogan with malicious amusement.

"You really think I want to get rid of you." His voice carried an edge of disdain. "On the contrary, I've had a growing interest in you for the last few years. You always had spunk, much more than Parnell. You've emerged into a strong-willed young man with the kind of courage it takes to survive in South Africa. I like that. I'd prefer a better working relationship with you. I have great plans for you, if you'll lay down your guard."

Rogan lifted a brow, making no effort to hide his caution and doubt. He believed none of Julien's flattery. His silence was suggestive.

"Very well," Julien said cheerfully. "I see I will need to work harder to convince you of my fair-mindedness. That I do indeed wish to be an uncle to you. I shall begin with Henry." He leaned his head back, looking toward the tent roof, and drew on the cigarette. The diamonds on his gold ring winked in the lantern light.

"Let's see… It was nearly two years after Henry left the Cape that I first returned to Rookswood to talk to him about his plans for an expedition to the Zambezi. By that time I'd heard the rumor of gold beyond the Limpopo, perhaps a new rand, so I knew I must begin to reconsider the reasons why I'd turned him down. Henry wasn't looking like such a reckless fool after all. I'd become an associate with Cecil Rhodes, and he'd convinced me of the need for British expansion in Africa. Some believe the Zambezi area is the golden Ophir mentioned in the Bible. Working with Henry on the expedition seemed a good way to benefit from his map. Now you own it, and again it is beneficial to work together for the good of Britain, the Company, and our family dynasty."

His explanation was consistent with the calculating way Julien would think and act. Rogan gave his uncle a measured look. Maybe… he was telling the truth for once.

"Henry turned you down?"

Julien crushed out his smoke. He stood again, hands shoved in his pockets as he paced.

"I was never able to talk with him about the idea. By the time I arrived in London, he was withdrawn, secretive, as though one matter or another was eating away at him."

"But you were in London the night of his death," Rogan countered.

"Quite so. It's also true that I've a credible alibi for the night of his death. Your aunt, Lady Elosia Chantry, informed the Scotland Yard Inspector that I was in her company from dinnertime—say 8:00?— until well after 1:00 A.M. We were playing a card game. Her butler, Mr. Ames, is a witness. He looked in and saw me sitting with my back toward him at the table. Since, according to the Yard, Henry was dead by 11:00 P.M., I couldn't possibly have left London and taken the train all the way to Grimston Way and Rookswood." He looked over at Rogan, and a faint smile touched his lips. "You see? All you had to do, all these years of dark suspicion, was check with the Yard."

When one of the Rookswood maids had discovered Henry dead in his third-floor office, the physician, Dr. Tisdale, had testified at the inquest that Henry had died between 9:00 and 11:00 P.M.

Rogan digested the news. So Julien's alibi was established by Aunt Elosia, of all unlikely people. He could hardly doubt his stuffy, highbrow maiden aunt!

Julien watched him. "You look disappointed."

"Someone murdered him. If it wasn't you, then who?"

"He took his own life."

"Rubbish, Uncle. You don't believe that any more than I do. We know Henry was too much a fighter to kill himself."

Julien didn't answer.

"All right, then, it looks for now as if you're in the clear, but what about the Kimberly Black Diamond?"

"I realized later Katie didn't steal it from Henry. But at the time, because Henry had lied to me so often, I felt I couldn't believe anything he told me. I thought they were in it together, that they had agreed to trick me. Katie, too, had often lied to me. Oh, I knew her well. I knew how strongly she felt about her baby."

Julien reached for the decanter of brandy and filled his glass again, his mouth tightening. "I was convinced she'd knocked Henry unconscious with the wooden club in the stables, then took the diamond. I believed it was buried in the massacre at Rorke's Drift. We all did, including Henry, so I never looked for it until near the end of his life." He stared at the amber liquid in the snifter. "Something changed his mind. He never explained what it was. I wish he had."

His interest aroused, Rogan stared at him intently. This he had never heard before.

"What could have changed his mind? There was no hint at all?"

"No, but I'm convinced something did." Julien set the snifter down without drinking it. "Unfortunately, I had no time to discuss it with him."

Rogan studied Julien's frown. *He's troubled. Now, this is curious... and unexpected.*

"But you did talk to Henry before his death. I saw you there for the London wedding."

Julien looked calm once more. "Yes, I talked to him. We were alone at Rookswood a few days before his death. That's when you must have seen me. Henry was in an intractable mood. He wouldn't tell me what was on his mind, but he did tell me he was prepared to come to Capetown and discuss the past with me."

"Rather odd, wasn't it? It was you who drove him out of South Africa to begin with. Why should he tell you he was coming back? And then there was the lack of money for the expedition. Henry didn't have it...unless he got it from..." Rogan's voice trailed off.

Julien noticed and looked up from the table. "From your father?"

Rogan didn't answer. His thoughts had suddenly stumbled.

"No, Lyle wouldn't have sponsored the expedition without telling me," Julien said. "And he never mentioned it."

Rogan's father, so firm on some matters, like the marriage of Arcilla, was negligent about others. He had long given up the hope of seeing his father stand up to Julien.

"No, I don't think Henry had an expedition on his mind," Julien said. "I wish he had trusted me, but he didn't."

"You've yourself to blame for that."

He waited for Julien to explode.

"Before I could talk to him again, he was dead." He picked up the snifter and gulped it down. He banged the small glass on the table and walked over to the tent entrance, looked out, then turned to face Rogan again.

Rogan watched him. Was he being forthright for once, or merely trying to fool him? Did Julien feel some guilt over his stepbrother's death? That emotion did not suit him. It would take more than regret and a pretended confession to convince Rogan, even though he couldn't discount some change in Julien. This surprised him, made him cautious.

"And the diamond?" Rogan reminded him.

"He'd become convinced Katie didn't take it. I could see he was troubled about having blamed Katie…as was I."

Rogan tightened his jaw. "Then why not tell Evy that now? She's still under that cloud cast on her mother's reputation."

Julien made a frustrated gesture and walked about. "I will tell you something, Rogan, that I didn't learn until after Henry's death." He looked across the tent at him. "The Kimberly Black Diamond, when taken from Henry in the stables, was carried to the Zulu King Cetshwayo, at Ulundi."

Zululand!

Cetshwayo had been defeated and exiled around the time of Evy's birth. Did that mean the Black Diamond was lost forever?

Wind sucked against the canvas siding, then settled. Far in the distance a hyena cackled.

Rogan considered Julien's murky disclosures as a duelist would test his opponent's skills.

"How do you know this? If the Black Diamond was brought to Cetshwayo, then by whom, and when?"

"I recently received a letter from Jakob van Buren. The fellow claims to be a cousin of Katie. He's an old man now, a cantankerous Boer, with a mission station in the north. He wrote me of Jendaya, a Zulu woman who once worked for me at Cape House. She fled to Dr. Jakob for safety after the Zulu defeat. She knew Katie, you see. He seemed the reasonable man to go to. Her brother Dumaka also worked for me when Katie was alive. Jendaya told Dr. Jakob it was her brother who stole the Black Diamond and carried it to Zululand. Dumaka was seen at Rorke's Drift when Katie and the Varley missionary couple were killed."

"And you didn't send anyone to meet Jendaya to find out whether it was true?"

Julien appeared to ignore the skepticism in Rogan's voice.

"You should understand well enough. Who can safari into that area at a drop of a hat?"

No one, obviously, which proved nothing.

"The van Buren station is somewhere on the Zambezi. This is another reason for both of us to support this expedition."

If what Julien said was true, yes. Rogan wanted to meet this Jakob van Buren as soon as possible and talk to the Zulu woman. Did Evy know she had a cousin? A missionary? He didn't think so.

"How did Jakob get his letter to you?"

"Always skeptical. Well, so be it. From what I hear, he comes in from the wilds now and then to visit his family in the Boer Transvaal Republic. There are a few other van Burens still farming in the area who are related to Katie."

Rogan remembered Heyden van Buren. He had never liked or trusted Heyden, a dedicated Dutch expansionist who loathed the British in South Africa. But Heyden was a cousin of Evy and would be related to Jakob van Buren as well. Yet not even Heyden had told Evy of her mother's cousin who ran a mission station on the Zambezi. It also seemed that Julien had kept this information from Evy. But then he'd kept a great deal from her.

"I've only recently received news of Jakob," Julien said. "And I knew nothing of the Black Diamond's being taken from Henry and carried by Dumaka to that savage Zulu king!"

Rogan believed him about Cetshwayo, but not about Jakob van Buren. Even when Katie was alive, he must have known she had van Buren relatives. But Katie, judging by her desperate actions, had not known, or she may have considered turning to Jakob for help when Julien insisted she give up her newborn.

"Naturally I went to see Jakob. He was staying at the van Buren homestead in the Transvaal. Heyden was there as well. Breathing fire against the British incursion into Africa, as usual. That young man is dangerous. He would even provoke a war between the Boers and the British."

"And the Zulu woman, Jendaya? I don't suppose you had the good fortune to question her while you were there."

Julien shook his head. "Jakob was alone. He claims he got up one morning soon after she told him about Dumaka's theft of the Black Diamond to find she'd disappeared. He doesn't know what happened to her, or even if she is still alive."

Rogan's optimism was fast turning into an extinguished flame. "And her brother, Dumaka?"

Again, Julien shook his head. "Jakob claims he's never met him. But Lobengula's tribe is related to the Zulus, as you know. Jakob is inclined to believe Dumaka may be among them in or around Bulawayo."

"If you had told me this sooner, I could have asked about Dumaka when I was there."

Julien dismissed Rogan's impatience. "You'd never find him. Dumaka was always insidious. Looking back now, I should have ordered him killed when I had the chance."

Rogan was not surprised by his bluntness. If only he'd known all this then.

"Too late now," Julien grumbled. "It is reasonable that he may have taken refuge with Lobengula after the Zulu defeat at Ulundi. He would be older now. I doubt I'd recognize him if I saw him face to face." He looked at Rogan sharply. "The induna who said he knew Henry… Jube…I wonder?"

Rogan mused over all this with growing frustration.

"So there you have it, Rogan. The story as I know it. And it's likely the Kimberly Black is lost to us forever. But not Henry's gold discovery."

"It would serve my interests to be able to talk with Jakob myself," Rogan murmured half to himself. He noted Julien's alert watchfulness after he'd spoken.

"That is quite possible. His compound is near our destination on the Zambezi."

They looked squarely at each other. Rogan realized he'd just been handed another reason for joining the BSA expedition. Rogan cared little about Julien's intentions. He had his own, and he wanted them fulfilled. He needed to talk to Jakob for himself. He owed it to himself and Evy.

"I agree with your conclusions about the Kimberly Black Diamond," Rogan told Julien. "In the British raid at Ulundi, it's likely Cetshwayo escaped with little. And whatever he had, the British would have discovered when they captured him—unless it was buried in the heap of ruins at his kraal."

Or a Zulu induna may have saved it and taken it away to who knew where? Lobengula? The person most likely to know its fate was Dumaka himself or his sister, Jendaya. Was it possible that Jube could be Dumaka?

Rogan made up his mind quickly. He would begin by meeting with the old Boer missionary, Jakob van Buren. And he would join Rhodes's expedition.

Julien, too, appeared to sense that his strong-willed nephew had come to the conclusion he and Peter had waited for. "Then we agree on some things, at least."

"A letter to Evy from you would mean much to her at this time," Rogan said. "There's no reason she must continue to live under the illusion that her mother ran off with the Kimberly Black."

Julien showed no positive response.

"It's wise, Rogan, for you to forget about Evy Varley. You need not worry about Katie's daughter."

Rogan didn't appreciate the cool dismissal of his request.

"If I don't trouble myself to be concerned, does this mean you will step up to the responsibility at last?"

At last. Those two words, calmly but decisively spoken, seemed to sting Julien, for he looked at Rogan even more intently.

"You're quite concerned about her, aren't you?"

Rogan kept silent.

"No need to worry, my boy. I'll soon be informing Evy of her inheritance in the diamond mines through Katie van Buren. In the meantime, a comfortable allowance will be set up with lawyers in London. It will allow her to remain in Grimston Way or move to London, as she chooses. But could you be apprehensive there may be a blood relation between the Chantrys and van Burens? And could it be, Rogan, you have long made plans to lay hold of the van Buren inheritance through marriage to Evy?"

The accusation jolted him. It was the last thing he'd expected Julien to say. Attraction toward Evy, yes—more than that; but in order to gain her inheritance? Until recently he hadn't known she had one.

Sensing weakness, Julien approached like a lion ready to pounce on its prey.

"Even as a young lad you were too inquisitive about Evy's status. I still remember Lady Camilla arriving at Rookswood with indiscreet whispers about a secret child. At once you began to suspect Evy. It's the van Buren inheritance that has always piqued your attention, that and the Kimberly Black."

Rogan reacted without thinking and grabbed Sir Julien by the front of his shirt, his fist ready to plow into him.

All of a sudden cool sanity rushed through his brain, clearing away rage.

Julien's cold, unblinking eye stared back with challenge.

Rogan's hand loosened from Julien's shirt.

Julien remained silent.

Rogan suddenly laughed, easing his own tension. "You're lying. It's the other way around, isn't it? It always has been. Even with Katie. Who knows what Carl van Buren truly entrusted to you until his child came of legal age? You wanted to manipulate Katie's marriage to keep authority over the van Buren share of diamonds. That she rebelled and went her own willful way must have infuriated you."

Instead of exploding with anger, Julien grew more cool, more precise, using words like daggers. "By the way, Lord Bancroft has written me recently about your scheme."

Lord Bancroft? Patricia's father… Their names tossed in Rogan's face momentarily blinded him.

"I brought the letter from Lord Bancroft with me from Capetown." Julien looked triumphant.

What could be in the letter that gave Julien cause to accuse him of wanting Evy's inheritance—and now, of all things, the Black Diamond! Until this moment the battle of wills with Julien had been all about Henry's map.

Julien brought the tips of his fingers together in a thoughtful pose. "Lord Bancroft fears you are in the process of betraying his daughter in exchange for Evy van Buren, the heiress."

This was the first time Julien had spoken of Evy using the van Buren name, and now he had added the word *heiress*. This final comment proved to Rogan that his uncle's actions were manipulative. One moment Evy was the forgotten daughter of Katie, to be left in the dark at Grimston Way. The next she was a diamond heiress, and Rogan was plotting to lay hold of her wealth.

Any quick denial of his intentions toward Evy would only serve to bolster Julien's attack. He could see where Julien wanted to take him, and he would avoid going there.

"If His Lordship has concerns about Patricia, he can write to me himself," Rogan clipped.

"Easily said, but you can understand his worries that you'll ignore the long-standing agreement made between you and his daughter."

"There is no agreement," Rogan stated coldly.

"Ah, but His Lordship feels quite differently."

"We can dispense with how His Lordship feels. It is my life, my marriage, and I will jolly well do with it as I please."

"And dispense with Lady Patricia's feelings as well? She is more than upset by your betrayal—"

"Betrayal, rubbish! Where is the letter? I want to see it for myself."

"She's become ill over your tacit decision to leave her dangling while you make plans to gain hold of Evy's inheritance. Very brutish of you, Rogan, my boy." Julien found the envelope, conveniently inside his pocket, and handed it to him with a disappointed parental frown.

Rogan snatched it from his hand, meeting Julien's single eye with a challenge of his own. He would not be bullied. If there was to be a betrayal, then he himself would not become the victim! He looked at the envelope and saw that it was indeed from Lord Bancroft and written to Sir Julien Bley.

"Lady Patricia is now staying at Rookswood with your aunt Elosia," Julien said. "Naturally, the young woman fled her whispering friends in London society. You can well imagine the embarrassment she must be suffering because of you."

Rogan was furious as he read the pompous tone of Lord Bancroft's ridiculous charge. The words were a worrisome tirade about a marriage to his daughter being "too long delayed." Something must be done "soon in order to save Her Ladyship's tarnished reputation in society." Already, Patricia was pale and wan and grieved for Rogan's return to assure her that his betrayal was not true. If Rogan would not come home to London to deal with his manly responsibilities, then Lord Bancroft would take this matter up with Rogan's father, Sir Lyle Chantry. Bancroft was disappointed over Rogan's heartless deception toward his daughter. He appealed to Sir Julien Bley, the patriarch of the extended family dynasty in South Africa, to speak sharply to his adventurous young nephew about his intransigence.

And leave Henry's map in Julien's charge while he went dashing back to London, no doubt. Totally absurd. He would not fall into Julien's cleverly laid trap.

Rogan tossed the letter onto the camping table in a gesture of irate independence.

"It won't work, Uncle. You won't use me as a chess piece to suit your purposes. You're already playing my brother for a fool with your cat-and-mouse game over marriage to Darinda. You also forced my sister into a marriage she didn't want. It ends there. I won't be maneuvered into a corner to marry any woman unless I decide she's the woman I want."

Julien claimed another Turkish cigarette, taking his time lighting it. "I'm afraid it is not so simple as all that, Rogan. Not where Evy is concerned."

"It will be as simple and straightforward as I choose it to be."

Julien shook his head. "You speak in ignorance. I didn't want to tell you this, but now I see I must. You've left me no choice. Her father, you see, shuts the door to any possibility of your marrying Katie's daughter. You had better settle for Lady Patricia and make the most of it."

Rogan looked at him, cautious again. He should have known the wily serpent had yet another threatening bite in his arsenal. Julien had never confronted him without being sure he would win in the end.

He assumed a sympathetic countenance, returning to his earlier more amiable yet condescending tone. "You see, my boy, I guessed your interest in Evy long ago. Learning she was Katie's daughter, with a diamond inheritance, only helped solidify your plans. I loathed telling you early on, as I somewhat admired your rugged tenacity."

"Forget the sentimentality. Get to the point."

"Henry was Evy's father."

Henry!

"Ah…I see this has been a shock. A devious blow. And with good reason. This is death to your plan to gain the van Buren inheritance."

Henry's daughter, Rogan thought again.

"We both know that Henry and Katie stole the Black Diamond together, and we know that Dumaka somehow snatched it from Henry in the stables. But what you didn't know was Henry and Katie's plan of escaping to raise Evy in America. Katie's death at Rorke's Drift changed everything for Henry. He was devastated. Since Dr. Clyde and Junia

Varley were relatives of Vicar Edmund Havering, Henry thought it best to bring his baby daughter back to England and make arrangements with the vicar and his wife, Grace, to raise Evy."

Rogan felt himself sinking under a flood of desolation. It was too much, and soon he would drown.

Julien was right as far as he knew. Rogan had wondered if there might not be more to Evy's birth than had been reported. When he was a geology student in London, he discovered that Evy had been at Rorke's Drift for only a month, which had raised doubts about Clyde and Junia Varley being her blood parents. He had learned through the records of the mission board that the missionaries were childless at the time. Later it was reported by Dr. Clyde himself that they were in the process of adopting a baby from Capetown.

He'd always been curious, yes. And suspicious. Especially when Camilla came to Rookswood. There'd been moments when he'd been forced to confront the possibility that Henry could be Evy's biological father. But he had swept these suspicions away because he didn't want to deal with them. That is, until now. Now Julien had uncovered the past with a victorious flair that left Rogan vanquished.

Rogan hardly noticed Sir Julien's placating smile. He only knew that he would not cooperate with Julien, regardless of becoming part of the Company expedition. He would do everything within his power to work against him.

"You have always been a practical young man, Rogan. I confess, if I'd not made Anthony my son and heir long ago, I'd be tempted to choose you, my boy."

Rogan felt the twitch in his cheek that bespoke boiling anger.

"I like a man with a strong will… I could almost wish you were interested in my Darinda rather than Patricia. That is a thought, you know. You cannot have Evy and her inheritance, but think of Darinda. She does come with her own share of diamonds from De Beers."

Rogan shot him a quick, calculating look. No thought for Parnell, of course. Julien would toss him aside in a moment if it enhanced his purposes. And what had suddenly annulled his concern over the betrayal of Lord Bancroft's abandoned daughter? Power and money. They were Julien's life's blood; like Rhodes and many others in the Company, Julien worshiped at the temple of diamonds and gold.

Julien was smoking, pacing. "One thing is certain, however. Katie's daughter is out of the picture. Lamentably, as much as this hurts you, you must forget her and build a new life here in South Africa. I will do everything in my power to see you prosper and grow stronger. Stronger in harmony with the determined purpose to turn Matabeleland and Mashonaland into Rhodesia."

Rogan did not trust himself to speak. At that moment he was so furious he could have crushed Julien. He lapsed instead into a quagmire of numbness and silence in order to escape his own anger. Later, yes, later he would make his own plans when he could think clearly, when his fevered brain cooled in the starlight.

Julien stood watching him, now showing some alarm.

The silence grew until Julien cleared his throat. He turned away from Rogan's even stare.

"I think it wise for all concerned that we forget the past and build upon a new foundation," Julien said, fumbling with some objects on the camp table. "Tomorrow we leave for Kimberly to begin preparations for the June expedition to the Zambezi." Julien turned his head toward him, adding a placating note. "Arcilla needs you. Peter will need your help too. So does my granddaughter."

Rogan looked at him for a moment. Then, without a word he walked past him into the late evening twilight and away from the camp.

He stood on the warm dusty plain. He was still thinking of the woman with amber eyes and tawny hair he had called the "rectory girl." He remembered how he had held her in his arms and how their lips had joined in a fiery kiss before he'd left her behind at Rookswood garden. From the first time he'd seen her in the woods at Grimston Way, he had wanted her for his own. Evy Varley, the girl from the rectory...now Evy "van Buren, heiress," and far worse, Evy "Chantry," Henry's daughter.

Rogan snatched Henry's old map from beneath his leather vest. In a harsh moment of utter frustration, he crumpled it in his fist. He might have hurled it into the fire to burn to a crisp if there had been one within reach.

Defeated and wretchedly disappointed, he stood in the deepening twilight, the wind brushing against him but not cooling his passions. At that moment he would have given all the gold of Mashonaland for just one opportunity to change the lineage of the woman he loved.

The wind rushed through the grass. The Southern Cross sparkled overhead like gleaming diamonds. As his thoughts drifted back to Grimston Way, Rogan agonized over the difficult decision he knew he must make. For her sake, as well as his, he must *never* see her again.

CHAPTER NINETEEN

London

A diamond heiress?

Evy could hardly believe her ears as she sat across the coach from Anthony Brewster. The horses plodded along London's cobbled streets into the swirling gray fog. He had called for her that morning to take her out in the coach for a ride and "a serious conversation."

Serious indeed! She had just been informed she was an heiress in the diamond mines at Kimberly, on equal footing with the Chantry children, Parnell, Rogan, and Arcilla. Evy was dazed. She hardly noticed that it was growing dim inside the coach due to the thick fog. She looked across at the rugged South African.

"I'm sorry it was necessary to shock you like this," Anthony Brewster said, concern etched on his face.

She shook her head, trying to comprehend the meaning of what she had just learned. "I didn't realize the van Buren family shared the ownership of the mines. It hasn't been that long since I learned I was a van Buren, and now it's even more surprising that I am actually considered an heir."

He nodded his head gravely that he understood her confusion.

"I can't say even I understand it all myself, Evy. Sir Julien is the one who controls these matters, and it hasn't been his purpose until recently to divulge this."

She noticed the unpleasant tone to his voice, making her wonder if there could be some kind of disagreement between them. She had always heard that Anthony Brewster was like a son to Julien Bley.

"Carl van Buren and Sir Julien had been partners in the early days of diamond discovery. They shared equal ownership. But after your grandfather Carl's death, Carl's closest relative, a cousin, sold out the van Buren family interest to Sir Julien. At the time Julien was a friend of Cecil Rhodes and others who already had diamond mines. Eventually, Julien bought in with Mr. Rhodes in buying up other diamond mines, forming what today is De Beers Consolidated. So you see, the van Burens made a grave mistake in selling early on to Julien."

Anthony went on to explain her inheritance, but from what she could grasp of all that he was telling her, she had no real control over her diamond shares. Sir Julien had final authority until she reached her maturity, which included marriage. Evy's heart sank. Whether or not she gained control depended upon a "suitable" marriage. Sir Julien, of course, would have final say in determining *suitability*, which would ultimately depend upon how well the bridegroom fit into the Company.

"What would happen to my inheritance if my marriage was not deemed *suitable*?" she ventured to ask Brewster.

"Then legal control of your portion remains under *family* control." He had said this in a matter-of-fact tone.

"But," he added, "regardless of that, Evy, you will always have suffi-cient finances from which to draw. You will be well taken care of, now and in the future. You will have a sizable allowance. Sir Julien has had his lawyer, Mr. Howard, set up a fund from which you may draw ex-penses at any time. I'm confident you'll find it more than adequately meets your wishes."

The facts ran crazily around her mind.

"Mr. Brewster, I don't know what to say to all this, really. I'm not going to marry to please Sir Julien Bley."

"My dear Evy, there's no cause to jump into this now. Of course no one in the family, including Sir Julien, wishes to force a match with a gentleman you don't approve of. The important thing now is that you continue to grow stronger."

For some reason she believed him. Anthony Brewster seemed kind, and his sympathetic smile and grave eyes made her feel…protected.

"We all think you should remain at Chantry Townhouse for the foreseeable future. Do you miss Grimston Way very much?"

Evy had to admit she didn't. Nothing seemed the same there, since childhood relationships no longer existed. Arcilla, Rogan, Derwent—they were all gone from her life, far off in South Africa. Except for Mrs. Croft, there were few ties that rooted her to the village. And then there was the incident she had yet to mention to anyone. She tensed, remembering, but he did not seem to notice.

She could easily have told him that she had no intention of returning to the cottage to live. Especially now, while she was dependent upon crutches. The thought of being there alone and unable to get around quickly sent a chill up her spine.

"Someday I'll wish to go back to teaching piano because music means so much to me, but as to where I'll reopen a school, I don't care to think about that now."

"That's well understood. I'm told you are quite talented. Someday perhaps you will play for me."

She smiled. "I will enjoy doing so, Mr. Brewster."

CHAPTER TWENTY

Limpopo River

The stars were still visible in the dawn sky as Rogan stirred awake. Derwent was shaking his shoulder.

"Thought you'd want this now, Mr. Rogan," he said and handed him a tin mug of black coffee. Derwent squatted on his heels as Rogan sat up and drank. "Wouldn't have wakened you, seeing as how you were up late, but Mornay's up to something I thought you'd want to know about."

Rogan was fast awake. Rolling out of his blanket, he grabbed his boots, shaking them out before pulling them on. A scorpion, tail up ready to strike over being shook about, confronted him. Rogan used a stick to get rid of it.

"What's our old cantankerous friend up to?"

"For one thing, he's quitting us. Thought he'd talk to you about it first. That's fair play, but he went and decided to join the BSA."

Rogan splashed water on his face.

Derwent scratched his russet hair. "You're sure enough taking the news calmly, seeing as how we needed him to be our guide. Thought you'd be as troubled as me when I told you. Think you can talk him out of it?"

Rogan frowned at his tin cup. How was he going to tell Derwent that he, too, had decided to sign on for the expedition to the Zambezi?

"I've been expecting Mornay to make that decision for some time now."

"You did? News to me."

Rogan felt his friend's troubling gaze and did not respond. Derwent removed his small Bible from his pocket and flipped through it, probably searching for a morning psalm to read to himself. Rogan felt a nip at his conscience.

"Looks like you and me and your hired Ngwato will have to go on that gold hunting safari on our own," Derwent continued.

"It doesn't surprise me about Mornay," Rogan went on, avoiding Derwent's statement. "He knows Frederick Selous, and they get on well enough."

"Selous? The big-game hunter who wrote the book?"

"Same gentlemen. Rhodes hired him for the pioneer trek. Julien told me the news yesterday. Mornay worked with Selous on several past expeditions. So it's not surprising he'd fall in with him now. The wage was good too. Better than I could pay."

"Seemed to me you offered him plenty."

"But not what Cecil Rhodes can pay."

"So that's why Mornay is teaming up, then. He's probably his right-hand man."

"Most likely." Rogan stood and looked down at him. He stroked his mustache thoughtfully, then said, "Derwent, you might as well know now. I've no choice but to go along with Sir Julien if I want to reach my goal on the Zambezi. The BSA owns the mining rights there under the Royal Charter from the queen. If I'm to locate Henry's gold find and collect any of it, I've no choice except to form a partnership with Rhodes's company. Besides that, there are a few people involved that concern Evy Varley and the Black Diamond. She has a relative thereabouts. A missionary doctor named Jakob van Buren."

He expected Derwent to be flabbergasted, but he wasn't. He remained calm and silent until Rogan became uncomfortable.

"Naturally, this doesn't end our relationship," Rogan said. "Working with the Company is simply a means and method to accomplishing the same goal." Did he really believe what he was saying? He went on smoothly, giving Derwent no chance to disrupt the flow of his argument. "I'll arrange with Julien for you to sign on as one of the two hundred pioneers. That will mean three thousand acres for you and Alice. Think of that. You always wanted your own farm—you'll have one of the best. The land, I hear, is very good. There's also fifteen shares in the Company gold mine, and I'll see to it that you receive a fair share of what's coming to me from Henry's map."

Derwent took his time to reply. He ran his fingers through his hair. "Three thousand acres and gold—why, that's more than I expected from this expedition, Mr. Rogan. But I thought we disapproved of the way Sir Julien was running things. Mr. Rhodes, too. From what I remember of just a few weeks ago, we were both bothered by the BSA's dealings with the Ndebele tribe. And there wasn't supposed to be any land given away, just some mining rights. When everyone got what they came for, we were expecting to go back to our own country and leave Africa to the Africans."

Though Derwent's words were calm and soft-spoken, they goaded Rogan's conscience. "I haven't changed my mind on any of that, but I haven't much choice. I've planned for this venture on the Zambezi too long to throw it all away now. Besides—the tribes can use some European civilization."

"Now you sound like men in the Company."

"Well, I can't help that. It's what I believe," Rogan said. He was starting to feel anger, since his reasoning didn't seem to be convincing Derwent.

"I didn't think we'd end up compromising to follow the dream through."

Rogan glared down at him. "I'll compromise nothing of what's truly important to me, Derwent. Don't forget that."

Derwent stood, fingering his small Bible. He stuffed it inside his pocket. "Seems to me we're both doing some compromising."

"Speak for yourself," Rogan snapped, chafing under his friend's lecture. He tossed his tin cup down. "Look, I'm going on the expedition, even if it means joining forces with them. When I reach the Zambezi, I'll follow Henry's map to the gold deposit. The BSA's giving me forty percent of the find and five thousand acres of land. That's an offer I won't throw aside easily. Without a partnership, I might as well toss the map to the flames and sail home to Grimston Way."

"It was you, Mr. Rogan, who insisted you wouldn't end up a Rhodes man."

"I'm not a Rhodes man," Rogan gritted. "I'll remain independent."

Derwent shook his head. "Joining forces is just that. You said you wouldn't lose your freedom, or sear your conscience by being bought."

In a sudden burst of anger, Rogan struck him. Derwent lost his footing, bracing his fall with one knee and a hand.

For a moment Rogan didn't move, so stunned was he by his own impulsive action.

Derwent recovered and got to his feet. He avoided Rogan's gaze, and shoving his hands in his trouser pockets, he walked away into the early dawn, head down.

"Derwent—" Rogan began and took a step in his direction, then stopped. He tightened his jaw. He looked down at his hand, tightly clenched. What had he done?

Frustrated, Rogan snatched up his leather hat, strapped on his belt, and strode off in a scowl to locate Mornay.

The sun climbed in its glory in a cloudless sky, and the camp was awake and stirring. The African workers were beginning to tear down the tents and load the wagons for the journey back to Kimberly.

Mornay, with the help of two Basuto servants, was loading his wagons.

Rogan stopped a few feet away. "So you've made up your mind too?"

Mornay's angular face was grim, his silver beard in contrast to his bushy black brows.

"It seems we have both counted our coins and come up short, monsieur. The BSA will not allow you sole ownership of any gold find, though the map is legally yours. Rhodes has hired Selous as guide to the Zambezi." He shrugged. "You are a clever young man, Rogan. You and I, we both know when the wall is too thick to butt our heads against. So we wisely seek a door."

Rogan didn't find the practical advice solacing, even if he agreed Mornay was right about bucking Rhodes.

"A man must make his way, and life…well, it must still go on," Mornay continued. "You and I, we make the best of it. Derwent, he is disappointed, but his conscience is more tender than yours or mine." He looked across the camp toward Derwent, who was rolling up his blanket and packing his things. "White is white, and black is black. But we see things sometimes gray."

Rogan drew his brows together. Mornay wasn't making him feel any wiser. He had no desire to see truth as a muddled gray. Did he?

"Derwent was raised a vicar's son. For him, compromising with what one believes is right is evil. On that, I believe as he does."

"Ah, *oui*…the end, it does not justify the means. Yes, that is how Derwent would say. But we know what we want, do we not? We know, and we seek it by whatever means we can. Then it will be right."

Rogan stood looking at Mornay and felt his scowl deepening.

Mornay cocked a brow, as though wondering what troubled him. "You have reasons to cooperate with Sir Julien Bley," Mornay said in a soothing tone. "For should you stubbornly proceed to resist the Company's plans, I would not wager that your head would remain long in place."

"You may be right, but I wager my head will remain in place awhile at least." He added dryly, "I and *only I* still possess Henry's map. Despite the blunder near Bulawayo to steal it."

Mornay rubbed his chin. "The Captain Retford and I, we both think it was Sir Julien's little granddaughter and your brother. We think you believe that too."

Rogan did think so. He also believed it wouldn't happen again. He turned and walked away, jerking his hat lower over his face.

Derwent was packing his satchel when Rogan approached.

"Appears that we'll be going to Kimberly, Mr. Rogan. I've got our workers loading our wagons now."

"Look, Derwent, about what happened a little while ago...I'm sorry. I didn't use my head. I won't let it happen again... I promise you. If it will help, you can go ahead and clobber me right now."

Derwent stood, wiping the dust from his hands. He grinned. "I've known you too long to think it would help, Mr. Rogan."

Rogan arched a brow, then laughed. He touched Derwent's shoulder. "Listen, why don't I arrange for you and Alice to return to England when we get to Kimberly? I've been thinking. You want a farm—I can have my father choose you some nice property around Grimston Way. You can help Vicar Osgood out at the rectory and be around all your decent friends again, instead of a ruddy lout like me."

"Oh no, Mr. Rogan—"

"If you and Alice settle there, I can transfer the ownership to you once I inherit Rookswood. Someday I am going back home...that, I promise you too. Our children will be friends, just the way we were."

Derwent ducked his head and fumbled with his gun belt. He shook his head and arranged his hat, looking embarrassed. "I wouldn't want to go back yet. Not without you. Neither would Alice. She'll come along on the expedition too, now that Miss Arcilla and Miss Darinda are going. If you're going with the BSA—then I'm coming with you. I wouldn't want to see you going on without me. Someone's got to be there when—" He stopped.

Rogan offered a faint smile. "When things fall apart? Perhaps they will. Another reason it may be best if you go back. What's ahead may not be pretty. In fact, I'm sure we will be facing even greater danger as we proceed."

Derwent shook his head. "If things fall apart, then that's where I need to be." He cleared his throat. "I'd like to go on, if you don't mind."

Rogan was touched by his loyalty, but he didn't want to get too sentimental. He'd already said more than he was prone to say.

"If that's what you really want, it's fine with me. Did you feed my horse?"

"He's full and raring to ride."

"Good. As you said, we've a lot to do before the pioneer trek begins in June."

Rogan walked away, feeling the sun warming his back and shoulders, aware of the map strapped safely under his canvas shirt. He could almost imagine it weighing him down a little more than when he had left England with it. His dreams were not so shiny as they once were. They had been tarnished now by Julien's. Setting his face with grim determination, Rogan would go forward with his plans. He believed he was now in too deeply to change course. If he went back to Grimston Way now, he would go back with near empty pockets and nothing to show for all his years of planning. He wouldn't end up following Henry's footsteps to defeat.

Yes, this was another reason for staying and fighting. He wanted to make his own way without any help, especially from his uncle Julien. It was one thing to acquire the estate and lands, but quite another to forge a name for himself with his own sagacity and hard work.

Pride, he thought sourly, could be costly indeed.

Nor was there reason to return home to England. His path must never cross Evy van Buren's in the summer garden at Rookswood, where he had held her and kissed her before sailing for Africa. Little had he known that it would become their final good-bye. He could lose himself in this expedition, and while there could be nothing between him and Evy, he wanted her to know the truth about her lineage—and her mother. He could also give her that much, at least. He could also give her a godly relative, Jakob van Buren.

Though this was the trekking season, Arcilla thought the morning of the twenty-fourth of June was hot and dusty near the Motloutsi River. The expedition was about to begin. Arcilla sat alone on the buckboard of the wagon she would share with Peter. It would be their home for months to come. She fanned her face, dreading the long ordeal that lay ahead. She already felt her muscles tense and her stomach become queasy, and the wagons had yet to start moving. Perhaps they wouldn't even make it to Fort Salisbury. Perhaps they would die on the way, horribly massacred by savages with spears just as it had happened years ago at Rorke's Drift. The thought sent shivers down her spine. She looked over at Alice Tisdale Brown in their covered wagon. Alice looked tense too, but also excited. *But not over visions of sugarplum fairies. She's dreaming of pockets full of gold,* Arcilla thought.

Alice hadn't changed much since the Grimston Way years, except that her disapproving mouth looked more puckered, and her strawberry-blond hair was more limp, though still wrapped around her head in a Boer fashion braid. Her skin was still sallow, Arcilla noticed, but there were freckles now. Arcilla was pleased her own skin was still flawless ivory, thanks to her wisdom in *always* remembering her hats, parasols, gloves, and potions. Poor Alice. She must have given up any concern for her appearance.

Ah, well…Derwent had freckles, too. But then, Derwent Brown had *always* had freckles. In fact, freckles looked cute on him. She smiled, rather liking Derwent. As a girl, she had thought him country. Now she thought him very polite and kind. He had deserved better than Alice.

Arcilla swished her fan and slapped at a persistent insect that buzzed around her face. She reached for the jar of repellent. Peter was right. It *did* work. Maybe she could pour some of her French perfume in the foul-smelling goop. Why, she could market the ointment and make millions! But no—that would mean working with the nganga. She shuddered. Witch doctors and bones…

Arcilla looked over at Cousin Darinda. She was the one who still looked cool and poised despite the dust and heat, and Arcilla hated her for it. Darinda's courage and handling of pistol and rifle goaded Arcilla the most. Darinda refused to squeal when a large spider or snake appeared. Arcilla was certain this was deliberate, just to make her look more courageous before Peter and the other men on the expedition.

"Just once I'd like to see her scream and faint!" she said to herself. Naturally, she wouldn't. Not the self-possessed Darinda Bley. Come to think of it, she was very much like her grandfather, Sir Julien Bley. A female Julien! Oh, save us! Arcilla threw her head back and laughed. She looked at Darinda again and saw her cousin watching her. Arcilla sat up straighter and smiled prettily at Peter as he rode past on a horse. Peter smiled and tipped his hat, then went on.

Arcilla looked back at Darinda, feeling smug. Darinda was looking straight ahead. She had no man now coquettishly strung on her leash. Not since she and Parnell had had a falling out. Parnell was deliberately keeping his distance from her, much to Arcilla's shock. Had he decided at last that Darinda was his cup of hemlock?

Rogan sat astride his horse, riding alongside Peter and Captain Ryan Retford to join the other officers of the Pioneer Column prepared to splash across the river on the northward push to Mashonaland.

The two hundred pioneer recruits, who had been personally selected by Frank Thompson to form the core of the new colony, were lined up along the river. The men had traveled by train from Kimberly, then ridden here to the dusty camp on the edge of Bechuanaland, a British protectorate. Like soldiers, the men waited to be addressed by the British officer Rhodes had arranged to send up from the Cape. They waited to hear the final flourish of trumpets to initiate the long-awaited expedition into the land of the Zambezi.

Peter had told him that Mr. Rhodes was not with the Company

leaders who would command the pioneer trek. A political crisis unfolding at Capetown had required Rhodes to take over the reins of Cape government as Prime Minister. He remained in Kimberly, his financial and political power base, located two hundred miles south of the Motloutsi River.

Rogan maneuvered his horse along the column, feeling relieved that the men looked capable. Garbed in tough brown corduroy trousers and digger hats, they sported new rifles. He noticed among the Englishmen that there were some Cape Afrikaners, Dutch, among them, all eager to begin the colony near Mount Hampden. The pioneers included doctors, engineers, ministers, military men, bakers, butchers, as well as the gold miners and farmers, all anxious to stake out their land claims provided by the Royal Charter.

"Can't say Frank Thompson hasn't chosen the lot well. We even have some cricketers," Peter said cheerfully. "Nothing like a jolly game of cricket, you know. We've a Jesuit priest as well."

Rogan was thinking not of cricket but of the godly old missionary Dr. Jakob van Buren and asked Peter about him.

"Jakob van Buren? Yes, he's a relative of Heyden," Peter said when Rogan mentioned the man. "He's from Holland, I think. Julien seems to think so, and mentioned it. He treats lepers, I believe. A brave man, from all I hear, and well respected in the area. His station was actually started by some English missionary back in the sixties. He'd been inspired by David Livingstone's expedition up the Zambezi to establish missions along the river. Unfortunately, that fellow was killed by the Africans. Jakob took over and has done quite a work there."

"Do you know Heyden van Buren? He's related to Julien's first mining partner at Kimberly, Carl van Buren."

"I met him briefly in London when I came to marry Arcilla. Heyden was with the Kruger delegation back then, but I've seen Heyden recently as well."

Rogan peered at him from beneath his hat, keenly alert now. "You saw him recently? Where? Kimberly?"

"No, actually it was Capetown. Strange you should mention Heyden. He spoke of a recent visit to Jakob van Buren. It was quite a trek for him. Some Boer guide brought him in. Sounds rather like your uncle Henry."

Heyden had gone to the Zambezi...

"What was Heyden doing in Capetown?"

"He was on his way to London to see his cousin." Peter looked at him thoughtfully. "The girl who played the piano, wasn't it? Very lovely young woman, as I recall."

Rogan frowned and toyed restlessly with the reins he held. "Did he say why he was going to visit her?"

"No. Is it important?"

Rogan had no ready answer. How could he admit how important it was to him, while also realizing he had no right to pursue Evy? But knowing that Heyden, whom he personally distrusted, would have access to Evy added to his frustration.

"I intend to visit Jakob van Buren when we get to the Zambezi region," Rogan told Peter. It was troubling to know that Heyden had recently visited the mission station. Had Heyden learned from Jakob that Dumaka had stolen the Black Diamond from Henry Chantry? Rogan began to think Heyden may have been told the same things that Julien had relayed to him back in April.

Peter changed the topic to the two hundred pioneers who had joined the venture. "They're risking their lives, just as we are. One can only think they are willing to do so for love of Mr. Rhodes and England."

Rogan winced. "Come, come, Peter. Don't wax too eloquent on his part, or theirs. I'll wager they're drawn by the three-thousand-acre spreads to be given away free."

"They'll be working hard for those acres, I can assure you. They'll be cutting the road all the way to Mount Hampden."

Rogan also saw hundreds of Africans hired for menial tasks. There were 350 Ngwato laborers, who would be hacking and clearing a road for the 2,000 oxen pulling 117 ox wagons.

They would work, all right. They all would. They would earn their farmland and their gold.

Along with the pioneers were five hundred men of the newly formed British South Africa Company police, who were being paid high wages to set up a security force in the new colony.

Earlier that morning, Rogan had inspected a naval searchlight powered by a steam engine that was to be pulled in one of the wagons by sturdy oxen.

"The nights will be long, sir," the man had said gravely. "Long, dark, and risky. This light will enable us to protect our camp from surprise attacks."

Right. Lobengula might decide the Company Pioneer Column was invading his territory after all, despite his earlier grudging consent. The old chieftain just might plan a surprise night attack by his impis.

Cecil Rhodes had already decided to bypass the much sought-after "road from Bulawayo," so as to try to avoid trouble with Lobengula. Instead, they would be cutting a path for the oxcarts along an old hunting track known by Frederick Selous and Mornay. It was believed the track would lead them right into Mashonaland.

"The British Government has agreed with this less obtrusive route. They've thrown their diplomatic support behind us," Peter said.

Rogan felt impatient with the whole thing. "I've always thought the old hunting track Mornay had in mind would serve us better than wrangling with Lobengula. It may have been the route Henry took with Mornay's father. Too much time's been wasted trying to negotiate. As it stands now, we may have already stirred up unnecessary trouble."

"Well, the Company's come around to see it that way now," Peter said. "Selous is a strong individual and was rather uncommunicative about the route he intended to take."

Rogan pulled his hat lower. "We should make use of every moment of peace we have with the Ndebele to get moving. The farther away from Lobengula we get, the better for the expedition. I don't trust him or his impis."

Rogan rode with Peter to the head of the column, where the lead men were gathered waiting for the arrival of a British official from Kimberly to send them on their way with the government's fanfare.

Rogan saw Dr. Jameson ahead. The doctor impressed him as a man who might act impulsively and at times, perhaps, unwisely. A forward push into hostile, unexplored country demanded cool-headed leadership. Mr. Rhodes, however, trusted Jameson and had sent him along as his special emissary from Kimberly. Jameson held perhaps the highest credential in the Pioneer Column. He alone carried Rhodes's power of attorney as managing director of De Beers. Peter answered to "Dr. Jim," and then to Sir Julien.

Julien was waiting for them at the head of the column, along with Parnell and Captain Retford.

"This is Rogan, my younger nephew," Julien told the group of men.

Rogan leaned across his horse and briefly shook hands with Lieutenant Colonel Pennyfather, young Frank Johnson, the contractor who'd been hired to arrange the journey, and the pathfinder Frederick Selous.

"Ah yes. The young man who'd been planning a private expedition to the Zambezi," Pennyfather said. He was an older man of dignified face and bearing and sat tall in the saddle.

So he knows too, Rogan thought. *I suppose they all do now.*

"Too bad we didn't meet first," Frank Johnson said with a meaningful grin, shaking hands with Rogan, who was near his age.

Dr. Jameson did not look pleased by Johnson's remark.

"Well, gentlemen, we're all in this together now. Whatever gold Henry Chantry discovered there in the seventies is needed by the Company, and we'll mine and transport it out by building a railroad. I doubt you or Frank could have pulled that off on your own."

"Not necessarily," Rogan said. "Chantry resources and determination could have accomplished more than Mr. Rhodes may think."

Sir Julien threw back his dark head and laughed.

"But alas!" Rogan smiled pleasantly at Dr. Jameson. "Her Majesty's award of a Royal Charter goes without dispute. As you say, sir, we're in this together—just as long as forty percent of the gold goes to the map owner, I will give the BSA little trouble." Rogan continued to smile as Jameson's hard eyes flickered.

Then Jameson laughed too. "Julien and Rhodes agreed. Forty percent. Who am I to protest? We need you along, Rogan."

Frank Johnson chuckled and relaxed into his saddle, and Captain Ryan Retford grinned at Rogan. But Peter said quickly, as though Rogan's banter might ruffle feathers, "And you know Mornay's good friend, Frederick Selous, our chief pathfinder."

Selous, a nice-looking man with a walrus mustache, was a stalwart South African with a shiny reputation and had a confident, quiet way about him.

"Mornay tells me you're a better pathfinder than he," Rogan said. "For a Frenchman to admit such a thing takes rare humility, so he must be right." Rogan shook Selous's hand.

The others laughed when Mornay, seated on his horse behind Selous, sniffed loudly and said something in French.

The brief introductions done, the conversation continued between the officials.

Frederick Selous then spoke up. "If all proceeds as planned, we should be beyond Bulawayo and as far northeast as Mount Hampden before the rains come!"

Chapter Twenty-One

"Here comes the official brass Mr. Rhodes said he'd send from the Cape," Parnell told Rogan.

Rogan's leather saddle squeaked as he turned to squint against the burning sun and dust.

Major General Methuen, apparently oblivious to the film of dust that covered his dressy red-and-gold uniform, came cantering toward them, as though just leaving a parade ground at the Cape. Behind him followed a large group of soldiers and African servants, all of them in parade dress as well. The Pioneer Column lined up for the final and formal send-off. Rogan sat in his saddle beside Peter and Mornay. Derwent was farther down the column among the pioneers. Rogan felt the wind blowing against him and the warm sun on his back, and he blinked against the dust that seemed to stir constantly. The wagons were neatly in line, and he glanced to see his sister sitting with straight shoulders and thought, *Well done, Arcilla.* Darinda, too, and Alice were at attention.

Then came a roll of drums, a blast of trumpets, and a show of colors. The Union Jack snapped proudly in the breeze, with the BSA flag alongside it, and then the guns fired a salute.

The official formalities over, Rogan turned his horse aside to go check on his supply wagon.

Derwent came riding up from his spot in the column. "Mr. Rogan, it's one of the Ndebele indunas. He's come from Bulawayo with a message from Lobengula, but he's asking to speak only with you outside camp. His name is Jube."

Peter was listening, but the others had not overheard. It was just as well, since Rogan did not want Julien to follow him and confront the induna, especially if Jube actually was Dumaka.

"I'll bring Retford and come with you," Peter said quietly.

Rogan, with Peter, Captain Retford, and Derwent, rode outside the camp to some white rocks that jutted upward like bleached bones. The wind whipped up the dust around the horses, and the sky appeared like an iron shield.

They waited astride their horses, keeping a watchful eye on the rocks around them. A few minutes later, Rogan saw Jube, the same induna he'd met at Bulawayo some two months earlier, step out from behind the largest white boulder. He was tall and dark. The leopard-skin draped over his shoulders moved in the wind. His hair, touched with gray, looked like a skull cap.

"I'll talk to him alone." Rogan swung down from the saddle and left the reins with Derwent.

Jube came toward him at the same moment, leaving three impis back among the white rocks.

Rogan stopped, seeing a slithering movement in the shade of a rock. A poisonous serpent watched him. The wind tugged at Rogan's leather hat. He kept a safe distance, while also trying not to give Jube the wrong impression.

After several cautious moments, the serpent slid away into low brush.

Rogan walked to where Jube stood.

"I see you, Jube."

Jube came toward him. He was very tall, well over six feet, thin and sinewy, and the skin on his fine facial features was drawn smooth and tight, giving his features the appearance of chiseled marble. As before he was unsmiling.

"The Ndebele king wants to know why there are so many warriors at Motloutsi. Has the king committed any fault, or has any white man been killed, or have the white men lost anything that they're looking for? How is it that the doctor agreed at Bulawayo to dig only at a place pointed out by the king?"

"I am not in command of this expedition, Jube. The decisions are not in my hand. I can tell them my ideas, but the doctor speaks for the white men. They say your king has signed a treaty for them to dig for gold. To dig for gold, we need oxen and wagons, and white men and Africans to work for us. We go far from your king's kraal at Bulawayo, beyond the Limpopo, to the land of the Shona people."

He had deliberately mentioned the Shona, hoping to show Jube that the Ndebele too had entered a land not theirs by birth and invaded and cruelly subjugated the Shona, reducing them to Lobengula's slaves.

For a brief moment Jube's eyes appeared to show contempt.

"Cetshwayo was my king. I am Zulu. Lobengula is related. When the white men invaded Ulundi and scattered the mighty Zulu, we went where we could go. Now Zululand is servant of the British queen. Cetshwayo was shamed and carried to a place he did not want to go. They put white man's clothes on him. He died in his heart. Now you want to do the same to the Ndebele."

Rogan caught the word *Zulu,* but affected no surprise. He measured Jube with a more careful eye.

"Why do you seek me out?"

Jube was silent and motionless for a long moment. "You are of the family of Julien Bley. Unlike him"—he looked over at Peter—"I have heard you are against Julien Bley. I am against him too."

"Jube is not your name, is it? You must be Dumaka."

Jube cracked his first smile, and it was unpleasant. "So you guessed. Yes, I am Dumaka. You tell Julien he has taken the bones from my hut at Cape House, but the curse he cannot take away and hide."

The bones…the bones Henry had written about in his diary. Could that be the cause for the look of consternation Henry had seen on Julien's face that day? Julien had found the bones of witchcraft in Dumaka's hut and taken them. Maybe Julien had understood the devilish belief behind them and recognized that Dumaka wanted to curse him with death.

"Why do you want to kill Julien Bley? The Black Diamond?"

"Yes."

Dumaka offered no more information. "Did you take the Black Diamond to King Cetshwayo?" Rogan persisted.

"Yes. But it was taken from Zululand the night of the battle."

"You took it?"

"I took it," he said proudly. "Now it is gone again, but it must be found. It must be brought to the sacred hills."

Dumaka looked away into the far distance, and Rogan followed his gaze to the southern end of the Matopos Mountains. *Witchcraft,* Rogan thought. Mornay had told him something about the mountains, which were considered sacred to the Matabele and Zulu, perhaps the Shona as well. There were secret caves there where the Umlimo lived, witch doctors who supposedly prophesied to the tribes. The Umlimo would yield to some sort of demonic oracle, giving forth dark sayings. Lobengula put great trust in the dark sayings, as did all the ruling indunas.

"The white man who once went to the Zambezi, your father, the hunter who drew the map, he told you where the Black Diamond was?"

So that was the reason why Jube—Dumaka—had sought him out at Bulawayo. Dumaka thought he might know who had the diamond. He had mistaken Henry Chantry for his father.

"I travel as a lone rider. It is gold I seek, not the Black Diamond."

"Hawk has the map?"

Caution…could it be? Could he possibly think Henry's map in some way led to where the diamond was hidden?

"I do not seek the Black Diamond," Rogan repeated. "I seek treasure from the earth of another kind, gold. But someone is blamed for stealing the Black Diamond, and a woman's reputation must be given back to her. She is the daughter of Katie van Buren, the woman your sister Jendaya protected."

At the mention of Jendaya, his smile left his face.

"Jendaya is cursed by the Umlimo."

"Where is Jendaya now? At Bulawayo? Bring me to her."

He shook his head. "She is not at Bulawayo. I will not bring you to her. I do not know where she hides." He turned to walk away and stopped, looking back at Peter and Captain Retford, then Derwent. "The one who is a friend of Julien, the warning is for him. The white men will die if they intrude into the sacred hold of the Umlimo."

Rogan was more interested in what he could learn than in responding to his threats.

"Umlimo?" he asked, pretending ignorance.

"The sacred speaker. The one who interprets the oracle. The great warrior spirits warn through the Umlimo that the white man brings a curse."

"Lobengula has signed with his own elephant seal the paper sent to the British government allowing the white men to come and dig for gold."

Dumaka's eyes fixed on Rogan, as though holding him responsible. "The doctor lies. Lobengula, he speaks well when he says fat is rubbed on their mouths. Be warned." He looked deliberately at Rogan's gun belt. "Go back."

Rogan frowned, holding back harsh words. He held up one hand to silence Dumaka. "Not all white men speak with the same words, but neither does any man welcome threats. Those who are my friends wish you no harm. And there are more like Moffat at Kuruman mission, and Jakob van Buren on the Zambezi, who wish you good from the God over all gods. But the men I travel with—none of us will allow ourselves to be killed. It is better we work together as friends, in peace."

"Friends? Peace?" Dumaka shook his head. "We are warriors!"

Peter maneuvered his horse closer, raising dust, and said loftily,

"That is a threat. You are a fool if you think we could not kill you now!"

Rogan made a sharp hand gesture to silence Peter, angry he had interrupted. Peter looked startled. Dumaka stared back. There was no hope for peace in his hot gaze. Rogan felt the hatred. Dumaka gestured to his impis to follow him, and like tall, ebony shadows they melted away among the rocks.

Peter now looked furious with Rogan. "I tell you, Rogan. You do not know these savages as we do. You made a grave mistake letting him speak that way to you. He takes your reasonableness for weakness. It only emboldens them to further provocations."

"If anything goads them to further provocations, it is suspicion and British presumption. I'm not worried about him mistaking my willingness to talk as weakness. He knows better."

Peter scowled. "Am I assistant commissioner or not?"

Rogan maintained a hard glitter of challenge in his dark eyes.

"I respect the fact that you were chosen to assist Jameson. I'm here willingly to assist you. That means my opinion is worth something if I remember what you told me at the Limpopo camp. If you expect a yes-man, Peter, then you no longer want me."

Peter's scowl deepened. He started to speak, then apparently changing his mind, he exhaled and paused before answering.

"When I said I respected your opinion, I meant it. I still do. I'll consider what you said. Otherwise, let's forget this dispute. We had better get back before we are missed."

Rogan turned his horse back toward the river camp. "Are you going to tell Jameson the induna threatened us?"

Peter looked at him as though he were a man with African fever. "But naturally I'll relay his threat. I must. It's my job."

"Why the need now? Are we not already on guard and expecting trouble?"

"Yes, of course, but Great Scott, man, I can't simply let the induna get away with this."

"He's getting away with nothing. What he said to me, he said on his own. Those were not the words of Lobengula. If you ride back in a ruddy huff, you'll only give Jameson and the others a reason to attack Bulawayo. Jameson is looking for an excuse. You'll give it to him if you go back there and play Dumaka's words for more than they were."

Peter's scowl had never diminished, and it didn't now. He said nothing in response and looked at him for a studious moment.

"Let it pass," Rogan urged quietly. "It's gold we want. Let's worry about finding it. The sooner we cross the river into Mashonaland and get farther from the old king's kraal, the safer we'll be—and the closer to our goal."

Peter did not reply, but Rogan thought he saw a relinquishing of his adamant mood.

"I'll think it over," Peter mumbled.

Rogan watched Peter and Retford ride alone back toward camp, dust flying from pounding hooves.

Rogan buried his face in his sleeve, sick of the unrelenting dust. A moment later, coughing, he walked back to where Derwent waited, holding the horses' reins. Derwent was scowling. Rogan knew he did not like the squabbles with Peter. Derwent quickly handed him a skin of water.

Rogan rinsed the dust from his mouth, then mounted and rode slowly across the dry field toward camp, Derwent beside him.

"I think we're making a mistake, Mr. Rogan. I think we ought to pack our bags and head back to Kimberly. The pioneers are as determined as bulls. But so are the king's indunas. I always say that when two determined bulls decide to face each other—"

Rogan pulled his hat lower and cantered a length ahead. At this moment he, like Peter, had little patience for another opposing view. If he was a determined bull, then so be it. He wanted to locate Henry's gold. Nothing was stopping him now, not even the Zulu. Dumaka was making a blunder if he, as Peter had said, mistook Rogan's cooperation for lack of resolve.

Chapter Twenty-Two

Rogan's frown deepened as he rode on, his thoughts swirling. Dumaka was a Zulu induna, so why had he been working on Julien's estate before the Zulu War in 1879? Their king, Cetshwayo, had been alive at that time, strong and greatly feared. No induna of Zulu blood would normally work for Julien at Capetown, yet Dumaka had done so. Strange... considering he hated Sir Julien and anyone now associated with him. What had happened at Cape House so many years ago when Katie van Buren escaped with Jendaya and Henry Chantry?

Could it be Julien hadn't realized who Dumaka really was but had mistaken him for a Bantu? Dumaka could have come to work there in search of the Black Diamond. That would surely suggest a different history for the diamond than what was presently thought. Could the diamond have been stolen from the Umlimo?

"I say, it was a bit strange, how Dumaka talked about Sir Julien and the Black Diamond," Derwent said.

"I wonder. I'm beginning to worry about its history."

"You mean, you think there have been some lies about how it was discovered at Kimberly?"

"Look, Derwent, forget everything we've been told. Now think. What if there's another story concerning its origin? One that Julien alone knows about—or maybe Carl van Buren, or even my grandfather, Sir George."

"You mean one of them could have stolen it—like a temple robber?"

"Something like that. Maybe there was something between the two partners we don't yet know. Van Buren, they say, was killed in a mine explosion at Kimberly."

"You questioning the report?"

"I don't know…but what if the report is hiding the truth? What if something else happened?"

Derwent pushed his hat back thoughtfully. The wind ruffled his russet hair. "Say, I never thought of that. I wonder. I see what you're thinking, all right. Maybe the two of 'em didn't find the diamond?"

Rogan was silent, thinking. *Or maybe only one of them?*

"That would certainly be an evil thing to lie about." Derwent scratched his long nose. "Your kin may have been thinking the wrong thing for two generations."

Rogan scowled. "The place to learn about this is Jakob van Buren's mission. I want to talk to him about a few things, including Jendaya and where she could be. Dumaka said he didn't know. He had an unpleasant look in his eyes when I asked him."

"Doesn't sound a bit good to me. Maybe she's hiding from him?"

Was she even still alive after all these years?

Rogan looked off toward the Matopos. "You see those distant hills?"

"Aye, a beautiful land, Mr. Rogan. Thought so the moment I laid my eyes on it."

"Somewhere in those hills, there's a secret valley and a cave—more than one, probably—that's considered sacred. It's a stronghold of demonic powers, with an Umlimo speaking all kinds of evil curses."

Derwent shook his head. "I heard all about the Umlimo. They use witchcraft—that's what it's all about. They seem to have certain powers, but I'm thinking Satan has his way in these parts, Mr. Rogan. It sure makes me feel good in my heart to know Jakob van Buren's a light for truth at his mission station. And Moffat's Kuruman, too. His son runs the station now. And I guess Jendaya is a Christian. Now, would that be enough cause for Dumaka to be angry with his sister?"

"Yes. And I think there could be even more to all this and the diamond than we dreamed of back in Grimston Way."

"Maybe it took our coming to South Africa to settle it. That would give us another reason for coming all the way on this expedition, wouldn't it? Maybe a more noble reason, I'm beginning to think."

Rogan looked at him, his serious mood gone, and irritation in his smile.

"Not beginning to feel guilty about getting a little gold in your hands, are you?"

Derwent shifted in his saddle. "No, not if it's all fair and legal. But look here, Mr. Rogan, things are getting a bit troubling. I don't know if I can trust the motives of some of those adventurers."

"Trouble is everywhere, friend Derwent. Maybe you're missing the life of a vicar after all."

"I don't think I'm called as a vicar... I don't have the way with words. I haven't changed my mind about getting land and some gold, either. But I admit to missing Grimston Way. And Evy. Wonder how she's doing? Must have gotten her music school by now."

Rogan forced Evy from his mind. He ignored Derwent's musing. "Trouble...is certainly bound to come to Rhodes's company. What worries me most is the hotheads in charge of the new colony."

"Aye, for sure. That Dr. Jameson is sure to cause trouble, if you ask me." Derwent shook his head again.

"If we're not careful, Jameson could do something reckless and virtually hand a lighted match to the indunas to set the whole thing ablaze. All it would take is for something to go badly, followed by a dark utterance from the Umlimo to stir the indunas to action."

"Aye." Derwent looked again toward the Matopos. "Still, it's only the beauty of the Creator's handiwork I see."

Rogan agreed. The sun shining through the spiraling mist cast the hills in a rosy glow that looked peaceful.

"It's just like the devil to take the good things that God made and try to get people to use them in ways that are twisted and destructive," Derwent said.

How true, Rogan thought as they rode into camp, but what about his own life? Could he keep his desires and ambitions from leading him in paths that were dark?

The Pioneer Column was ready to move out. Nothing, it seemed, would halt the expedition now. Their destination was Mount Hampden—before the seasonal rains came.

The first horseman splashed across the Motloutsi River, followed by the Pioneer Column, their wagons and oxen, and a host of African laborers.

After months of planning, the expedition had finally begun. The BSA had leaped over the two Boer Republics—the Transvaal and the Orange Free State—as well as Lobengula's Matabeleland. Their intent was to form a new country between the Limpopo and Zambezi rivers three hundred miles north of the Transvaal. It would be called Rhodesia, in honor of Cecil Rhodes. After crossing the river, the long Pioneer Column was soon enveloped in a great dust cloud, which trailed behind them, visible for miles, until it was at last borne away by the wind.

The company moved forward, and wagons creaked and shuddered under heavy loads. Arcilla groaned as she thought of the weeks of riding in a wagon that lay ahead. Each bump and clank of the springless axles jarred her teeth as wagon wheels jostled across the expansive empty veld and over rocky stream beds. The dry season brought dust everywhere. Unlike the children of Israel who were safely led by God's pillar of cloud, everyone in this column was hounded by the swirling clouds of dust. From the first covered wagon to the men bringing up the rear—all were smothered in dust. For one of the few times in her life, Arcilla prayed without her prayer book, "Oh God, help us, protect us, and help Peter to be wise. In the name of our Savior, amen."

✤   ✤   ✤

In July the Pioneer Column reached Tulie, where they began construction of their first fort, a place of rest for those who would follow in coming years to join the new colony of Rhodesia.

"Sorry you came along, Miss Bley?"

Darinda, weary and exhausted, was looking on the ground where she'd lost a button from her jacket, knowing she'd not likely find it or get another to replace it in a very long time. She straightened and looked up at Captain Ryan Retford astride his horse. It was irksome that he looked confident, relaxed, and at home in such wild territory. His hair glinted in the sun, and she found the cleft in his chin attractive. The last time she had talked to him was on the other side of the Limpopo weeks ago. She had parted from him in a rage, humiliated by her indiscretion that he so bluntly pointed out. Since then she had stayed far afield of him, Parnell, and Rogan Chantry as well. She refused to even think about the ruddy map. So far it had only caused trouble for her.

"I'm not in the least sorry, Captain," she said coolly.

He smothered a smile and touched his hat in salute, his dark blue eyes glinting with humor. "I suppose not. If you ever need any help with anything, just call."

"I'll manage on my own, thank you."

"This is a far cry from Cape House."

"If you will excuse me?" She started to sidle past him.

"I understand why you've avoided me on the trek, Miss Bley, but what's happened between you and Parnell Chantry?"

"That, Captain, is none of your business." And she brushed past him.

"Wait—"

She slowly turned. He'd swung down from his saddle and picked something up from the ground.

"Looking for this, Miss Bley?"

He walked up to her and extended his palm. Her golden button gleamed in the sunlight.

He would have to be the one to find it. Darinda snatched it from him and was turning away when she glanced up at his face. As his dark blue eyes flicked over her, she felt herself flush. She jerked her shoulder at him and walked away.

"You are welcome," his calm, amused voice followed after her.

She gritted her teeth.

After building the fort at Tulie, the Pioneer Column pushed forward, mindful of the inclement weather to come.

The Ngwato laborers hacked out bush for the wagon roads. The pioneers rode and marched along this track, sweating in the southern hemisphere winter sun, alert for possible surprise attacks by Lobengula's impis.

At night Rogan helped Mornay and Derwent hobble the horses. Peter and Captain Retford oversaw the grouping of the wagons to form a laager. Each evening before darkness closed in, the men set up the naval searchlight and fired up the steam engine to power it throughout the long night.

Rogan and Parnell helped lay charges of dynamite farther back so that the explosions thundered a stern warning to the Ndebele. Rogan had seen the impis secretly following at a distance, ominously shadowing the column.

Arcilla snuggled deeper into the blankets inside the wagon. "Suppose they break through?"

"Don't worry, darling. We've posted guards all around the laager."

"Peter, I feel sick. I want to go home to England."

"Arcilla, my dearest, we cannot go home. This is our new home. Things will be better at Fort Salisbury, I promise."

Arcilla was sure things would be worse. She longed for Aunt Elosia, pampering her again as her mother had. She remembered her charming bedroom at Rookswood and how all the maids—even chatterbox Lizzie, Mrs. Croft's niece—would rush to meet her every whim. Now she woke up to warmed-over mealies and dark, bitter coffee. No wonder she was getting thin. "I'll die here," she told herself one night as she listened to the calls of the wild animals. "They'll bury me in Mashonaland."

By August Frederick Selous had halted the Pioneer Column at Lundi. This was south of the main mountain range that Rogan had studied on Henry's map. The range separated the bush veld from the high plateau of Mashonaland.

Rogan and Derwent climbed through the bush to explore. When they reached the summit, Rogan pointed at the open veld below.

"This is it, all right," Rogan said. "This is one of the areas that Henry drew on the map." Frederick Selous had called this area Providential Pass, since it opened up the main range.

They trekked still deeper into what they called the Zambezi region, though the Zambezi River itself was far distant. On the sixth of August, they resumed their steady advance and reached the main plateau on the fourteenth. Here they built a second fort and named it Fort Victoria, and in September they reached their destination, the site chosen for the new British colony, in sight of Mount Hampden, and christened it Fort Salisbury, after the British prime minister.

The next day Rogan took part in the official ceremony to commemorate the end of a long journey and the beginning of a new British colony. He stood with Peter and Arcilla, Sir Julien, Darinda, and Parnell. The entire Pioneer Column soon gathered, with Lieutenant Colonel Pennyfather dressed in full military garb. They stood solemnly as the officers of the British South Africa Company hauled out two Union Jacks: one belonging to the Cape government and the other to Her Majesty Queen Victoria's Government of Great Britain.

They located the straightest tree and trimmed its branches. Then they all stood at attention as the flags were solemnly hoisted. Two seven-pound cannons shot off a twenty-one gun salute. Mr. Balfour, the chaplain of the five-hundred-man BSA police, prayed for God's blessing and gave thanks.

Arcilla felt a tingle of excitement run down her spine as a deafening cheer reverberated across the veld. Peter stood beside her with his shoulders back and a glow in his eyes. "This will one day be called Rhodesia," he told Arcilla, pride and pleasure in his voice. He drew her aside and planted a kiss on her forehead. "We made it, my dear. I told you we would. We'll be happy here. You will try, won't you, Arcilla?"

"I'll try, Peter. I promise you I'll do my best."

"Darling, that's all a man could ever ask of his beloved wife."

"Oh, Peter…" She went into his arms, and Peter enfolded her closely.

Darinda turned to her grandfather, Sir Julien, and they embraced as well. Then she turned to Parnell, and laying her palms on his forearms, she smiled up at him. Parnell's eyes took on new life, and some of the old sparkle appeared to come back to his face. "You did wonderfully well, Darinda. You did better than I did on the trek."

She laughed, and her eye caught that of Captain Ryan Retford. He stood with the soldiers, watching her and Parnell, and a small smile showed on his tanned face. Darinda turned toward Parnell, looping her arm through his, and met her grandfather's gaze; he had followed her eyes across the dirt yard to Captain Retford. She turned quickly toward Alice and Derwent Brown.

"Well, Alice, we are finally here in Fort Salisbury. Did you ever think we'd make it, all of us?" Darinda said.

"There were times when I told Derwent we'd all die for sure. But Derwent was right. He said God would bring us here, and He did." She looked at her husband and smiled.

"What will you do now, Derwent?" Darinda asked amiably.

"I'll be going with Mr. Rogan, Miss."

"To look for gold," Alice said cheerfully. "Oh, wait till I write to Mum."

"I'm afraid that'll be a long time," Derwent said quietly. "Until Mr. Rhodes sends along more pioneers and opens a better road, we're completely isolated. We'll have to make things do."

Within a few days the column was disbanded. Frederick Selous and Frank Johnson were paid for their work by Rhodes's partners in the BSA, and the pioneers scattered to stake out their farms and ranches.

Rogan stood with Mornay and Derwent. Despite all the obstacles that had crossed his path since he had sailed from England, he was finally here. He pulled out Henry's map and grinned with confidence.

"Well? What are we waiting for? The land is before us. We'll join forces to stake our own claim in Rhodesia."

Six Months Later
Near the Zambezi

Rogan had left his base camp and ridden out with Derwent and Mornay. He stopped his horse and looked up and around him, swiveling in the saddle as he studied the layout of the land.

"This could be the place, all right," Rogan told Derwent and Mornay as he looked at the map. "See that ridge over there?"

Derwent Brown squinted, following where he pointed. Mornay, too, looked off, puffing on his pipe.

"Shall I ride back and tell 'em to break camp?" Derwent asked.

"Let's have a closer inspection first," Rogan said, folding the map and tucking it inside his shirt.

Mornay nodded sagely as they rode forward.

Months had passed since Rogan and the others first arrived with the pioneers in Rhodes's company to form the British colony. The pioneers had spent long days building farm huts and tilling the land so they could plant crops. Some had brought along chickens and pigs, and cattle and oxen roamed the cleared land.

"The more I compare Henry's checkpoints with the area before us, the less I'm convinced we're here, Mornay."

Mornay nodded gravely. His silver-bearded chin seemed to bristle, and his inky brows pulled low over his eyes. "You could be right, monsieur, The area traversed by my father and your uncle Henry. This might not be the land of the map."

Rogan looked at the hills and rock formations again, still unsettled, despite what seemed to be ample evidence. Despite Mornay's knowledge of geography and his own of geology, Rogan still had questions. He removed the piece of quartz from his pocket that he'd taken from the ridge in question yesterday and compared it with the quartz rock Henry had left him. Rogan's studies at the geology school in London convinced him of the promise of gold in this ridge. But one thing troubled him: *the symbols Henry placed on the map of the bird, the lion, and the baobab tree. What could he have meant?* Rogan had looked the area over for weeks now and could see nothing that resembled the symbols. He also noticed that the two quartz rocks were different. Was there more to Henry's map that he had yet to discover in the months ahead?

Back at camp he would discuss his find with the newest man on this enterprise, a geologist he'd hired named Clive Shepherd. The man had ridden in a few weeks earlier on a private trek following the Pioneer Column.

Rogan continued to ponder the ridge that rose before him. He turned in his saddle and with narrowed gaze studied the land, as he had been doing for days. His mouth hardened beneath his dark ribbon mustache. He patted his pocket where he had returned the piece of jagged quartz he'd taken from farther up the ridge.

"We'll have a talk with Shepherd to see if he backs us up. There's no geologist I trust more than him. Let's go back to camp," he said briskly.

Rogan now had some fifteen Shona working for him in a land where the Matabele warriors frowned upon the white man's incursion. He'd learned it was useful to use Africans from other tribes as workers and guards, for many of the tribes looked upon one another as the greater enemy. Several African kings had signed treaties with the British government to protect their land from Africans and Boers alike.

That night at their base camp, Rogan, Derwent, Mornay, and Clive Shepherd sat around the fire, discussing the prospects of the site.

Shepherd was shrewd on the subject of mineral discoveries due to his broad experience in the field. A regular bloodhound when it came to sniffing out gold deposits, he was even said to be "canny." Such men appeared to gravitate to other men like Rhodes and Sir Julien Bley, but Clive Shepherd had wanted to work for Rogan.

While a student at the geological school in London, Rogan had noticed several of Clive Shepherd's treatises on gold, emeralds, and diamonds. It had seemed a stroke of luck when two months ago Clive had ridden into Fort Salisbury with a new group of pioneers, some fifty in number. Peter had introduced him to Rogan one night at supper.

Rogan reached into his pocket and removed the piece of quartz he'd chipped from the ridge. He looked across the campfire at Shepherd.

"What do you think, Clive?"

Shepherd caught the rock Rogan tossed him.

"This looks very promising."

Rogan wasn't surprised over Clive's conclusions. They confirmed his own findings, but he didn't believe he'd found Henry's deposit.

"This outcrop might run for miles. It could go very deep," Rogan stated intently.

Shepherd, a tall, gangling man with a high forehead and a jutting chin, blew smoke rings into the darkness.

"I'm a cautious fellow, Chantry, but I think you've got something here."

Mornay squatted on his haunches before the fire, his white hair gleaming. "Yes, do not forget, *mon ami,* how the BSA holds a large portion of whatever is discovered."

Rogan did not like to think of that, but Mornay was right. Rogan put down his empty cup and stood. He thought of Evy and the Black Diamond. He knew a great deal more about the van Burens now that he had visited Dr. Jakob van Buren at his medical mission station farther up the Zambezi River. Jakob had told him about Heyden's earlier trip to locate Jendaya and demand that the Zulu woman contact her brother Dumaka to bring the Black Diamond. Dr. Jakob worried that Heyden might be planning to use Evy in some way to get Jendaya to cooperate. "It would be dangerous," Jakob kept telling him, "much too dangerous."

Rogan's thoughts flew back across the sea to Grimston Way, to a girl with green-flecked amber eyes and hair the color of a lion's mane. A woman he should not think about but who filled his memory at night beneath the lonely stars.

"Don't worry," Rogan said abruptly. "We'll all get our share from the Company. The BSA needs us more than we need them. We're all in this together now." The arrangement he had been forced to accept disturbed him, but he had settled into it for lack of any way out. And he wanted the gold, regardless. *But...those symbols on Henry's map.*

"We'd better turn in early," he said. "Come sunrise, I want those prospect holes sunk from here to the hills north of us, along the Zambezi."

Next morning, when the dawn painted a crimson sky, a rider on horseback from Fort Salisbury entered the camp. It was Captain Retford, Peter's military assistant.

"A letter for you, sir. Mr. Bartley thought it might be important."

Rogan took the envelope and saw that it was from Capetown, sent by Lady Camilla Brewster.

Rogan frowned. Why would Anthony's wife be writing to him?

He opened the letter and read:

Dear Rogan,

My Christian conscience will not permit me to sleep well without alerting you to two important facts that affect your future happiness and Evy van Buren's. Evy has had a dreadful accident. Anthony has sent a wire to Sir Julien, telling him about Evy's fall. It seems she tripped down the attic steps at her cottage. She's been in the hospital for a month and is in a slow recovery. There is a fear she will never walk again without crutches.

Rogan's heart stopped. *Evy.* He read on:

The second important fact is crucial to both of you. Evy is not the daughter of Henry Chantry. She is Anthony's by Katie van Buren. Of course, sadly, Evy has not been told this news. I realize Julien has lied to you, insisting Henry is her father. He has done this because it is his aim to keep you separated from her on account of the diamonds and her inheritance through Katie. But I have long believed you cared for her. Now I have told you the truth. What you do with it is your decision. I wish you well.

> *Yours truly,*
> *Lady Camilla Montieth Brewster*
> *Cape House*
> *Capetown, South Africa*

Rogan was still standing there in the warm wind when Derwent came up beside him. The paper scuffled in the wind.

"Bad news, Mr. Rogan?"

Rogan looked at him, hearing Derwent's worry. He set his mouth in a confident smile.

"Both bad and good, Derwent. I must drop everything and return to England immediately."

Derwent looked at him, stunned.

"I'm turning matters here over to you, Shepherd, and Mornay."

"Not a funeral, Mr. Rogan?" Derwent asked anxiously.

Rogan folded the letter and put it back into his leather pocket. "Not if I can help it, Derwent. Rather, a wedding."

Derwent looked after him as Rogan strode off to find Mornay and Shepherd. Derwent scratched his angular nose. Now what could that mean?

CHAPTER TWENTY-THREE

London
Chantry Townhouse

When Mrs. Croft handed Evy a letter just delivered and postmarked Grimston Way, the incident on the attic stairs, never far from Evy's mind even here in the rich surroundings of the townhouse, came to a head.

"From those Hooper twins and Wally. They must be wondering when you're coming back. Miss their piano lessons, is my guess."

Evy opened the envelope and took out the small sheet of paper. Neatly printed at the top in Beth's hand read: "Hooper Detective Agency." While their title brought Evy a smile, their words did not.

Dear Miss Varley,

We've been waiting for you to come home to Grimston Way so we could talk to you. Wally agrees with us that we'd better write you.

Wally was the first to enter the cottage to find you had fallen down the attic steps. Mrs. Croft sent him to check up on you when you didn't show at the church supper. In all the rush afterward, Wally says he forgot to mention something that we think you should know about. We want to talk to you about it soon as you come back to the village.

Mary and Beth Hooper, detectives,
and Wally, our helper

Evy didn't realize she was standing there staring at the letter in silence until Mrs. Croft addressed her.

"Is it bad news, Miss Evy?"

"Hmm? Oh. No, Mrs. Croft… It's interesting, is all…actually, quite interesting." *What did Wally know?*

Mrs. Croft looked dubious. "Those Hooper twins are double trouble, if you ask me. And that Wally is always poking about where he shouldn't."

Evy made up her mind quickly. "Mrs. Croft, there's something I haven't told anyone about the afternoon of the storm when I returned to the cottage."

Mrs. Croft's tufted grayish brows waggled. "Oh? Something worrisome, then, is it, child? If that be the case, then maybe I should set out some tea first."

No matter the situation, be it lighthearted or serious, Mrs. Croft trusted in steaming black tea with a splash of milk to add the calming touch that hastened wisdom.

A few minutes later Evy joined her in the warm, fragrant kitchen, where the smell of cinnamon wafted temptingly on the air. Simms, the butler, had gone out with his daughter to do the shopping, and Evy and Mrs. Croft were comfortably alone.

Evy sat at the table watching Mrs. Croft pour tea and stack the buttery cinnamon cakes on a pink rosebud platter. It was very much like old times, except Evy was grown and Mrs. Croft had more gray in her neat bun at the back of her head. But Evy's spirits were, nonetheless, in need of as much uncritical acceptance and motherly advice as ever. Actually, it was surprising how little had changed across the years, and yet how shockingly different the circumstances were.

"I'm going to tell you the truth, and if you don't believe me, I don't know who will."

"Now, of course I'm going to believe you. Why wouldn't I?"

"Because what I'm going to tell you is frightening and sounds daft at the same time. I trust you know me well enough, Mrs. Croft, to understand I'm not daft."

Mrs. Croft made a throaty sound and poured Evy's tea, then her own. "You have my full attention."

"Though this is very distressing, Mrs. Croft, I need to share with you that I did not accidentally fall down the attic steps. Someone *pushed* me—deliberately. There's no doubt in my mind; it was deliberate." Evy lifted her chin, trying to show calm resolve. "Someone hoped that that shove backward would leave me not merely injured…but dead."

Mrs. Croft gaped at her, then her cup rattled on the saucer as she lowered both to the large kitchen table. She released a deep breath.

"Child, you *do* know what you're saying?"

"Yes, I know what I'm saying. I lived through it as surely as we're sitting here now."

Again Mrs. Croft stared at her, her brows wrinkling and her head shaking as she struggled with Evy's bold disclosure of what had really taken place that horrible night.

"I know what you must think," Evy said quietly, "but I assure you I'm quite sane."

"I don't doubt it a minute. You've always had a sensible head on your shoulders, not like that frivolous Miss Arcilla. Now if she were telling me this, I'd throw it all out the window with the mop water. But still, Miss Evy, you're positively sure?"

Evy tasted her tea. Somehow nothing tasted as it used to, not even the warm crumpets.

"Quite sure. Someone was in the attic, but I thought maybe it was just my imagination because of the storm. And like a fool, I thought I'd prove my courage to myself by going up there to confront whatever it was. But when I reached the top"—her cup shook a little, and she lowered it quickly and leaned toward Mrs. Croft, who hung on every word—"the door flew open, and some *thing*, some *person* rushed at me like a giant bat. Before I could think or even react, strong hands shoved me backward down those steps." Evy's voice dropped breathlessly. "It was horrid," she murmured, staring at the tea in her cup. Then her gaze rose toward her crutches leaning against the kitchen wall within reach. "I don't remember anything after that. Not even the week you said I spent in my old room at Rookswood. I remember waking several times in the London hospital, then everything seems hazy, until Lord Brewster stood at my bedside."

Mrs. Croft's wan and distressed face twitched with some inner turmoil. "Oh my, oh my... This is much worse than I thought, than I dared to think. Child, you are *sure* you didn't have nightmares after the fall, so as to make you think it happened like that?"

Evy shook her head firmly. She lifted her cup and drank the sweet, milky tea. "No. It happened just as I've told you. Just as sure as those crutches are leaning there. The result of being shoved down the steps. It's all very real...and terrible."

Mrs. Croft appeared to accept that, though struggling, perhaps not so much from disbelief, as from horror that it could be so.

"And you don't know who it was?"

"No. Some kind of dark cloak hid the person's head and shoulders. Why, I can't say."

Mrs. Croft shuddered noticeably. "If that be so," she murmured, "then it could mean the person expected to be recognized without some kind of disguise."

"That's what makes this all so horrid."

"My dear, why didn't you let anyone know sooner?"

"Oh, Mrs. Croft, I didn't know if anyone would believe me," Evy said, looking down at her teacup.

"We need to bring in the police, Miss Evy, and let them know so they can begin an investigation."

"No, we can't, not yet. There's no proof. You know as well as I they wouldn't believe me. The first thing they'd say was that I was ill and hallucinating, or something of that insipid nature. 'Suffering from a bump on the head, the poor dear.' Oh no, I haven't said anything, and I won't. Not until I can prove it."

"That's playing with fire, child. Anyone that violent wouldn't wait to strike again if they thought—" The normal pink of Mrs. Croft's cheeks gave way to a sickly pallor.

Evy nodded. "Exactly so, If they thought I remembered. And that's why I haven't said a word to anyone except you."

Mrs. Croft laid her elbow on the table, a palm to her cheek, and shook her head in dismay. "Yes, we don't know whom we can trust." She looked up quickly. "Blessed be the day. I'm thankful you're here instead of in that dreadful cottage all alone. We've got to do something to protect you, child. We can't go on taking chances as though it didn't happen."

"No, Mrs. Croft, I don't think someone was waiting to deliberately kill me. But I do think I'm being watched to see if I'm suspicious of anyone in particular."

"Well, sure now, but—"

"True, that seems normal. Friends and acquaintances calling to wish me well. But I can't be totally sure of any of them, either."

"But if someone was waiting for you to come up those steps, then it was deliberate," Mrs. Croft said as she nervously twisted her napkin in her hands.

"I think I surprised whoever was up there. I should have been at the Allhallows Eve Supper, so I wasn't expected home."

"I see what you're getting at. Yes, that's for sure. The supper, I'd forgotten that." She frowned and picked up her cup. "Then someone knew enough about your schedule—for that matter, everyone's schedule—for the evening."

"Yes. And I interrupted someone's plan by coming back unexpectedly. The storm was so noisy by that time that whoever it was didn't hear me come through the front gate and up to the door. And that's probably why the gate was unlatched. Someone had been in a hurry and didn't bother to latch it. The window in the parlor was open—that's probably the entry that was used, because the front door was locked.

"When I came inside, I changed out of my wet clothes and made tea before I heard footsteps in the attic. And whoever it was also didn't hear me until I started up the steps—at least that's what I think now." Evy quickly finished her tea and poured more, her hands shaking a little. She was determined not to panic.

"Until I do think things through carefully," she said, "it's wise to behave as though I don't remember a thing."

Mrs. Croft answered with a moaning sound and a shake of her head.

"It had to be a thief."

Evy dismissed the hopeful emphasis in her voice, but Mrs. Croft persisted.

"It's that no-account newcomer, Jeffords, I'll wager. That man's naught but a thief. I told the vicar so from the beginning, but he's bent on keepin' him around the rectory as a gardener, Trying to help him. Doesn't have all his mind, the vicar keeps saying. So all the more's the reason to be rid of him. Why, Jeffords was caught red-handed snooping 'round Miss Armitage's cottage just weeks before Allhallows. She chased him away with her broom."

Evy could see Mrs. Croft was still shocked by what she'd told her and didn't want to believe the worst. It was more comfortable for her to believe something less sinister. Evy didn't fault her for that. At least Evy had finally told someone about what had really happened after all these months.

"We ought to write Vicar Osgood about this," Mrs. Croft continued. "If it was Jeffords, the Yard ought to question him on where he was that afternoon. He wasn't at that supper, to be sure."

Evy looked at her with alert interest.

"Yes, everyone was at the supper. Of course!"

"But Jeffords wasn't, is what I'm saying, child."

"I see what you're saying, but it wasn't Jeffords."

"Now, how can you go saying so?" Mrs. Croft looked perturbed. Obviously she *wanted* it to be Jeffords.

"Because he has the best possible witness. Me." Evy turned her lips into a rueful smile. "I saw him wandering the village green on my way to the cottage. There was no way he could have gotten there before me. Besides, the vicar is right, Mrs. Croft. Poor Jeffords is harmless and in need of mercy. I even have my doubts that he was out for mischief when old lady Arm—I mean when Miss Armitage ran him off with her broom."

"Well, if that's so, then that's that."

Yes, that was indeed the end of that, but not the end of her interest in what Mrs. Croft had said earlier. "You say everyone else was at the church supper?" Evy asked.

"Well, most everyone, it seems. I didn't exactly nose count, if you know what I mean. I was so busy helping to ladle the soup. But most, I'd say, were there."

Evy looked at her intently.

Mrs. Croft squinted thoughtfully. "I'll try. Let's see, now. I remember Vicar Osgood and Missus Martha, the Tisdales, the Stewarts. Even Wally's father was there with the boy. The Hoopers was there, so was the Tuckers, the—"

She went on reading off her alphabet of familiar, trusted village names, people Evy had known all her life and had affection for.

Mrs. Croft sighed and drew up her shoulders. "Only ones who wasn't there was the squire and Lady Elosia. That is, Sir Lyle came in late, but Lady Elosia didn't come at all on account of the sudden storm. And Sir Lyle wouldn't have no interest in snooping about your attic. And Lord Anthony Brewster, he was still here in London until, as you said, he called at the hospital, due to that telegraph from Sir Julien Bley."

Evy nodded thoughtfully. "Well, it is all quite silly and bizarre at the same time." But someone had been in her attic.

"Just for the sake of eliminating folks, seems to me the squire's a mite moldy when it comes to some things, like Lizzie says. He locks himself in his library and studies till all hours of the night, even needs to be rung twice by the dinner bell to get him to come to supper. But he's a gentleman, that one. Not much like that scoundrel son of his, Master Rogan. Seems wicked to even suggest the squire would do such a thing."

Evy agreed. Sir Lyle Chantry was rather elegant and certainly not violent.

"And Lady Elosia—well, she can't get around much faster than me. Doubt if she could even climb them steep steps without huffing and puffing."

Yes, of course, quite ridiculous to even consider Lady Elosia Chantry.

But whoever it was had been afraid of being recognized, enough to cover his or her face with a blanket. And whoever it was had—and still did have—a desire to kill if cornered.

Evy shuddered.

"I still think we should talk to the police."

Evy shook her head firmly. "Don't you see? They'll attribute what I'm saying to some deep depression I'm suffering over my injury. And suppose they spoke with Vicar Osgood. He'd have to tell them how depressed I was when he and Martha visited, and that's all it would take."

Mrs. Croft used her thumb to smooth the frown from between her brows, as though her head ached. "Much as I hate saying it, I think you're probably right. A young woman losing her ability to get around the way she used to, and then a lot of time's passed too. They'd be wanting to know why you just now told them."

"Exactly, Mrs. Croft. That's just what they'd ask."

"Then what do we do, child?"

Evy shivered when she heard the fear in Mrs. Croft's voice. She reached quickly across the table and took her hand, so rough and callussed. "We take the initiative. We won't panic. We're going to Grimston Way."

"Good grief, girl! You be out of your mind?"

Evy smiled crookedly. She leaned back and held up the letter from the Hooper twins. "Maybe. But listen to this."

She read the twins' little letter, and Mrs. Croft fidgeted uneasily as she listened.

"What do you think Wally could've found?"

"I've no clue at all. But I'm going to find out soon."

"If you think you're going back—"

"I've got to, to learn what really happened. Take courage, Mrs. Croft. Was there *anything* unusual about Wally when he returned to the supper at the parish hall? Did he have anything in hand, or say anything to you that you might have ignored at the time, thinking it didn't matter?"

Mrs. Croft sat scowling to herself. "No, nary a thing that I can recall now. Wally was out of breath and upset terrible like. By the time I got up the road to the cottage and into the pantry, Dr. Tisdale was there and so was the squire. They was already moving you to your room. I don't recall a thing more." Her suspicious scowl only deepened the lines in her face. "So I wonder what he and the twins have in their minds?"

Evy tucked the letter away into her skirt pocket, reached for her crutches, and stood from the chair. She squared her shoulders beneath her neat white blouse with high, lacy collar and bodice.

"I don't know. But I'm sure it has to do with what happened that night. And I need to know why they wrote me this letter."

"Evy, don't you go meddling in anything that could kindle more risk for you. There's such a thing as walking too close to the fire."

Evy drew her mouth into a tight smile. She was determined now, perhaps more than at any time since her fall.

"I need to go to Grimston Way, regardless. There're the trunks from Uncle Edmund and Aunt Grace, and his parson's desk. I won't part with those. I'll need to have them moved to storage, or even here to London. Lord Brewster told me the owners of the cottage have decided not to let it out to strangers again—meaning me. So everything I still have there must be moved."

Mrs. Croft stood, looking unhappy but also determined.

"Well, if that's the way of it, then I'm going with you. I'm not letting you out of my sight for a second. I've as good of an excuse as any. Lizzie's been after me for weeks now to come see her and the family. And I'll get some of the family boys to move those things from the attic."

"I think Vicar Osgood will be kind enough to let me store them at the rectory. There was always plenty of room there. That will give me a good reason to be at Grimston Way without arousing undue curiosity. A little meeting with the twins and Wally should be easy to arrange."

"I just hope this isn't one of their foolhardy whims, child. They've all three got themselves as big an imagination as Miss Armitage, with the strings of garlic she hangs out to keep vampires away."

Somehow Evy believed there would be more to her meeting with the youngsters than superstitious games. She would find out soon enough. First thing in the morning, she was going to make arrangements for a train ride to Grimston Way.

Chapter Twenty-Four

A sudden summer storm drenched the dark London streets. Gas lamps swayed in the rain-laden wind, casting their flickering glow precariously over the walkways. At Chantry Townhouse the wind tugged at flowering vines and small trees, threatening to uproot them.

Evy was in the parlor reading when, during a lull in the storm, she heard the front gate swing open and shut. She put her book on the table beside her chair and glanced at the clock on the fireplace mantel...a little before nine o'clock. The sure but hurried tread of footsteps sounded upon the walk and up the porch to the front door. She held her breath. A moment later someone grasped the solid brass knocker and rapped several times.

Who would come calling at this hour, and in such inclement weather? She rose with the aid of her crutches and moved to the hallway that led to the front of the house.

Simms the butler was already in the entrance, sliding back the heavy bolt on the front door.

A gust of wind invaded the hallway, stirring the yellow summer skirt around Evy's ankles, filling the hall with a muggy dampness and the smell of rain.

A man in a heavy black coat with a hat pulled low over his brow stood on the threshold. He carried no umbrella, alerting Evy that he was not English. He removed his dripping slicker and left it on the porch. He shook out his hat, handing it over to Simms.

Evy broke into a smile when she recognized the unexpected caller. "Heyden van Buren."

His South African tan had turned his fair hair into a halo, and his light blue eyes stared at her, transfixed. His gaze dropped reluctantly to her crutches. The line around his mouth tightened. He came toward her with both hands extended almost in apology. His manner caused her to stiffen, and heat rose in her cheeks.

"Cousin Evy *van Buren,* my dear. How are you?"

Evy forced herself not to flush upon hearing her mother's name spoken to her for the first time, though she had thought it a hundred times since learning the truth.

He took her hands into his and squeezed them reassuringly, looking down at her gravely. "I came as soon as I learned what happened to you."

"Do come into the parlor, Heyden. What a surprise. A pleasant one, I should say."

"I'm happy you think so."

"Simms? If Trudy is still up," she said of his niece, "would you ask her to bring tea for Mr. van Buren?"

"Yes, at once, Miss."

"I wondered if I would ever see you again," Evy told Heyden while feeling his stricken gaze. She held her head and shoulders straight as she labored on her crutches into the parlor with what dignity she could muster.

He followed as Evy went to the chair by the window and sat down, casually leaning her crutches within reach.

Heyden stood in the middle of the parlor. "I was wondering myself. It's been over two years, hasn't it?"

She sat looking at him in the brighter light from the lamps. He was as she remembered, of medium height, in his early thirties, and he appeared somewhat more muscular than she recalled.

"What have you been doing with yourself these years?"

"Oh, one thing and another. Do you mind?" He had taken out a silver cigarette case, and it glinted in the light from the lamplights on the wall. She shook her head, and he struck a match. "I visited a cousin of ours in the Zambezi region of South Africa for a few months last year."

"Another cousin?" she asked, interested.

"Yes. Jakob van Buren. I shall tell you about him later. When I left Jakob, I made my way back to the Boer Republic. I'm here on political business for our President Kruger. I only just arrived on Monday."

As a Boer, Heyden firmly opposed British expansion in South Africa and their policies with the African tribes.

"The British government simply refuses to understand that the two Boer Republics will not surrender our sovereign rights to their queen."

She was not surprised by his dislike of the queen's government. She remembered how coldly Heyden was received by the Chantry family on his first visit to Rookswood Estate, especially by Rogan.

But there were other reasons the family disliked Heyden, personal reasons that reached out to affect Evy. She recalled that Rogan had actually paid Heyden to leave England and stay far away from her. Yet here he was, just a few years later, as bold in behavior as though he belonged to the Chantry family.

Evy could hardly contain her curiosity as their conversation paused upon Trudy's entrance with a tray of tea.

He glanced at Trudy, then sat down in the chair opposite Evy. "I was at the Parliament building this afternoon, and lo and behold, I was surprised to run into Lord Brewster. He told me about your unfortunate accident, and it became even more important that I come straightaway to see you. You're the other reason I've come to England, Cousin."

She concealed her surprise.

A little while later, they enjoyed tea as rain lashed the windowpane. Evy restrained herself from asking the barrage of questions that burst upon her mind while Heyden explained the reason for his visit.

"I'd not have called you a van Buren if there'd been any chance you still didn't know that you're Katie's daughter. When I found out you knew the truth about your mother, I had to come and see you again."

"You knew Katie van Buren was my real mother even when we spoke years ago." She kept any accusation from her voice.

He was unsmiling now, and his wintry gaze bore a sadness. "Yes, dear, I did. When we met at the museum at the diamond showing, I realized you mistakenly believed Dr. and Mrs. Junia Varley were your parents. I couldn't burden you with such a formidable pronouncement then and there. It would've been rude. I thought I would explain what I knew when we were to meet at Regent's Park, but—" He set his empty cup down. His mouth formed a hard line. "Rogan Chantry threatened me. He had his own reasons for wanting to keep you in the dark about your mother's identity. At the time I just didn't know what his plans were, or I would have never permitted him to use me the way he did."

His words were confusing, raising unwelcome doubts. "What do you mean, he had his own reasons? That he used you?"

"For wealth—money," he stated. "I'm sorry to be blunt, but it's time the truth came out, Evy."

Evy felt the muscles in her jaw tighten. "Yes, he paid you several hundred pounds to keep silent and go back to the Cape."

He pushed back his chair and stood looking down at her, his wintry eyes like marble. "Are you mad, Cousin? Is that what he told you?" His anger was followed by a glimmer of obvious disdain. "And you believed him?"

She disliked the way he had managed to put her on the defensive. "I hardly knew you, Heyden. I still don't know you well. But I have known Rogan from the time we were in school."

He blinked and slowly sat down again. "Yes, yes, of course."

"Rogan told me he gave you money before he left two years ago."

The subject appeared to put Heyden under strain.

"If that's what he told you, he lied to you. I left of my own accord to voyage back to the Cape with the Kruger delegation. Why he'd say such a demeaning thing is unclear to me, but I'll find out when I return."

"Heyden—"

He would not be restrained and stood, ramming his hands into his pockets, displaying his fury. Her smoldering doubts about Rogan were more easily fanned into flames of late, since he had failed to write her as he had promised. *Why would Rogan have misled me?* she thought as more doubts assailed her.

She decided that whatever the reason, it hardly mattered now. Rogan apparently had no further interest in her except for getting back the money he had loaned her to start her music school. Satisfaction washed over her. At least now, as an heiress, she could pay him back promptly and relieve herself of the debt and sense of obligation she carried. She promised herself she would do just that and ask Mr. Harris, the Chantry family lawyer, to reimburse Rogan at once.

"The reason he'd say that no longer matters to me," she told Heyden. "I shall never see Rogan Chantry again. Nor do I wish to."

His eyes flickered with interest at her comment, but he didn't ask why. "Allow me to disagree, Cousin Evy, about the reason no longer mattering. It does to me. And it will to you once you know what's been going on in Capetown these last few years."

What could be going on? she wondered.

"The reason for his blatant dishonesty is clear to me now." Heyden stood glaring into the flames at the hearth, then he looked at her sharply. "He hoped you wouldn't try to contact me in South Africa, and I wasn't wise enough to see it. I would have contacted you if I had known Grace Havering had recently told you who your mother was. I only found out from Sir Julien Bley just before I sailed from Capetown."

"You'd better explain," she said, folding her hands in her lap.

He faced her, looking stern.

"That's why I've come. It's important you understand the dislike Rogan and Sir Julien Bley have for me. They're both cut from the same piece of cloth, though neither trusts the other. They are, however, both loyal to the British throne. They're doing everything in their power to cooperate with Cecil Rhodes and his 'gold and diamond bugs' to provoke our president of the Boer Republics to war. They want the Transvaal so the English can control the wealth on The Rand. Since Rogan knows I'm loyal to our president, Paul Kruger, ruining my honor is in keeping with his self-seeking ambitions."

"All I want is the truth about Katie—and the Kimberly Black Diamond. I even wrote Sir Julien Bley a year ago—before my accident—but he didn't answer. I wrote Lady Camilla as well. She'd shown some rather strange interest in me when she came to stay at Rookswood years ago, but neither did she answer my inquiries."

"It's no wonder you haven't heard from Camilla," Heyden explained. "She's ill, but Sir Julien could have answered. I'm not surprised by his silence, though. He's always known you were a van Buren and deliberately hid the fact to keep you from inheriting a good deal in diamond shares through Katie."

"I know that now. In fact, Lord Brewster has taken care of all that at Sir Julien's wishes."

He looked at her. "Has he? And none too soon. He's been fair, I hope?"

She merely looked at him, unwilling to reveal her personal affairs to him until she knew and trusted him far more than she did now.

"The van Burens have been robbed of what rightfully belongs to us all," he said. "Sir Julien cheated us. All the van Burens have a right to diamond shares through Carl, your grandfather.

"Lord Brewster insists the van Burens sold out to Sir Julien after Grandfather Carl was killed in the mine explosion. All, that is, except what he left to Katie. Julien will say what suits him if it serves his purpose. If anything, he and the others in the diamond company stole Carl's rights and managed to hide it…"

Evy wondered if it was true. She had no liking for Sir Julien. "It is obvious he kept me from knowing the truth all these years." When she looked back to the financial struggles she and Aunt Grace endured through the years after Uncle Edmund's death, it was clear Sir Julien had deprived her.

"There is still the matter of the Black Diamond, isn't there? With your mother yet blamed for its disappearance."

"Katie didn't steal it. Not even Rogan thinks so. He said so before he left."

"Did he?" Heyden looked thoughtful. "That doesn't surprise me either. I told you the last time I saw you in London that I'd been looking into its disappearance, as I have for years. Even as a boy, I'd heard about its theft from members of the van Buren family. Inga was Katie's maid at Cape House, and she was even present when you were born. She helped Katie escape, knew about her plans, and helped her contact Henry Chantry when he was in Capetown to see Sir Julien." Heyden walked over to her. "Well, Inga was a van Buren.

"Even Katie didn't know Inga was related. Inga kept it a secret because she feared Julien didn't want a possible heir caring for Katie after your grandfather Carl was killed in the mine. Inga was Carl's cousin. And I am Inga's son," he finished quietly.

She studied his face for clues. Did he think this was important to her? Evy knew little about Inga's relationship with Katie during the time her mother had managed to escape from Sir Julien's house on the night the diamond was stolen, so she accepted the news mildly that Heyden was Inga's son.

"Inga told me about that night Katie ran away with Henry Chantry," Heyden went on. He looked at her. "Inga left Katie's bedroom door unlocked when Sir Julien demanded it be locked from the outside."

Evy leaned forward. "Julien locked my mother indoors?"

"Inga told me that Julien suspected Katie would run off and try to find you."

Evy felt indignant, yet grieved, too, for what her mother had suffered.

"Inga learned where you were and told Katie."

"Was it Inga who told you about Jendaya?"

"Yes, my mother had smuggled a message to Henry Chantry that Katie wanted to meet him at the stables that night."

Evy had heard before about the Christian Zulu woman Jendaya who had rescued her during the attack at Rorke's Drift, but each time she heard the story, it seemed new and warmed her heart. She wished she could meet Jendaya to thank her and also to hear from her own lips all that had transpired.

"You told me in London two years ago you'd met Jendaya," she reminded him.

"I did. I found her in Zululand. By then the war with Cetshwayo was over. Zululand had become a British protectorate, so it was safe to go there. Katie didn't bring the Black Diamond to Rorke's Drift, and Henry didn't have it when he was at Rookswood. I think Jendaya knows more than she's willing to tell me. She's quite old now. She was living at Jakob's mission station on the Zambezi River. I spoke to her again and was close to getting more information, but the next day she left the station without letting me know. She can't be trusted."

"Jendaya? But—"

He shrugged off the incredulity in her voice. "My dear cousin, I know these tribal savages. Their character is such that it's questionable whether the missionaries should even attempt to convert them."

"I can hardly believe my ears! Not bring the knowledge of Christ's forgiveness to the Africans? Why, it's repulsive to even say such a thing."

"You'll get on well with Cousin Jakob. He feels as strongly as you do."

"A great many of us feel this way. Who wouldn't wish to bring light into darkness?"

Heyden shook his golden head. "Never mind about that. I'm sorry I mentioned it. But getting back to Jendaya, I'm certain she knows more about the Black Diamond than she'll tell me. It has something to do with the Zulu and her brother, Dumaka. He was an induna among his Zulu people before the Zulu war."

He turned to her. "Evy, if she'll tell anyone where the diamond is, it's you. Think of what this would mean. You'll clear Katie's name for good, and you can meet Jakob van Buren, a man you would warm to. He's everything you'd approve of, and very zealous about his mission.

He works with some of the lepers at his private medical mission. Not only that, but I've told him about you, and he longs to meet Katie's daughter."

He suddenly caught up her hand, his wintry blue eyes warming. "Evy, will you come with me back to South Africa to meet Cousin Jakob? And talk to Jendaya? Everything depends on your cooperation. And there are other van Burens, too. My family lives in the Transvaal. They're farmers and they want to meet you."

Evy's heart began to beat faster. She had *family*, and one of them was Dr. Jakob, a medical missionary? Her heart seemed to take wings. *I must see Jakob…and Jendaya.*

"When I last spoke with Jendaya, she told me Rogan Chantry came to see her and that he wanted the Black Diamond."

Her breath paused. "Rogan—he was at Jakob's mission station?"

"Yes. So now you should know why he hasn't been in touch with you all this time. There's little else on his mind but the gold discovery on Henry Chantry's old map and the missing Black Diamond. He'll do anything it takes to get it from her. He's not told Sir Julien, but that doesn't surprise me. He has his base camp near Fort Salisbury now. He certainly doesn't need the diamond. It's just greed on his part. They say he's already struck gold and intends to lay claim to even more on the Zambezi River."

So Rogan wanted the Black Diamond too! And that was the reason he hadn't contacted her? She looked across the parlor at Heyden. "How did Rogan learn Jendaya may know where it is?"

"The same way I did, asking questions, putting two and two together. He was after the Black Diamond when I first arrived at Rookswood to see him. Why do you think he threatened me? Wanted me gone from London? At that time we both mistakenly believed the diamond could be hidden in Rookswood. He pretended it was only the map that interested him. But there again, he lied. He's after Jendaya now. He'll force her to tell him where it is. She's an old woman now and wouldn't be able to put up much resistance."

Evy felt the tension in her face. "Has Jendaya told any of this to Sir Julien, or Jakob at the mission station?"

"No. She refuses to talk. She's afraid. But when I told her about you, Cousin Evy, it seemed as if new life entered her old body. 'I must see Miss Katie's daughter,' she told me. She repeated this to me several times until she persuaded me to bring you to South Africa to see her before she dies."

Heyden took both her hands into his. His earnest gaze searched hers. "Say you'll come, Evy. Come to the Boer Republic to meet some of Katie's relatives. As I said, Jakob also has a longing to meet you. He's a good man. You'll like him. He's like an uncle. And there's Inga, my mother. She can tell you all sorts of stories about Katie, and there's Inga's granddaughter, Katrina. They'd more than welcome you to Katie's old home."

Evy was overwhelmed by all this news of relatives longing to meet her. "I was never told any of this."

"Both Rogan and Sir Julien knew of us in the Transvaal all along, but they've deliberately kept you away. Now Rogan wants to get the Black Diamond for his own selfish plans, which also include Lady Patricia Bancroft. I'm afraid, Evy, you've been played for little but a pawn. We both have."

Her back stiffened at the thought of being used. New thoughts trampled through her mind that only added to her anger.

"Rogan knows Katie and Henry didn't have the diamond when they left Cape House that night. He's spoken to Julien about it too. But now it serves his purposes for the old tale about Katie and Henry and the Kimberly diamond to survive, obviously to keep others from finding it. And of course he doesn't want you there talking with Jendaya."

She turned away, her emotions churning.

"It's time you came to South Africa, Cousin Evy. Please say you'll come back with me."

Her hand went to her forehead. "I must think about all this, Heyden. But if what you say is true, I will want to find out for myself. Not just for Katie's reputation, but to discover the truth about my father, too." She looked across the room at him. The lamplight cast dancing shadows on the wall behind him.

"Do you know who my father was?"

He was very still, watching her thoughtfully. The troubled frown slowly vanished from his brow. His face was smooth and blank.

"Jakob can tell you for sure. And that's another reason for you to come to South Africa."

"If Jakob thinks he knows, then it's likely he also told you."

He walked over to her. "Yes. He said it was Henry Chantry."

She stared at him a long moment while everything she had dreamed about and prayed for suddenly turned into ashes. It seemed as though the storm crooning around the house swept those ashes to the four winds.

"Then...I am a Chantry?"

He nodded in silence.

She gripped the sides of the chair. "I see..."

"Cousin Evy, I fear my words have affected you. I'm deeply sorry for that. You must still care for Rogan Chantry."

She blinked rapidly, keeping back the stinging tears. She said quickly, firmly, "No—not any longer. It's over now."

He nodded gravely. The wind moaned and continued to hurl the rain against the windowpane. A horrid sensation ran over her. That wind, that rain, that silence, and unease—it reminded her of that dreadful afternoon at the cottage in Grimston Way.

An expression of wonder crossed his face. Then he looked away and threw his cigarette into the fireplace. "It was so unfair of Sir Julien not to tell you about Henry all these years," he said angrily. "He knew you were involved with the Chantry children, Rogan included. I suppose that's what we should expect from that sort of ruthless fellow."

Evy calmed her heart. She'd been foolish to react in such a guarded fashion toward Heyden. It was from the memory of the frightening ordeal, of course. Sometimes it came rushing back without warning. She prayed that she would eventually get over it.

She said in a low deliberate voice, "Someone murdered Henry Chantry thinking he had the Black Diamond. That could not have been Rogan. He was a mere boy at the time. Though I've no doubt that he would have wanted it. Someone else those many years ago did it, and whoever it was must be brought to justice."

Heyden folded his hands, fingers intertwined, and brought them to his chin, his eyes fixed upon her as she sat in the wing-backed chair near her crutches.

He nodded slowly. "I'm relieved you think your father was murdered. I feared to add that burden to those I've already placed upon you. Yes, I've always thought someone took Henry's life. I wouldn't be so quick to eliminate anyone, though, if I were you, Cousin."

"What do you mean? Surely you don't think Rogan—?"

He drew in a deep breath, let his hands fall to his sides, and shrugged. "It's been known to happen before. A boy who can and does commit a dreadful crime. He was in Rookswood that night. He had opportunity and cause."

Every fiber of her body and spirit resisted his implied accusation.

"No, impossible," she said, shaking her head.

"Not so impossible as you might think. He wanted both the map— and the diamond. Rogan's always been fixated on that map from boyhood, hasn't he?"

She knew that was true, yet she couldn't...wouldn't accept the worst.

"I see this is too much for you. Well, that's understandable. We won't discuss it any further. Except to say that I do think Rogan is capable of doing whatever it takes to accomplish his goals. He's been that way since childhood. And I wouldn't simply discount him."

"That also goes for everyone in the extended family. None of us can be excluded."

"You're right. Anyone old enough at the time could have done it, perhaps even Lord Brewster—or his wife, Lady Camilla. She's a little unbalanced, you know."

She nodded. "So Sir Julien claims."

"Not only Julien. Everyone who knows her says so. She's kept in her room at Cape House most of the time now."

Evy reluctantly recalled what her aunt Grace had said about Camilla's delicate mental balance. Was it possible she'd become unstable only after murdering Henry?

"But what reason would Lady Camilla have?"

Heyden did not flinch. "Didn't anyone ever tell you it was Henry Chantry she wanted to marry, and not Anthony Brewster? Oh yes, after Henry's first wife died of African fever on the Zambezi, Lady Camilla had hoped her father would arrange a marriage with Henry. He had been attentive to her in the past, you see, and she loved him. Again, it was Sir Julien Bley who managed to have Camilla's father give her in marriage to his nephew Anthony Brewster."

Evy was stunned.

"So you see, it could be any of the Chantrys, Bleys, or Brewsters."

"You're excluding the van Burens," she said quietly, calmly meeting his eyes.

He smiled wryly. "Yes, although we'd have less opportunity. None of the van Burens were in England when Henry was murdered. And that can be proven."

Thunder rumbled outside. Reminding her again of…*someone in the attic of her cottage…someone in Grimston Way.*

"If you go to see Jendaya, I think the truth will at last be known," Heyden was telling her. "It will be up to you and me to bring the truth to Sir Julien. Naturally, Rogan Chantry will do everything he can to stop you, to stop us both."

She knew her amber eyes must be glittering, and her face felt warm with emotion.

"We're in this together, Cousin Evy. I'll do all in my power to back you up and see you have what is yours by right of birth."

It wasn't her "rights" that Evy wanted to fight for but the truth about Katie and whether her father was Henry Chantry.

Her thoughts of Rogan now brought pain to her heart. The memory of his warm lips on hers had been with her through the long, lonely nights. But if Heyden was right, Rogan was absorbed in pursuing his passions, gold and the Black Diamond. Somehow she was not entirely surprised by this. Had he not always been willful and determined about Henry's map? But he must have kept his secret desire for the Black Diamond hidden.

She thought of South Africa. If only she hadn't injured her spine when she'd fallen. Would her physical limitations even permit such a long and arduous journey?

Heyden had not mentioned her crutches. He had shown discomfort at first seeing her with them. But he had seemed able to dismiss them from his thinking, almost as though denying reality. No doubt he'd done this out of regard for her, to convince her nothing had changed. If that was his intention, she felt grateful. She didn't want anyone's pity. She wanted God's grace and strength upholding her, confirming that He was at work in her life, that her impairment did not make her a candidate to be placed on the shelf as an unused vessel.

He smiled. "You look so much like Katie. I have seen her photograph. Jakob has it. You have her tawny hair, her eyes, her spirit. You will come, won't you? To your people, and to the Transvaal? It will be good to come home to where you belong."

Home? Evy was not able to agree, not yet.

"I can't give you an answer now, Heyden. I need to think this over, to pray before I come to a decision. This is so sudden, and there is much to think about. I'm going to Grimston Way for a few days with Mrs. Croft. After that, I'll let you know my plans."

"Yes, you'll need to think about it. When are you leaving for Grimston Way?"

"Tomorrow."

"You're going back to the cottage where you had the accident?" He frowned. "Do you think you should?"

"I'll be staying with Vicar and Mrs. Osgood."

He nodded his approval. "Then I'll see you in a few days." He handed her a calling card showing his hotel and number.

"I do hope you'll decide to return with me, Cousin Evy."

She smiled as he squeezed her hand.

When Heyden had gone, her smile disappeared. In spite of everything he'd told her, she still remained uncertain about South Africa, about her abilities, and about Heyden.

Late that night she found she was unable to sleep as more unsettled questions tossed in her mind. Since Katie had relatives in the Boer Transvaal, then why had she become the ward of Sir Julien Bley? Why hadn't she been sent to Carl van Buren's relatives instead? And why did Katie not flee with her baby to the van Burens? Because of her love for Henry Chantry?

CHAPTER TWENTY-FIVE

Evy arrived in Grimston Way with Mrs. Croft the next afternoon. "You sure you won't settle in with me and Lizzie?"

"Thank you just the same, Mrs. Croft. I'm planning to stay at the rectory, since Vicar and Mrs. Osgood have already asked me." It would bring back so many memories staying in her old bedroom again.

"I'll be there to fix breakfast. You won't be meeting with the twins till tomorrow, will you? I don't like you going off alone without me, dearie."

"Don't worry, Mrs. Croft, I'll be careful. There's one thing about these crutches—I can't run off easily." She smiled, trying to lighten Mrs. Croft's worries, but the woman had remained somber ever since learning the truth about her fall the night before.

"Well, I won't worry so long as you're with the good vicar and Martha, but promise me you won't go to the cottage alone for your things."

"I promise. Without help I can't do much about the trunks and Uncle Edmund's desk anyway. And believe me, I've no wish to mount those attic steps alone!"

Vicar Osgood had come to meet them in his jingle. After speaking to Evy and telling her that Martha had her room ready, he winked, and turning to Mrs. Croft, he said, "I'm glad you're home again, Mrs. Croft. No one in the village can come close to baking as you do. I'm looking forward to your hot fresh bread with butter while you and Evy are here."

Vicar Osgood drew up at the rectory, and Mrs. Croft went off to the cottage in search of Lizzie. Evy worked her way toward the rectory while the vicar went ahead carrying her two small bags. Evy paused at the gate, looking toward the familiar rectory where she'd grown up. Aunt Grace's crimson roses were in full bloom, nodding their heads in the breeze. A mockingbird went through his medley of songs in the apple tree, and the white ducks quacked and waddled across the yard toward the pond.

Her heart swelled with warm, nostalgic memories. Derwent, with his russet hair and freckles, seemed to come from the trees smiling as ever. She could almost hear Aunt Grace calling her indoors to supper while Edmund studied his Bible at his parson's desk, his spectacles slipping down his small pug nose. If she turned toward Rookswood, she could envision a young Rogan Chantry riding his black horse, handsome and arrogant as ever.

A deep sigh came from Evy, and she was aware of the crutches pressing into her arms, of her fingers tightening on the handle grips. She blinked hard. *Don't be a fool. Why torture yourself like this? Life moves on, so keep going. Jesus has not changed. Depend on His faithfulness, His love, His good plans for you. He hasn't ended your life—nor is it His will for you to surrender and give up.*

She drew in a breath and walked forward, the flowers along the walkway nodding in agreement and sending their sweet fragrance her way. A blue and yellow butterfly gently flitted past her. Bees hummed contentedly at their work. A summer cloud drifted by, and for a few minutes the afternoon sun was masked. A strange sensation ran along the back of her neck. She turned her head to look toward the road where hemlock trees grew tall and shadowed the area. The branches sighed in the wind. A foreboding came with the wind that blew lightly against her face, flipping the brim of her stylish hat.

"Psst!"

Evy turned back to the garden and looked toward the Jacaranda tree, where the hiss seemed to come from.

"Over here, Miss Evy. It's me, Wally," came a whisper.

She could not see him but assumed from the direction of his voice that he was behind some bushes, keeping out of sight.

She glanced farther ahead toward the rectory, but neither the vicar nor Martha had yet appeared. Evy left the pathway and walked toward the bushes, as though enjoying the blooming daisies and periwinkles in their display of white and blue.

"This way, Miss, by the privet hedge...I can't let anyone see me. Someone's been trailing me all week. Got my goose flesh up."

This news alerted her greatest fear. "Are you sure? Who?" she whispered, bending over a yellow rose.

"Can't say. Someone's been watching me for two days now. Whoever it is won't catch me, though."

She hoped Wally's notion was merely his and the twins' detective imagination, but it worried her, nonetheless. This was no game, as her crutches proved.

"Be careful, Wally. Don't take chances. And whatever you and the twins do, don't upset anyone with your snooping."

"Oh, we're careful, all right, don't you worry none. And Hooper Detective Agency ain't snooping, Miss."

He head popped up between some bushes, his straight brown hair ruffling in the breeze beneath a droopy forest green felt hat. He grinned. "Miss, can you meet us at the pond in an hour?"

"Yes," she whispered. "I'll be there, but remember what I said about being careful."

"Sure, Miss Evy. We'll be there too. Say, welcome back, Miss."

Evy heard the vicar calling, and Wally quickly dived back into the bushes.

"Coming, Vicar," she called over her shoulder and walked back to the pathway.

Soon after luncheon when the vicar took his afternoon snooze and Martha was busy at the back of the rectory, Evy was able to slip away from the house and make her way into the familiar garden and down the path to the pond. Thankfully, it was only a ten-minute walk, and she was able to get there without stopping to rest. She was becoming more accustomed to the crutches, and her daily exercises to strengthen her back and spine seemed to be helping. Perhaps one day she would, as Dr. Harris had said, need but one crutch—or only a cane. *Please, Father, let it be so.*

The pond was a pleasant retreat this summer afternoon. The white swan was out gliding on the water, doves were lying in the sun on the warm ground, and sparrows chittered, perched high in the trees overhead.

She walked to the stone bench and set her crutches down, looking around for Wally and the Hooper twins. The pond was a sheltered area, enclosed with hedges and birch and elm trees. The weeping willow fluttered its branches in a swaying dance over the pond. The gray water rippled contentedly below a clear sky.

Evy sat down on the bench and waited, glancing about for some sign of the children. All was silent and peaceful. She had left a few minutes early, so she tried to relax and soak up the sunshine. How nice it was to be back home.

The branches scraped behind her, and she turned her head.

"Psst, it's me again, Miss. Is it all clear?"

"Yes. Are the twins with you?"

"No, their mum kept 'em in for piano lessons. Since you left, Mrs. Tisdale's been giving them their lessons. But it's okay, because they don't know any more than I do. And I'm the one who has the stuff hidden."

A moment later he stood up from the bushes, a tall boy for his fourteen years, with long arms.

"Maybe it would be best if you'd come back here so no one can see us, Miss."

Evy stood and made her way into the cluster of trees and bushes. Wally's eyes glistened and his face was flushed. He gestured to a sack that he had under a bush.

"It's in here, Miss. A dark blanket of some odd sort."

Evy felt a wave of repulsion. Yes, that awful dark thing the intruder had worn for concealment.

"It was this way, Miss…"

Wally told his tale of what had happened that frightful afternoon back in October.

He had left the parish hall at Mrs. Croft's request to go to the cottage to see why Evy hadn't come to the supper.

"By the time I got there, I was soaked. I hammered on the door, but you didn't answer. So knowing as how Mrs. Croft would've sent me back anyway if I'd just gone back to the supper saying you didn't answer the door, I went ahead and tried the knob.

"Well, it was unlocked, and I went inside. I stood there and called to you a couple times, but you didn't answer. First, I thought Mrs. Croft was wrong, that you might've been at the supper, and we just didn't see you. But that didn't make no sense, either. Then I smelt smoke. It came from the kitchen. So I walked there, still calling your name. When I got to the pantry, I saw you lying there at the bottom of them attic steps. I was scared to death, Miss. You looked dead to me. It was a week or two later I got to thinking about how things were. And it seemed a bit strange to me. So I talked it over with the Hooper twins, and they thought the same thing."

He swallowed, and Evy asked, keeping her voice calm, "What did you think was strange, Wally?"

He took a step closer, lowering his voice even more, and glanced around the trees and bushes as if someone was following him.

"Well, it was the lamp you had, Miss. The one you must've brought with you up them attic steps."

"Yes, I carried a lamp…"

"Well, I remembered there was something about how it was lying on the floor that bothered me. Well, when I mentioned this to the twins, we all three decided it was time to go back and have a look. So we went back there and got in through a window. The first thing I looked for was pieces of the lamp, but the broken glass had been swept up since that awful night. Mrs. Croft probably swept up after you was taken up to Rookswood and London. But we three had us a careful look around the attic steps and—hope you don't mind, Miss, but even up in the attic, and…well, we found a thing or two that made us more curious."

"Go on, Wally," she said breathlessly.

"I found that blanket up in the attic. You want to see it, Miss?"

Evy looked at him for a long moment.

"Wally, what was it you remembered that bothered you about the lamp?"

He scrunched up his eyes. "Well, the biggest pieces was far away from the smallest pieces—like they was moved to the other side of the room or something. And the lamp must have made the fire on the floor when it fell beside the stairs, 'cause of all the smoke I smelt. Well, later on I kept wondering why the fire went out. After we went up the attic and found the blanket, it smelled like smoke and kerosene. When I looked at it, I saw some charred cloth. I thought maybe someone had used it to beat out the flames from the broken lamp. But I didn't see the blanket when I found you at the bottom of the stairs. Then, I asked myself, now how did it get up the steps into the attic?"

Yes, that seemed to fit. Whoever had pushed her had to contend with the kerosene fire. So they used the blanket to beat it out, then in a frenzy must have brought it back up to the attic, not realizing it would be noticed.

"You were very clever, Wally."

He grinned and dug the bag out from the bush. He opened the top and pulled out a dark blanket. She forced herself not to recoil. Yes, that was the one she'd seen on the intruder. She took it gingerly and smelled it. Yes, kerosene and smoke… She touched the charred spots near the hem. Evy's hand tightened on the cloth.

"And this was up in the attic?"

"Aye, by your uncle Edmund's desk, sort of tossed aside on the floor. But that ain't all, Miss. The Hooper twins found *this*." He pulled something else out of the bag. "Don't know if it means anything or not. The twins kept it for you. Beth smuggled it out to me awhile ago when she told me she and Mary couldn't come here to see you."

Evy took the old envelope.

"But there's nothing inside," he said. "Beth thought there was at first. She found it crumpled on the floor under the desk, as if somebody kicked it aside. Looks like it was written to your uncle, Vicar Edmund."

Yes, and sent from Henry Chantry. How interesting, and how odd. What could Henry have written Vicar Edmund? Had Aunt Grace been privy to the contents? There was no postage on the envelope, which meant it must have been written here in Grimston Way and sent to Uncle Edmund by a message boy. Henry must have written it before his death. But why had Uncle Edmund never said anything about its contents if it was important?

Then again—if it wasn't important, why had someone wanted it? Or was she jumping to conclusions? Had the intruder she'd interrupted in the attic been after this letter or something else? Perhaps he, if it was a he, had merely tossed it aside hastily to locate something else. But if so, why bother to crumple it? The fact that the letter was missing convinced her it had been sought.

But only the letter? There must have been other items taken, which made her rebuke herself for not having gone through her uncle's desk long ago. She'd told herself there was nothing important, just mementos about his work, and she hadn't wanted to deal with the emotions it would bring her.

Evy held the envelope in her hands. "Wally, you've done a grand job. So have the twins. I'm not sure what it all means, but it strengthens my case that I—" She stopped. No, it wasn't safe for Wally and the Hooper twins to be told she'd been pushed down the attic stairs. Containing that secret was too much to ask of three young detectives bubbling over with childish enthusiasm. If it was true that Wally was being watched these days, as he'd said earlier, she must get them disengaged somehow. For their own safety.

"Have you mentioned any of this to anyone?"

"Oh no, Miss. That would have landed us in the crick for sure—especially me. The twins can worm their way out of most things with Mrs. Hooper. They just keep talking circles around her. By the time they're done, Mrs. Hooper, who's none too clever about talking, don't have a clue what's going on. But me, I'd end up getting blamed for luring her daughters into mischief like Mrs. Hooper always says. But I tell you, Miss. It's mostly the other way around. And if my pa finds out—well, I'd be in a bucket of trouble for sure."

"My lease of the cottage hasn't run out yet," she assured him. "And in my judgment you've not broken in. I'm pleased you found this blanket. And the twins, the envelope—though I'm not sure what the envelope means, if anything...but if you hadn't gone back to the cottage—" She hesitated again, reminding herself that the less the children knew, the better for now.

In fact, she thought warily, *the intruder may well have gone back after things settled down, thinking of the smell of kerosene on the blanket.*

Wally's eyes narrowed as he glanced again about them, then watched her.

"Miss Evy, what I don't understand is how did you beat out those flames?"

Her mouth tightened. She remained silent, fingering the blanket.

"Well then, who did it, Miss?"

She avoided his suspicious gaze. "Maybe someone found me before you did and put out the fire, but failed to get to the parish hall before you. Maybe you outran them, arriving first to tell Mrs. Croft and Dr. Tisdale."

"Now, Miss." His voice seemed hardly more forceful than an indulgent parent.

Evy felt her mouth turn into a wry smile. "Don't think it's possible?"

"No, Miss. I didn't see anyone on their way to the parish hall when Mrs. Croft sent me to the cottage. I was the first one to find you—except whoever put out the flames with this." He pointed deliberately to the blanket.

Evy placed the blanket back inside the bag. She wasn't going to admit someone had pushed her and beat out the flames. The story would spread quickly around the village. But Wally was already getting too close to the truth. He watched her alertly.

"Miss? Shouldn't you talk to the Yard about this?"

"I'll look into all this," she said evasively. "In the meantime, Wally, please don't mention this to anyone. That goes for the Hooper twins, too."

He nodded and shoved his big hands into the pockets of his worn breeches. "We kept it quiet so far, Miss."

"Yes, and that was very wise of you three. Did you actually see someone following you?" she asked again suddenly.

"I didn't see no one, but Digger did."

She looked at him. "Digger? Oh, your dog."

He nodded. "Digger was growling the other night outside the bungalow, so I got me up and out to see if I caught a rabbit in my trap by the barn. Then I saw Pa's barn was open, with all his carpentry tools. I went to shut the door, but I knew I closed it before supper like I always do. It was then I saw someone run away. I think he'd been in the barn."

"What makes you think it had something to do with you and the blanket?"

"Uds, Miss. That's where I was keeping this here bag all the time! Up in the loft, under the hay. Maybe whoever I saw peeping about thought to find it. Maybe he saw me bring it in there. I don't know for sure, Miss, but that's what I'm supposing. An' it's a good thing Digger was carrying on like that. 'Cause when I lit the lantern in the barn, I saw someone had brought the ladder up to the loft and must've been ready to climb himself up and have a look, but Digger's barking scared him off. Well, that was three days ago or thereabouts. After that, I brought the bag into my room and hid it under my bed."

Evy's alarm grew. At least now the bag would be in her care, deflecting any more attention from Wally.

"I've both the blanket and the envelope now," she stated. "Perhaps the safest thing is to let others know about this, after all. Whoever left them up in the attic will now see it's too late to come back for them. They'll then know it's wiser to step back into the shadows."

"Then you're thinkin' like me and the Hooper detectives. That someone was up to no good, Miss Evy. And you never did say how you fell down them steps."

"Wally, it's best not to discuss that now. I've decided to tell the vicar. Maybe Lord Brewster as well."

"I'd feel better about it after that, Miss."

She picked up the bag and took her crutches from Wally.

" 'Tis a shame about your back, Miss. We're all praying you get strong again."

She managed a smile. "Thank you, Wally. But even if I don't, God will remain faithful and have His good plans for my life."

He nodded. "Then if you be needing me for anything, or the twins, well, just let us know."

"I will. And thanks again."

He grinned and stepped out of her way. "Shall I walk back to the rectory gate with you, Miss?"

"No, that's not necessary. I'm fine. Getting stronger each day that passes. Besides, I don't want us to be seen together."

"Aye, but that bag's sure to have folks seeing it."

"It doesn't matter now. As they say, the cat's already out of the bag."

Wally grinned and chuckled. "G'day, Miss Evy."

As Evy walked back to the rectory, she carefully made her plans. She would need to return to the cottage to arrange for the transport of the trunks and desk to the storage room at the rectory. The sooner, the better. She wanted to look around the attic one more time for herself as well. Just what had Henry written to Uncle Edmund? Why did someone feel it important enough to enter her attic secretly? Had Henry written to confess to being her father? That, in itself, seemed no cause for breaking into her cottage. But…perhaps it was. She was sure the Chantry family would not approve of her discovering she was a relative.

As such, she even had rights to live at Rookswood! Not that she would ever demand such a thing. But if Sir Lyle Chantry's brother had heirs— then perhaps she could inherit from that end of the family just as she would from her mother Katie van Buren.

Why, I could very well be an exceedingly wealthy woman. The idea was numbing.

She would tell Mrs. Croft at breakfast tomorrow that she wanted to go to the cottage.

When she neared the rectory, a familiar shiny coach waited, attended by a man dressed precisely in uniform, not a hair of his waxed mustache out of line.

"Hello, Mr. Bixby."

Lady Elosia's footman tipped his tall hat and bowed his head. "A fair afternoon to you, Miss Varley."

Varley. At least everyone in the village continued to call her by the name she'd grown up with.

"Lady Elosia has requested you come up to Rookswood to see her this afternoon if possible."

Curious, she could read nothing in his face, but one never could with Bixby.

"She wishes to see me now?"

"For afternoon tea, Miss, if you would be so inclined."

She smiled but saw his gaze drop to the bag she held pressed against her crutch, then he looked away. Did he recognize it? Or did it merely look out of place here in the gardens?

"I should be delighted to take tea with Lady Elosia, Mr. Bixby."

"Then I shall wait for you here, Miss."

"I shan't be long. I'll tell Mrs. Osgood."

"Very good, Miss."

Evy was staying in her girlhood room. She refused to loiter amid melancholy memories and went straight to business. She concealed Wally's bag in her wardrobe on a back shelf not easily noticed, then turned her attention to choosing a suitable afternoon dress. She settled on the summery blue pastel and arranged her tawny hair in a becoming upsweep. She stared at her image in the mirror. Standing here as she was without the crutches, she looked as she did a year ago. *Only a year?* It sometimes seemed a decade.

She picked up her crutches, squared her shoulders, and refused to look again.

She turned her thoughts to the tea with Lady Elosia Chantry. What could the formidable woman want to see her about? Perhaps just a kindly invitation to see how she was recovering, or was there something more serious on her mind?

Chapter Twenty-Six

Rookswood looked just as Evy remembered it as they approached. Mr. Bixby drove the Chantry coach through the tall arched gateway beneath overhanging oak branches. Mrs. Croft's cousin Harley, the old gate-keeper, had died not more than ten days after Hiram Croft the sexton, and now Harley's son, Harry, stood near the small rose-covered cottage he occupied. Harry grinned and lifted his cap, then shut the gate after them.

Inside, the road changed from dirt to small cobbles. Evy looked upon mounds of green turf that gently rolled toward a horizon of trees on the perimeter by more private woods. The land went even farther back beyond the woods to farmland cultivated by workers employed by the squire.

The shrubbery along the lawns was meticulously manicured, the handiwork of Mr. Tibbs, Rookswood's main gardener. Not far from the gate was a familiar narrow lane—the route to the bungalow where she and Aunt Grace had lived until her death. And ahead, within sight, were the luxuriant Rookswood gardens where she and Rogan had said their good-bye over two years ago. Her heart hid its silent disappoint-ment. A disappointment she must not feed with memories, for she was Henry Chantry's daughter. It caused her no uncertain pain to learn from Heyden that she had been used by Rogan.

The coach bore her along the S-shaped carriageway to the mansion, rimmed on one side with white birch and on the other with elm. When the horses at last came to the end of the S, Mr. Bixby brought them to an easy stop. Evy looked up at the forbidding mansion. Some of it was twelfth century, with crenelated towers and turrets. The same old gargoyles with bulging eyes and evil scowls glared down at her.

Mrs. Wetherly remained as the Chantrys' housekeeper, wearing black bombazine and a stiff white apron, and she smiled warmly as Evy entered the Great Hall.

"How wonderful to see you looking so much stronger, Evy."

"Thank you, Mrs. Wetherly. I do feel much more optimistic. I'm here to have tea with Lady Elosia. Is she in the parlor?"

"Her Ladyship's not come down yet. I'll show you to the parlor, where you may wait."

Evy had not done much socializing in the parlor while Aunt Grace had worked as governess. She well remembered the time Lady Camilla Brewster had asked her to come down for tea and Sir Julien Bley had unexpectedly walked in on them. He had confronted Lady Camilla, wife of Lord Anthony Brewster, with uncalled-for rudeness. Sir Julien had been overbearing with her. To this hour Evy still wondered if Camilla might not have been contemplating telling her that her mother was not the missionary Junia Varley who had been killed in the Zulu War, but Katie van Buren. Evy also recalled how Sir Julien had faced her in the glaring lamplight, had cupped her face in his hand and boldly searched her features. Now, of course, she knew why he'd done so. He had been making certain in his own mind that she was Katie's daughter. Even so, he had done nothing about it until recently. If she allowed her emotions free rein, she could become very upset over the injustice that had been done her by the secret kept hidden for so many years.

The dark wood furnishings in the parlor were done in burgundy and gold. She moved across the thick rugs to an array of family paintings staged grandly above the huge fireplace mantel. It did not take her long to find Henry Chantry—with his rugged dark features and that somewhat arrogant smile that reminded her of King Charles—and Rogan Chantry. Strange, she had always thought there was some resemblance between Henry and Rogan rather than Rogan and his father, Sir Lyle. How odd that it was *she* who was related to Henry.

She tried not to look at Rogan's handsome face, but instead she concentrated on Henry. She walked up close to the painting and stood staring at it intently, as though she could will the truth from those dark eyes, that enigmatic smile.

Are you my father?

Moments slipped by, and she was still standing there when a voice said, "A man who did not live out half his days."

She turned, surprised to see Anthony Brewster. He followed her gaze to Henry's painting as he walked up beside her and stared.

She remembered that Lord Brewster had business that would have brought him here to Rookswood.

"I heard Henry was an adventurer…a bold man with a restless spirit."

"Yes, he was that."

"You knew him?"

"I knew him well. I was at Cape House the night Katie ran away to Rorke's Drift looking for you. I was with Sir Julien when we found Henry in the stables. He'd been knocked unconscious and claimed the Black Diamond was stolen from him by Katie."

"But I think that's not true about Katie."

"No…she did not steal the diamond from Henry. Someone else did that."

"You were there too?" she asked, knowing she was being unwise. She continued to look at Henry's likeness, ignoring the veiled suggestion.

"As I said, I was there with Camilla. We'd returned from here in London to marry at Cape House."

She noted the lines between his brows.

"Who do you think knocked Henry unconscious and took the Black Diamond from him?"

"There's some suggestion it could have been Jendaya, or her Zulu brother, Dumaka. This was before the Zulu War, and Dumaka was a young induna."

"That seems odd, then, that someone of noble position would be working for Sir Julien Bley, doesn't it?"

"Exceedingly so. I could never get a straight answer from Sir Julien. He claims Jendaya had become a Christian through Dr. Clyde Varley at Rorke's Drift Mission, and Dumaka, in loyalty to her, had come with her to live among the whites."

"Do you believe that was the real reason?" she ventured.

"No, I think there was something more to it. Something more sinister." He looked at her, and his hard eyes softened. "It's no concern of yours, Evy. You've enough problems on your shoulders. You know what Elosia will ask of you, don't you?"

She had warmed to his unclelike concern. "No, not at all."

"I should let her explain, then, and whatever you decide, I will stand beside your decision."

Lord Brewster amazed her. Why this sudden interest in her?

She looked back at Henry's picture and said with boldness, "Lord Brewster, have you any idea who my father was?"

He was silent. She sensed a rigidness come over his stance.

"I suppose you will always wonder. It's natural you would. Knowing that Katie was your mother, you'll never be satisfied until all the truth is uncovered."

"You don't blame me, do you? If you were in my shoes, wouldn't you wish to know everything?"

He hesitated, then exhaled. "I don't know if I would or not, Evy. You see, I've never learned who *my* father was. And my mother died before I was mature enough to try to persuade her to tell me. I was raised here in England until I was fifteen, going from one school to another until Sir Julien sent for me. I worked in the diamond business for Julien until my marriage to Lady Camilla Montieth was arranged."

Lord George Montieth, Camilla's father, was the number two man in the FO, the Foreign Office, dealing with all colonial affairs. Evy knew how Sir Julien had deemed it important to have marriage connection to those in the British government whose personal views favored British expansionism in Africa. The debate continued to rage in Britain: "If we don't take the initiative, the German government will, or Portugal." The one good thing Evy could see in the forward thrust of the Union Jack into places like Africa, India, Hong Kong, and elsewhere was that it permitted the missionary movement to follow, even though it was often true that the British colonial governments in those countries frowned upon the missionaries. Still, God was sovereign in His dealings with the nations, and the missionary movement was growing.

"Another arranged marriage by Sir Julien Bley," she said. "At least I'm safe from such concerns," she commented wryly.

His brows rose. "Do you think so, my dear? I'm not at all convinced of that."

Her gaze, against her will, strayed to the painting of Rogan Chantry. Lord Brewster noticed, and he searched her face until Evy looked away from Rogan too quickly, feeling the heat in her cheeks. No matter what Heyden had recently said of him, or how hard she tried not to think of him, her heart kept him close to her thoughts.

She moved away from the proud gallery of Chantrys. "I'll never allow Sir Julien to make me marry a man I don't love. Anyway, in my situation..." She looked at her crutches.

He did so as well, and his look grew serious. "Don't be foolish, Evy. Few good men would turn and walk away just because you have a limp. You are a very beautiful young woman with character and, yes, an inheritance. I would think a gentleman of both family and importance would be anxious to marry you. Besides, you'll get stronger. I talked with Dr. Harris before leaving London. He assures me you are still improving. Who knows? The day may come when you may not need crutches at all."

"You're kind to say all this, sir. I suspect you're trying to make me feel better." She smiled.

"Nonsense," he said. "I mean every word of it."

"But I still won't marry to please Sir Julien Bley."

Unconsciously, she betrayed herself again by glancing at Rogan's painting.

"You've heard Rogan and Lady Patricia will marry?"

She tried to sound glib. "Of course, who has not? It's been arranged for years, if my memory is correct."

"You do know she's here?"

Here in Rookswood? No, she hadn't known. Her muscles tensed. She did not want to run into Patricia now. Evy remained silent.

"Then you have not yet heard. Rogan has arrived in London too. He should be here soon at Rookswood, perhaps tomorrow. The marriage is to take place shortly, from what Elosia tells me."

He had said all this quietly, as if to soften the blow. But Evy remained a little dazed. *Rogan...here. I won't see him. I won't!*

At the sound of a swish of skirts, Evy turned, expecting to see Patricia gloating.

"Ah, there you are, Anthony, dear," Lady Elosia said. "Lyle is waiting to discuss the diamond sale with you in his office." She entered the spacious parlor and gestured to the plush divan. "Evy, do sit down, please. The maid will be coming with our tea momentarily."

Elosia was a woman with a certain aloofness about her that reminded Evy of chilly elegance. The possibility that this woman could be her aunt by blood through her brother Henry seemed as remote as her glance that swept over Evy.

"A pity about the need for crutches. Ah, well. You've always been a strong girl. You'll adjust."

"It comforts me to know you are so convinced, Lady Elosia."

Lady Elosia shot her a glance. Evy was nettled by the woman's indifference. Strange how easily she could assure her of victory over a trial, when Lady Elosia would feel very differently if so afflicted.

Elosia's hair was a sculptured gray-gold, her complexion white from years of staying out of the sun, and her skin was painted expertly with pink rouge and lip-tint. Her brows were darkened and arched somewhat complacently above almost pearl-gray eyes. She and Sir Lyle could have been twins.

It amazed Evy to think of the darkly exciting Rogan as the son of Sir

Lyle and the now deceased Lady Honoria, who had much in common with Lady Elosia. How they had produced the willful and sparkling-eyed Arcilla and the adventuresome Rogan seemed a mystery.

Lady Eloisa looked to Evy as though she rarely laughed, as if it were inappropriate to do so. Her determined demeanor set Evy on edge, adding to her discomfort at being called here, and making her feel as if her crutches were an impediment to refinement.

What could she possibly want of me? Evy wondered as she sat there under Lady Elosia's scrutiny. Certainly this wasn't a social call just to see how she was recuperating. Lord Brewster would have told her all she wanted to know, which Evy was sure did not amount to much.

Evy was unsure how much Lady Elosia knew about Evy's link to the family through Katie, and perhaps Henry Chantry. The family had shown no interest all these years, so there would be little if any reason to believe their attitude should change now, unless it was affected by the van Buren wealth. The Chantrys would know about the diamond inheritance coming to her through her mother, Katie. And how Sir Julien had directed Lord Brewster to set up a financial account on her behalf through his barrister.

A maid Evy did not recognize brought in a silver tea tray with refreshments. The tea was one of the strong Indian varieties. A china serving plate was neatly arranged with some heart-shaped watercress sandwiches and some liver and onion paste. It was all Evy could do to swallow her tea.

"I shall come straight to the point, Evy. Pretending otherwise would not benefit either of us. We are both direct, I believe."

"Yes, I think you are quite right. Does this have to do with your niece, Arcilla?" Lady Elosia seemed surprised. "Arcilla is the one person I can think of who forms even a thread between me and the Chantrys."

Elosia thoughtfully slid her spoon once through her cup before laying it aside.

"You are correct," she confessed. "It concerns Arcilla...and Peter as well. Arcilla is like a daughter to me, and you *know* what Arcilla is like," she said, as though Evy would understand everything.

Evy did *know* the manner of woman Arcilla was, but she did not understand Lady Elosia's troubled expression. She went on before Evy could respond.

"I understand that it was the wish of Sir Julien that you at last know who your mother was. As to whether that was wise—"

"I beg your pardon, Lady Elosia, but of course I should be told. I should have been told from the very beginning, even when I was a child at the rectory. And the inheritance rightfully belonging to me through Katie van Buren *should* have been shared in part with Vicar Edmund and Grace Havering, as well as to help pay my schooling. When I look back and see how difficult it was for us at times—especially after Vicar Edmund died—I feel the deliberate silence was unjust. Grace had to scrape together her meager earnings to send me to music school at great cost to her, and to me emotionally. If it hadn't been for your nephew Rogan, I wouldn't have been able to finish my final year at all."

Evy had not planned to say all this and was surprised herself at her sudden boldness. But now that her emotions were out in the open, she wasn't really sorry. She wasn't the only one who had suffered because of it. Uncle Edmund and Aunt Grace had suffered from the injustice, and she wanted them to know she understood it quite well. But of all that she said, it was the mention of Rogan's name that seemed to shock Lady Elosia the most, and she set her tiny porcelain teacup down with a rattle. Her pearl-gray eyes widened unbecomingly.

"Rogan? What has he to do with you?"

"He loaned me the money to finish my schooling in London, and then to open my short-lived music school here in Grimston Way. Surely you were aware? Everyone else in the village seems to talk about it."

"My dear! I am quite above the common gossip that flits about Grimston Way. As Sir Lyle's sister, I am much too busy assuming many of the important duties of the wife he no longer has."

It was time to make amends. "And very wisely too, Lady Elosia. You are much respected in the village for all you have done."

She looked slightly mollified. "I did not know about any such loan from Rogan or that he would deign to involve himself in your private matters, Evy. If I had known, I would have discouraged it at once. There is already too much chatter in London about his wandering ways. But thank goodness he's about to arrive and silence the doubters, where our dear and darling Patricia Bancroft is concerned." She drew a lace handkerchief from her cuff and dabbed pointedly at her nose, as though tried beyond endurance.

"A marriage," Lady Elosia continued with a dignified tone, "is soon to come. By September is my hope. Patricia is here, of course, and—"

"Were you speaking of me?" came Patricia's voice.

Evy and Lady Elosia looked across the parlor. Lady Patricia had entered through a side door and stood elegantly, the picture-perfect future lady of Rookswood who would one day assume Lady Elosia's position, overseeing all the social affairs of the ancestral Chantry estate. Her auburn hair was arranged elaborately, and her lips formed a rosebud smile.

"Oh, Patricia dear, I was just telling Evy about your upcoming marriage to Rogan."

Patricia walked over to the tea table and looked Evy over with obvious concern. "I've heard you'll never walk again? I am so sorry for you, my dear. It must be horrid." She reached down and picked up a chocolate Florentine and bit into it with her white teeth.

"I am walking quite well enough. Thank you for your concern."

The auburn brows arched. "I can't imagine myself hobbling about on crutches for the rest of my life. You must be brave, Evy. I don't think I could *endure* it."

Lady Elosia cleared her throat and glanced from Evy to Patricia. "Dear, Evy and I are in a business discussion. Perhaps it would be best if you joined us later?"

Patricia smiled sweetly at Lady Elosia and then Evy. "Will you be staying for dinner tonight, Evy? Rogan should be here by then. He arrived in London a few days ago and is on his way to Rookswood this very moment to see me. I'm sure he'll be pleased to see the little girl who lived at the rectory."

Did Patricia know she was now a diamond heiress? Evy didn't think so. Lady Elosia changed the subject quickly, as though she feared Evy would announce her new family position. Evy forced herself to keep silent. She was fuming inwardly at Patricia's overbearing manner, but she did not want to strike back. God would not approve of a vindictive tongue. She already felt a bit guilty for honestly stating her views earlier to Lady Elosia.

As Patricia strolled confidently from the parlor, Lady Elosia sighed. For once that Evy could recall, she actually appeared ashamed.

"You must overlook Patricia. Please do. She has gone through such emotional turmoil of late over Rogan. The scoundrel left her high and dry and sailed off to Capetown, and she's been upset ever since. Society can produce such nasty little gossips, you know."

"Yes, I *know*," Evy said with emphasis.

Lady Elosia looked at her quickly and then changed the subject again.

"Arcilla is expecting a child. She's with Peter at Fort Salisbury. A bleak, forsaken place, so Arcilla writes. Peter's been sick with numerous ailments since he arrived a year ago. She's not about to leave him now, of course. She couldn't if she wanted to, but Peter wants her with him, as is only right."

Evy felt herself smile genuinely for the first time. "Arcilla's going to have a baby? Oh, I'm so happy for her. When is it due, if I may ask?"

"Five months or so. She's in an absolute tizzy. She won't hear of *any* nanny coming to be with her. She has requested that you consider going to help her at this time."

Evy lifted her brows. "I'd love to see Arcilla, but I don't plan on becoming a nanny—"

"No, naturally not. It was merely a term she used. She desires you as a companion, just as she was also very close to Patricia while they were growing up in London."

Evy knew that, as well as how Arcilla had wanted to marry Charles, Patricia's brother. All that was old history.

"Arcilla is looking for a good English nanny, and I promised her I'd have one sent out to the Cape."

"Then she's living at Fort Salisbury? Lord Brewster had hinted the Rhodes colony was coming along quite successfully."

"Arcilla has no plans to leave Peter until after the baby is old enough to travel that difficult route back to Capetown."

Lady Elosia studied Evy now with some curiosity.

"Arcilla is hoping you'll come, perhaps traveling back with Rogan and Patricia after their wedding. Patricia would then go on with Rogan to Fort Salisbury when he returns to his work. From what I'm told, the gold operation is proceeding well."

Evy was dismayed and not just a little nettled, but then she understood that Lady Elosia could not possibly have known about her feelings for Rogan. Evy wisely refrained from saying anything in haste and formed her expression into noncommittal interest.

"Arcilla made it clear to Sir Julien that it was you she wanted with her."

And what might Sir Julien's response have been, she wanted to know, not that she anticipated going through with this. And there was still Heyden's invitation to return with him to the Transvaal to meet the van Burens. If anything, meeting her mother's relatives held more interest than going to Fort Salisbury to see Arcilla. She would not mention this to Lady Elosia just yet.

Lady Elosia set her china cup aside, and Evy noticed an exquisite bracelet of small black diamonds and wondered where she had gotten them. It seemed frivolous to Evy that she would even wear such a bracelet for afternoon tea, especially after the unhappiness, scandal, and even death surrounding the disappearance of the Kimberly Black. At the very least, it was an ostentatious display.

Lady Elosia saw her looking at the bracelet. A lively pleasure showed for the first time in her expression. At least there was *something* that appeared to excite Lady Elosia: diamonds, black ones at that. Evy more thoughtfully considered the woman.

"Lovely, are they not? A gift of Sir Julien many years ago."

Julien! "Are they of the quality of the Kimberly Black Diamond?" Evy saw her tense, or did she imagine it?

"I would hardly know that, since the Black Diamond disappeared a generation ago. But getting back to Arcilla, I understand she has always thought well of you."

Evy covered a smile. Hardly *always*. Their friendship did not get off to a good start, as she recalled Arcilla's demanding ways when she first came to Rookswood, but it had strengthened as they grew into their girlhood, and later at school in London.

"I've missed her," Evy said sincerely.

Again, that troubled look flickered in Elosia's eyes. "You might as well know that she and Peter are having marital difficulties over living in South Africa, especially over the Zambezi area—Fort Salisbury."

The news did not really surprise Evy. She had suspected trouble when Arcilla stopped writing to her from Capetown. Arcilla was not an easy person to live with, but Evy suspected that neither was Peter Bartley. When Evy met him, he had seemed totally dedicated to the British cause in South Africa.

"Arcilla would like to come home, but of course, Peter can't support that. His position as assistant commissioner of the new colony demands his presence. Dear Arcilla has interests of her own, some of which the family, Julien in particular, disapproves, but you know our Arcilla. She has always cultivated her dabbling in this little preoccupation or that." She smiled, showing her teeth for the first time.

Evy could smile wryly about "our Arcilla," who was indeed known to have her little preoccupations. But Arcilla had known about Peter's responsibilities in the British South Africa Company before she married him. Sir Julien and Peter had made those clear.

Evy now worried about what new "preoccupations" Arcilla could be cultivating at gold-and-diamond-rich Capetown.

"Peter sympathizes with her, but there is nothing he can do. Sir Julien insists she remain with her husband."

Evy could envision Arcilla throwing one of her tantrums and, as usual, getting her own way. Evy wondered again what manner of man Peter might be.

"Since you are without close family, we are all the more hopeful that you will find this arrangement agreeable. Arcilla is most anxious that you come and stay with her. I promised her I would do my best to encourage you to do so. The only question is whether your health will permit such rigorous travel at this time."

She lifted a letter from the divan. "From Arcilla. It's personal. I am certain she's done her best to talk you into going to Capetown. You may read it at your leisure. If you decide to accept, you could voyage back with Patricia and Rogan."

Evy accepted the sealed envelope, recognizing Arcilla's showy handwriting that was so much like her personality.

Lady Eloisa stood, and Evy gathered that their little tea party was concluded. Evy was anxious to make her departure. Bidding her hostess good-bye and promising to let her know her decision about Capetown, she left Rookswood as unobtrusively as she had entered.

As Mr. Bixby drove the coach through the Rookswood gate with its gargoyles poised for action, she leaned back against the seat and removed Arcilla's letter from the handbag. Voyage to the Cape with Rogan and Patricia? Not even a team of a dozen horses could get her to do such a thing!

Dear Evy,

If you won't leave England to come and stay with me for our old friendship's sake, then do consider coming to stay at Cape House to teach music to Susanna Bley. She's Julien's youngest granddaughter and nothing like her sister, Darinda. Darinda, who's had her eye on Rogan for months now, is a positive bore. She actually delights in the politics surrounding

the new colony, Fort Salisbury. Alice is also here with Derwent. They
have two children now. Can you believe it?

Susanna is completely unpolitical, and a gentle soul. You'd like her.
And she adores the piano. She reminds me of you when we were girls.
Now! As for my situation—help! The baby is growing, and I feel as
though I weigh three hundred pounds. I'm bored to death. I desperately
need my prudent friend from the rectory. So you must come soon.

Love, Arcilla

Evy smiled. So very like Arcilla.

As the horse's hooves clomped down the road back toward the rectory, she sighed over her dilemma. She was beginning to think her future might point in another direction. This realization brought both excitement and some anxious dread.

The steps of a good man are ordered by the LORD...

The divine promise brought comfort. Where would His hand lead and guide her? For what purpose was she to take this new road? Faith said it was enough that He knew. If trouble waited, as it had already awaited her in the past, then she must continue to go forward, believing that God had only good plans for her, even through trials. Evy believed there just might be a divine reason for the restlessness that urged her onward to Cape House.

Suddenly, she longed to meet Cousin Jakob van Buren. She wanted to go to his medical mission station and help him in some way. But if this was not to be, at least she could contact relatives on her mother's side—maybe even her father's?

Nothing will stop me. Not now.

"I'll go," she said aloud and lifted her chin.

The answers to many of her questions awaited her in South Africa.

CHAPTER TWENTY-SEVEN

The envelope... What had Henry written to Uncle Edmund so many years ago? And why did someone think it important enough at this late date to come looking for it? Evy studied it as though the handwriting itself would tell her what she wanted to know. She shook her head, frustrated with the impasse. She stood from the chair in her rectory room and, snatching her wrap and a hat, made up her mind quickly. She would return to the cottage to search through those trunks and the desk for herself. It wasn't likely she'd find anything after all this time, but she'd have a look anyway. She wished ardently that she had not let her feelings of loss keep her from doing so earlier.

She would need Mrs. Croft for the visit to the cottage, but before she set out, she wanted to visit the cemetery and Aunt Grace's and Uncle Edmund's graves. This was a time for her to be alone, so she managed to avoid Vicar and Mrs. Osgood as she slipped into the big country kitchen. Mrs. Croft had not yet arrived, and Evy quickly wrapped her breakfast, a leftover scone with jam, and went out through the back door.

She had left a note on the kitchen sideboard for Martha and Mrs. Croft to find, informing them she was on a spiritual pilgrimage of sorts to the cemetery, and that she desired solitude. She would be borrowing the jingle for the morning but would return by luncheon.

With her Bible and the key to the cottage in her handbag, she left the rectory.

The summer morning was cool and quite pleasant yet, with a clear sky and a few small clouds over the green hills. The birds were twittering, and blue lupine flowers grew freely along the dirt road winding down from Rookswood. The scene gave no evidence that all was not right with the world, the wider world as well as her own narrower one. She reminded herself that her Shepherd was sovereign over both domains. While so many things seemed to be coming apart like a worn-out garment, her Divine Shepherd neither slept nor slumbered.

She quietly sang a childhood hymn she loved particularly:

"Savior, like a shepherd lead us,
Much we need Thy tender care;
In Thy pleasant pastures feed us,
For our use Thy folds prepare:
We are Thine; do Thou befriend us,
Be the Guardian of our way;
Keep Thy flock, from sin defend us,
Seek us when we go astray:

Blessed Jesus, blessed Jesus,
Thou hast bought us, Thine we are;
Blessed Jesus, blessed Jesus,
Thou has bought us, Thine we are."

Yes, she was *His*, crutches and all.

A short time later, Evy parked the jingle under the huge pepper tree and, with studied determination, climbed down from the seat, holding a crutch for support. She made her way to the grave sites for Edmund and Grace Havering, the only parents she'd ever known. She owed them an everlasting place in her heart—for love never dies—faith, hope, and love—but the greatest of these is love. They not only cared for and loved her, but they had brought her into a knowledge of Jesus Christ. She didn't know whether Katie van Buren had been a sincere believer, and she knew even less about her father.

So she was indeed blessed to have been raised as the Vicar's niece. As she stood there, her heart was flooded with bittersweet memories of great loss and immense gratitude. Evy was fully aware that she had much to thank her heavenly Father for. *Suppose I'd been born a Zulu with no knowledge of the true God?*

She began to think of her mother's cousin, Jakob van Buren, and his mission station somewhere in the distant wilds of the Zambezi region. More and more she wanted to go there to meet him, to glean all she could about her mother and family members, and—was it possible?—to even help him in bringing the Good News to those who needed to know her gentle Savior.

I am a debtor...both to wise and to unwise.... For I am not ashamed of the gospel of Christ, for it is the power of God to salvation for everyone who believes... The words of Saint Paul in the first chapter of Romans chimed clearly through her mind and soul. So much so that Evy stopped on the summer grass and turned toward the distant chapel. As those words rang upon her mind, she wondered if Vicar Edmund might have been pulling the rope hanging down below the bell tower.

She stood silently, hearing with her earthly ears only the warm, sweet summer wind whispering along the tall green grass, brushing like angel's wings through nodding heads of flowers and tree branches. The skirt around her ankles lifted and nudged the summer hat at her side. A peace moved through her spirit, bringing an unexplainable joy—unexplainable because her circumstances were unchanged. She felt herself smiling and even glanced up toward the blue sky with puffy white clouds, as though God's love had unexpectedly embraced her.

"Here am I, Father God," she said out loud. "Do with me as You will. I know I can fully trust You. Faithful and True are among your wonderful names."

Evy laid a cluster of wildflowers at the grave sites of her uncle and aunt. She was under no illusion that the real Edmund and Grace were here, for she knew that believers in Christ were in His presence. *To be absent from the body, is to be present with the Lord.* Only their earthly remains were buried here, awaiting the first resurrection. *O death, where is your sting? O grave, where is your victory?* Christ had conquered both by paying the penalty for sin. Evy knew that the last enemy that shall be destroyed is death.

She sat down on the grass to read and pray, enjoying the solitude, feeling no superstition over mere burial plots.

A while later she heard footsteps and turned her head. The Hooper twins stood there looking somber. Their matching green skirts flared in the breeze. They both wore spectacles, and their corn-colored hair was in looped braids. As usual, Mary wore a ribbon in her braids, this one green.

"Hullo, Miss Varley," she said.

"Why, hello, Mary, Beth. Come sit down."

Beth shook her head, looking glum. "We don't like tombs, Miss Varley. They say when a person visits a tomb and sits for more than an hour, the ghost will follow you home."

Mary lifted her necklace watch and squinted through her thick glasses. "You've been here almost fifty-five minutes."

"So we've come to warn you," Beth said and reached down to tug at her arm. "Oh, come away, Miss Varley, do come now."

Evy smiled, and her first response was to protest, but their disturbed faces drew from her a sigh instead.

"I don't believe a word of it," she said, getting up from the grass. "If I didn't know better, I'd think you were listening to silly stories told by Hiram the old sexton."

"He's dead," Beth said soberly. "Did Wally give you the envelope we found under the attic desk?"

"Yes, and did you look about the floor to see whether the letter might have been wadded up or tossed aside?"

"Hooper Detective Agency wouldn't make a mistake like that, Miss Varley. I looked all around the floor. So did Beth."

Beth nodded gravely. Her eyes were curious and thoughtful beneath her glasses. "You will search again. You think something important was in that envelope."

She was more discerning than Mary. "I don't know if there was or not, but you're right. I'm going back to the cottage. Perhaps this morning with Mrs. Croft."

"Wally saw Mrs. Croft busy with Hulda's new baby," Mary said.

Hulda was Lizzie's younger sister. If Mrs. Croft was busy helping with a sick baby in her family, it wasn't likely she'd have time to go with her to the cottage. Let alone that she might think it unwise and refuse to go. Evy could go there on her own, of course, and she wasn't afraid. But could she manage the steps to the attic? Perhaps she should just square her shoulders and go ahead by herself. The more independence she could manage, the less mental stress she would have to confront.

"We can go with you, Miss Varley," Mary offered. "Can't we, Beth?" She looked at her sister, obviously expecting agreement.

Beth did not look so willing. Evy wondered if the girl was afraid to return there, but that was not likely, since both delighted in their pretend detective agency. They'd certainly had the courage to go the first time. Perhaps there was some other reason for her hesitation. Wally, maybe? Had Wally told Beth about the incident in his father's barn? Mary, on the other hand, did not seem the least bit wary. Perhaps he had not told her.

"We'll both come with you, Miss Varley," Mary said again. "Just in case you need help getting up the steps. They were very steep, I remember. All I can say is, I sure wouldn't want to trip and fall down them."

"That's a silly thing to say now," Beth told her with an injured look.

Mary looked at Evy with sudden contrition. "All I meant to say was—"

"I do understand Mary's caution," Evy said smoothly. "Look, girls, perhaps you shouldn't come. Mrs. Hooper isn't likely to approve of your activity. I'll wait until Mrs. Croft is free and go another time. Was Hulda's baby very sick?"

"They called Dr. Tisdale to their bungalow, so I think so," Mary said.

They were walking back across the grass to where Evy left the one-horse jingle.

"Oh, look, there's Wally. Excuse me, Miss Varley. I'll just go and see what he's doing this afternoon. I think he said his pa was going to let him go hunting in the Grimston Woods. Come on, Beth."

Mary ran ahead, but Beth did not follow. She walked alongside Evy in silence. She was a much more quiet, studious girl than her twin and seemed to pick things up by observing people and situations from afar. Evy was curious about the change that came over her when the attic was mentioned, and she tried approaching her on the subject while they were momentarily alone.

"You don't seem as anxious to return to my cottage as Mary. Is there a reason, or do you have something more fun to do this morning—with Wally, maybe?"

Beth turned pink but shook her head no. "I'm not going fishing with Wally. I don't like catching fish. I hate watching him put worms on his hook. And when you pull fish from the stream, they wiggle all around."

Evy glanced at her. "Jesus helped His disciples catch a huge net of fish."

"Yes, I remember that story from Sunday school. In South Africa the hunters do horrible things to the wild animals. They shoot elephants and lions just for the sport of killing. I think that's wrong."

"If it's not for food, for clothes, or because of danger to human life, yes, I agree. God told mankind to be responsible for the animals. We should never kill any of God's creatures just for sport."

"Did you ever see a sjambok?" Beth asked.

"It's a short whip, isn't it? Made from rhinoceros or hippopotamus hide?"

"Yes, but have you ever seen one?"

Evy was surprised at the girl's knowledge of something from so far away. That was a curious question coming from a girl who'd never been out of Grimston Way.

"No, and I don't suppose you would have either. Why do you ask? Odd that you'd be studying about such things in school. I didn't know Curate Farley held any particular interest in South Africa."

Beth did not answer and looked down at the grass. "Miss Varley? Why do you suppose Mary said what she did about not wishing to fall from the steps?"

Another sudden change of subject. "I suppose it was because I stood up from the grass and used these crutches. It's not something any of us would want, if we had a choice. I'm sure it made Mary uncomfortable. She'll get used to it," she said with more determination than she felt in her heart. Would anyone get used to seeing her like this? "But life is a journey with unexpected turns, Beth. That's when we must cultivate the knowledge of who God is, and why He is trustworthy, because most of the time we're not ready for the kinds of changes that come to us."

"It must be awful to let go of plans you really want," she said quietly.

"Especially when we've nurtured them for many months or years. That's when we need to be open to letting God show us the new plans He has for us."

"I don't think God has any plans for me."

"God has plans for every one of His children, Beth, even when disappointments come. When Israel was taken captive to Babylon, their lives were greatly troubled, but God still loved them more than they deserved and told Jeremiah to write to them, 'For I know the thoughts that I think toward you, says the LORD, thoughts of peace and not of evil, to give you a future and a hope.' And now we know about God's love for us even more surely than Jeremiah did, because we can read that 'He who did not spare His own Son, but delivered Him up for us all, how shall He not with Him also freely give us all things?'"

Beth looked thoughtful. She nodded.

"What about your plans, Miss Varley? What are you going to do now that you have to use crutches every day?"

"I have a couple of choices to consider. Lady Elosia has asked me to go to Capetown to stay with Miss Arcilla until her baby is born and old enough to travel to Rhodes's new colony. And…" She halted a moment, wondering if she should mention the van Burens. She was sure many in the village knew she was not a Varley, but to admit it aloud remained uncomfortable.

Beth did not seem to notice, but her manner had changed back to what it had been earlier when she'd asked about the sjambok.

"I don't think you should go, Miss Varley. I think you would be safer to go back to London." And upon that wary and unexpected statement, she added, "I'm going to go find Digger, Wally's dog." And she ran off in the direction of the trees and disappeared, leaving Evy to look after her in surprise. What was bothering Beth? Whatever it was, she wasn't even sharing it with Mary.

A few minutes later Mary and Wally walked from the village green to meet Evy. "Wally's going to take us to the cottage, Miss Varley. He can take us now. Isn't that right, Wally? Oh, say, where did Beth go?"

"She ran off into those trees. I think something is troubling her. Do either of you know what it could be?"

Mary pursed her lips. "Is she acting daft again? I *do* wonder what's come over her. Mum says she's the one twin who has a melancholy personality. I'll find her."

Before Evy could ask her not to, Mary ran toward the trees, calling her twin sister impatiently.

Alone, she looked at Wally. He removed his green felt hat and rubbed his locks.

"Do you know something, Wally? If you do, please tell me. It may be important for Beth's sake."

He shrugged his skinny shoulders and shifted from one foot to the other. "Can't say as I do, Miss. Beth's been acting different lately."

Evy didn't like the sound of this. "In what way?"

"That's just it, Miss. I don't know exactly, but lately she's just more quiet and not wanting to talk to me anymore. She's more interested in looking after Digger. I guess it's her mum, too. She's been after Beth to stay clear of me for months. Guess it's getting worse. Anyway, I noticed it these last weeks."

"Did she mention a sjambok to you, or killing animals in Africa?"

He tapped his forehead with his thumb. "A sham...what? Nary heard of no sham—whatever you called it, Miss."

"Sjambok. It's a South African whip used by the Boers, people of Dutch ancestry who migrated to the Cape in the sixteen hundreds."

Wally looked at her, thoroughly confused. Evy dropped the subject, realizing Beth had not discussed it.

"You say she avoids you now because of Mrs. Hooper, but you are still friendly with Mary. Could it be that Beth's strange manner is due to something other than her mother's wishes?"

"You're right there, Miss. Hadn't thought of it that way."

"Tell me, Wally, did you mention to Beth about being watched recently?"

He squinted thoughtfully. "Maybe I did. Yes, last week, after Sunday school, I think it was. I told her where I'd hidden the blanket in Pa's barn because I thought someone was watching me. She didn't say anything, though."

"Was Mary there when you told this to Beth?"

He hunched his shoulders. "Don't think so, Miss. Are you saying Beth's scared? Is that why she ran away just now?"

"I don't know why she ran off, but I think she wished to be left to herself."

"She does that more and more lately. Never thought I'd see the day when her and Mary weren't as thick as milk and cream." His eyes were alert. "Say, Miss, should I come with you to the cottage now? Pa's let me have the afternoon to dally. An' it don't look like neither Mary nor Beth is coming back."

Perhaps having Wally with her would be more helpful than the twins or Mrs. Croft. "All right, if you want to come with me, we'll go now. I have the vicar's jingle."

"Shall we wait to see if the twins come back?"

"I think it's best if we don't involve them further right now."

He looked at her curiously, but said nothing and trotted ahead to get the jingle ready for the short ride to the cottage.

Evy could tell something was troubling Beth, perhaps even frightening her. She must think of a way to get Beth to confide in her. But she wouldn't think of that now. Her thoughts were on searching the attic. If someone was still prowling about, then it might mean the intruder was still looking for something important.

There was something she had never mentioned to anyone, not even to Aunt Grace. She had once walked into Uncle Edmund's office to see him seated at his desk with a small drawer open. Though she hadn't understood back then, she now thought that drawer could have been a hidden compartment. Uncle Edmund had looked up to see her standing in the doorway watching him. He made nothing of it, but he had slowly pushed the little drawer closed and, smiling at her, asked if she wanted to talk with him.

The long-ago incident had been kept deep in her childhood memory until recently. When the intruder searched the desk and located the contents of the envelope, had he also opened a hidden compartment? Or was something of importance still waiting there?

Crutches or no, I'm going to find out.

CHAPTER TWENTY-EIGHT

Evy arrived at the cottage with Wally a short time after leaving the cemetery. Except for the season, everything was much as she remembered it
on Allhallows Eve. The summer day sparkled with sunshine, and the
crimson and yellow roses were in full bloom. Even the scraggly gera-
nium cutting that she had taken from Aunt Grace's rectory garden had
snapped out of its gloom, and a brave cluster of blossoms was about to
burst forth into a cheery pink. A mockingbird in the apple tree was
singing merrily at a lookout perch near the top, hopefully serenading a
prospective mate.

Evy glanced up toward the attic window. The green shutter remained missing, and the familiar dark pane looked down on her.
The sight awakened the same sensation of watchfulness that she'd felt
months ago.

Evy walked up the garden path to the front door, Wally following
behind her. She sensed that he, too, had become wary, though there was
little but suspicion to justify their uneasy emotions.

She unlocked the door, and it opened, beckoning her inward.

The dimness of the rooms struck her. She told Wally to draw some
drapes back. As light flooded in, the shadows fled.

She entered the pantry, which remained dim, and Wally lit a lamp
and held it toward the flight of steps.

The sight of those steps built along the wall affected her more than
she had expected. She managed to hide her sudden pang of fear from

Wally, aware that he could already sense the moment's drama. Just what did he suspect might happen?

"Can you climb up, Miss Evy?"

Wally's nervous whisper caused her fingers to tighten on her crutches. Could she? She knew she must confront her limitations eventually. Did she even have the nerve to climb upward again—toward that closed door? The memory of it flying open, with that dark, ugly blanket rushing at her, left her heart pounding.

She must face that stairway—of steps toward her affliction. What had transpired here was to her an emotional barrier, strewn with fears out of the past.

"I can do it with one crutch," she insisted, aware her voice was tense but steady. "I can use my free hand to balance along the wall. You go ahead with the lamp, Wally, and I'll follow at my own pace."

"If you're sure, Miss."

He climbed slowly as though he, too, were facing an unknown danger that might suddenly jump out at him from the shadows.

Wally was already inside the attic lighting a second lamp when she entered. He'd leaned her other crutch by the door, and she took it and went across the wooden plank floor to Uncle Edmund's desk.

"Everything looks the same, Miss. Nothing different since me and the twins was here."

She looked around carefully to make her own assessment. She couldn't tell if the desk had been tampered with or not, but she checked both trunk lids and found them still locked. It would seem normal for an intruder to have pried the lids open to search the contents. Had the individual known just what to search for and exactly where to search? That gave her pause. If that was so—her gaze went to the desk, her heart sinking—had the intruder known then about the secret drawer? The envelope must have come from there. She moved toward the desk, her eyes searching the area where she remembered seeing Uncle Edmund's hand—

Wally breathed in. "Did you hear something, Miss, from below?"

Evy stood still, listening. At first she heard nothing, just ordinary creaks as the sun beat upon the roof. Then, lightly…the sound of footsteps. There'd been no one here just minutes ago, and she hadn't heard anyone arrive out front of the cottage.

She moved to the shutterless window, looking toward the dirt road that led up to Rookswood, seeing the line of trees bordering Grimston Woods.

"See anything, Miss?" Wally whispered.

His whisper sounded nervous. Except for the vicar's jingle, she could see no other vehicle or horse near the gate.

"It could be one of the twins…or we imagined it. The wind is rising. You know how old wood creaks." She spoke quietly, discounting her assessment even as she spoke. Surely, no one would try anything harmful now, not with the two of them here. It was too easy to let her imagination run in the wildest directions.

But it was too soon for the Hooper twins to have gotten here, and Wally knew that also.

"They'd've hollered up, Miss. An' I doubt Mary's even found Beth yet."

Evy was beginning to think Wally did indeed have suspicions about whether or not she had fallen down the steps the night of the accident. This was no time to feed his fears. She was about to turn from the window when she saw something in the bushes directly below her that halted her. *What was that?*

Wally hurried beside her. "What do you see, Miss?"

A horse stood tied near the wall of the cottage, partially concealed by thick bushes.

Wally looked toward the bushes. "Say, that horse…"

The excited recognition in his voice alerted her.

"You've seen it before?"

He nodded at her low voice. "Yes, a fine horse he is, too. I was passing time with Tibbs the other day. Tibbs's pa is head groom at Rookswood. He was rubbing him down and saying what a fancy one he was."

"A Rookswood horse, then?" What could she make of that?

"Aye, Miss, a Rookswood horse, aright. That's King's Knight. He got a ribbon in a show some years ago."

"The Dublin horse show?" she asked quickly.

"Aye, it was, Miss. You know the horse?"

It belonged to Rogan Chantry. Rogan had won that ribbon. When she made no comment, Wally went on. "I'd recognize King's Knight anywheres, 'cause of that white diamond on his black head. A beauty, he is. Odd why he'd be here, Miss."

She leaned closer to the window, trying to catch a glimpse of anyone near the horse.

Odd, too, that whoever was riding King's Knight had not cared to draw attention to himself, but tied the horse here, instead of the front gate. The question was, how long had the horse been there? A few minutes, or since before she and Wally had arrived?

"The rider musta rode here through the back lanes from Rookswood property, Miss."

Yes, perhaps through the back woods, which was a longer route. Was someone just out for a pleasant afternoon ride? She was fooling herself. Then why *hide* the horse?

Maybe someone was already inside the cottage when she arrived with Wally a short while ago. But the front door had been locked. Perhaps the back door by the kitchen? There would be no difficulty getting a second key, since the owners were friends of the Chantrys. If everything was innocent, then why the cautious tread of footsteps? There was no reason for anyone from Rookswood to keep their presence secret.

"Shh, the footsteps have stopped."

"Yes— Look, Miss! *There!*"

She saw the stirring of bushes from below where the horse was tied. Evy strained, seeing only the back of the figure that emerged. The stealthy movements sent a tingle along Evy's skin. The nightmare of last October was still too fresh upon her mind not to react to the creaks and events around her. She must see who the person was. Her gaze riveted upon the figure, presumably a man, wearing a hat that concealed his hair and, although a warm day, some sort of riding jacket. As though sensing her unwavering gaze, the figure's head turned, and the side of his face momentarily came into view.

Evy stepped quickly away from the window, drawing Wally with her.

Lord Anthony Brewster. When she carefully inched forward again to look below, she saw Lord Brewster leading King's Knight away from the trees and bushes toward the back of the cottage, where she assumed he would ride through the woods to Rookswood.

But why?

"Did you recognize him, Miss? Seemed a bit familiar to me."

Evy turned away without speaking. She must be careful before giving Wally suspicions about Lord Brewster.

What had Anthony Brewster been doing here, and why had he gone to such care to keep from being seen? The questions nagging at her only increased. If those were his footsteps they'd heard, why hadn't he spoken when she came in? He would have heard her and Wally enter the cottage through the front door and climb up the stairs. They hadn't tried to keep quiet. Maybe Lord Brewster had been searching for something too.

The implications were disappointing, unpleasantly so. Yet she wanted to give him the benefit of the doubt. His motives might be honorable. She liked the gentleman. He'd been kind to her. She pushed troubling suspicions from her mind and focused her attention once more on looking through Uncle Edmund's desk.

"Rather strange, isn't it, Miss? What do you think it all means?"

"I'm not at all sure. Perhaps it would be best if you went below and kept an eye out. If the Hooper twins decide to show up, better send them back home. I don't think it's wise to have them wandering around. Check the back kitchen door, too. Since the front door was locked when we came in, he may have come in that way. See if you notice anything unusual out back, but stay close to the cottage."

"Yes, Miss, just as I was thinking. But you don't think that fellow was up to any ill, do you? Not someone from Rookswood, Miss?"

She heard the incredulity in his voice.

"Yes, it does sound incredible, doesn't it?" Her voice was toneless.

Wally looked at her a moment, bewilderment on his young face, then she looked away and heard the sound of his footsteps clattering down the stairs.

Evy went to the parson's desk and began a quick search to locate the secret drawer, praying it hadn't been a childhood fancy. She fussed for about fifteen minutes, pushing and shoving here and there, opening drawers and feeling behind them for knobs and levers, yet finding nothing. It proved a daunting task, especially as she became emotionally absorbed in old letters and sermon notes from the vicar's younger years. All in all, she had discovered nothing that would give even the slightest indication either of the contents of that envelope or of any secret drawer.

Frustrated, she paused long enough to open the attic window, letting in the summer breeze and the singing of birds. In this environment it appeared, even to her, that the recent events of her life might merely be illusory. Her crutches, however, propped against the wall, countered that possibility. One thing she was certain she could not have imagined was the sinister figure rushing at her from the attic door.

She turned away from the little window to resume her search. *Lord, if there really is a secret drawer...if I didn't just imagine it as a child...please help me. The desk is small enough. Surely locating it can't be that difficult.*

She sat staring at the desk, rubbing away the crease between her brows. Her gaze fell on the smooth strips of wood below the rim of the desktop. The strips looked like parts of the structure, but what if one of them could slide out?

Evy pulled on them, but nothing moved. Could there be a release somewhere? She began pulling out the drawers again and feeling inside for anything unusual. Within the top right drawer, her fingers reached up and brushed against a small lever connected beneath the desktop.

Was this it? She pulled it toward her and heard something click. One of the strips had snapped out about an inch, startling her. It had to be! The hidden drawer! As she pulled it farther out, she saw a long envelope lying in the thin drawer.

With glee she stared at the yellowed envelope. *Thank you, Lord.* She snatched it from its compartment and compared it to the wrinkled envelope Beth Hooper had found.

Her hopes crashed. The writing was not from Henry Chantry. It was just Uncle Edmund's handwriting. She fingered the sealed envelope—perhaps several pages inside.

Had Uncle Edmund intended to deliberately mislead someone? Perhaps what she now held was what the intruder had been searching for. Had the intruder only found a decoy back in October? Had the thief believed he had found the real letter when he hadn't? Her hopes revived. Uncle Edmund with his gentle ways and spectacles always slipping down his nose may have been more shrewd that anyone had suspected.

She was beginning to open the sealed flap when she heard the sound of the front gate clicking shut, followed by footsteps up the walkway. Bold footsteps! Quickly she stuffed the sealed envelope down her bodice and arranged the front of her dress. Drawing in a quick breath, she hobbled to the window and peered below.

Heyden van Buren. He must have decided to leave his hotel in London and join her here. He would be pleased to learn Lady Elosia also wanted her in Capetown. Pleased, too, that Evy had made up her mind to go. Maybe she ought to tell him everything. But no, she wasn't that trusting yet. Until the whole truth was known, everyone was suspect.

At least he was making no effort to be elusive. She'd certainly had enough of stealthy footsteps and creaking wood for one day. She walked to the attic door and prepared herself for the visit, waiting for Wally to open the front door and let him in.

Evy was still standing there a moment later when she heard Heyden below her.

"Hullo, up there, Evy?" he called from below the attic steps.

Where was Wally?

"Up here, Heyden!"

She caught her breath. *What!* Challenging voices—a thud, followed by a scuffle, then the cracking sound of something breaking—*furniture?*

Wally! With heart pounding she moved through the door to the small landing and looked down into the pantry. Her breath sucked in. Wally was nowhere in view. It was Rogan! And Heyden, in a savage fight.

Rogan's fist smashed into Heyden's belly, followed by a chop to the back of his neck, bringing him down on one knee, but Heyden came up again and rammed Rogan, sending him slamming against the wall. A picture crashed to the floor.

Heyden took a swing at Rogan but was met with a blow to the chin that sent him backward against the stove. The collision sent a kettle clattering to the wall. Heyden slumped to the floor. This time he moaned but did not get up.

Evy stared at the scene in confusion. *What is going on!?* Her gaze swerved to Rogan. Could she trust him? What if—

He came to the bottom of the stairs and looked up at her. His dark, earthy gaze held her captive.

She hardly recognized him. He was tanned deeply from the African sun and now wore a small mustache. Although Rogan had never lacked masculine appeal, he was even more handsome now.

"Rogan! What are you doing?"

Rogan's eyes hardened into rock. He started toward Heyden again.

"No," she cried, and he looked up at her, and for the moment she searched his face, his gaze told her nothing.

"My one regret, Evy, is that I wasn't here to protect you from him."

Evy looked from Rogan down to Heyden. From him?

"What are you saying?" she whispered.

"I believe it was Heyden who came to Rookswood years ago to confront Henry, believing he still had the Black Diamond. They had a row and things went badly, and Henry was shot, but I've no solid evidence to prove it."

"And you never will," Heyden countered suddenly. "You're lying through your teeth. Don't fall for his schemes, Evy."

Heyden caught the edge of the table and pulled himself up from the floor. He leaned there, his lip cut, looking up at them with a thunderous scowl. "It's the diamond he wants, Evy, not you. Don't you see? The Black Diamond. He knows now that you're the one van Buren heiress. The one person Jendaya will trust to tell where the Black is hidden."

Rogan went toward him. He grabbed Heyden by the front of his shirt and jerked him forward. "You're lucky you're still alive," he said through gritted teeth. "If I were you I'd sit down nice and quiet and start worrying about being hanged."

He pushed Heyden into a kitchen chair and leaned toward him.

"You think I don't know it was you who killed Henry that night? You were convinced he had the Kimberly Black, but you were wrong. But by the time you discovered you were wrong, it was too late. Henry caught you red-handed in his study, and you decided to silence him."

"I don't know what you're talking about. You're raving like a lunatic. Evy, go for Lord Brewster at once."

"Stay where you are, darling. Heyden van Buren is a murderer."

Darling. Evy couldn't have moved if she wanted to.

"You're out of your mind," Heyden sneered. "I was a boy when your uncle was killed. I was in the Transvaal and can prove it. If anyone killed him, you did. You and your obsession for his map and the Black Diamond."

Evy snapped awake. Which man should she trust with the sealed envelope? Rogan, of course—but was she absolutely certain? Her love must not get in the way. She would remain silent for now.

Heyden's use of the term "a boy" struck her. What had he told her the other night in London at Chantry Townhouse? Even a boy was capable of murder? Yes, that was it. Even a boy…

"I wasn't old enough to confront Henry," Rogan said, "but *you* were. But I'll admit there had to be someone else older and wiser who put you up to coming to Rookswood that night. Someone who also believed Henry had the Black Diamond."

"Keep talking. You're only making a fool of yourself in front of Evy."

"Who was it, Heyden? Out with it! Julien Bley? No, not Julien. You despise him and his plans for British expansion into Boer territory. Was it Inga?"

Heyden's defiant smile was fixed. "If Mother and I decided to take back the diamond, why not? It came from the Transvaal Republic, Dutch territory. Territory stolen by the British. That diamond was a van Buren discovery. Julien stole it from Carl. Yes—from Evy's grandfather. Julien even arranged for Carl van Buren to be killed in that mine explosion to take control of the discovery."

Could that be true? Evy wondered.

"I've no particular love for Julien, but there's no reason he would have arranged Carl van Buren's death," Rogan said.

"I wouldn't put it past him. Inga thinks so. My father was killed, too, in the same explosion with Carl. Had I held onto the Black Diamond in the Cape House stables that night, it would have gone for a good purpose, to finance a war with you cursed English! We will yet have one, and we will win."

"Then you admit knocking Henry unconscious in the stables?"

"Yes. But I didn't kill him that night at Rookswood. I wasn't anywhere near Grimston Way."

"So that was your motive…to use the diamond to finance a Boer war? You're crazy if you think you could have sold that on the international market."

Heyden glared at the scorn in Rogan's voice.

"That's where you're wrong, Chantry. We could do it all right, and we will. We'll get the diamond yet."

"You were around fourteen when Katie van Buren escaped Cape House to meet Henry in the stable. How did you manage to knock him unconscious?"

"I was hiding in the stables before Henry came in. I knew Katie was coming to meet him there. Katie had Inga send Henry a message at Capetown harbor to come meet her. I was the messenger boy, though Katie didn't know it. Before Henry arrived, I chose a spot where I could overhear everything they said. I heard them plotting about the Black Diamond and running off with it. But Katie wanted to go to Rorke's Drift first to get Evy. When Katie and Henry came back from the house with the diamond, I was ready. He saw me when he came in for the horse, but he underestimated me. He thought I was on his side. He asked me to see to his golden gelding in the stall. When his back was turned, I clobbered him. I had the Black in my hand when I went out the back stable door with his horse. But someone jumped me from behind as I was mounting. I know now it was Dumaka.

"When I awoke I was lying in a ditch behind the stables. Henry's horse was still around somewhere. I heard Anthony looking for the horse. A short while later, when Anthony and Julien were accusing Henry of stealing the diamond, I was able to get back to the house to my mother, who fixed the bruise on my head. She hid me for a few days so Julien didn't notice. He was always so occupied he never paid much attention to what Inga was doing anyway. There was a time when Inga tried to steal the Black, but she couldn't find it, though she often searched. Katie was the only one who figured out where he kept it."

"So Inga was in on the whole thing," Rogan said.

"Absolutely. The entire van Buren family is dedicated to the Boer Republics." He hastened a glance toward Evy. "But Inga loved Katie. She had no intention of hurting her, but she knew that Boer independence took precedence over everything else."

Evy remained silent, studying both men.

"Then we both know that it was Dumaka who took the Black from you at the stables," Rogan said. "You tried to get information about Dumaka from Jendaya at Dr. van Buren's mission, isn't that right? But she didn't trust you and got away that night."

Heyden gave him a measuring glance. "You were at Jakob's mission?"

"I was there a few days. He told me everything he knew. He said you were looking for Dumaka and the Black. When I put two and two together, I knew the reason you were coming back to England was to find Evy and bring her back to South Africa. You were hoping to use Evy to gain information from Jendaya, but the woman was too smart to trust you."

"Jendaya should have cooperated with me. If she had, I wouldn't have needed to bring Evy into this at all. Jendaya knows where Dumaka is. She's just a stubborn old Zulu."

"She was wise. And she's come to faith in Christ, and she wouldn't have cooperated with you anyway. She ran away because she guessed you would use Katie's daughter to get information to take them to Dumaka. That it would be a dangerous and foolish move on your part. I know Dumaka. I've already spoken with him. He's a warrior. And he's fanatical about his spiritual beliefs. Beliefs that concern that Black Diamond. I've thought long and hard about why Dumaka would have worked for Julien Bley at Cape House. He's an induna. With Jendaya it was different. She was a Christian, and she was recommended to work for Julien by Dr. and Mrs. Varley, who were at Rorke's Drift at the time."

Heyden narrowed his eyes. "Dumaka knew Julien had the Black and was just waiting to find its location before he took Julien's head for a trophy. Lucky for Julien he never did. Why Dumaka let me live, I don't know, but it didn't have anything to do with sentiment. He was probably just short on time."

Heyden looked up at Evy. "You accuse me for wanting to bring Evy to meet Jendaya, but Evy wants to meet her, and Jakob as well." He turned a sharp glance on Rogan. "It would have worked, too, if you hadn't come back with your meddling. You're after the diamond too. Why not be man enough to admit it?"

"Why did you think it was Henry and not Dumaka who took the diamond from you at the stables that night?"

Heyden shrugged. "I didn't think of Dumaka then. I thought I might not have struck Henry hard enough to keep him down. That somehow he'd managed to come to and jump me from behind. Later,

Inga figured out it was Dumaka. He disappeared from Cape House that same night. He was seen among the Zulu fighting at Rorke's Drift. Jendaya told me when I talked to her at Jakob's mission."

Silence filled the dim pantry for the first time.

"Then you didn't kill Henry Chantry at Rookswood that night?" Evy asked her first question.

"No." Heyden looked at Rogan. "There's your murderer right there."

"If that were true, I wouldn't waste my time talking to you," Rogan said dryly. "But you haven't convinced me, Heyden. I think you did come to Rookswood that night. You didn't know about Dumaka back then. You thought Henry had the Black."

There was a commotion at the front door. Wally rushed in, dragging Beth Hooper behind him. Both were flushed with excitement and their eyes wide.

"Tell 'em what you know and seen, Beth. Don't be afraid."

Beth looked up at Evy. "I've seen Mr. Heyden around the village the last few weeks, Miss Varley. I even talked to him down by the inn. He told me all about the Boers and said the British are cruel and unjust to them. He talked about a whip called a sjambok, saying they would whip the British into obedience with it in the next war. He said if I told anyone what I saw at the barn that he would use that whip on Digger, Wally's dog, and kill him."

Wally glared at Heyden.

Heyden started to get up from the chair, but Rogan shoved him back down.

"Go on, Beth," Evy urged. "What did you see at the barn?"

"I saw Mr. Heyden around the carpenter shop in the barn belonging to Wally's father the day before I saw him at the inn. Mr. Heyden came riding by, keeping close to the woods, as if he didn't want anyone to see him. Then I went to hide behind a tree. I saw him sneak in through a window. Then Wally's dog Digger started to bark. Mr. Heyden took off in a hurry, got on his horse, but he saw me as he rode off into the trees.

He was gone before Wally arrived. But the next day Mr. Heyden found me alone and said what I just told you about Digger."

Evy was furious. *To threaten a child with killing a pet!* Her eyes shot from Heyden to Wally. "That was where you hid the sack with the dark blanket, wasn't it, Wally? In the barn?"

"It was, Miss. I told you yesterday someone's been following me for two weeks or so, and it was him." He pointed at Heyden. "I'll wager he was trying to find out if I suspected anything. If I still had the blanket, and if I did, where I put it. I recognize his yellow hair."

"You are certain, Wally?" Evy asked, keeping her emotions under control.

"Yes, Miss. Sure of it now."

Rogan's dark brows were drawn together with intense curiosity. "Blanket? What blanket?"

But before Evy or Wally could say anything, Heyden gave an icy stare at Wally and Beth. "You both think you're ruddy clever little brats, don't you?"

"Intimidate the children again, Heyden, and you'll soon be missing a few teeth," Rogan warned, his voice cold and steely. "All right, out with it. You did come to Rookswood on the night Henry was killed."

"Absurd! I wasn't anywhere in England that night. I've already told you. I didn't kill him."

Rogan's dark eyes were glittering. "I think you did, Heyden."

"You're mad, Rogan. See for yourself, Cousin Evy. Yes, quite stark raving mad. He is the insane one in the family."

Evy felt drained. "I don't think so, Heyden. Rogan, I have something I think is important. I found it in Uncle Edmund's desk." She turned her back to them, and when she faced them again, she held the sealed envelope.

The two men looked up at her. Rogan watched intently. Heyden seemed to stop breathing, and his gaze dropped to the envelope.

Heyden cried out, "Careful, Evy! That's exactly what Rogan's been looking for." He stood, and this time Rogan didn't push him back down into the chair, for he was staring at the envelope.

"Rogan's been in Grimston Way for weeks now, sneaking about. Just as he did when he was a boy. And yet he dares to accuse *me*. He's the one who really killed Henry. I told you Rogan was here, didn't I? I warned you. I was right, wasn't I? Don't let him get that envelope, Evy. It was Rogan who was searching the attic for something incriminating when you came home unexpectedly on Allhallows Eve. It threw him into a panic. He lost his head. And when you started up those steps, he was so frightened you'd recognize him that he pushed you down! You're on crutches now for the rest of your life because of him."

Rogan whirled and looked at her in shock. "Pushed?"

Heyden went unexpectedly pale.

Rogan took a threatening step in his direction. "*You* just stated that Evy had been *pushed* down those steps."

Heyden was speechless.

"Yes," Evy cried. Her gaze fixed on Heyden. "How would you know I was pushed, Heyden? How would *you* know?" she repeated. Her heart thudded as she started down the steps without her crutches, leaning against the wall for support, emotion seizing her. "I've kept that horrifying nightmare to myself. I've told no one except Mrs. Croft, and she would *never* tell you. She doesn't trust you. It was you, wasn't it? I never thought of you, but I did fear it could be Lord Anthony Brewster.

"And now—it was this letter you wanted, that you were searching for when I came home and surprised you. It was *you* who lost your head and came at me in a panic...with the blanket over your head. That hideous dark blanket that came at me...and shoved me backward. But Uncle Edmund outsmarted you! The letter you found in his desk was a decoy. The right envelope, but the wrong letter. Henry's letter to Edmund is here inside this envelope. Edmund outsmarted you—good was wiser than evil. Uncle Edmund was as wise as a serpent, though harmless as a dove."

Rogan seemed to be in shock for a moment more. Then, blazing with anger, he turned toward Heyden, but too late. Heyden caught up a chair, bringing it down with a sickening noise against Rogan's head.

Evy thought she screamed but heard nothing come from her throat, just the pounding of her heart in her ears. She watched in frozen horror as Heyden kicked Rogan in the head and then started toward her with wild eyes. Wally and Beth tackled his legs and brought him tripping to the floor with a *thud*. Wally swung a chair against him, but not powerfully enough. Beth began hurling cups and glasses and pans at him as Evy fought her way up the steps with the letter to lock herself inside the attic. As Rogan started to stir, Heyden decided to flee while he had the chance. He broke from the pantry, rushing through the parlor like a crazed demon. Wally went out after him.

Rogan pushed himself up from the floor, staggering, trying to regain control. He went after Heyden and Wally.

Evy came back down the steps, her hands trembling, gripping the envelope.

Wally burst back into the pantry from the front parlor.

His eyes were wide and his face flushed. He pointed behind him. "The blond fellow jumped on his horse and took off. Master Rogan did the same, and now they've galloped off into Grimston Woods. Rogan was close behind him. That black horse of his rides like the north wind!"

Evy sank to the step. She couldn't think clearly. Heyden, a murderer—

And Rogan—

And she loved him desperately, but—

She dropped her head into her palms and out of desperation started to pray. "Oh, Father God, help Rogan, protect him, help us *all!*"

She felt Beth's trembling arm around her shoulders and raised her face. The girl's eyes were anxious, and she was trembling and breathing hard. "Don't be afraid, Miss Varley. He's gone now. Master Rogan will stop him. Remember what you told me about God having plans for us, even if they're different than we expected? They're good plans, because God loves us."

Evy's heart melted. She put her arms around Beth, and they held on to each other tightly.

"Thank you for being brave enough to speak up, Beth. You did the right thing. And you were right to hurl those dishes at him. Even if we won't have any more cups and saucers for a while." She laughed nervously, and Beth suddenly grinned.

Beth touched one of Evy's crutches. "There's a reason for painful things, even if we don't always know what it is at the time. You were right, Miss Varley."

"It's the Lord who is right," Evy said. "He will be our confidence."

Wally came up and grinned at Beth. "Say, Twin, we done pretty good together, didn't we?"

"We did. How's Digger?"

"Chewing on a bone."

"You both are heroes," Evy said with a smile. She held up the envelope intact.

"Are you going to open it?" Wally urged.

"No. I'll wait for Rogan. We know Heyden was the culprit, but we still don't know if he killed Henry Chantry. I think this letter will answer that question."

Mary Hooper came rushing through the parlor. She stopped short when she saw the broken furniture and dishes.

"Drat, I missed it."

"We'll tell you all about it, Twin," Wally said. "Won't we, Beth?"

Beth nodded. Mary sighed. "Mum's having a fit. You better come with me. You, too, Wally."

Beth followed her twin sister, but Wally shook his head. "Not till Master Rogan gets back. I'm staying with Miss Evy."

"Tell Mrs. Croft to come here to the cottage," Evy said to the twins as they went out.

"Yes, Miss Varley," they called in unison over their shoulders.

When Wally came down the steps with her crutches, Evy walked into the parlor and sank tiredly into a chair to wait for Rogan.

CHAPTER TWENTY-NINE

When Rogan rode into the front yard an hour later, Wally called out from the parlor, "Master Rogan's back, Miss. He's alone. Everyone's saying Mr. Heyden got away."

Evy waited anxiously. Beth had gone home, and between Beth's and Wally's reporting, the village was astir with the news. A "cracking fight" had occurred in the cottage between Master Rogan Chantry and the newcomer, Heyden van Buren. Already people were out in the lanes talking about it, and a small gathering stood in front of the gate. Wally said Lord Brewster was contacting Scotland Yard.

Mrs. Croft had come hurrying over with Vicar Osgood, who consoled Evy and persuaded himself she was doing well. Afterward, he'd taken the jingle and returned to the rectory to be with Mrs. Osgood, who was down with a summer cold and quite upset that she hadn't been able to accompany him to the cottage.

Mrs. Croft muttered to herself as she cleaned up the mess of broken porcelain and glass in the pantry so she could get tea on. Always the practical one, Mrs. Croft had managed, on her way over with the vicar, to bring a plate of cakes and sandwiches from the rectory kitchen.

"I always knew it was that blond Dutchman," she had commented to Evy. "Never trusted him. Gave me the willies when he'd come calling to see you in London."

Evy was feeling so much better now that the ordeal was over that she let the exaggeration pass.

Rogan entered the front door looking grim. His shirt was torn, and he had dried blood on his temple and forehead. But his unwavering gaze told her not to be alarmed.

"He fired his pistol, first at me, then at my horse. He grazed the stallion's leg, but I think he'll come out of it all right."

His horse, his beautiful black stallion, the one she'd first seen him riding when they met years ago in the woods. "Oh, Rogan, I'm so sorry."

A hint of a smile appeared. "Just like us, isn't it? We're both more worried about my horse than Heyden getting away." He touched his head and winced. "But I'll hunt him down. He'll try to get out of the country and back to the Transvaal."

Then he looked at her...

Weakness washed over her as his dark, earthy gaze caught and held hers.

He came toward her and stopped midway as his eyes deliberately confronted the crutches she held beside her.

She cringed inside. This was the moment her pride had recoiled from, had dreaded to confront—face to face with Rogan Chantry.

Rogan took the remaining steps two at a time until he stood before her. The warmth in his eyes could not be denied. His arms encircled her waist, pulling her to him as she looked up into his face. His aggressive approach sent her head spinning.

He cupped the back of her head and brought her face to his as their lips met passionately. Abandoning her crutches, she wrapped her arms around his strong shoulders in a moment charged with wild sweetness.

"Darling, remember I told you to wait for me? That I would come back?"

"Rogan..." she whispered, holding him tighter, resting her head against his chest. "It's been dreadful...without you."

"I'm sorry I'm so late returning," he whispered warmly against the side of her face. "There were reasons I can't explain now, but they were chains that bound me, that kept me from you. But I'll allow nothing to tear us apart again, Evy. You're mine. You've always been mine from the first time I saw you in the thunderstorm in Grimston Woods. I've loved you ever since then. And I'm going to love you forever."

Her heart wanted to burst. She must tell him about Henry, but she couldn't swim above the sea of emotion that was drowning her into silence. *I love you!* She could barely keep from declaring her heart.

"I'm in love with you," he said. "You care for me. I know you do. And I won't take no for an answer."

He held her close. Here was the man she loved, the man she wanted, and the man she might have to refuse. She couldn't handle the thought of loss now and held him tightly.

"Now, what was this about your being pushed down those steps?" His look grew sober.

"I'll explain everything, but first let's tend to that head of yours!" Worried about his head injury, she tried to lead him to a chair, but instead he grinned at her and, catching her up, set her in it instead. He turned to Wally.

"It's Wally, isn't it?"

"Yes sir. It's me."

"Good lad. I've got a task for you. I need you to go bring Tibbs's father from Rookswood. Tell him to bring his bag of medicine over here and see to the stallion."

"Yes sir!"

"Then go to Rookswood and tell Mrs. Wetherly to send Bixby down with the coach. From there, go to the rectory and inform the vicar and Mrs. Osgood that Evy will be returning to Rookswood with me."

Rogan looked over at Evy with a slight smile. "You don't mind staying at Rookswood?"

She smiled and lifted a brow. "You seem to know what you're doing."

"Yes. And Wally, I'll send Bixby down to the rectory later to bring Miss Evy's bags up to the estate. Got it?"

LINDA LEE CHAIKIN

Wally grinned. "Got it, sir."

"Good. And don't think I've forgotten you, Wally. You'll be rewarded later for your friendship to Miss Evy. You and your father, Harold. I understand he wants a new carpenter shop with the latest tools from London?"

Wally sucked in his breath. He looked from Rogan to Evy and back to Rogan again. His grin widened. "Yes sir!"

When he'd gone running out the front door, Evy managed a smile at Rogan. "That was good of you."

"Just preparing the soil. I'll be Squire of Rookswood one day."

"You forgot to tell him to send for Dr. Tisdale. Those bruises on your head must be treated. I'll get some antiseptic and some wet cloths from Mrs. Croft. She's in the kitchen making tea."

"I'll wait until we get to Rookswood. I've learned a lot about survival on the trek to the Zambezi."

As independent as ever.

"No, you don't, Master Rogan," Mrs. Croft said firmly. She entered with tea and the plate of sandwiches and cakes and clucked her tongue over Rogan's condition as she hustled off for wet cloths and salves.

He smiled toward Mrs. Croft, then sat down beside Evy. Putting his arm around her, he drew her to him and kissed her.

"That should make my aching head feel better before we talk," he murmured.

"Mrs. Croft will be back in a moment…"

"She'll need to get used to my adoring inclinations…"

"I'm not sure it's going to help me concentrate…"

Mrs. Croft brought a basin of water, cloths, and a bottle of ointment and fussed over Rogan while Evy smiled and poured the tea.

Mrs. Croft carried away the basin, and Evy handed him the cup of tea.

"And now! Business. Those crutches… I was told by Lady Camilla in her letter that you'd fallen and hurt yourself seriously and were in the hospital in London, but she didn't say you'd been attacked."

"She couldn't have known. No one knew the truth but Mrs. Croft. I didn't know whether I could trust anyone."

"That was wise, not only for your sake, but if the story had gotten out, you wouldn't have been able to trip up Heyden for knowing too much about the incident. Anyway, I came at once. I've been here for a week because I've suspected Heyden of Henry's murder all along, and I was hoping to catch him doing something incriminating. But the first thing I did on arrival in London was talk to your physician, Dr. Harris. He believes you'll get stronger with time. Someday you may walk again with only a slight limp."

If only...

"Lady Elosia said you were due in from London today or tomorrow. She didn't know you were here?"

"No. I kept things to myself. I was staying at the inn where Heyden is. I disguised myself coming and going. I searched his room when he was gone but came up with nothing. I saw him follow you and Wally from the cemetery earlier today. He arrived just after you and Wally, but he concealed himself in the trees. As an afterthought, I don't think he would have harmed you again. His present obsession was to get you back to South Africa to talk with Jendaya, as he admitted. But at the time I didn't know that. As soon as he saw Anthony Brewster leave with King's Knight, Heyden left the trees and came here to the cottage, as bold as you please, pretending he'd just ridden up."

Evy suddenly sat straighter. "Yes, Lord Brewster, I'd forgotten." She told him about having seen King's Knight tied below the attic window in the trees and how Lord Brewster had left the cottage. "Then you saw him, too?" she said.

"Only when he rode away."

"He left the cottage quite stealthily too, and I wondered why. Why didn't he want me to know he was here?"

Rogan stroked his mustache, regarding her thoughtfully.

"I don't know, but I think I shall have a talk with Lord Brewster tonight."

She wondered at the grimness in his voice, as though something bothered him about Lord Brewster. "But he's been quite kind to me. Remember the gentleman I came across in Grimston Woods when I was a girl? Did I ever tell you about it? It was the day I first met you. The gentleman turned out to be Lord Brewster. He told me so himself."

Rogan looked at her sharply. "What did he tell you about himself?"

"Not much, actually. He came to visit me in the hospital and arranged for my stay at Chantry Townhouse. As I said, he's been unexpectedly nice to me recently."

"Has he?" Something in his voice made her pause and look at him, but he merely watched her, alert. "Did he tell you anything else?"

Rogan must be asking about her inheritance. "He explained that I'm the van Buren heiress through my mother, Katie. But it seems I can't do much with the inheritance unless I marry. That will make me a prime target for more of Sir Julien's planning," she said wryly. She was determined not to do as Julien wanted. "I do have funds for living expenses now, very handsome ones, actually. That reminds me, I can now pay you back the loan you gave me."

"Evy, I've struck gold on the Zambezi. I don't need anything of yours from the van Buren side of the family. When Heyden went on that hysterical rampage about my wanting the Black Diamond, he was spewing forth the greed of his own heart."

She smiled. "Rogan, you needn't tell me that. I know you better than you think. For one thing, you've too much pride to want to succeed in life on van Buren diamonds," she said ruefully. "Besides, Rookswood will be yours—and the gold you've discovered. I didn't believe what Heyden said about you."

He stood and offered a bow. "Thank you, Madam. And may it be known to you that I will endeavor to win more of your confidence and trust."

"You're welcome *Sir* Rogan," she said primly.

She told him how Heyden claimed she had other van Buren relatives in the Transvaal, and about Dr. Jakob van Buren and his mission station near the Zambezi. "You said you spoke with him."

"I did. Julien first told me about him, and about Heyden's visit there with Jendaya. When our pioneer expedition arrived at Fort Salisbury—now it's usually called Rhodesia—I went to look up Dr. Jakob. He's a good man, Evy. You'll like him. He's eager to meet you. He gave me information on Heyden and Jendaya that got my suspicions up about Heyden. When I returned from the visit to our gold camp along the Zambezi, there was a letter waiting for me from Capetown, from Lady Camilla Brewster. She informed me of your *accident*. I came as soon as I could."

"Oh, Rogan…"

He squeezed her hands in his. "I'm only sorry I couldn't have gotten here in time to stop Heyden. But he'll get justice for what he's done to you, and to Henry. Can you tell me what happened?"

For the next half hour Evy told him all that had happened since that dark night in October, beginning with her return to the cottage from the village green on Allhallows Eve. She went through every terrifying detail about the attic door flinging open and a darkly garbed figure storming out at her like some winged gargoyle.

"He was covered with a dark blanket."

Rogan was angry but restrained. "The blanket Wally had? You still have it, I hope?"

"Yes, in my bedroom at the rectory."

She went on telling him the details of what had attracted Wally's curiosity enough to mention it to the Hooper twins, and then how the three detectives had returned here to the cottage to search.

"Wally discovered the blanket in the attic still smelling of kerosene, and with charred edges. It's the same blanket. I recognize it."

He scowled. "Do you remember seeing Heyden around the village or the rectory when you were younger?"

Evy thought back to those early days. She shook her head. "Not that I can recall."

"I think I may have."

That surprised her. He explained.

"On the night Henry was murdered, I was at Rookswood. I don't recall anything that happened. I must have been dead asleep. But most everyone else in the family had gone to London for the marriage of some relative. I think it may have been a sister or cousin of Lord Brewster. Heyden had opportunity to be in London that night, and it's a short train ride here to Grimston Way, not more than an hour and a half."

"He claims he was in Capetown."

"He can claim anything. After what he's done to you, I think we both agree he can be ruthless. Thinking back, I believe I saw him around the village that afternoon. I can't prove it. I was young, but I think he was here. It would have been easy enough to hide out in the woods until he could come to Rookswood without being seen. The servants and I were the only ones still in the house. Arcilla was in the nursery asleep with her nanny, old Miss Hortense."

The idea that Heyden may have been about the village now and then while she grew up gave her a chill. She was beginning to think Rogan was right in his earlier assessment, that Heyden might be a little daft.

"I'm also remembering some things Julien told me in South Africa as well. He told me that when he called on Henry shortly before he was murdered, Henry appeared to be onto something. He'd even made plans to make a trip to South Africa."

"You think Henry may have suspected Heyden?"

"I'm beginning to think so. Where's the envelope from Vicar Havering's desk?"

"Right here." She reached into her handbag and brought it out, still sealed.

He studied the writing on the outside. "This must be the vicar's handwriting."

"It is. Henry's letter should be inside."

Rogan opened the envelope and removed a single-page letter from Vicar Edmund Havering, and a second, smaller sealed envelope.

"This is interesting," Rogan murmured, turning the smaller envelope over in his hand. "It's from Henry all right, but it's addressed to *me*."

Evy was startled. "To you?" She looked at the envelope and saw that it was addressed to "Rogan Chantry, Rookswood Estate." And it was signed by Henry Chantry.

"So this is what Heyden was after," Rogan said, a thin edge of surprise in his voice. "I'd not have guessed anything like this."

Rogan handed her the single page from Uncle Edmund, while he opened the flap on the small envelope addressed to him from his uncle Henry.

They each read alone, in silence.

The letter from Edmund was not a letter at all, nor was it written to anyone in particular. It read more like a small diary.

As a safeguard, I am taking extra precautions with Mr. Chantry's letter. I have left it sealed, as it is not for me to know what he has written within. Mr. Chantry and I met alone two weeks ago. He gave me two envelopes. One, he said, was merely a decoy. The important envelope is to be kept for Rogan Chantry when he comes of age. But Henry has suggested to me that a young lad named Heyden van Buren could pose a problem. I was told that he is a cousin of sorts to Evy, but Mr. Chantry feels it best not to involve Evy at this time with the van Burens.

He has asked me to keep the decoy envelope in my files, but not so that it is impossible to find. I have done so. The important letter from Henry to Rogan is to be protected at all costs and turned over to Rogan Chantry on his twentieth birthday. Naturally, I will do so. I feel that I have obliged Mr. Henry Chantry accordingly, as he has ardently requested.

These are strange days, and one never knows what troubles are brewing. It is my desire, as well as Mr. Chantry's, to see that little Evy is allowed to grow up in Grimston Way with as few burdens as possible.

12 September

I have seen a young stranger in the village recently. I believe he is Heyden van Buren. He came to call on me last night when Grace was at the ladies meeting and Evy was asleep. He is from the Transvaal in Africa, inquiring about a letter that Henry Chantry had left him. He claims Henry wrote to him to come and claim this particular letter upon his death. I knew the lad was lying because the letter is Rogan's. Why he would know of this letter, I cannot guess. I have decided to put the letter for Rogan in my secret drawer and leave the decoy in my files just in case this fellow breaks into my office.

15 September

Heyden van Buren has been pestering me again. He's threatened me if I don't turn the letter over to him. I told him there is no letter. This is true, because the letter is not his but Rogan's. I informed Heyden that his soul was in a bad way with his Maker and that he needs to make peace with God through Christ. I offered to pray with him and read the Scriptures, but he railed at me. I do believe he could be dangerous. I warned him I would contact the London authorities if I saw him in the village again. He's been inquiring about Evy, and this troubles me deeply. I've not told Grace any of this. It would frighten her.

Late October

Heyden van Buren is back. He's changed his behavior. He has apologized for his rudeness and asked to meet me at the Inn of the Woods. Since I will be going that way to see Farmer Withers on October 25,

I shall oblige the strange lad. He wishes to pray with me. I will go meet with him as he has asked. It is my Christian duty to do so.

Evy sucked in her breath. October 25! That was the night of the storm when Uncle Edmund's buggy overturned and he was found dead.

Evy stared down at the letter, a pang of anxiety in her heart. It was his last entry.

Had they met? Had they talked? What had Uncle Edmund said to Heyden? Had he convinced him there was no letter from Henry Chantry? Heyden had not come back to the rectory searching for any letter. There had been years of silence until last October when she had surprised him in the attic going through Uncle Edmund's desk. What had happened during the long interval to change Heyden's mind and convince him to return and search for a letter from Henry?

She looked at Rogan. He was grim. They exchanged letters. Henry wrote:

I am on my way to South Africa to see Dr. Jakob van Buren. I think I am close to solving the mystery of what happened to the Kimberly Black Diamond. The young Heyden van Buren attacked me in the stable that night and took the diamond. He worries me. He is obsessed with the Boer cause and holds a deep resentment toward England. He has written recently, threatening me, accusing me of taking back the Kimberly Black from him. Actually, I suspect that Dumaka must have taken the diamond from Heyden.

Jakob wrote me months ago, suggesting I should be wary of Heyden. I wrote Jakob back and informed him that I had already received a threatening letter. Heyden demands I turn the diamond over to him. I have enclosed young Heyden's letter with this, my own letter, as evidence of his threats against me.

I am now taking the precaution of writing this brief letter and giving it to Vicar Havering. I have asked the vicar that should something unpleasant come my way on the expedition to South Africa to see Jakob, he is to guard this letter indefinitely. It is to be given to my blood nephew Rogan Chantry when he is old enough. I think he will know what to do. We have had too much scandal in this family already. And for little Evy's sake, I want no more. I want her to grow up in the healthy, cheerful family of the vicar and the honorable lady, Grace Havering.

It is my hope that Rogan Chantry will take it upon himself when he grows older to see to Katie's daughter in the years ahead. I wish for her a happy life. Katie would want her daughter to grow up with a Christian faith as strong as that of Dr. Clyde and Junia Varley.

Henry R. Chantry

Evy stared at the letter. She swallowed back the emotion welling up in her heart. Had Henry loved Katie?

She looked at Rogan. He had finished Uncle Edmund's letter and was reading the short message that Heyden had written to Henry. Rogan's jaw flexed. He finished reading and handed it to her.

"This is what Heyden was looking for."

Dear Henry Chantry,

You knocked me unconscious in the stables at Cape House the night Katie ran away to Rorke's Drift to find her baby. You stole the Kimberly Black Diamond from me. You will either turn it back over to me, or I swear I shall make you pay with your life for cheating me! You greedy British are all the same. You and Julien Bley and all the Chantrys! Greedy swine! Either return it, or you will pay!

Heyden van Buren

There was silence. Evy drew in a breath. "He wrote this before discovering Dumaka had the diamond. Do you think Heyden murdered Henry?"

"Yes."

She shivered. His terse voice reinforced her own convictions. She struggled to get the next words out. "And...Uncle Edmund?"

"Yes. When he grew older, he must have understood he had written his own arrest warrant."

She trembled, and Rogan seemed to notice at once and drew her into his arms. "It's over, Evy. The past cannot be changed. But I'll find Heyden again. He won't get away with this." Rogan sank into a chair, rubbed his head, and closed his eyes.

Evy went to him and put her arms around his neck. "I must get you back to Rookswood. Mr. Bixby should be here soon."

His gaze held hers, and he smiled. "Did I ever tell you how beautiful you are? I've missed you more than you'll ever know. On many of those warm, starry nights in Africa, I dreamed about you, having you there with me, holding you, kissing you—"

She felt the heat filling her cheeks, and her eyes faltered. "There's something I should have told you at once, Rogan."

His lashes narrowed thoughtfully, and a brow lifted. "Don't tell me you've fallen for the farmer's son, because I won't accept that, and your kiss denies it." He cupped her chin.

She looked at him. "Yes, I do love you, but love isn't enough."

"Look, darling, Derwent's been talking to me quite a bit recently, and don't forget I was raised in the church the same as you. Granted I'm not the saint that you are, or Derwent, but I confidently trust in Christ as my Savior."

She laid a loving hand against his bruised temple. "I know that... now. But that isn't the problem, Rogan." Tears came to her eyes, and she tried to stand quickly, nearly losing her balance.

He reached and steadied her, looking up at her. "What is it?"

She turned her head away. "I know who my father is... Your uncle—Henry Chantry!"

He stared at her for what seemed to Evy an eternity. His hand caught up hers, and he smiled as he brought it to his lips.

"Who told you that lie? Heyden?"

Lie? She continued to look down at him, her eyes searching his. "If it were just Heyden, I would have reason to doubt. But Lord Brewster also told me so."

He dropped her hand and stood, his mouth grim. "Anthony told you Henry was your father?"

"Yes," she admitted, aggrieved. "I came right out and asked him. After my hospital recovery, he arranged for me to stay with Mrs. Croft at Chantry Townhouse. I was there for a few months. He would come often and visit with me. Once I asked him, and he said that it was Henry. Oh, Rogan! How bitter life can be!"

"That's a ruddy lie, and if anyone knows it for sure, it's Lord Anthony Brewster—Lady Camilla, too."

"What do you mean? Why, Lady Camilla—" She stopped abruptly and her breath caught. *Camilla and her tale of a secret child...* Evy continued to stare at Rogan.

"Evy, darling, I was told the same story. Julien clobbered me with it just before the pioneer expedition to the Zambezi. He told me Katie and Henry had been in love and were planning to run away with you to America. Well, it's not true. I've a letter I could show you, but I want to give someone a last chance to show that he has the courage expected of a man. But trust me, darling, we are not related by blood."

She wanted to believe him. Her heart cried out that he was telling her the truth. A letter? From Lady Camilla?

"When I told you earlier," Rogan went on, "that there were chains that bound me from contacting you, I was referring to the lie Julien told me about Henry. I believed him and felt the only thing to do was to make sure we never saw each other again."

"But if Henry isn't my father, why would Sir Julien say this to you? And why would Heyden reinforce it?"

"Seems quite clear to me. The last thing Julien wanted to contend with was the effect our marriage would have on the family mine holdings. You know Julien. He arranges marriages to benefit the Company, but also to keep his hands on the reins. He knows we're both independent and won't tolerate his whip. And darling, Julien would have liked to keep you from ever inheriting Katie's wealth. As for Heyden, he probably understood Julien's wish to keep us apart, and thought that telling you I was a ruthless adventurer out to take advantage of you would make it easier for him to convince you to visit Jendaya."

"Yes, I thought that, but I did believe Lord Brewster about who my father is."

His jaw tightened. "Never mind Brewster for now, all right? We'll get all this cleared up shortly." He turned toward the open window. "That's Bixby now. The sooner we can get up to Rookswood, the better. My head is killing me."

Bixby came to the door and knocked. "Come in, Bix!" Rogan called.

Rogan turned to her, taking her shoulders and drawing her to him. "We still have much to talk about. Your health is most important. I want to talk to your London doctor myself so I can understand what's possible. But get one thing straight, sweetheart. Nothing is going to keep us apart. Not ever."

Emotion overwhelmed her. She came into his arms. "Rogan, darling…"

He kissed her, his embrace tightening. Her mind swam giddily.

"Ahem," Bixby discreetly cleared his throat. "I beg your pardon, sir."

Evy drew away from Rogan, and he smiled. "Hello, Bix, old boy. You're looking at the future Mrs. Rogan Chantry. Beautiful, isn't she?"

Bixby's dignified brows rose. "Quite so, Mr. Chantry. A very wise choice indeed."

CHAPTER THIRTY

Evy was shown to one of the guest bedrooms, where she freshened her face and hands with a cloth dipped in cool lemon water, then was served tea and cakes. She was not surprised to see that Lizzie, Mrs. Croft's niece, had managed to relieve the kitchen maid and bring the tray upstairs herself. One look at the young woman's eyes, shining with shrewd excitement, told Evy the young woman had a "bit of story" to pass along.

"Thought you'd care to know that the Lady's upped and gone back to Heathfriar, Miss. She left last night."

"Lady Patricia?"

"Indeed, she took every last one of her frocks and boxes of powder and rouge, she did. She was a mite upset too, I don't mind telling you, Miss. Like one of them hornet's nests my Jim has to clear outta the attic eaves every summer. She was riled, and she told Master Rogan a thing or two no respectable lady ought to repeat to another lady." Lizzie touched her white dust cap. "I can tell you Lady Elosia was in a state of shock herself. Thought she'd faint there and then, dead away on the rose-patterned carpet. It was Master Rogan himself who found her smelling salts and fanned her with that black lace fan she carries in the summer. Then he carried Lady Elosia to the divan. 'Now, Auntie,' he kept saying, 'I've always told you I wouldn't marry a woman I didn't really want.'"

Lizzie chortled. "Oh, Miss, if it weren't all so upsetting, it woulda been a cause for laughing. Him, so calm and determined, and Lady Elosia an emotional tizzy, and Lady Patricia throwing things at him from across the parlor. She had some letters that she just ripped up in front of him. She walks up and tosses them in his face. 'Cad,' she called him, and 'knave of hearts.' You know what those letters was, Miss?"

"I've no idea." Evy sighed. *Poor Rogan.*

"It was letters he'd written you while in Capetown. She'd come to visit on and off at Rookswood ever since Master Rogan left, and she musta sneaked them out of the morning mail basket in the hall."

Evy was at least thankful to learn that he had indeed written her during the long absence.

"Then Lady Patricia broke one of them glass cherubs that's been on the table for as far back as I can remember! That made Lady Elosia mad, it did. She sat up and shouted, 'How dare you break my heirlooms!' And then Lady Patricia called her an old hen and stomped out, shouting for Annie—that's her private maid—to pack her things. They was going to Heathfriar then and there."

Evy sank to a chair, palm to forehead. "Oh no, what a debacle. Oh, I'm so sorry it turned out badly. It sounds dreadful. There must have been some way for it to work out graciously."

"Not with Lady Patricia, Miss, oh no, not her! A whirlwind of fury, that one. She even slapped Rogan. He remained the perfect gentleman and told her how sorry he was, but life would go on. That really made her mad, Miss."

Evy groaned. She took no pleasure in Patricia's loss, but at the same time she thought the young woman was quite spoiled and immature to carry on like that. And Rogan hadn't mentioned a word of this to Evy at the cottage.

Lizzie grinned, her round cheeks flushed. She snapped her fingers. "Just like that it was, Miss. All this was said before the squire, too. He just threw up his hands and walked to his study with his books and closed the door. Lord Brewster seemed upset...and thoughtful. Then he left too. But not before Master Rogan talked with him alone, just the two of 'em. I couldn't hear what those two said to each other," Lizzie said, showing grave concern over not having listened to the whole thing.

Lizzie stopped to catch her breath and lay out the tea on the table. Evy could feel sorry for Patricia, but not extremely sorry.

"So Lady Patricia's gone, Miss."

Evy drank her tea, relishing every bit of it. A knock came on her door. She braced herself for a cool reception by Lady Elosia, but when Lizzie opened the door, it was another of the maids, Hulda.

"His Lordship wishes to speak with you in the parlor, Miss Varley, just as soon as you have your tea."

"Lord Brewster? I thought he went to London, to Scotland Yard."

"No, Miss, he sent a telegraph at the train depot, then came home. He's been with Master Rogan."

Evy smoothed her tawny hair into place, and after straightening her dress, she went to the stairway.

Rogan waited below. He had changed into a spotless white shirt and black trousers. He smiled and came up the stairs to meet her. Tucking her arm under his for support, he ushered her down the staircase as she gripped the banister.

"I talked to Anthony. He went to the cottage to have a discussion with me about you, but he left when he saw I wasn't there. He wanted to avoid you."

"Avoid me? But why?"

"He wasn't ready to face you yet."

They walked slowly together into the parlor, where Lord Anthony Brewster stood waiting below the portraits of the Chantry men. Evy's eyes strayed to the picture of Henry Chantry. She felt a bubble of suspicion and glanced quickly at Rogan. His confident gaze assured her. He escorted her to one of the comfortable chairs, and she sat down.

"Shall I leave you two alone?" Rogan asked Anthony quietly.

Anthony shook his head. "Do stay, Rogan. You should be in on this, although you know what I'm going to tell Evy."

Rogan gave a nod of his dark head and stood behind Evy's chair. She felt his warm, strong hands on her shoulders.

Anthony drew in a deep breath, and looking down at his polished black shoes, he took a turn up and down the floor in front of the great fireplace below the paintings on the wall. Evy watched him, trying to remain calm, although her heart was thudding with each breath.

Anthony stopped before Henry's handsome portrait and gestured. "I can assure you, Evy, that Henry is not your blood father... I am." He turned slowly and looked down at her. His face was taut, and his eyes anxiously searched her face.

Evy stared at him. *My father...Lord Anthony Brewster.*

"I won't ask you to forgive me, Evy. I don't ask anything of you, for I am keenly aware I don't deserve to." He paced again, his shoulders stooping, then he threw them back and went on quietly, not looking at her, but at the carpet as he paced up and down.

"I loved Katie van Buren, and she loved me, but we knew Julien was against the marriage. For a time we planned to run away to America and marry and turn our back on diamonds and power...but Julien found out. He threatened me. Said if I went against his will that he would send me to prison. Yes...I stole diamonds from the mine when I was around seventeen...and I was afraid of Julien. Katie didn't know, and I didn't want her ever to find out. I was sent away to London to finish at the university and was taken into the Montieth family, where a relationship with Lady Camilla was arranged. I still saw Katie each summer, and she did not know about Camilla... I was unfair to Katie, but I told myself I couldn't give her up... I admit it was selfish and immature. I didn't know she was expecting a child when I returned to London one year later to work with Lord Montieth in the Parliament. Julien got in touch with me and told me not to return without Camilla... When I did go back, Katie had given birth to you, and Julien had already given you up for adoption to a missionary family serving at Rorke's Drift. I never saw Katie again.

"You know the rest of the story. Camilla never knew, and Julien was determined to make sure she never did. At first we expected children of our own, but when that didn't happen, Camilla grew quite unhappy. I approached Sir Julien several times with the idea of bringing you to Capetown and introducing you to Camilla, but he would have none of it."

Julien, Julien, Julien.

"Camilla learned from Inga that Katie van Buren had a child by me, but she could never be sure you were the mystery child until she came here to Rookswood. By then you were already a growing young lady, and she held back from telling you for several reasons. One of which was Sir Julien's presence. Another reason was a request from Grace Havering. She wrote to me several times through the years to ask that the secret remain. She begged Camilla when she was here not to tell you. Grace believed it would do you damage to know. I understand that she did tell you on her deathbed that Katie was your mother. By then Camilla was ill and confined to her room much of the time. She, too, thought it best to keep silent."

And the silence remained as Evy sat there. She felt the pressure of Rogan's fingers on her shoulders.

"Was it the van Buren inheritance that kept Julien from letting the truth come out openly?" she asked. "He didn't want Katie to have an heir?"

"Yes. And the Brewsters. You're an heiress on two counts, Evy."

"Three," Rogan stated.

Anthony looked at him, and Evy turned her head. "Why three?"

"Because, darling, since returning to London, I've found out from my new lawyer, Mr. Billings, that Henry had also left half the gold deposit on his map to you. Some white diamonds as well. Billings is looking into the facts about how and why this escaped the old family lawyer, Mr. Scruggs. Scruggs died last month. He was eighty." Rogan bent down and planted a kiss on her head. "And you could say you're an heiress on *four* counts, since you'll soon be Evy Chantry."

Anthony had lapsed into melancholy silence. Could she forgive him? There was so much to forgive, and not just on his account, but also Julien's. How could she forgive such neglect, pain, and disappointment? And yet she knew that carrying such a heavy load of resentment would burden her and imperil the happiness that lay ahead with Rogan.

Could she forgive? Yes, as God's forgiving Spirit mended her heart and washed away the dark stains of the past, she could open her fists and let the anger of loss slip away. If she were to reach out to the future, she could do so only with hands that did not grasp the old hurts.

"I don't know about being a diamond and gold heiress," she said quietly, "but today's treasure far outweighs the sacrifice and loss of the past."

She got up from the chair and walked haltingly to where Anthony stood. "Knowing that I have a father today is a blessing I never dreamed I would realize. Let's leave all that's happened in the past and begin again." Her eyes were moist, and so were his. They reached out at the same moment, and their fingers intertwined.

"Hello, Father. My name is Evy, and I'll be proud to be called your daughter."

Tears suddenly coursed down his cheeks. He tried to speak, and when he could not, he threw his arms around her and wept.

THIRTY-ONE

In the happy days that followed, Evy wrote to Lady Camilla and thanked her for contacting Rogan at Fort Salisbury. "I look forward to seeing you again after these many years when I arrive with Lord Brewster—*my father*—and with Rogan. Rogan and I have our wedding day planned for a week before we sail for the Cape. I have gained so much in these last months—a father, a stepmother, and a husband. Truly God has been good to me. My health is also improving. Rogan has done so much to help me with special exercises. I am now able to get around with one crutch. Rogan insists I will walk on my own again someday."

Evy also wrote to Arcilla to let her know they would soon be sisters by marriage. Arcilla sent a wire almost immediately after receiving the letter:

I am thrilled. I always knew that Rogan had a crush on you even when we were all young. I count the days until you both arrive at Capetown. I wish I could be there for the wedding. But at least you and Rogan will be here for the birth of your niece or nephew.

Love, Arcilla

There had been no mention of Peter.

Even Lady Elosia had recovered from her shock and fainting spell to actually show some enthusiasm for Rogan's wedding. Evy smiled to herself when she overheard Lady Elosia say to Mrs. Tisdale, "I always believed dear Evy was the perfect young woman for our Rogan. She will make him a far better wife than Lady Patricia. Such a temper! Tosh, the girl actually broke my French cherub—an heirloom, mind you. I cannot imagine dear Evy throwing things at Rogan. And he's so devoted to her. Such a handsome couple."

There was more pleasant news. King's Knight was walking again, and Rogan believed he would be strong again in the next few months. Truly, as the days drew near, her wedding plans were turning brighter still. Wally's father, Harold, was building a modern carpenter shop on Grimmes Street. Beth and Mary Hooper were hanging up a homemade sign, which Wally had made, announcing their Hooper Detective Agency. Mrs. Hooper was even permitting the twins to have Wally over for an afternoon tea. And Wally told her that Digger had a new blue collar and a large bone from Gifford's meat shop.

Only one dark cloud remained on the horizon, foreshadowing events of the future. Anthony—her father—had told them at breakfast one morning that Scotland Yard had been unable to locate Heyden. Prevailing opinion was that he had somehow managed to get out of England by private ship and sail to Scotland. From there, Rogan believed he would return to South Africa. Evy feared they might cross paths with Heyden again.

The mystery concerning the whereabouts of the Black Diamond continued. The murder of Henry and perhaps even Vicar Edmund had as yet gone unpunished. Rogan, she knew, was determined to find Heyden in South Africa and bring him to justice. The idea was frightening, but she did not care to burden herself with it now. Today the sun was shining. She wanted to relish these happy times as much as possible.

At last Evy's wedding day arrived. She had ordered her wedding dress from London. It was of white satin and lace, and her veil trailed behind her, carried in procession by the Hooper twins. When Evy looked upon Rogan, her heart throbbed with joy and passion at the young man to be her bridegroom. The ceremony took place at the parish chapel, and the entire village turned out for the joyous celebration. Even old Miss Armitage, now in her late eighties, showed up.

"I always told you to watch that scoundrel," she told Evy. "And now you've gone and married him."

Evy laughed, and then Rogan came up and led her away as her beautiful long dress masked her limp. With his strong arms for support, she was suddenly lighter. She found she was dancing the first waltz as though she had no need of crutches ever again. She had sprouted wings, and heaven was smiling down upon her.

Mrs. Croft looked on, beaming with as much pride as if Evy were her own granddaughter. She would be going with Evy and Rogan to Capetown. Adventure awaited them. Mrs. Croft said she was coming to keep them all out of trouble.

Evy looked up into Rogan's dark eyes as he smiled down at her. "You are beautiful, my dear Mrs. Chantry. Are you ready for our adventurous life in South Africa?"

I love you, her eyes told him. "With you, darling, and with God directing our paths, I am as ready as I can be."

He drew her closer, his embrace protective, his gaze warm and promising. "You're everything I want, Evy. With you, my life is just beginning. You're the one treasure that fills my heart. In all our days it will always be so."

Evy's heart sang in harmony with his. *God be with us,* she prayed. *In all our days.*

Author's Historical Note

Dear Reader,

Writers who enjoy researching history generally accumulate more information than can be incorporated into a novel. I have, therefore, found it practical to choose certain events from a rich and varied time period which were particularly representative but which did not always fall into a chronology. In *Yesterday's Promise,* I was able to condense into a manageable period some of the key events of history which shaped the struggle to form the nation called Rhodesia.

Rogan Chantry and others are now able to take us into South Africa's color and controversy, and though the time period is condensed, the history I have incorporated into the East of the Sun trilogy is accurate, the historical individuals are genuine, and the fictional lead players are representative of the times in which this novel takes place.

In the interest of accuracy, I have included a list of historical dates and other facts used as the background for both *Tomorrow's Treasure* and *Yesterday's Promise.*

Historical Dates

1600s	Protestant Dutch, later called Boers, arrive at the Cape in much the same time period as the Pilgrims arrived in America, both seeking freedom from religious persecution in Holland and England.

1795–1803	The British capture the Dutch East India Company and form their Cape Colony.
1817	Robert Moffat (1795–1883) was a Scottish pioneer missionary to South Africa who arrived in the Cape in 1817. He and his wife Mary opened mission stations in the interior, and their eldest daughter, Mary, married explorer David Livingstone. Mr. Moffat translated the Bible into the language of the Bechuanas. He served for 53 years and his model Kuruman station was a focal point of the Gospel.
1835	The Boers begin their Great Trek across the Orange and Vaal rivers to be free of British rule and to farm.
1849–50	Explorer and missionary David Livingstone's first expedition and discovery of Lake Ngami.
1852	Sand River Convention confirms the Boer Transvaal's independence.
1854	Independence of the Dutch Orange Free State.
1867	Diamonds are discovered in Cape Colony at Hopetown.
1870	Lobengula becomes chief of the Ndebele tribe. He moves into Mashonaland and makes slaves of many of the Shona, and resists Dutch and British from the area.
1870	The big Diamond Rush
1871	Kimberly founded (spelled Kimberley and Kimberly by some.)
1871	England annexes the diamond area, despite protests from the Boers in the Orange Free State.
1872	Cape Colony is given governing rights by Her Majesty.
1879	Zulu War
1883	Paul Kruger elected president of the Transvaal for the first time.

1884	A London convention on the Transvaal gives limited Boer independence.
1886	The great gold rush to the Transvaal begins, Johannesburg is founded.
1887	England annexes Zululand.
1888	Portugal refuses weapons to be delivered to English missionaries struggling against slavers on Lake Nyasa.
1888	Cecil Rhodes and allies gain a monopoly of the diamond mines at Kimberly and form De Beers Consolidated.
1888	Cecil Rhodes wins exclusive mining rights in Mashonaland and Matabeleland from Lobengula.
1888	Her Majesty awards a royal charter to form his British South Africa Company, BSA.
1889	Rhodes becomes prime minister at Cape Colony.
1889	The Pioneer Column sponsored by Rhodes's BSA make their trek into the Zambezi region (Mashonaland) to establish Fort Salisbury and eventually form Rhodesia.
1891	Her Majesty's Government permits the British South Africa Company to extend operations in Barotseland, which later becomes northern Rhodesia.
1893	Kruger is elected for his third term as the Transvaal president.
1895	Kruger ends isolation of the Transvaal by opening a railway from Pretoria and Johannesburg to Delagoa Bay in Mozambique.
1898	Kruger elected president of the Transvaal for fourth term, war with England.
1899	Boer War
1902	Peace Treaty signed at Pretoria between England and the Boers.
1910	Union of South Africa formed (31 May).

Dear Reader,

I hope you will look for the third book in the East of the Sun trilogy in 2005, when the story of Evy and Rogan Chantry completes their destiny in Rhodesia.

I would be pleased to hear from you. You can write to me through my publisher:

Linda Lee Chaikin
c/o WaterBrook Press
2375 Telstar Drive, Suite 160
Colorado Springs, CO 80920

Sincerely,

Linda Lee Chaikin

ABOUT THE AUTHOR

Linda Lee Chaikin has written eighteen books for the Christian market. *For Whom the Stars Shine* was a finalist for the prestigious Christy Award, and several of her novels have been awarded the Silver Angel for excellence. Many of Linda's books have been included on the bestseller list.

Behind the Stories, a book about writers of inspirational novels, offers Linda's personal biography. She is a graduate of Multnomah Bible Seminary and taught neighborhood Bible classes for a number of years before turning to writing. She and her husband presently make their home in California.